W9-BZO-915

DESTROYER
OF WORLDS

ALSO BY MARK CHADBOURN

The Dark Age

The Devil in Green
The Queen of Sinister
The Hounds of Avalon

The Age of Misrule

World's End
Darkest Hour
Always Forever

Kingdom of the Serpent

Jack of Ravens
The Burning Man
Destroyer of Worlds

Underground

Nocturne
The Eternal
Testimony
Scissorman

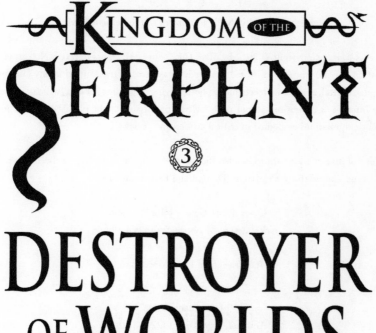

KINGDOM OF THE SERPENT

3

DESTROYER OF WORLDS

MARK CHADBOURN

an imprint of **Prometheus Books**
Amherst, NY

Published 2012 by Pyr®, an imprint of Prometheus Books

Destroyer of Worlds. Copyright © 2012 by Mark Chadbourn. All rights reserved. No part of this publication may be reproduced, stored in a retrieval system, or transmitted in any form or by any means, digital, electronic, mechanical, photocopying, recording, or otherwise, or conveyed via the Internet or a website without prior written permission of the publisher, except in the case of brief quotations embodied in critical articles and reviews.

The right of Mark Chadbourn to be identified as the author of this work has been asserted by him in accordance with the Copyright, Designs and Patents Act 1988.

Cover illustration © John Picacio
Jacket design by Nicole Sommer-Lecht

Inquiries should be addressed to

Pyr
59 John Glenn Drive
Amherst, New York 14228–2119
VOICE: 716–691–0133
FAX: 716–691–0137
WWW.PYRSF.COM

16 15 14 13 12   5 4 3 2 1

Library of Congress Cataloging-in-Publication Data

Chadbourn, Mark.
    Destroying of worlds / by Mark Chadbourn.
        p. cm. — (Kingdom of the serpent ; bk. 3)
    Originally published : London: Gollancz, an imprint of the Orion Publishing Group, 2009.
    ISBN 978–1–61614–617–7 (pbk. : acid-free paper)
    ISBN 978–1–61614–618–4 (ebook)
    1. Gods—Fiction. I. Title.
PR6053.H23D47 2012
823'.914—dc23

                                                    2012000383

Printed in the United States of America

CONTENTS

For Liz, Betsy, Joe and Eve

THE FINAL AGE

I am the Caretaker. I keep a light burning in the darkest night. I serve all who come to me, whether their hearts are filled with hope or tainted by despair.

Here I stand, at the end of the world, where the night is darker than ever, and the lamps have gone out, one by one. What lies ahead is mystery. But the road to the end is clear.

It began one misty morning, close to Albert Bridge in London, where Jack Churchill wandered, lost in the depths of grief for his dead girlfriend, Marianne. Drawn by the sounds of struggle, Jack—an archaeologist known as Church—stepped away from his world and into a stranger and more real one when he encountered one of a race of shape-shifting creatures from the depths of Celtic mythology: the Fomorii, also known as the Nightwalkers. Though the creature fled, Jack met the woman who would become the great love of his life, Ruth Gallagher, and together they uncovered the first signs of an invasion by the Fomorii.

But Church and Ruth were also inducted into a greater and more uplifting mystery, that of the Blue Fire, an energy that ran through the land along leys, its power focused at ancient sacred sites. For more than two thousand years, this force for Life—Existence—had chosen groups of five champions, the Brothers and Sisters of Dragons, who would fight to protect the land. Bound together by the Pendragon Spirit, Church and Ruth were only the latest members, and they soon met the other three of their team: an Asian mystic, Shavi, the acerbic Laura DuSantiago, and Ryan Veitch, a tough ex-criminal from South London.

The Fomorii were engaged in battle with their ancient race-enemies—the Golden Ones, the Tuatha Dé Danaan, who had been the gods of the ancient Celts. Many of these golden-skinned gods were contemptuous of humans—Fragile Creatures, as they named them—and manipulated them to their own ends. The Tuatha Dé Danaan, however, had an odd, symbiotic relationship with their mysterious shape-shifting companions, the Caraprix, which at times appeared to be more powerful than the gods.

With the Brothers and Sisters of Dragons in the middle, this war thrust Britain into an Age of Misrule. Science and reason were overthrown, and magic returned to the world.

Church and his comrades found their abilities honed in the crucible of battle. Ruth became an exponent of the Craft, drawing on the long heritage of wise women tapping into the power of the land. Laura became more nature spirit than human under the guidance of the Celtic god Cernunnos, also known as the Green Man. Veitch found his destiny as a powerful warrior, and lost a hand in the process. Shavi grew into a role as seer and wise man. And Church became the great leader the world needed.

In their quest, they were accompanied by their elderly guide, Tom, who had been kidnapped from his home in the Middle Ages and altered by the gods at the terrifying Court of the Final Word to become the great hero of myth, Thomas the Rhymer, who had the power of prophecy.

He was not the only human to be caught up in the gods' manipulations. Callow, a bitter wanderer, joined forces with the Fomorii and almost caused the downfall of the Brothers and Sisters of Dragons.

As the war raged across Britain, the Brothers and Sisters of Dragons overcame numerous hardships. Shavi was killed, but Veitch journeyed to the Grim Lands, the Land of the Dead, to reclaim his spirit and return him to life. This heroic act, however, had unforeseen and devastating consequences.

Callow was eventually killed, but he was not the only one; Tom, too, gave up his life, as did Niamh, one of the Tuatha Dé Danaan, who had fallen in love with Church. And in the Battle of London where the Fomorii were finally defeated, Ryan Veitch lost his own life. A tragic figure, Veitch had been manipulated by the gods to betray the Brothers and Sisters of Dragons.

In the cataclysmic battle against Balor, the great god of the Fomorii, Church was flung back through the ages, separated by more than two thousand years from Ruth, the woman he loved.

Though victorious, the Brothers and Sisters of Dragons had paid a high price. The survivors went their separate ways, and Existence set about forming a new band of Five who could be champions in the devastated world that remained.

But these Brothers and Sisters of Dragons would be different. Veitch's journey to the Grim Lands had broken one of the great rules and thereby attracted the attention of a terrible dark force beyond the edge of the universe: the Void, also known as the Devourer of All Things, the dark reflection of Existence, Anti-Life, the true ruler of the universe. Through the Mundane Spell, it kept humanity in thrall and deflected it from magic and wonder, which could eventually lead to the dark god's rule being usurped. Now that the Void had noticed magic had returned, it was coming back to Earth to ensure the Mundane Spell remained unbroken.

And so Existence needed to find five Brothers and Sisters of Dragons who could operate beyond the attention of the Void. From another reality, it plucked Mallory, who had killed himself in his own world after committing an undisclosed terrible crime. In Salisbury, Mallory joined the ranks of the new Knights Templar and learned to become a warrior. There he met the first Sister of Dragons, Sophie Tallent, who had mastered the Craft, and Miller, whom Existence had gifted with the power to heal.

Meanwhile, rural doctor Caitlin Shepherd also became a Sister of Dragons, after a plague claimed the lives of her husband Grant and son Liam. Caitlin escaped the Void's attention because her consciousness was fragmented: known as the Broken Woman, she developed several distinct personalities and was eventually possessed by the Morrigan, one of the Tuatha Dé Danaan, the goddess of death and violence, sex and life.

In her travels, Caitlin encountered several helpers, amongst them Carlton, a young boy who was killed during their quest; Jack, who, like Tom, had been kidnapped by the Court of the Final Word and had the destructive force of the Wish-Hex embedded inside him; Jack's sociopathic girlfriend Mahalia; and their guide, the dissolute academic Crowther.

The final two Brothers of Dragons were Hunter, a Government Special Forces officer and trained killer, and Hal, a lowly clerk, so insignificant that he escaped the Void's attentions completely.

The Void eventually realised that the only way it could maintain the Mundane Spell was by completely changing reality back into its familiar form, the age-old ways of money and power, where magic and wonder did not exist. All the Brothers and Sisters of Dragons were locked into fake, mundane lives, forgetting their true heritage—except Hal, who gave up his corporeal existence to become part of the Blue Fire. His mission was to seek out Church, the true "king," and help bring him back from the past to defeat the Void.

In the Iron Age, Church had been adopted by a Celtic tribe in the village of Carn Euny, in what would become Cornwall. He lived a simple life, but the Void recognised him as a threat and set out to destroy him. Through time, it despatched its agents, the Army of the Ten Billion Spiders; the Libertarian, a sardonic, brutal killer with lidless red eyes; and one other: a rejuvenated Ryan Veitch, corrupted by hatred, who blamed Church for his death and the loss of the woman he truly loved—Ruth.

Time became the battlefield. In different ages, Church fought the Void's agents, while in the modern world, the Brothers and Sisters of Dragons began to awake from their fake lives.

Paradoxically, Church established the line of Brothers and Sisters of Dragons in Carn Euny, long before he was chosen to be such a champion. But the first group were killed by Ryan Veitch, and eventually reanimated by the Void as the Brothers and Sisters of Spiders to help Veitch destroy Church.

The paradoxes continued thick and fast. Church was taken to the mysterious Otherworld, also known as the Far Lands, by Niamh, who would fall in love with him over time, and there he also encountered Tom in his younger days. In Niamh's court, Church befriended Jerzy, the Mocker, a surgically altered Fool who would play a large part in what was to come.

The magical Far Lands were timeless, and Church realised that he could while away his days there while centuries passed in the real world, and eventually return home when his own age rolled around again.

On occasional trips back to the real world, under Niamh's control, Church encountered many other Brothers and Sisters of Dragons. In Roman York in AD 306, he met the Dacian barbarian Decebalus, and the Roman Briton Aula Fabricia Candida, both of whom returned with him to the Far Lands when they discovered that Ryan Veitch was systematically killing off the line of champions. Over the centuries, Church rescued many others and brought them back to the Otherworld, where they formed an Army of Dragons in waiting.

The Great Powers continued to manipulate humans to their ends. The Void controlled many human leaders through the spiders, while gaining power over several gods from other pantheons in Earth's mythologies, amongst them the dual-faced Janus, god of doorways, and Loki, the Norse trickster god.

In Elizabethan times, Janus arranged the capture of many humans to be slaves in the Void's Fortress in the Far Lands. Amongst them were the New World colonists of Roanoke, including the young girl Virginia Dare, the first European to be born in the Americas.

Meanwhile, the Tuatha Dé Danaan continued their own manipulations. Dian Cecht and the gods of the Court of the Final Word were involved in a desperate attempt to probe the heart of Existence, not only to ensure their survival in the face of the Devourer of All Things, but also to prevent the Golden Ones from being supplanted by Fragile Creatures. In one of their experiments, they inserted a Caraprix inside Jerzy's head, to control him and use him against Church.

In 1851, at Stonehenge, Jerzy mysteriously disappeared from Church's side. He had been kidnapped by the shape-shifting trickster Puck, also known as Robin Goodfellow, one of the Oldest Things in the Land, to undisclosed ends.

As Veitch, the Libertarian and the Army of the Ten Billion Spiders continued a campaign to stop Church, they also launched a search for a world-shattering magickal artefact, the Extinction Shears, which could cut through all reality. Locating them, the Void's forces used the Shears to sever the Blue Fire from its source and condemn the world to the Mundane Spell. But after this act, the otherworldly Market of Wishful Spirit reclaimed the supremely powerful artefact, and disappeared with it.

At the Woodstock Festival in 1969, the Libertarian offered a world-weary Church a deal—if he allowed himself to be placed in the Sleep Like Death, and locked forever in a casket in the Far Lands, Ruth, Shavi and Laura would not be killed. Church believed this was the only way to save his friends.

As Church slept in the casket, events he had previously experienced continued apace. The Fomorii invaded, and his past-self fought them through the Age of Misrule. Tom and Niamh died. The Battle of London took place.

Locked inside his head, Church experienced what he thought was a dream or a hallucination: he met me, and the Daughters of the Night, the true owners of the Extinction Shears, and then he was guided to a cave that housed the Axis of Existence, which he perceived as a great reality-altering machine. Using the Axis, Church changed events in the same way that the Void had done, though not as catastrophically: both Tom and Niamh returned to life. But there was a price to pay, as there always is for these things, and Niamh became an agent of the Void.

Returning to the fray, Ruth, Laura and Shavi rescued Church from the casket in the Far Lands and returned to Earth for a final confrontation with Veitch. In the battle, Veitch was killed, his body taken away by the Brothers and Sisters of Spiders.

But now the Brothers and Sisters of Dragons faced their biggest test: to destroy the Void before it could reshape the world in its image for all time. From the depths of the Blue Fire, Hal told them what they would need: the missing Extinction Shears; and the Two Keys, two humans, one with the power to create life, the other with the power to destroy, hidden by Existence somewhere amongst the world's billions.

Church knew that they could not complete this quest alone, and so he set out to locate Mallory, Sophie, Caitlin and Hunter, still living the fake lives the Void had given them. With Tom once again joining them, they split up into two teams. Mallory, Sophie and Caitlin travelled to the Far Lands in search of the Extinction Shears, under the guidance of a returned Jerzy.

With the Libertarian hounding them at every turn, Church and the others raced to Norway in search of the First Key. But there they discovered why they had encountered only the Celtic gods during the Age of Misrule: each pantheon of gods from Earth's mythologies had their own Great Dominion over which they ruled. For centuries, they had slept, but every time the Brothers and Sisters of Dragons trespassed in a new Great Dominion, they woke the old gods.

In Norway, Church and his team were confronted by gods from the cold northern climes, including Tyr and Freyja. To save the lives of his friends, Tom agreed to an undisclosed but clearly tragic deal with Freyja, who gave him the cursed ring Andvarinaut to help them locate their hearts' desire—in this instance, the Two Keys.

Veitch, meanwhile, had returned to life through a ritual in the Grim Lands, and with the help of the Brothers and Sisters of Spiders, he kidnapped Ruth. Feeling even more betrayed and bitter, Veitch had turned his back on the Void and was now determined to bring all of reality crashing down around him.

In Oslo, Veitch found the First Key before Church—Mallory's former friend from Salisbury, Miller, who was using his Existence-given power to heal the sick. And so the Brothers and Sisters of Dragons set off across the world in pursuit of Veitch, Ruth and Miller, awakening the gods of several Great Dominions in the process.

In the Far Lands, Mallory, Sophie and Caitlin had fallen under the manipulation of Niamh, not realising that she had become an agent of the Void. The influence of the Devourer of All Things was spreading across the Otherworld: its Fortress was growing, the Army of Dragons was missing, as were many of the Tuatha Dé Danaan, and the Enemy's forces were on the march, destroying everything they encountered. Meanwhile, at the Enemy's Fortress, the Burning Man was being created, a giant, flaming matrix that would contain the essence of the Void on its return.

At the last, Niamh's corruption was exposed and the Army of Dragons and missing gods were discovered, but at a terrible price: Niamh used a magickal artefact to wipe Sophie from Existence, a fate truly worse than death, where the Sister of Dragons would never have existed and therefore be forgotten by everyone who knew her. Niamh escaped, and though Mallory liberated her court, he failed to find the Extinction Shears. Unbeknownst to him, they had been hidden with the Market of Wishful Spirit somewhere in the Grim Lands.

Back on Earth, the Brothers and Sisters of Dragons closed in on Veitch, Ruth and Miller. Though Veitch was still bent on revenge, Ruth's influence gradually began to strip away his encysted bitterness, allowing his former heroic nature to surface. In the process, the pair grew closer.

In Egypt, many of the old gods had agreed to help the Void, and were destroyed by the Brothers and Sisters of Dragons. Only Seth escaped, vowing revenge.

Soon after, in the Forbidden City in Beijing, the gods revealed to Church a shattering truth: the Libertarian was Church's future self. He was given a vision of the moment when he would transform into the psychopathic killer, thus betraying Existence and ensuring victory for the Void. Church's only hope was that in the fluid nature of time, the future could be altered and his vision would never come to pass.

In China, the Brothers and Sisters of Dragons did claim one great victory: the connection to the source of the Blue Fire was reopened and magic flooded back into the world.

The Second Key was hidden in New York: Jack, Caitlin's former associate, who still carried the vast, destructive force of the Wish-Hex. Here, Veitch finally overcame his hatred and agreed to help his former comrades, though he was still treated with suspicion by all.

Realising it faced defeat, the Army of the Ten Billion Spiders set about remaking the world, in the process closing all the gateways to the Far Lands. With hardly any time to spare, Church and the others escaped Earth on the supernatural Last Train, ready for the final battle with the Void.

And so the pieces move into place for the final battle at the end of the world.

PROLOGUE
THE WORLD-TREE

> "The snake came crawling and struck at none. But Woden took
> nine glory twigs and struck the adder so it flew into nine parts."
>
> From the Anglo-Saxon "Nine Herbs Charm"

1

It is the beginning of the end.

"Church! Church! Wake up—you're dreaming! Please wake up, Church!"

"Maybe it's just time."

It is the beginning of the end.

"Where is the meaning in life?"

"What is real?"

"There are signs, certainly, but in the end, who knows?"

"You don't have to leave me, Church."

It is the beginning of the end.

"So cold. Oh, please, why are you letting this happen?"

"Everybody describes it differently . . . like a shadow falling over them, or a jolt of electricity. I wish I could be more helpful."

Chilled to his bones and aching, Church wakes; and then he wakes again, and there is the rhythm of the train, like the pulse of blood.

It is the beginning. Of the end.

2

Snow falls. A flurry caught in the unforgiving wind blowing relentlessly across the frozen wastes that stretch to the horizon. In that wind, there are whispers, lost souls, telling of the end of the world, of all worlds. Their stories are caught in the ruddy glare reflected in the rolling snow dunes and the crested waves of ice.

High in the silver sky, the Burning Man looks down on this place, and the shimmering city of gold and glass at its heart, as he looks down on all places, waiting to cast the final judgement. The towering outline of fire is still waiting to be filled, but it will not be long now. It is the twilight of the gods, and men, and all living things.

Ragnarok.

Dreaming, yet awake, you understand this as you move out from the confusion of the World-Tree's branches and drift across the desolate landscape. The whispers have told you what was and what will be, what is real and what is not. You move on quickly. You want to see more. Worry knots your thoughts, that perhaps this time it will not be all right.

3

See there, at the top of the tallest tower of the City of Marvels, where Hunter looks out at the seething figure and feels its words in his heart. His quarters reveal that he is treated with respect. Sumptuous furnishings fill the chamber, furs piled across the wooden floors and tapestries hanging on the walls, while floor-to-ceiling windows on three sides give a grand perspective on the world. But though a great fire blazes in the hearth, Hunter still feels the chill.

Like the city, Hunter's appearance belies the true nature beneath—rakish, piratical, a flair for flamboyance concealing an iron will.

"Intriguing. You still believe there is hope. Is this what it means to be a Brother of Dragons, then? Faith over reason?" Math, the great sorcerer of the Tuatha Dé Danaan, stands beside the stone fireplace, oblivious to the heat. Sometimes Hunter wonders if there is a person inside the black robes and the brass mask that rotates every minute or so to reveal one of its four faces: boar, salmon, falcon, bear.

"Reason is overrated." Hunter pours himself a goblet of fruity wine and downs it in one. "What's the point in sitting on your arse and ruminating on the logic of what is, by any rational person's yardstick, complete bug-eyed, screaming craziness? Life's for living. When some git's swinging an axe at your head, or a woman is pressing her lips against yours, you feel it and you react. You start reasoning about either one, you're a dead man." He pours himself another goblet of wine, drinks it quickly.

"Your drinking is a mask, like mine," Math notes wryly.

"We're just two peas in a pod."

The long wait ends as the door opens silently to admit the goddess Freyja, wearing a black dress to mark the gravity of the occasion. Her delicate features are emphasised by the thick animal fur she wears across her shoulders. For once, her potent sexuality is tightly controlled; another sign of respect for the visitor.

"The Council of Asgard is convened," she says. "Brother of Dragons, and cousin—" she nods to Math "—you will accompany me."

Past hissing torches, she leads them down the majestic staircase to the great meeting hall of oak and glass. At one end of the room, an enormous window looks across the expanse of snow to Bifrost, the Rainbow Bridge, shimmering like the aurora borealis. Its far end hangs in tatters; Earth cannot be reached.

The hall rings with the voices of gods bellowing at each other, or flirting, or fighting. Hunter's senses take a moment to adjust to the combined presence of the powerful beings, faces slowly arising from a swirl of impressions: features he vaguely recalls from childhood stories or dreams; fiery red beards and wild-man hair, glittering lupine eyes that have seen seas of blood flow over the rocks and ice of the northlands, women with hair glowing like the sun and a beauty primal and terrifying and sexual. Muscles like iron and hideous, jagged scars. They carry weapons—nicked axes, great swords—or pluck on ancient stringed instruments. Everything about them speaks of blood and battle and sex and honour.

Hunter feels quite at home.

"Let the council begin." The crowd falls instantly silent at Freyja's command, and all eyes turn towards Hunter.

Freyja gestures towards the great empty throne at the far end of the hall. "These are dark days. The All-Father's whereabouts are unknown. He has followed his ravens, Hugin and Mugin, to an uncertain future. And so this decision falls to us, now. Before the All-Father departed, he placed his trust in the Brothers and Sisters of Dragons, and so we must give fair hearing to their plea."

A murmur races around the room. Support or dissent? Hunter cannot tell.

"There's a war coming," he begins. "The war to end all wars. You know it. This is the final battle foretold in all your old stories."

"Ragnarok," one intones gravely. Red-haired, he is taller and stronger than all the others, and from the enormous hammer that stands by his side, Hunter knows he is the thunder god, Thor. "It blows towards us like a storm at sea. Inevitable, inescapable. The end of us all."

"The Norns will be gathering around their well beneath the roots of Yggdrasil," sighs an elderly man with a long, white beard. Unconsciously, his fingers play over the strings of the harp in his lap. "Urd, Verdandi and Skuld, who hold us all in their hands."

"Hush, Bragi. This is not a time for your eloquent misery." Tyr stands, his scarred, hairy body now recovered from the terrible injuries Hunter had seen inflicted on it in Norway. "That sly trickster Loki has not been seen for a season," Tyr continues. "If we find him, and carve his body with my axe, Ragnarok will not unfold. Simple."

"It's too late for that," Hunter insists. "Loki is already with the Enemy, and he's not alone. A lot of others, from across the Great Dominions, are under the Enemy's control. They're all following the lead of Janus, two faces, neither of them pleasant."

"If it is too late, what is the point of this council?" Bragi asks.

With a roar, Thor crashes his hammer Mjolnir on the stone flags and sends lightning flashing across the hall. "The Aesir have never turned from battle, even when all hope appeared lost. We fight, and if the Norns so decide, we die!"

Thundering his support for Thor, Tyr drives the gods to their feet with a deafening martial clamour.

With a sigh, Hunter waits for the bravado and bloodlust to subside.

Freyr, the Shining Lord and brother of Freyja, says, "Why do we need to listen to you, Brother of Dragons? What can you possibly offer the Aesir?"

"Allies. The Enemy force is greater than you can imagine. However powerful you think you are, you won't be able to hold them back. Alone. But with an army of gods, from all the Great Dominions . . . now, that would make a difference." Hunter gestures to Math, observing silently with his hands folded in front of him. "The Tuatha Dé Danaan have already agreed to stand with us. I have a message from Lugh guaranteeing the support of the Golden Ones."

"An army of gods?" Tyr's laughter roars to the rafters. Thor, though, remains grave as he considers Hunter's words.

"You're facing the true, organising force of the universe. The god above gods," Hunter continues. "The Void represents the opposite of Life. And it's slowly focusing its attention on us through that Burning Man you can see from your windows. Once that receptacle is filled, it will act."

"But until then there is an opportunity?" Thor asks.

"Not for any of us alone. Even together there might not be a chance—"

"Hold!" Pressed against the great window, the goddess Frigg looks out across the wintry wastes. "Something approaches."

The horizon is a blur in the blizzard that rages constantly around Asgard, but gradually shapes coalesce in the snow, moving towards the city. A handful at first, then a score, then hundreds. Brutish figures range speedily ahead of the main force: Redcaps wearing their clothes of human skin and organs, followed closely by the shimmering, insubstantial Gehennis tearing at their wild hair, and the shrieking, vampiric Baobhan Sith. Behind them, a great army pulls slowly out of the storm, dead yet alive, axes and swords and lances merged with their limbs, armour rusted and bloodstained. Purple mist drifts around the Lament-Brood, and even at that distance their keening song of despair is clear.

"They attack us here, in our home?" Thor intones incredulously.

"We fight!" Tyr bellows. "Now."

"I don't want to pour cold water on your war party," Hunter says, "but this is where I advise you to run."

4

Across the Far Lands, ashes drift in the wind. In your dreams, you taste the bitterness on your tongue. Listen. There is a sound like a heartbeat throbbing behind the breeze, under the rustling of the leaves, deep in the land itself. It is the sound of war drums, it is the sound of a heart. It infects your dreams so that you cannot sleep peacefully, for you know what it is, and from where it comes.

Against one of the foothills of the great mountain range sprawls an enormous walled city. You stare in awe at its jumble of buildings, its winding streets, its towers and turrets, gambrels and chimneys, ramparts and spires. Once you would have been troubled by its claustrophobia, the darkness beneath the upper storeys of the buildings overhanging the cobbled streets. But no more. Now the streets are flooded with light, and a new mood of hope fights to establish itself; the Court of the Soaring Spirit has a new lord. You see his long dark hair and the note of irony in his dark eyes, but most of all you see the unfathomable sadness in his heart. Despite that, Mallory, Brother of Dragons, possessor of Llyrwyn, one of the Three Great Swords of Existence, projects only optimism, a necessary quality, for his city now lies on the brink of destruction.

The Palace of Glorious Light lives up to its name. Golden illumination shining from every window, it is a beacon that can be seen far and wide across the Far Lands, and it rings with beautiful music, earthly songs that Mallory has taught the strange band of musicians drawn to him from across the city. He hoped it would ease his emptiness. It has not. But all the other residents will never forget its joy.

Yet still it faces destruction.

At the heart of the palace is a formal garden, tranquil amongst its honey-scented alyssum, spicy lilies and sweet, strong jasmine, its sparkling fountain, its elegant statues and winding walkways. Amidst the fluttering butterflies and the lazy drone of bees, Caitlin Shepherd, Sister of Dragons, practises a relentless series of martial routines with her axe.

From the upper cloisters, Mallory watches her brown hair flying, her fragile features tense and determined. "No peace," he mutters. "Ever."

As if to underline his words, Decebalus, the Dacian barbarian, marches up. "Another attack is imminent," he growls. "I have ordered the sounding of the alert."

Mallory curses. "We need to get everyone indoors. Man the defences—"

"Already done." Decebalus nods towards Caitlin in the garden below as they march to the stairs. "You are concerned about her?"

"It's just difficult to get used to the new Caitlin. There was always something gentle about her. A healer, not a fighter."

"Gentle she remains, deep inside. But she is so much more now. So many people in one small body."

"Five personalities. It's not the human ones I'm concerned about—Caitlin herself, Amy, Briony, even that old crone Brigid with her doom-mongering and predictions."

"It is the Morrigan." Decebalus nods. "A human possessed by a god. What good can come of it?"

"Not just any god. The Morrigan is terrifying. Blood and death——"

"And sex and life," Decebalus interrupts with a wink.

"No. I love her dearly, but not like that. She's a friend."

As they hurry along the cloisters where beams of sunlight and deep shadow form a complex interplay, they pass Brothers and Sisters of Dragons hurrying towards the rooftop defences, an Army of Existence brought to the Far Lands from their own long-gone times. To a person, they look to Mallory with hope and respect as he passes.

"The Brothers and Sisters of Dragons are ready for the fight ahead," Decebalus observes.

"They shouldn't be. They don't stand a chance."

"Do not let them hear you say that," Decebalus cautions sternly.

"I'm not stupid. But I'm really not comfortable sending them all to their deaths."

"This is their sole reason for existing. More than two thousand years of history... the shaping of the Brothers and Sisters of Dragons... it has all been leading to this point. Live or die, this is what they were made to do. It is their destiny."

"I don't believe in destiny."

"You are a strange and troubling little man. You do not believe in anything. I am a poor, uneducated barbarian, yet even I have learned to understand the thing you call 'reason.'"

"It's overrated."

Decebalus curses under his breath, but his mood is too vibrant to be constrained. "You should see them when they train," he says, a twinkle in his eye. "The very air of the room becomes alive... the iron smell of the Blue Fire, so powerful." He smacks his lips. "It makes my skin tingle and my heart sing. Existence chose well, all of them. And it is not just the Pendragon Spirit! Their hearts are strong. They will face any odds. They will risk their lives for what Existence requires of them. You should be proud to be a part of it, Mallory."

"Yeah, they're heroes. So who's killing them, Decebalus?"

High overhead, the alert sounds, a lone, tolling bell that ignites in Mallory the chill of dread every time he hears it.

"Two dead," he continues. "Holes punched in the centre of their foreheads. Church didn't save them from slaughter in their own time only for them to be murdered here."

"You know there is an enemy in our midst. The force we oppose attacks from without and within. It will not allow us the space to take a stand. Time is running out—"

"I know!" Mallory snaps. "You don't have to remind me every damned minute of the day." The bell tolls again, and again, turning his stomach. "I'm sorry. It's the waiting. For Hunter to build his coalition of gods who refuse to acknowledge each other's existence. For Church and the others to find the Two Keys. For the location of the Extinction Shears. For us to do anything before we get wiped out." Frustration drives an edge into his voice.

"You are a man of action, I understand that. This period is difficult. But soon there will be action enough for all of us."

Stepping onto the palace roof, Mallory sees that the defences are already in place, here and on the other highest points around the city. He knows Decebalus has trained them well since the first attack that had killed so many. Ranks of golden-skinned archers from the elite forces of the Tuatha Dé Danaan face the roiling black clouds on the distant horizon. Behind them, the Army of Dragons prepare to use the bizarre but devastating weapons created in the vast armoury of Goibhniu, Creidhne and Luchtaine.

The tolling bells continue to sound. Clang, clang, clang. In the city below, the streets clear rapidly in a mood of fear and desperation. Doors and shutters are bolted.

Mallory watches the black clouds move slowly across the great plain. "I don't know how much more of this we can take," he says. "We can't just sit here under siege until every building is reduced to rubble."

"Huh. The Enemy's full army has not arrived yet," Decebalus grunts.

"Thanks for the reassurance."

As the storm clouds near, they part to reveal the creatures at their core. Three Riot-Beasts, each with twin leonine heads, eyes rolling with idiocy as they silently roar, their big-cat bodies covered with scales, feathers and fur. They are engines of destruction, throwing out crackling bolts of energy more devastating than any missile. Each time he sees them, Mallory is unnerved by the way they float without wings or any other visible means of staying aloft.

The day becomes like night as the storm clouds fill the sky, and a low bass rumble vibrates through everything. As the Riot-Beasts reach the city walls, plasma balls sizzle erratically, exploding rooftops and sending out waves of superheated air. Towers crash to the ground in a rain of masonry as the creatures blunder across the city.

"Now!" Decebalus roars, and a hail of arrows arc majestically. Some hit their target, but the Riot-Beasts show no pain, if they can even feel it.

Mallory nods, and Decebalus orders the firing of the greater weapons from the vaults of the Tuatha Dé Danaan. The air becomes glassy or boils in a wave of fire, and bolts of energy shriek like banshees. Sometimes the Riot-Beasts are knocked off course. Mostly, they continue on their paths of destruction, occasionally bursting into flame until the wind or gusting rain extinguishes the blaze.

"We haven't got anything that can hurt them," Mallory says redundantly. His anger boils within him, but he maintains a cool demeanour for the sake of his troops.

"Whatever, we send out a message," Decebalus replies. "We will resist unto death."

"Very poetic, with an unnerving knack for premonition."

The battle continues for fifteen full minutes. Across the city, buildings collapse and roofs are torn off. Many die. Finally the Riot-Beasts drift away as if they are leaves caught on the wind. The storm clouds follow, the thunder's rumbling decreasing, until the sun eventually breaks through.

"As soon as you have the figures, let me know how many died this time," Mallory orders.

"Why do you punish yourself?"

"Because until I find a proper defence, I'm responsible for every one."

They wait until their exhausted troops file off the rooftop before making their way down. There have been too many attacks, and little chance to rest.

Now the attack has passed, you prepare to move on. You are unsettled; the threat here is palpable. But you know there is still more to see. The Far Lands is a place of subtlety and intrigue, and many things shift behind the surface of all that you see.

5

In the ringing corridors of the palace, a woman staggers, blood streaming from a gash on her temple. Her name is Marie, a scullery girl in a large London house during the Regency period of George IV; ignored by those who believed themselves to be her betters, she gained renown as a brave Sister of Dragons. Here, though, she is disoriented, terrified; the world has shifted beneath her feet.

As Mallory and Decebalus come down from the roof, engaged in deep debate about tactics, she comes to a halt, wide-eyed. Seeing her wound, Mallory and Decebalus rush to her aid, but she only shrieks and presses against the stone wall as if hoping it might swallow her.

An accusing finger points at Mallory. "Stay back!" she says, and then to Decebalus, "He tried to kill me!"

"When?" the barbarian asks.

"Not five minutes ago, during the attack."

"Impossible. Mallory was at my side then, up on the roof."

Marie wavers, her eyes flashing from side to side. "He tried to kill me, I tell you!"

Decebalus motions for Mallory to step back as he attends to the young woman. "This is not the truth, Marie. Either you are mistaken, or it is some kind of magic."

"Magic, then!" She stares at Mallory accusingly. "His face, Decebalus. He came at me as the fire rained down, in the dark of the upper floors. Instinct made me turn at the last. Good fortune was all I had, but it was enough. I did not see his weapon, but I felt it as it tore through my flesh. I did see his face." She points again. "And I ran . . . here—"

"Think, Marie," Decebalus says sharply. "You ran into us—Mallory was not pursuing you. He was ahead."

The woman wavers, tries to make sense. "Then who . . . ?"

"The one who's already killed two Brothers and Sisters of Dragons," Mallory says. "The Enemy's sent an assassin to pick us off one by one."

"If it uses your face, then it attempts to undermine our spirit," Decebalus says gravely. "If it can use any face, then who can we trust?"

Troubled, Mallory and Decebalus deliver Marie to a healer and then seek out comfort and the sun in the herb garden, which lies beyond a maze of lavender in a walled area at the rear of the palace. The air is heavy with rich perfumes. Decebalus and Mallory find Aula tending her herbs, as she does at that time every day. At first Mallory does not recognise her. Her blond hair shimmering in the sun, the Roman Briton's face is strikingly peaceful as she immerses herself in the garden's atmosphere, a far cry from the fierce looks that usually accompany her caustic tones. Her mask returns when she sees them both.

"So little to do you must trouble me here?" she says tartly. "No wonder we face disaster."

"Your day would be bereft without a visit from the one who gives your life meaning," Decebalus replies with a broad grin.

Aula snorts unconvincingly then turns to Mallory. "She plays in the maze," she says.

Past clouds of honeybees, Mallory weaves through the heavily scented bushes and eventually sees the top of a young girl's head in the centre of the maze. Virginia Dare never smiles. Occasionally, a heartbreaking, haunted look will appear in the depths of her eyes. In that moment it is possible to comprehend the many atrocities she has witnessed since the Army of the Ten Billion Spiders kidnapped her and her fellow settlers from Roanoke in the New World almost five hundred years ago. She has spent her formative years in the heart of horrors, the Void's Fortress on the edge of the Far Lands, until her escape. Though only eight years old, her eyes say she is a hundred.

"Is it time?" She cradles a doll made for her by one of the kitchen staff who had hoped it would bring back some aspect of childhood.

"Not yet. But soon. I need to ask you if you are prepared to do it."

"You have asked me twice already."

"Now I'm asking you a third time."

"Yes," she says without hesitation. "I will travel with you to the Enemy Fortress, and show you the secret way I discovered under the walls."

"You know what it will mean?"

"You want to protect me, Mallory," she replies in too-old tones, "but it is too late for that. I am ruined."

Mallory cannot look in her face; it makes him too desperately sad.

"She'll be fine."

Frequently, these days, he never hears Caitlin come up on him. She stands at the entrance to the maze's central rest zone, still slick with sweat, holding her axe loosely. Mallory searches her eyes to see who is in control this time. He doesn't know why he tries, for even when he sees the bright innocence of Amy, there is always the dark of the Morrigan just behind.

"It's me, Mallory. Caitlin. The one, the only, the original." She smiles, kisses him on the cheek.

Virginia hugs Caitlin tightly, the first time she has looked like a little girl. "Have you come to play with me?"

"I said I would, didn't I?"

With a whisper of desperate thanks, Virginia buries her face in Caitlin's midriff. "No hide and seek," she says. "I don't like that."

When Virginia has raced away to fetch a board game from her room, Mallory observes, "She likes you."

"We have an understanding."

"I still don't want to take her to that place."

"She's tougher than you think, Mallory. When it comes down to it, we all are."

He watches the bees, and the clouds scudding across the blue sky. "Do you think it's enough?" he enquires. "Wanting to do the right thing?"

"No, it's not enough," she replies. "But we do it anyway."

6

And so you move again through the twisting, ever-multiplying branches of the World-Tree, and now you watch the walls of Asgard crumble. From out of the swirling blizzard, blazing rocks crash with a steady beat of destruction. The Enemy's siege machines never rest. The monstrous troops wash out of the snow in a black tide that Hunter wills to ebb but which never does. They swirl around the foot of the walls, throwing up ladders as quickly as the Aesir can despatch those who scurry like insects to the ramparts. But their greatest weapon is insubstantial: a potent atmosphere of despair radiating from every fibre of their being, infecting any who allow their defences to slip; a moment's doubt is all that's needed. Hunter sees shoulders sag, heads bow, weapons fall to their sides.

"It is only a matter of time before we are overrun," Baldur mutters in a daze of abject disbelief.

"This is a taste of what's to come," Hunter intones above the din of battle cries, clashing weapons, the screams of the dying and the constant howl of the icy gale. "Nobody survives on their own."

Amidst peals of deafening thunder, a storm cloud races along the ramparts towards them, lightning bolts flying in all directions. Only when it nears does Hunter recognise Thor, his face consumed by volcanic fury. Swinging Mjolnir with the devastating force of a hurricane, he shatters the face of a Redcap attempting to climb over the wall. The god grips the siege ladder and thrusts it back out into the blizzard. Howls rise up from those falling below.

"Asgard shall not fall!" he bellows to the wind.

At intermittent points along the walls, the lie is being given to his words. Hordes of decaying Lament-Brood haul themselves over the ramparts, losing an arm here, even a head there, but continuing relentlessly. Aesir warriors run to confront them at the points where they have broken through the defences, but the Lament-Brood attack the moment their feet touch the walkway.

An Aesir warrior is impaled on a rusty sword embedded in the handless wrist of one of the Lament-Brood. The sword is roughly twisted and the warrior explodes in a cloud of golden moths gleaming against the white snow, a single moment of beauty at the instant of his death.

All along the walls, the Aesir stop what they are doing and watch, aghast, disbelieving, fixated on each individual moth as it struggles to pick a path through the gusting snowflakes.

A single teardrop rolls slowly over Thor's cheek.

And then along the ramparts bursts of golden moths rise up here and there, the interval between each explosion growing shorter, like bursts of smoke and light in a magician's stage show.

"No!" Thor thunders, and renews his furious hammer-attack.

The Aesir return to action, blades and axes flashing, but Hunter can see something has gone out of them. Their attacks are less sure; they glance at each other, seeking reassurance, finding none.

Forseti, one of the younger gods who had been responsible for justice in the city, is surrounded by six Redcaps. Before Hunter can react, the god is hacked to pieces.

As the moths soar, Baldur cries out, "My son!" Consumed by grief, he races towards the Redcaps.

"We must leave." At Hunter's shoulder, Math's four-fold mask turns implacably. "There is no hope left here."

From his backpack, Hunter removes a silver-scaled gauntlet with brass talons. "It would be impolite to leave at the height of the party."

"What is that?" Math asks suspiciously. "A weapon?"

"The Court of the Final Word called it the Balor Claw." Gritting his teeth, Hunter slips on the gauntlet. "And now it's mine."

He arrives at the fray as the Redcaps surround Baldur, as they had done his son. One sweep of the Balor Claw takes the first Redcap apart. Another falls as he turns, the Claw breaking the bonds of his body at the molecular level. After his slaughter in the Court of the Final Word, Hunter has grown used to the sight of bodies unfurling, but the other Redcaps are, for the first time in their existence, rooted. In a frenzy of despair, Baldur despatches three with his sword and Hunter kills the last. Catching his breath, the god represses his grief and looks Hunter deep in the eyes. In that one moment, he accepts everything Hunter has attempted to communicate to the council.

"The age of gods and men is passing," Baldur admits. "It is time to make the final stand."

The Aesir fight furiously, but the Enemy keep coming, devoid of fear, wave after wave with no purpose save destruction. Their atmosphere of despair is corrosive. The clouds of golden moths are now indistinguishable from the snow.

"Fall back!" Baldur yells. "To the Groerland Square!" Piercing the crackling lightning, he grips Thor's arm. "This is no place to make a stand. We must leave with the Brother of Dragons."

"But the Golden City will fall!"

"Stone and wood, brother. It can be rebuilt. The true glory of the Aesir is a light that must never be extinguished."

Thor weighs the words for only a second and then roars, "Fall back! Do as the Bleeding God says!" He grins at Baldur. "Lead the way, brother. I will protect your back."

Baldur snatches the horn from his side and blows one blast, loud and clear, rising up above the howling gale and the thunder of battle. Along the walls, the gods retreat, down the steps to the avenues of Asgard radiating out from the Groerland Square.

"You've made the right choice," Hunter says as he and Math follow Baldur into the streaming mass of warriors.

"Asgard is surrounded. You can free us from this place?"

"As long as your man with the hammer can keep the Enemy off our tails for a little longer."

"He does not stand alone." Baldur indicates a balcony on a tall tower where Freyja stands, arms raised to the sky. "She uses her seior in the city's defence." The direction of the wind changes suddenly, hurling many of the Enemy to their deaths from the walls.

The Aesir will make good allies, Hunter thinks, but will even they be enough?

In the Groerland Square, a large public space centred on a statue of the World-Tree, Yggdrasil, the axis mundi around which all reality turns, the gods silently look towards Hunter, the unfamiliar expression of confusion etched in their faces. The only sound is the heartbeat of the Enemy's missiles against the walls.

"Are you sure you can take them all?" Hunter asks.

"We shall go by Winter-side," Math replies. "There will be no Enemy there yet."

At the foot of the Yggdrasil statue, the sorcerer utters an incantation in a language Hunter does not recognise. Amidst a sound like rending metal, a section of air as big as a barn door shimmers and appears to become a two-dimensional sketch of what had previously been there. Math pulls it open to reveal a cavernous darkness.

"We go into the World-Tree, to follow the branches to other worlds," Math explains.

"It's just a statue," Hunter replies.

"The depiction of the reality is the reality. Have you not learned any-thing?" As Math beckons, Baldur hesitantly leads the Aesir into the dark.

Hunter waits until Thor and Freyja come running from the battle-lines. Tears stream down the thunder god's face.

"The Eternal City is falling," he says. "How can this be?"

"You'll get your chance to make amends," Hunter replies. "This isn't the end."

Along the western wall, a sheet of flames rises up. They watch it for a moment and then step into the dark. The door that is not a door closes behind them, and the snow fills their footprints, and for the first time there is silence within the walls of the Eternal City.

7

In your dreams, you see these things. Across the worlds, there is a sense of winter approaching, of the dying of the light. The steady rhythm in the ground and behind the sky now sounds less like a heartbeat and more like the ticking of a clock, growing imperceptibly slower.

You see all this. You know. You are now a part of it.

8

You travel across the infinite Far Lands to a point that is neither here nor there, that anomalous place on the distant edge, where the Otherworld breaks up and opens onto another infinity.

Words mean nothing here. Ideas have more substance than things. But you see as you move that numbers underpin everything. Repeating patterns that form the basis of a greater pattern. At a distance, the mathematical complexity creates the illusion of chaos. It is all random, you would have said in another time, under other circumstances.

Move closer and you see the truth. The structure. The plan. You understand the mechanics of Chaos Theory, without needing to know the name, that within seemingly chaotic systems there is a hidden order, masked by a complexity so great our brains cannot comprehend it.

Five, you say. That is one of the numbers. It is familiar by now. Comforting. You know it well.

But there is another important number, too. Hidden till now, waiting to be called into the Light.

Odin, the great god of the Nordic lands, hanged himself on the cosmic ash tree Yggdrasil for nine nights in order to learn the wisdom of the dead.

That great tree of life, around which all reality revolves, sheltered nine worlds beneath its branches.

Nine books of wisdom tell a story that is more than a story, in which you now play a part. Nine symbolises completeness in the Bahá'Õ faith. To the Celts, the ninth wave is the boundary between our world and the Otherworld. King Arthur was brought in on the ninth wave. The Chinese consider nine to be lucky because, in their language, it sounds the same as the word for "long-lasting." The Japanese consider nine to be unlucky because it sounds like the Japanese word for "distress" or "pain." The cat is believed to have nine lives.

The Forbidden City in Beijing is filled with the number nine. It is linked with the Chinese dragon, a symbol of power and magic. There are nine forms of the dragon. It has nine attributes, and nine children.

There are secrets here, you realise, if only you could divine them.

But you are distracted by a terrible sight. The Fortress of the Void sprawls across a blasted, desolate terrain of rocks and dust. It is bigger than any city you have ever seen, as big as a country, and from a distance it resembles a gigantic squatting insect. Indeed, part of the city appears to be organic. Amongst the walls of fused volcanic glass and the detritus of failed civilisations are areas that appear to be constructed from spoiled meat. It continues to grow by the day, new wings, new towers spreading in all directions, consuming the land.

The Fortress swarms with the worst that the universe has to offer, not just the Lament-Brood, the Redcaps, the Gehennis and Baobhan Sith, but things worse still, things you cannot bear to examine for fear you would be driven insane.

And above it all towers the Burning Man, so close you can feel the heat from its blazing outline. Here is the place where it was born. Within the Burning Man you can see writhing figures being consumed. These are gods, or ones who consider themselves gods, providing the fuel that gives the Burning Man shape, and allowing it to shine like an infernal beacon across all worlds. You cannot hear their screams, but you can see their mouths fixed in a continual "O."

On a balcony overlooking the suffering stands a man living a new life of perpetual cruelty, a mirror-image man who still sees echoes of his former existence; but he can discard them, for he is better, at peace now, unlike before. He emphasises his flamboyance, wearing all black like a silent-movie villain, or all white, however the mood takes him. His eyes are blood-red, with no lids, so he can never shut out the horror he sees, the horror he causes. He is wedded to the idea of peace and stability through control, not the torments that come from the uncertainty of free will. He believes hope is a debilitating virus, and love, and that contentment only comes from not looking to the distant horizon. It is a simple philosophy, but many things spin from it.

"They may be the most efficient warriors in all the worlds, but they could do with a few tips on interior design," the Libertarian says. He takes a deep draught of sour air and turns back to the austere chamber where fires rage continually in the braziers, a futile attempt to bring warmth to bodies that can feel none.

Niamh, former queen of the Court of the Soaring Spirit, now truly queen of the Waste Lands, wears a black headdress with six horns, like the arms of Shiva, and ebony armour etched with silver. She is filled with spiders. She considers a geometric design that resembles a mandala, or a Mandelbrot set, revolving slowly in mid-air. It glows gently with a rich, white light. Though you only see three dimensions, she sees more. It is a map of the worlds, and the trail they make through time. Her brow knits, for what she sees changes continually. Nothing is fixed; everything is fluid. She finds that puzzling.

The Libertarian takes her hand and pulls her away from the map and into his arms. "Don't you find that all this power and destruction make the sap rise?" he says, pressing his groin into hers.

She smiles, not without affection. "I find the patterns of Existence a mystery. My heart yearned for you from the earliest times, in your past life, and we danced back and forth across the ages, until it appeared we would never share the same space. Yet here we are."

"All good things come to those who wait."

"Together now, and always, and in all time before this moment."

A headache stabs briefly at the Libertarian, a nagging thought, hardening by the moment, of troubled times ahead, sights, disturbingly, that he cannot see, an area of insecurity, of disconnection.

A tolling bell echoes dully through the Fortress.

"It's time," he says.

Niamh nods, takes his hand. They make their way along corridors of pulsing meat, down echoing stone steps, until they come to a hall so large that the far walls are not visible.

You will not want to enter. Even in your dreams it affects you, the stink, the feeling of subsonic vibrations in the pit of your stomach, but most potently a dread so terrible it would drive you insane if you lingered. You want to shut it out, pretend you never experienced it, but it will haunt you for the rest of your days. Amidst a seething mass of shrieking foul creatures floats the great god Janus, his two faces switching back and forth, black on white, white on black. He holds aloft the golden key to open the doors and then the ironwood stick to drive away those who have no right to cross the threshold. The monstrous beings shriek louder, the noise rising and falling, and you realise that hideous sound is singing, a form of celebration. In their ecstasy, they fight and tear at each other like animals in a pit. In a circle around Janus's feet lopes the god Loki, part-man, part-wolf, his head rolling as he mouths incantations, lost to the ritual, lost to the dread and the frenzy, round and round in circles.

Niamh smiles, closes her eyes and breathes deeply of the foul atmosphere. "You can smell it. An ending," she says. "And a beginning. The serpent eats its own tail."

Janus raises the key once more and a door opens behind him. Listen. That beat, steady, growing louder. It is the sound that lies behind everything you see and feel.

"He is coming," Niamh says.

The Void, the Devourer of All Things, the essence of Anti-Life approaches the door, preparing to coalesce in this place, this time, and fill the receptacle that has been made for it: the Burning Man.

For once the Libertarian has nothing to say. A tear stings his eye. It could have been joy had he not relinquished that emotion long ago.

Niamh claps her hands. "It is over," she sighs.

Quickly. You must leave before it is too late for you.

The pounding grows louder, and the beasts fall silent, and still, and look towards the door, and wait.

CHAPTER ONE
GOD ONLY KNOWS

1

The Last Train thundered out of the world. Behind it, swarming spiders tore apart the land and rebuilt it with a boiling intellect and a cold eye. Hope and wonder and magic could not survive under that scrutiny. The unequivocal image of the Void was all that would remain.

Through the carriage window, Church attempted to see some pattern in the dark pressing in on all sides, but the dream was still heavy on him, distracting, haunting. Lying on some kind of bed or trolley or bench, faces loomed over him uttering familiar yet unrecognisable voices. On awakening, he had been convinced of some life-changing meaning just beyond his grasp, but it was slipping further away with each moment. It felt very much like a death dream.

His reflection in the window revealed the burden of responsibility carved into his brooding features. There was too much darkness about him, from the black hair, to the eyes lost in shadow, to the hollowness of his cheeks. Was this the chrysalis state before he would emerge as the Libertarian, bloody eyes staring from the gloom?

Veitch came up silently behind him. His features carried the hardness of a life lived on the street, his eyes registering every hurt, every betrayal, every disappointment, all too close to the surface. Church still didn't know how much he could trust him.

"You know what we need? Some music," Veitch said.

"Sinatra," Church replied.

"Nah. Something . . . something sunny. A bit of heart, bit of hope. I've got this Beach Boys song stuck in my head. Can't remember what it's called." He quietly hummed a few off-key bars.

Lounging back in a seat, Veitch's silver hand caught the lamplight, the glow illuminating another hint of uncertainty in Veitch's eyes. "Laura's never going to accept me," he commented.

"Surprised? She never liked you much before. Now she knows you've killed about ten times as many people as the worst serial killer in history, all of them Brothers and Sisters of Dragons."

Veitch gave nothing away.

"Any regrets?" Church pressed.

"I did what I did."

"You had the spiders whispering in your ears—"

"Don't blame them. I knew what I was doing."

"The Void deals in despair, Ryan. Once you get infected with that you can believe black is white and up is down. Nothing looks right."

"You're the one always banging on about accepting responsibility. What I did felt right then. Now . . ." Veitch gave a shrug that was supposed to represent easiness. "All that matters is I did it. I'm never going to put it right, no chance. I've got to accept what I did and live with it." Veitch rolled up his shirt to reveal the mass of colourful tattoos that covered his torso. He indicated a Promethean figure strapped to a rock being attacked by ravens. "See that? That's me. Being punished forever for what I've done. No relief. Just pain. You fuck up like I did, you deserve to pay the price."

Church felt a pang of pity. "You're here now when we need you most."

"So you trust me?"

"I do."

"You're an idiot, then. Even I don't trust me."

Their eyes locked, and Church was acutely aware of the weight that lay between them. Veitch loved Ruth as much as he did, and neither of them was wholly sure where Ruth stood. What would happen when the time came for choices to be made? Could he trust Veitch to walk away? Could he trust himself?

His transformation into the Libertarian would be sparked in some way by his relationship with Ruth. Before, he couldn't comprehend how that could possibly happen. Now he could see with startling acuity the road begin to appear before him. The question was clear: how far would he be prepared to go for the woman he loved?

Something similar unfolded in Veitch's face.

"None of us are heroes, mate," Veitch said quietly. "In the end we just do the best we can."

"And sometimes we fail."

Veitch nodded.

"But that's the thing about five. If one screws up, there's always someone else to make sure the job gets done."

Veitch pondered this for a moment. "We've all got a part to play. Thinking about this too hard does my head in, but it's like even bad stuff is important. Like you couldn't have had some of the good if the bad things hadn't happened to cause it. So it's all linked. Pull back a bit and you start seeing things for what they are. They're just part of some . . ." He struggled to complete the concept.

"Pattern?"

"It's like we're so far inside it we don't see how it all fits together, but if you could float above it somehow . . . you know . . . Listen to me—I sound like bleedin' Shavi." He laughed. "Looking forward to spending some time with that fucker. I missed him. He keeps me calm."

"We go well together."

"Yeah. We do."

Outside the carriage, the impenetrable black was like deepest space, punctuated every now and then by a burst of fire in the far reaches, a beacon crying for help, quickly extinguished. Briefly, a vast mountain of stone came into view, topped by a sharp spire with gargoyles and carvings and windows but no sign of life: the Watchtower between the Worlds.

"You think Miller and Jack are enough to stop the Void?" Veitch was lost to the gloomy view.

"Not without the Extinction Shears. Maybe not even then."

"It's not going to end well for us, is it?"

"No happy endings."

"I never expected that for me, but you lot . . . you deserve better. You've fought hard."

"Maybe dying won't be so bad. I just feel so tired. All this running, and fighting."

They were interrupted by the silent arrival of Ahken, the host of the Last Train, his heavy-lidded eyes staring from a skull-like face. His black robes were pristine, but he smelled of the grave, and when he clasped his hands before him in a show of obsequiousness, it hid something darker. "Brothers of Dragons," he said. "Is there anything that would make your final journey more pleasurable?"

His words chilled Church.

"Yeah. Some dancing girls," Veitch replied.

Ahken smiled slyly. "You feel at home on the Last Train."

Veitch stroked the leather seat. "It's weird. It feels a bit Egyptian, some Chinese, Arabic, Victorian."

"Oh, the Last Train is very old," Ahken said. "It was here in the earliest time, before the Golden Ones, before even the Drakusa."

"Before the Oldest Things in the Land?" Church asked.

Ahken did not reply.

"What are you going on about?" Veitch asked.

"There's a hierarchy. The gods manipulate us. The Oldest Things in the Land manipulate the gods and us. Puck, the Caretaker . . ." With an involuntary shudder, Church recalled the two figures he had seen, or imagined, hovering over the cauldron that was not a cauldron while he suffered the Sleep Like Death in the casket of gold and ivory. "There's always something higher. Apparently."

Defiance hardened Veitch's features. "Humans are on the way up, and we're not taking any bollocks from anyone any more."

Church nodded in agreement. "This whole period is ushering in the next step of our evolution, if we can follow the right path. Not Fragile Creatures any longer. A lot of the ones above us don't like that." He eyed Ahken, who smiled, giving nothing away.

"So does that mean we get one of those little silver rats like all the gods?" Veitch said.

"A Caraprix?"

Ahken flinched.

"You know something about them?" Church asked him.

"I know the Last Train, and that is all," Ahken lied.

"The Tuatha Dé Danaan can't live without them," Veitch said. "But what use are they? They change shape, yeah, but I mean, so what, right? It's not like they serve up your dinner. They're like pets."

"Except I can never tell which is the pet—the Caraprix or the god," Church said.

2

Laura kept one eye on her reflection in the window of the adjoining carriage as she teased her white-blond hair. "The end of the world is no excuse for looking less than perfect," she hummed.

Further down the carriage, a piper played a heart-wrenching lament to the four lost cities of the homeland of the Tuatha Dé Danaan. The king of the Seelie Court maintained a cold dignity, but the queen's head was raised, eyes closed, tears streaming down her cheeks.

"Do you miss Hunter?" Shavi sat cross-legged on the opposite seat.

Laura noted the tinge of rawness around his left eye where the stolen alien orb had been inserted, but it only emphasised the beauty of his bone structure, the gleam of his black hair, his flawless skin. "Like I miss crabs."

His smile revealed he recognised the truth behind her words.

"All right, so he's not a complete loser. And trust me, I've shagged enough of those in my life to tell one at fifty paces."

Shavi continued to smile.

"Will you stop that?" She sighed. "He's not had the experience we've had. I mean, we've all died and come back, for a start."

"He is a strong and capable man. There is little in the Far Lands that would give him pause."

"I'm going to be really pissed off if he goes and dies on me. At least before I've managed to suck the life out of him."

"You deserve a little happiness."

"Yeah. Tell that to her." Laura nodded towards Ruth, who stood apart from the strange members of the Seelie Court, lost to the music and her thoughts. She leaned on the Spear of Lugh as if it was a crutch.

"Ruth does not think badly of you."

"She doesn't like it that I'm not a frosty, miserable moaner. And she envies my beauty, wit and charm."

"You know, you do not have to be afraid to be honest about your feelings."

"I've never been honest in my life. Why start now?" She fixed him with a telling gaze, but for once Shavi did not notice the subtle signs.

"When are you going to tell us your real name?" he asked.

"It's DuSantiago."

Shavi nodded; another faint smile.

"So how's the new eye? Causing you a great deal of pain?"

"It appears to have settled in remarkably well. For an eye stolen from an otherworldly construct to replace the one it stole from me."

"Shame." She saw the briefest shadow cross Shavi's face. "What's up?"

"The eye doesn't always show him things he wants to see." Ruth stood in the aisle. Laura felt a charge in the air, as if Ruth were some kind of generator. It was both comforting and unsettling at the same time.

"So what are you seeing, Shavster? Or should I cross your palm with silver?"

"Nothing."

Laura grew serious. "I'm going to throw back at you all that shit you tell me about friends. You shouldn't keep all this stuff inside you. It'll eat away at you and drive you mad. Trust me, I know."

"She's right, Shavi," Ruth prompted.

"I do not see specifics, just fleeting images, impressions." He shrugged.

"He sees death," Ruth said.

Shavi flinched.

"How do you know that?" Laura asked.

"It's circling all around us. Can't you feel it?" Ruth hugged herself. "A coldness, that brief feeling of a shadow passing over you?"

Laura shook her head. "What do I know? Thanks to Cernunnos I'm more plant than human. A beautiful little nature sprite."

"Maybe it's my Craft," Ruth accepted. "Come on, Shavi—share your burden."

Reluctantly, he replied, "Yes, death is all around. As it comes closer, symbols of its presence will arise, as they always have done, but we are usually oblivious to their presence."

"You're creeping me out now." Laura said. "What are you talking about?"

"In life, death is an anomaly. It is like a weight dropped onto a taut rubber sheet, bending the patterns all around, throwing up indicators of its presence. In the midst of them, we discount them as coincidences, randomness. Only after death has passed do we see those things for what they are."

"Patterns," Ruth said. "Symbols. That's where the true magic lies."

"Who dies, Shavi?" Laura said sharply.

"The Pendragon Spirit responds to the gravity that lies ahead."

"So if I can cut through all your verbal wankery," Laura said, "you're saying Brothers and Sisters of Dragons. Us. One? More?"

"The details are not clear."

Laura couldn't tell if he was lying.

The musician came to an abrupt end of his piece, and with silent awe the Seelie Court moved to one side of the carriage. The Last Train emerged from the gulf into a crepuscular zone and then rapidly burst into a blaze of colour and detail. They had arrived at the distant edge of the Far Lands.

But the members of the travelling court were not entranced by their return to the land the Golden Ones now called home. Their apprehensive attention was fixed on the Fortress that sprawled to the lip of T'ir n'a n'Og, as big as several cities and growing with every moment as armies of labourers relentlessly scurried with ant-like organisation to erect annexes, walls, towers, courtyards, keeps. From one angle, it didn't resemble a fortress at all, but an enormous insect squatting on the land. All around was blasted, dry and dusty, and devoid of life. And over it all loomed the Burning Man.

Everyone remained silent until the Fortress had passed from view, and then they returned to their seats, muttering darkly to those beside them.

3

The Last Train moved rapidly across the blasted zone, past the long columns of monstrous beings marching out from the Enemy's Fortress. Their great war machines shook the ground as they rumbled towards the centres of habitation. Soon the train passed onto rolling downs, where the breeze-blown grass looked like waves on a green sea, and then to misty valleys and tree-covered slopes.

In the carriage beyond the one occupied by the Seelie Court, Tom perched on a seat, studiously constructing a roll-up from the small tin he carried in his haversack. With his silver hair tied back in a ponytail, he still carried with him the spirit of Woodstock. "Scared?" he said.

"No, of course not." Crowther watched the passing scenery intently. He was a big-boned man, wrapped in a voluminous overcoat topped with a wide-brimmed hat that made him appear even larger. "I have been here many times. In my dreams—"

"Nightmares."

"Speak for yourself. Our world is a place of low horizons. Here, anything is possible."

"Yes, death from nowhere, torture, the dismantling and rebuilding of the body in infinite, agonising variations. It's one long, fun-filled holiday of the mind."

"If you don't have the intellectual capacity to see the possibilities," Crowther sniffed, "there's little point in discussing it further."

Tom eyed him coldly. "Intellect is a poor substitute for experience."

"As people without intellect always say."

"Oh look, the old folk are arguing again. This journey is like one never-ending visit to a rest home. You'll be fighting over the Rich Tea biscuits next." At sixteen, Mahalia had the cut-glass tones of an expensive private education, but her eyes suggested easy violence and a much greater age.

"Oh yes, the teenage delinquent," Tom said. "Move along. No mobile phones to steal here."

"For God's sake, don't engage her." Crowther sighed. "You'll only find ground glass in your food."

Mahalia snorted. "I can be much more inventive than that." Her hardness fractured briefly as she glanced back along the carriage to where her boyfriend, Jack, sat in gloomy conversation with Miller. At seventeen, with his shock of blond hair and healthy farm-boy appearance, Jack was a stark contrast to the older Miller's sickly pallor, only emphasised by the lank brown hair falling around his ghostly face. "You need to do something about those two. They've got some kind of death wish," Mahalia added.

Realising they were the subject of the conversation, Jack and Miller approached.

"Tell them!" Mahalia pleaded with Tom and Crowther. "Just because they've been given these special abilities doesn't mean they have to go out fighting."

"Don't, Mahalia." Jack had a world-weariness that belied his age. "Everyone can see how this is going to turn out."

42

"No, they can't!" Refusing any sign of weakness, she quickly brushed away a tear.

Jack took her hand. "My memory's back now. I know what happened. Snatched from my mum when I was a baby and taken to the Court of the Final Word where they worked on me."

Tom winced.

"They made me into a weapon," Jack continued. "The ultimate weapon. The Wish-Hex that they buried inside me is like . . ." He fumbled for words to describe a concept he could barely comprehend.

"Like a nuclear bomb that can devastate the very fabric of reality," Crowther interrupted.

"So it's there," Mahalia said. "So what? That doesn't mean it has to be used. You can have a normal life—"

Jack silenced her with an affectionate squeeze of her hand. "You know I've got a part to play."

"All right!" she snapped. "So you release the Wish-Hex. There has to be a way you can do that without destroying yourself."

Jack's sad smile stung more than any words could have.

"We all want a little happiness, but sometimes we have to give that up so everybody else can have a chance to be happy," Miller said. Tom saw in him an echo of Shavi's inner peace.

"Shut up, you simpleton." Mahalia sighed.

Refusing to be deterred, Miller took a seat across the aisle. "I've got something inside me too, but mine heals. You don't know what it's like to have these gifts, Mahalia—"

"Gifts!" she snorted.

"They are! Jack's too, though it's hard to see it at the moment. They speak to us in a way I can't explain and they tell us we've got a job to do. If there's a chance we might be able to stop the Void—"

"Might, might, might!"

"We've got to try! To have an ability and not use it . . . and everybody suffers because of it—how could you live with that?"

"I could," she said.

"We're the Keys," Jack said. "Miller . . . me . . . there's no chance of winning without us."

"There's no chance with you!" Mahalia stormed down the carriage so no one could see her tears. Jack and Miller followed, trying to comfort her. Crowther watched Tom's face and saw an echo of Mahalia's desire for peace and happiness after a long period of responsibility.

"They say you have the Second Sight," Crowther said.

"One of my many wonderful attributes."

"And the tongue that never lies?"

"Oh, yes. But that doesn't mean I have to answer."

"Can you see how all this plays out?" Crowther asked hesitantly. "Victory or defeat? Who lives, who dies?"

Tom smiled tightly, rose and made his way to the opposite end of the carriage where he sat with his back to the others and closed his eyes. The gentle rocking of the train should have calmed him, but nothing did any more. Instinctively, his fingers went to the gold ring in the shape of a dragon eating its tail that the goddess Freyja had given to him in Norway. Known as Andvarinaut, it was cursed to bring misery to anyone who owned it. He had bartered away his future to help Church, Laura and the rest, and soon enough he would be forced to pay the price.

"Don't worry."

Jerked alert by the voice, Tom saw a boy of about nine or ten sitting opposite him. He was black, his hair shorn to a bristle, and a little overweight, but he had the most expressive eyes Tom had ever seen.

"Who are you?" Tom growled.

"My name's Carlton."

Tom glanced back at Crowther and the others.

"They can't see me," Carlton said.

Tom searched the boy for any suspicious signs. "You don't look like one of those damnable fairy folk."

"I'm not."

"Then you're with the Enemy."

"I'm a friend. I've come to help you."

Carlton's face was open and honest, but Tom wasn't going to be fooled. He smoked, and waited.

"Time is running out. The Devourer of All Things is almost here. His army sweeps across the Far Lands. His assassins are abroad, attempting to kill or disrupt key elements of your opposition."

"You know, little children do not talk like that," Tom noted acidly.

"But there is one important thing you must know: in the battle to come, there will be people you can trust, and people you can't."

"And you're going to tell me which is which, I suppose."

"Even those closest to you are not above suspicion."

Tom snorted.

"I want to help—"

"You'll forgive me if I don't trust you." Tom returned to Crowther and the others, and when he glanced back, the boy was gone. When he described his encounter, Mahalia's face filled with sadness, and then anger.

"You're lying." Her voice broke. "That can't have been Carlton. Carlton's dead!"

4

In the great debating hall in the Palace of Glorious Light, Mallory and Decebalus were distracted from their strategy meeting by cries coming from the direction of the city gates. A crowd of excited Tuatha Dé Danaan flooded into the courtyard outside the palace where Lugh and an anxious cadre of the city guard waited uneasily for a caravan speeding up the winding streets. The golden-skinned outriders wore heavy armour, their faces grim, but several of the horses had empty saddles. Behind them, the royal carriage clattered so wildly over the cobbles that it was in danger of careering into the surrounding buildings.

"The first of them," Lugh said when Mallory arrived at his side. The god stood tall and handsome and was filled with the burning power of the sun, but since he had discovered the true extent of his sister Niamh's betrayal, it was as if a dark cloud had gathered within him. "The twenty great courts of the Golden Ones are answering our call."

"All of them?"

Lugh still barely believed he had gained the support of his unruly people. "We have received responses from all, save three," he replied. "The Seelie Court, who wander the worlds eternally; their dark brethren, the Unseelie Court, but they will never follow our path; and the Court of the Final Word."

As Lugh watched the gathering riders, the weight of his leadership lay heavy on him. "I am concerned. We sent a messenger to the Court of the Final Word, but he reported it sealed and silent and cold. I fear the worst."

Reining-in their mounts, the outriders leaped down as the royal carriage skidded to a halt. With a resounding crack, the rear axle shattered, the carriage sagging, the horses rearing up. Guards ran to help the occupants. The remainder of the caravan trailed through the palace gates and down the steep hill to where they had entered the court from the Great Plain, aristocracy and soldiers, merchants, musicians and magicians.

"Who are they?" Mallory asked.

"The Court of the Yearning Heart. Beware them, Brother of Dragons. Though they are my people, they are sly, untrustworthy and dangerous."

From the carriage climbed the queen, exuding a supernaturally charged eroticism so powerful that a tense silence fell over all those present, of either sex. She wore a transparent gown that only served to draw attention to her breasts and pubis.

Accompanied by two young women-in-waiting, she approached Lugh. No love was lost in the curt bow they exchanged, but she found time to cast a curious, sexually predatory gaze towards Mallory.

"I trust your journey was safe," Lugh enquired.

"It was not. We left as my court was overrun, and from there to here we were harried continually. Many of my subjects were slaughtered in the process," she noted without a hint of sadness. "Imagine—Golden Ones eradicated! How can this abomination come to pass?"

"There are worse things ahead, I fear."

"Is that a Brother of Dragons I spy?"

"Leave him alone," Lugh said sharply. "He is an ally."

The queen snorted contemptuously.

"More than an ally," Lugh continued. "He may well be our saviour, and he has more to concern him than being idle sport for you. The season has turned, sister, and Fragile Creatures have joined our kind at the high table. You must adapt to this new arrangement."

The queen batted a dismissive hand. "See also what has been wrought upon our kind."

She marched to a covered wagon surrounded by heavily armed guards who kept the curious at bay. Haughtily, the queen snatched back the cover to reveal six of her guards writhing in indescribable pain. Their bodies had been transformed by some disease, sprouting scales, horns, patches of exposed bone and weeping sores.

"What could do this to our kind?" the queen asked.

"Rangda."

Behind them stood a young man of about twenty, tall and thin, dressed in a green, crushed velvet suit with a hat, a cane and sunglasses. The whiff of the sixties lay heavily on him.

"What can you tell us, Doctor Jay?" Mallory asked.

"We had a run-in with her in Haight-Ashbury in sixty-seven." The Doctor tapped the brim of his hat with his cane to emphasise his words. "The demon-queen of Bali, they call her. She leads an army of evil witches and spreads plague wherever she goes. The Enemy sends her out to spread chaos." He peered into the back of the wagon. "There's nothing you can do for them. It's just a matter of time."

Refusing to believe, the queen raged impotently. Mallory, Decebalus and Doctor Jay left Lugh trying to calm her and returned to the Doctor's chaotic apartment in the palace. It was packed to the brim with magickal items, crystals, boxes and parchments, potions, candles and skulls, all moved from Math's tower before the sorcerer had departed with Hunter. The curtains were drawn and it was too hot and claustrophobic.

Jerzy moved studiously around the room, reading from several volumes as he mixed a concoction, his bone-white skin and rictus grin glowing spectrally in the half-light. When they entered, he gambolled over and danced around them like a child. Mallory had a sense of a second Jerzy behind the fool he had been made into by Niamh and the Court of the Final Word: secret, real, serious and hidden, with his own agenda.

"Are you ready to try again, good friend?" Jerzy said to Doctor Jay.

"We'll give it a rest for a while, Mister Mocker. I need to refuel my mojo, if you know what I mean." The Doctor flopped wearily into a large chair and put his head back. He kept his sunglasses on despite the gloom.

"Still no success?" Mallory prompted.

"Man, if you only knew what I'd achieved here," the Doctor replied. "Wonders and miracles! It's this place...the Blue Fire...all stirred up together. I'm supercharged!" He sat cross-legged. "But yeah, you're right—not the wonders and miracles we need."

Decebalus growled an epithet. "You cannot contact the king? Church?"

"I can't contact Earth, man. It's like it's closed off, all the shutters pulled down. The Void's made sure no one's getting in or out of our home, at least not yet. And no information's getting through, either."

"We don't even know if Church or the others are still alive," Mallory said.

"Good friend, Jack Giant-Killer will not be defeated. He will be with us soon," Jerzy said.

"Is that a platitude, or a snippet of information from your mysterious friends and allies?" Mallory asked suspiciously. "Those higher powers you're secretly working for?"

Jerzy looked hurt.

"Sorry. I'm an idiot. Ignore me." Mallory rested one hand on his sword, Llyrwyn. In times of stress, it calmed him, whispering mysteriously through the Pendragon Spirit they shared. "You think there's hope for Church?" he asked the Doctor. "Because if he doesn't turn up with the Two Keys, there's no hope for us, even if by some miracle we do locate the Extinction Shears."

Doctor Jay shrugged. "I've been reading, researching, talking to people out in the city. All the races out there have their own myths about these times. The End of the World myth, you know? They're all in code, like all stories, but with the information we've got now, you can read them in the right way. It's all the same story, just told with different emphasis. The battle between two great kingdoms. The light and the dark in the Tuatha Dé Danaan version. The fight between a spider and a snake that destroyed the universe, for Jerzy's people."

"The Christians talk of the Apocalypse . . . and the Antichrist," Decebalus mused.

The Doctor nodded. "It's all over our world too. Prophecies . . . hints . . . Who is the Antichrist, or is that just another symbol?"

"The Libertarian?" Mallory suggested.

"Revelation talks of the people of God opposing the Evil, and two prophets called the two witnesses. Is that the Two Keys?"

"I thought Revelation was supposed to refer to some Roman Emperor or something back when the Bible was written?" Mallory mused.

Animated, the Doctor fetched more books from the shelves. "The patterns, man. They're everywhere. The true template behind reality. See the patterns and you get what it's all about. A trip, the biggest trip of all. Numbers are the key, see." He giggled. "The key. Numbers are the key in music. Music is the key to the universe."

Mallory sighed. "You're having a rush, Doctor."

"Sorry, man, sorry. But it's the numbers! Science and magic . . . maybe it's the same thing. The pattern is everywhere. The Aztecs had the Legend of the Five Suns. Five was an important number to them. Each sun was an age, and when a sun died, there was chaos and the gods destroyed the world and started again. We're on the fifth sun now. The last one. This is the sun of movement, Tonatiu, the Rising Eagle, and when it's over the world gets torn apart."

"If that's a prediction, it doesn't sound like they've got a lot of faith in us," Mallory said.

Doctor Jay hesitated. "Maybe we don't fail. Maybe we cause it."

"Your brain is addled," Decebalus spat.

"The Indian myths are like the Aztec one, in a way. The universe goes through cycles of birth and death and rebirth. The Hindus believe that Vishnu, the Preserver of Order, comes during times of chaos to save humankind. He appears in a different form each time . . . an avatar . . . and he will appear in ten forms before the universe ends."

"You're saying that number is significant?" Mallory asked. "Like the number of the last two groups of Brothers and Sisters of Dragons. Except . . . except there are only nine . . ." He rubbed his forehead where the familiar painful emptiness had risen again.

"Don't know, man. But Vishnu has appeared in nine of his forms already. For the tenth, he will come as a man riding on a horse, to destroy the Earth."

They considered this for a moment. Sensing a darkening mood, Doctor Jay moved on. "The Norse had their myths of Ragnarok, the end of gods and humans, when the world is destroyed after a final battle. There's more, from all over the world, but I think you get the picture."

Decebalus snorted. "Patterns can be broken. And stories are like the gods. They tell you one thing but mean another. The truth is slippery."

A sudden crash made them all jump. Jerzy had pitched forwards, sending phials and bottles flying. Spasming on the floor, his eyes rolled back so that only the whites were visible. Mallory, Decebalus and the Doctor struggled to stop him hurting himself.

"A seizure?" Mallory said as Jerzy finally grew still.

"The Court of the Final Word changed him so much, it's impossible to tell what's going on inside him," Doctor Jay said.

Jerzy remained unresponsive. But as Mallory carried him to the bed in the adjoining quarters, a low-pitched hum emanated from the Mocker, growing more intense by the second until it set all their teeth on edge.

"What the hell's that?" Mallory reeled away from the bed.

Doctor Jay clamped his hands over his ears. "Strange days are upon us, man. It sounds like some weird radio signal."

All attempts to revive Jerzy failed. A silvery substance, like mercury, emerged from his tear ducts and slid across the surface of his eyes until they were like mirrors, reflecting the troubled faces of Mallory, Decebalus and Doctor Jay.

"Get all the court's medics together," Mallory said. "I want to know what's happening to him, why it's happening now and what it means."

5

With a screech of metal and a billowing cloud of hissing steam, the Last Train juddered to a halt at the gates of the Court of the Soaring Spirit.

"You ready to face all those bastards again?" Leaning on the window, Veitch watched the massive obsidian gates creak slowly open as puzzled guards emerged, weapons drawn, to investigate the arrival.

"We're on the same side now," Church replied. "This war is going to make a lot of difficult allies."

"Tell me about it." Veitch flashed a knowing glance at Church. "Common aims, right?"

"Whatever's happened, you're one of us, Ryan. You always were and you always will be."

Veitch grunted noncommittally, but the brief glance he exchanged with Laura as she made her way along the carriage ahead of Ruth and Shavi spoke clearly of the problems ahead.

"Congratulations, dude," she said. "You finished a whole train journey without killing one of us."

"Leave him alone," Ruth snapped.

"Oh, yeah, you would say that. Is there a man around here you haven't tapped?"

Her cheeks flushing, Ruth's eyes flashed angrily. Shavi stepped in with a gentle hand on her arm. "It's just Laura," he said softly.

Amidst an odour of loam and a sound like dry insect casings rattling, Ahken arrived, his obsequiousness undiminished.

"Your journey on the Last Train is over," he said, "and it is time to make payment." As he spoke, Tom, Crowther and the others made their way into the carriage.

"What's the price?" Church asked.

"More than you can bear!" Tom raced up, thrusting himself between Church and Ahken.

"Most peoples of the Far Lands and the Fixed Lands only ride the Last Train once, and their destination is always the same," Ahken continued with an unsettling edge to his voice. "Out of deference, I have allowed the Seelie Court free passage on their flight back to their homeland. They will join me again shortly. But you, Brothers and Sisters of Dragons, have journeyed on the Last Train three times, and three times is the limit."

Outside the window, on the dusty approach to the city, the members of the Seelie Court waited curiously for the other passengers to join them. Instinctively, Church felt that the train had already started moving imperceptibly, gradually building speed.

"You must let them alight," Tom insisted. "You allowed them passage from the Fixed Lands—"

"The Last Train was summoned by blood," Ahken said.

"You cannot take them to the Final Destination! The survival of everything depends on them!"

As Ahken's smile broadened, Church had the uneasy feeling that something was squirming just beneath his skin. "Your kind has little respect for the eternal patterns of Existence and the great inviolable rules. That one—" Ahken pointed to Veitch "—transgressed the ultimate law when he travelled to the Grim Lands to bring back this one." Ahken indicated Shavi. "That has not been forgotten. Indeed, the current crisis that grips all the lands is a direct result of that action. You are architects of this suffering."

Church and Veitch stepped forwards, hands on their swords. Tom held them back. "Don't," he said quietly. "You can't hurt it. What you see is not what is."

"You were our only chance to escape Earth when the spiders came," Church said. "We had no choice but to call you."

"Every action has repercussions, seen and unforeseen. You must take responsibility for them."

"Wait," Tom said. "They are too important for their lives to be forfeit—"

"No one is too important." There was a crack like thunder to Ahken's voice.

"Take me in lieu," Tom pressed.

"I have you anyway, True Thomas. You knew the price asked the last time you travelled with me. But you have traded away your future, and now you are worthless to me."

Recognising that Ahken would not back down, Church part-drew Caledfwlch and the Blue Fire fizzed and crackled around him. The gravity surrounding Ahken grew by the moment, and Church was now in no doubt as to whom he represented. They could not defeat such a force.

"Quick, now! Be swift, like mercury, like the wind!" The voice rose up around them before Church caught a glimpse of a figure slipping low and lithe along the carriage, more mischievous grin and sizzling eyes than substance.

At the same time, Ahken was altering into something that filled Church with dread. Clasped hands became hooked claws and the smell of the grave intensified, but Church only had an instant to glimpse it, for there was a flash of blinding light and then utter darkness.

The carriage door opened with a sound like escaping steam, and Church instinctively propelled those nearest to him out into the bright daylight. As he sprawled in the dust, he saw the others urged unceremoniously out around him, before a flash of brown sealskin bolted out to pause close by his ear. He looked deeply into yellow eyes and saw world upon world before their colour changed.

"Grasped from the jaws of dark disaster. You, merry wanderer, are the Puck's prime spark. Enjoy your good fortune, happy fool and lover, for falling so neatly in my purview."

"Thank you," Church said, still shaken by what he had sensed in the carriage.

"No, thank you, Brother of Dragons. It serves me that you serve me, but the Puck cannot always be on hand to pluck you from the fire. The end can only be achieved by your own devices, and perhaps not even then. That is the way of the weft and the weave, and we are all at its mercy, even the Oldest Things in the Land."

In the space between thoughts, the Puck was gone. He had saved and guided them several times, but Church feared he was shepherding them towards an uncertain future that would benefit only the Puck.

With a belch of steam, the Last Train raced away. Amidst the billowing cloud and the rising dust, Church had the impression that it wasn't a train at all, but a long black insect scurrying across the land, the roar of its wheels an angry cry that promised retribution another day.

"I saw the Puck, too," Shavi said, helping Church to his feet. "He plays a long game, but at this moment I am glad he has chosen to act as our protector."

"Until the time arises when he needs to sacrifice us to achieve his ends," Church said. "We're always pawns and I'm sick of it."

The now-excited guards hastily ushered the Seelie Court through the gates, while others rushed to collect Church and the others. To one side, Etain and the other Brothers and Sisters of Spiders stood, stiff and isolated by death and their former allegiance. Church hadn't even realised they were on the train.

He tore his attention from Ruth wiping the dust from Veitch's cheek and turned to Tom. "What did Ahken mean, that you've traded away your future?"

"Stop asking fool questions!" Tom adjusted his glasses in a manner that Church had come to recognise as defensive.

"You can't keep secrets from me any more, Tom."

"I can do what I damn well like. I should be dead by rights, and you've made my life a misery by bringing me back. I've got no purpose here now. So don't you start telling me I need to speak my mind to you. It's you that owes me to keep your nose out of my business. It's the least you can do for the pain you've caused."

Church winced, and Tom instantly appeared to regret his words. "There's a more pressing matter," he said. "On the train, I encountered a boy who, I'm told, is dead. He said his name was Carlton, and he told me something you ought to consider."

Church saw that Tom's hand was trembling. He tucked it quickly in his jacket pocket.

"He said, in the battle ahead there are people we can trust and people we can't."

"You believe him?"

"Who knows what to believe in this madhouse? But if I were you, I'd keep a close eye on those around you. And the ones at your back."

6

The streets of the Court of the Soaring Spirit were filled with a cheering throng that left the Brothers and Sisters of Dragons baffled and embarrassed by the obvious adulation they were receiving. Many of the disparate races of T'ir n'a n'Og were represented, from the Tuatha Dé Danaan, whose calls had an uneasy edge of desperation, to animals that walked and talked like men, squat, dour mountain folk, bat-winged, sable-skinned people from the Forest of the Night, short, tall, fat, thin, bizarrely attired.

Veitch was surprised by his reaction. He had forgotten the peculiar, rich, uplifting qualities of the Far Lands, the potent scents—spices, fruit and perfumed candles—colours more vibrant than his home and the rich textures of the stone, metalwork and carvings demanding that he touch them. It felt as if he was in a dream; it felt like coming home.

"What are you smiling at?" Ruth asked him between nods to the well-wishers lining the way.

"Do I need a reason?"

"You? Usually."

At the Palace of Glorious Light, drenched in the mid-morning sunlight, they were guided to chambers that had once been occupied by Niamh, the court's former queen, where Mallory, Hunter and Caitlin now waited.

"I didn't believe it when the guards told me," Mallory exclaimed. He shook Church's hand forcefully, and then the two groups hugged and greeted each other like long-lost friends.

Laura and Hunter adopted a blasé attitude, but were soon sequestered together deep in conversation, their eyes gleaming, oblivious to the high emotions that whirled around them.

After the reunion, Mallory said, "We couldn't find the Extinction Shears. We failed. I failed."

"That's because you were looking in the wrong place," Church said reassuringly. "The Market of Wishful Spirit is in the Grim Lands."

"Why on earth would it be in the Land of the Dead?" Caitlin asked.

"It doesn't matter. We'll start working on a plan to get to them immediately," Mallory said.

"Not going to be that easy, mate," Veitch interjected. "We come in and out of this place like it's a tourist destination, but there are strict rules about getting to the Grim Lands. I've been there twice. The first time I brought the Void back and caused all this mess. And the second time I had to die to get there."

Leaving the others to share stories, Mallory led Church along the sun-drenched corridors to Doctor Jay's laboratory. As they neared, the constant low-pitched hum set their teeth on edge.

When Church saw Jerzy, unconscious, silver-coated eyes wide and staring, his heart went out to his friend. "What's wrong with him?"

"I've got Math . . . everybody . . . working on it. No one has any idea."

"It's got to be linked to the Void's return in some way."

"Yeah, but . . . Jerzy? What could he have to do with anything?"

"The Puck took an interest in him. Even kidnapped him for a while. That could be it—" He cursed under his breath. "I'm useless. All these important details, and I never see them at the time. Why didn't I question why the Puck got involved with Jerzy?"

"What would you have been able to do?" Mallory led Church out of the chamber and closed the door to muffle the unsettling noise. "All these connections . . . half the time they could be random. No one sees their importance till after the fact."

"I hope he's going to be all right." Church cast one last glance back at the door separating him from his friend; it had been too long since they'd spent time together.

"Yeah, he's one of the good ones," Mallory replied, "so this is going to sound harsh, but we've got too much else to worry about right now. Doctor

Jay is doing what he can for Jerzy, and if there's any significance to this change we'll find out quickly."

"We saw the Enemy's army all over the Far Lands," Church said.

Mallory nodded. "They'll be here soon. We've already been softened up by the Riot-Beasts. The Enemy's going to throw everything at us. There's an assassin loose in the city, trying to pick us off one by one. We've got strategies in place to tackle it—no Brother or Sister of Dragons travels alone, trebling patrols—but sooner or later someone will make a mistake."

"Tonight we rest, and plan," Church replied. "Tomorrow we start fighting back."

7

Too many suspicious glances from the others eventually drove Veitch out into the deserted corridors, where his incipient guilt over the last few violent months gradually subsided. For a while, he wandered, deep in thought about Ruth and his belief that if he had any chance of redemption, it was through her, until a faint echo told him he was not alone.

He waited, watchfully, and when no one materialised, he slipped around a corner, ready to draw his sword. Hesitant footsteps heralded the cautious approach of a woman of around twenty-five, her delicate face framed by blond ringlets in an old-fashioned style that Veitch had seen many times during his stays in Victorian London.

"Oh," she said, startled that he was waiting for her.

"Why are you following me?" Veitch growled.

"You are Ryan Veitch?" she replied in a cockney accent. "That's what the guards say. All the fellers and the girls are talking about it downstairs."

"What's it to you?"

She smiled. "Let me tell you, ducky."

Rough hands grabbed Veitch's arms and threw him against the wall. Three men had come up behind him with the stealth of Brothers of Dragons, strong arms, strong faces, sharp eyes, but he could see the hatred in their eyes. He struggled to throw them off, but in a second the woman had a knife against his throat.

"Name's Cathy, lovey, and as God is my witness, I'm going to carve your flesh for what you did to me."

"I've never met you before."

"Which is why I'm still here. I'm one of the lucky ones. But back in my old time, you murdered three of my Brothers and Sisters. We never got the chance to be Five. And I'm not alone there."

"You've got a lot of blood on your hands, Ryan Veitch," a voice said at his ear. "Good, decent people, just trying to do their bit for Existence. I saw my fair share of twisted slaughter at Dunkirk, but nothing like what you did. You betrayed the Pendragon Spirit. You betrayed everything Existence stands for. You killed people who would have been our friends and lovers. And now you're going to pay."

Veitch opened his mouth to account for himself, but Cathy pricked the knife deeper into his flesh. "No lies," she hissed. "Just a quick cut and you won't be hurting any more of us."

Before she could thrust, there was a shift in the quality of the light and shadows appeared, source unknown. A background drone swelled, like the hum of a generator, a charge to the very air itself.

Ruth rounded the corner, eyes crackling with an unearthly power, hair snaking around her head as if it was alive. From her outstretched hands whirled a storm of blue light. Veitch had seen her like that once before, during the Battle of London when her Craft had consumed her and she had become a lethal weapon that could destroy friend and foe alike.

Cathy's knife slipped from trembling fingers as a gale flung her and her three helpers across the flags. The knife whisked up and embedded itself to the hilt in the thin join between two wall-stones.

"You're protecting him?" Cathy raged.

Ruth's appearance slowly normalised. "He's working with us now. No one forgets all the people he's killed, but we need him."

"We don't need him!" Cathy shouted. "He'll always be a danger. At the end, he'll turn, you'll see."

Veitch winced when Ruth cast an unguarded glance his way.

"See? He knows it himself!" The three men helped Cathy to her feet, their expressions no less murderous. "We owe it to all the others to kill him before he destroys everything. Never forget, never forgive!" Tears of anger streaming down Cathy's face, she ran back along the corridor, with the others close behind.

"Thanks," Veitch said. "I should have expected that."

"Probably best if you don't go wandering off on your own from now on."

Veitch tried to put out of his mind how much he had thrown away, the camaraderie, the sense of being on the side of right, respect, love, all for some immature desire for revenge that had become more undefined with each passing day. He felt pathetic. He hated himself.

Seeing some of this in his face, Ruth's expression softened with pity, and that made him feel even worse. "Don't worry," she said. "It's going to be tough, but people will come around."

"You know what? I don't care. I've got a job to do—that's the important thing. The sooner I can start using this blade to cut things down, the better."

A window framed the distant shape of the Burning Man, hazy in the mid-morning sky, and for the briefest instant, Veitch thought it was looking deep into his very heart.

8

Fiddles and pipes and voices created an exuberant music that rippled out from the Palace of Glorious Light across the rooftops of the night-shrouded city and raised the spirits of everyone who heard it. The celebration centred on the great hall of feasting, though the thronging revellers spilled out into corridors and antechambers. Musicians from the Court of the Yearning Heart and the Seelie Court took it in turns to play. The former chose long, rich, dense reels that exuded eroticism and could ignite passion with a simple run of notes, while the latter selected uplifting melodies that exhorted the listener to love life and focus on higher purpose. Dancers whirled continually, collapsing in corners when exhausted for new couples to take their place.

The sprawling kitchens at the heart of the palace had been working all day to prepare the feast, in clouds of steam and ferocious heat from the ovens that left every worker stripped to their underclothes. Pies and roasts and delicately spiced dishes, stews and soups, fruits and cakes and sweetmeats were piled high on the tables around the edge of the hall. Goblets were never empty; a small army of servants moved steadfastly around with flagons of wine and ale.

The atmosphere was one of wild abandon, from the dancers to the staggering drunks to the couples who made love in the shadows, not caring who saw them. The festivities had been called to celebrate the reunion of the Brothers and Sisters of Dragons as they prepared for the next and final stage of the campaign, but it was also a statement: that even in the sight of the Burning Man, life was a powerful driving force.

Shavi, mildly drunk and happy, watched the proceedings with one foot on a beer-washed table and a goblet clutched tightly to his chest. "This is the reason why we do what we do," he said.

Sipping his ale, Mallory watched Laura grab Hunter by the hand and drag him behind a pillar. "Free booze?"

Shavi laughed. "We lived in a world where strange and wonderful things happened on a daily basis, yet we barely raised our eyes from our work to see them. We were truly blessed to exist in the Fixed Lands. Everything that is writ bold here in the Far Lands was there, moving quietly on the edge of our vision, just waiting to be discovered."

"I never saw that much of it."

"Then you never looked. Every magical thing is invisible until you find the right eyes to see it, whether it be love, or joy, or friendship, or a small flying pixie."

"Do you ever get depressed?"

"If you saw the world as I did, you would not. Yes, there is hardship. Yes, there is pain and suffering, and if you focus on each instance in detail then the only thing you will find is pointless misery. But the mysteries of cause and effect are far beyond our abilities to understand them. Because we love science so much we believe there is a process where a simple action has a straightforward reaction. But the system in which we operate is massively complex, and what may have started at the beginning of time caused a billion, billion connecting reactions that are only now bearing fruit. Pick any point along that chain and you would not see what came before or what the final result would be, only that instant, good or bad in and of itself."

"Oh, yeah, the Butterfly Effect. Flap, flap, big storm a world away."

"Indeed. We fool ourselves into believing we understand cause and effect, but we see nothing, we know nothing. That is why you cannot plan to influence the world, for good or bad, in the same way that the butterfly cannot plan to create the storm. No one can predict the repercussions in a complex system. In the end, all you can do is trust your heart and hope."

"Then why are you so upbeat? It could all be trending towards misery."

"Because if you examine your own life, you will see that the universe is kindly and that it does its best to help you."

"Laura's right. You really are an old hippy." Mallory sipped his ale, thoughtfully. "So nobody knows anything, and we just trust our instincts?"

"Our hearts."

"I wish I'd had somebody like you on our team to keep the morale up."

"Hal would have fulfilled that role if he had not become part of the Blue Fire."

"Be kind of good to get him back." Mallory stirred uneasily. "I still don't understand why there's only four of us. Every other team gets five, but us . . ." He shrugged. "I keep expecting somebody new to walk through the door. I can't shake the feeling that something's missing."

"Perhaps it was simply meant to be that your team has only four members."

"Why? I don't get it."

"That is my point. We cannot see the patterns. We can only trust that things will work out for the best."

"I really wish I could see the world like you do, Shavi. I just feel . . . sad."

"We all have our pain, Mallory, because in the vast, indecipherable pattern we are all insignificant, while at the same time we are each and every one hugely significant, for our actions, small and large, make up that very pattern. We are threads in the warp and the weft."

In the centre of the room, Caitlin danced alone, lost to herself, the Morrigan's love of sex and life evident in each seductive movement.

Loading his plate with roast meat, Veitch ignored the pointed stares of the other Brothers and Sisters of Dragons from across the ages. They milled around the hall as they tried to avoid being dragged into Decebalus's ribald revelry as he stalked back and forth, swilling ale by the flagon while indulging in outrageous flirting to make Aula jealous.

For much of the evening, Church and Ruth had been involved in intense conversation, but they broke off to join Veitch as he made his way over to Shavi and Mallory.

"You know how to throw a good party," Church said.

"One of the perks when you get your own Great Court," Mallory replied.

"I still can't believe the Tuatha Dé Danaan let you take over." Ruth laughed.

"They owed me big time."

Church surveyed the Brothers and Sisters of Dragons with pride. "They seem like a great crew, from what I can tell. Brave, fierce—we'll do well with them on our side."

"Would you expect the Pendragon Spirit to choose any other?" Shavi said.

"You think they're formidable, you wait till you see the gods," Mallory said with a sly smile. "Norse, Greek, Chinese, the whole terrifying, insane collection."

"Where are they?" Ruth asked.

"We've got them in their own separate camps outside the city walls. If you think the Tuatha Dé Danaan are fractious when they get together, you really don't want to see this lot mixing with time on their hands. They'd be at each other's throats in a second."

"Imagine them side by side on the battlefield," Church said. "Whatever troops the Void can throw at us are going to be up against it."

"As long as our lot don't kill each other first."

The revelry was disrupted by the crash of the main door slamming open. In staggered Ronnie Kelly, a Brother of Dragons in a field uniform from the Great War, his expression devastated. He flailed for a moment before raising his hands in a silent plea. They were covered in blood.

"Murder," he eventually stuttered. "There's been a murder!"

The band came to a sudden halt. Church, Veitch and Mallory raced towards Ronnie before the others realised what he was saying. In one of the branching corridors off the main approach to the hall, a woman in a pink satin Georgian dress was sprawled, eyes wide open. A neat hole had been punched in the centre of her forehead.

"Marie," Mallory mouthed. All he could think of was her accusation the previous day that he had attacked her. Haunted, he dropped to his knees to check her pulse, though it was clear she was dead.

Angry voices rose up from a small crowd of Brothers and Sisters of Dragons further down the corridor. A man in a Georgian morning suit pointed an accusing finger at Veitch. "He did it. He killed our Marie."

"No." Church stepped quickly between Veitch and the group. "He's been with us all the time. Don't jump to conclusions."

"Why not?" The man brushed away a stray tear. "That is what he does."

Fearing they would attack Veitch, Shavi held up his hand and drew all attention to him. On the periphery of his vision, his alien eye glimpsed hidden shapes, and amidst the dislocation, he heard the distant whispers of the Invisible World. "The murderer is still here in the palace. And more. . . We are under great threat!"

"Fan out across the palace," Church said. "Stick to the core groups that Decebalus has defined for you. Nobody goes alone."

Reluctantly, the Brothers and Sisters of Dragons moved off along the echoing corridors.

"This wasn't me," Veitch said, eyeing the body.

"We know," Church replied. "I was stupid to think the Enemy would give us time to regroup. Come on."

Shavi followed Church, Veitch, Ruth and Laura along the corridor. Mallory, Hunter and Caitlin headed for the stairs to the next level. As the groups separated, Shavi heard a rasping, unfamiliar voice issuing from Caitlin that chilled him to the bone. It said, "Death is circling. Blood will come!"

9

Navigating the deserted, barely lit upper reaches of the palace was not easy. Hunter led the way with a torch snatched as they climbed the stairs in the east tower. To his left, Mallory's sword provided its own blue light to guide them, while at the rear, the Morrigan had risen in Caitlin, who now moved like a jungle cat. The possession brought physical change too, her eyes becoming a deeper black, her muscles tauter. Gripping her axe effortlessly, she appeared to hear things beyond even her comrades' sharpened perceptions.

Climbing the last flight of stairs, they entered an echoing loft space beneath the ancient oak rafters that supported the palace's pitched roof. Sleeping birds rested on every beam and in every nook and cranny above their heads, the floor white with their excrement.

Caitlin rested an unnaturally cold hand on Hunter's shoulder, her head half-cocked as she listened. "There's someone up ahead."

"You need to get yourself a sword," Mallory said.

"Don't you worry about me," Hunter replied. "Now, who loves the stink of bird droppings enough to hide out up here?"

The loft area branched right and then broke off in three directions over the palace's wings. As they reached the junction, an ear-splitting, high-pitched shriek ripped out of the dark. The birds erupted from their roosts, driving Mallory, Hunter and Caitlin apart as they surged around the enclosed space.

One glimpse of Caitlin wielding her axe in a cloud of feathers and blood reached Mallory before he was driven away by talons and beaks, bodies battering him like stones. Disoriented by the beat of wings, he staggered back until he felt the wall against his shoulder.

Amidst the chaos he glimpsed a figure ahead, seemingly unmoved by the storm: a woman's hair, a cheek, an eye. In the gradual accumulation of information, a deep cold ran through him, driving out all rational thought. He propelled himself through the birds towards her.

His worst fears were confirmed: a woman in her late twenties stood before him, blond hair tied back, face weary from too much struggle too soon. A woman from his old life, before he was a Brother of Dragons, forced to endure an atrocity of Mallory's making that ironically set him on the path to becoming who he was.

The emotions her face dredged up blinded him to the knowledge that she couldn't possibly be there. He grasped her hand, desperate to tell her all the things he should have said but never had the chance, but all that came out was a weak, "I'm sorry."

The woman's eyes glittered hatefully. Through the haze of his crushing guilt, Mallory finally noticed something off-kilter about her. Pain jabbed into the back of his hand, drawing his attention to fingers that were no long the slender, pale ones he had grabbed but made of twisted blackthorn. A drop of his blood gleamed on the end of one sharp protrusion.

The woman's face unpacked, altered, until what remained was a head that appeared to be constructed of crumpled paper with black, blinking eyes hovering above a malicious grin. The body was now constructed wholly from the same twisted strands of blackthorn.

Mallory threw himself back. "I saw you. In Ogma's library."

The creature lifted its hand high, tilted back its head and dripped

Mallory's blood into its open mouth. "Now we are joined for all time," it said in a voice like rustling paper, "and that will not be for long." It advanced on Mallory, one finger outstretched as if accusing him.

Scrambling to his feet, Mallory hacked off the blackthorn creature's arm. With a crackle, the forearm regrew from the stump, the index finger extending into an even more brutal point.

"You cannot stop me," the creature said. "Nothing ever stops me."

Mallory lopped off the arm again, but it grew back just as quickly.

From out of the whirling birds, Hunter exploded into the creature. An instant later Caitlin was at his side, axe at the ready.

"Should have brought some defoliant." Hunter watched the creature pick itself up and turn those chilling black eyes upon him.

"Take it easy," Mallory said. "Your weapons can't hurt it."

For a second the creature weighed an attack, and then another high-pitched shriek increased the birds' wild activity. Battering her way through the wall of feather, beak and talon, Caitlin searched for their adversary, but there was no longer any sign of it.

They retreated to the only entrance to the loft space and waited until the birds had calmed and returned to their roosts. A careful investigation throughout the branching wings of the loft found only a ragged hole into the night and a potential escape route across the roofs of the city.

As they looked out over the lights of the Court of the Soaring Spirit, Hunter said, "You hear that?"

At first they thought it was the thunder of an approaching storm until faint metallic notes rose up amongst the pounding. "The Enemy," Caitlin said. "They've reached the Great Plain. It won't be long before they're at the city walls."

Mallory's attention was caught by the distant outline of the Burning Man simmering in the night sky. "The fire's rising within it, see?" he noted. "It's nearly done. Soon the Void will here, and when that happens the clock stops. It's the end of the world for all of us."

CHAPTER TWO
TEN DEGREES OF HELL

1

From the window, it appeared as if a black cloak had been laid across the rooftops surrounding the Palace of Glorious Light. As the night receded with the first silvery light of dawn, that cloak gleamed with an oily sheen that eventually revealed itself to be thousands of ravens perched in eerie silence. The beady eyes of the *Morvren* all turned towards the palace.

"What is it with birds?" Hunter said. "Since that thorny bastard attacked last night, I've spent all my time picking feathers out of every crevice. And now this."

"Blame Church. They're his." Laura carved her name in the stone with a small knife.

"I think he might debate the ownership issue with you. A supernatural omen of death following you around to pick the bones of the fallen isn't quite the same as a budgie."

"Looks like there's more of them," Laura said, casting a bored glance out of the window.

"They know something we don't."

"You're lucky you've got me to protect you, then."

"Sorry? Did you say 'torment'?"

A gong resonated along the silent corridors, summoning them to a gloomy chamber where the walls and windows were hidden behind purple and scarlet drapes. Magickal artefacts were piled high on the tables and floor, suggestive of some hidden ritual pattern—skulls, crystals, athames, statuettes, jewels, candles and more. Parchments and books were stacked head-high in one corner. With a long, delicate brush, Math carefully inscribed protective runes on a section of wall that would soon be hidden again behind the drapes. His four-faced mask turned slowly and deliberately.

Even though Church and Shavi talked intensely in one corner, there was an unshakable feeling that something had just departed the space.

"Nobody thought to lay on a muffin basket?" Hunter said. "You can't have a breakfast meeting without muffins."

"Funny man." Laura shied away from Math and went to annoy Tom, who had just lurched in, grumpy and tired.

Soon the two teams and Tom were gathered, with Math observing silently from one corner. All of them were aware of the bond they shared, despite their personal differences. The air was electric with the Pendragon Spirit.

"What lies ahead is more than we've ever faced before, and there's a strong possibility that none of us will be getting out of this alive," Church said. "It's important we're under no illusion about that."

"It's the job," Hunter said. "No point grumbling about it."

"That's easy for you to say. You've got a death wish," Laura said tartly.

"We know where we stand," Mallory said. "The question is, where do we go? And just as importantly, what do we do about that thing we found in the loft last night?"

"If, as you describe, it can change appearance at will, it could remain amongst us, picking us off one by one," Shavi mused.

"Who's to say it's not here now?" Ruth said. They all shifted uneasily.

"Math, what did you find out?" Church asked.

"The creature is known as the Hortha." Math's voice echoed hollowly from behind his mask. "It is mentioned many times in our histories, as an agent of destruction and death and chaos."

"An agent of the Void," Caitlin added.

"The Hortha is a hunter, a tracker. Once it has identified its prey, it cannot be deterred or stopped. It will continue until it has killed."

"Okay, you got a load of gods lined up out there ready to fight for the cause," Veitch began, "but from where I'm standing, the biggest threat to the Void is the Army of Dragons. If I was the Enemy, I'd send that thing out to pick the whole lot of us off one by one. Cut out the heart."

"We're not going to be sitting back, letting the Hortha get on with it," Church said. "Ryan?"

"So, what, he gets to call the shots now?" Laura said.

"We're all here because we've got individual strengths that benefit the group as a whole. Veitch—and Hunter—they're the strategists."

"What am I? The cheerleader?" Laura said sullenly. "Give me a C-U-N—"

"Let's focus, shall we?" Church insisted.

"We're taking the fight straight to the Void," Veitch said, "starting right now. Decebalus is going to lead the Army of Dragons, the gods and the Tuatha Dé Danaan against the Enemy forces."

"Our troops can be organised before the Enemy reaches the city?" Ruth asked.

"I reckon. Decebalus is a big bastard. He's not going to let people drag their feet. In the meantime, we're going to split into two teams. One lot is going to get the Extinction Shears. Once they've done that, they're going to rendezvous with the other group, who are going straight into the Fortress of the Void."

"When you say it like that, it sounds simple." Hunter looked around the room. "Does anybody else fancy some wine?"

"Hunter's right," Laura said. "You've already made it clear: the rules say nobody gets into the Land of the Dead. And that Fortress must be swarming with the Enemy, never mind the Burning Man hanging right over the top of the place. What are you going to do—walk up to the front door and ask nicely?"

"Actually, we'll be using the back door," Church said. "A group of colonists in Roanoke back in Elizabethan times were kidnapped and taken to the Fortress. One of them was Virginia Dare."

"That little girl?" Laura said.

"She escaped from the Fortress," Church continued. "She knows a secret way back in—"

"You can't take her back there," Ruth protested. "Laura and I both spoke to her last night. She's completely traumatised by what happened to her in that place. It would be cruel to make her go back."

"It's not like I haven't wrestled with this, Ruth—"

"Church. No."

"We don't have a choice," he said firmly. "There's too much at stake."

"She's just a little girl."

"She's stronger than you think," Caitlin said. "If this has to be done, we'll protect her as much as we can."

"So it's a suicide mission," Hunter said. "Into the Fortress, blow up the Burning Man. Last post and medals all round. Delivered to the ones we leave behind, of course."

"And what part do Miller and Jack play in this?" Shavi asked.

A touch of weariness was evident in Church as he shook his head. "Math's been trying to work that out. All we know is that the Two Keys are needed along with the Extinction Shears to stop the Void."

"So we're winging it," Veitch said, with what the others thought was an alarming note of relish. "We trust our instincts once we get in there. That's what we do, right?"

"I usually prefer what we in the security business call a 'plan,'" Hunter said. "But I'm willing to try your way for the novelty."

"Death wish," Laura muttered.

"I'm going to take Virginia, Miller and Jack to the Fortress alone—" Church began.

Mallory, Hunter and Veitch all cut him off but Ruth's voice was louder. "You don't get to play hero on your own," she said.

Church saw the truth in their faces. "You don't trust me," he said. "You know I'm fated to turn into the Libertarian and you think I'm going to sell you all out."

"It's not that," Mallory said unconvincingly. "We just don't want to take any risks. The more of us we can get in there, the better chance we'll have."

The sting of betrayal was evident in Church's face for a brief moment before he continued, "Then we all choose the two teams. I'm going to the Fortress, so the other team needs a leader. Mallory?"

Mallory nodded. "I've seen Stoke. After that the Grim Lands is the only place left to visit."

"Ryan?" Ruth suggested. "You told me the dead worship you as some kind of hero. Sounds like you could use that to our advantage. They should know where the Market is in their own home."

"No," Mallory said firmly. "I don't need to be looking over my shoulder all the time in a place like that."

"Fair enough," Veitch replied. "Your loss, mate."

"I'll go." Caitlin flashed a brief smile at Mallory. "We make a good team. We trust each other. And two of us should be enough. Travel light, travel fast." Mallory began to protest, but Caitlin silenced him. "Don't try to protect me. I've got a goddess of death inside me, you goon."

"Okay, that's a plan," Hunter said. "And it only leaves one question outstanding. How do they get to the Grim Lands?"

After a long moment of silence, Veitch said, "The same way everybody else does. They die."

2

The great council chamber in the Court of the Soaring Spirit was almost as large as the Colosseum, with marble pillars supporting a domed glass roof that brought shafts of morning sunlight onto the chamber floor. Bas-reliefs of events from the long history of the Tuatha Dé Danaan lined the walls, and high overhead Gothic carvings of strange beings echoed the works of the master medieval stonemasons. The building's enormous scale generated a reverential atmosphere, and even though it was almost full, barely a whisper ran around the tiered seating.

Caitlin stood on the floor of the chamber next to the Speaker's Wish-Post, turning over what Veitch had said. The chatter of her three personas had stilled for long periods since the Morrigan had joined with her, but she could always feel the goddess's brooding presence at the back of her head. The Morrigan was a being of contrasts: cold of will and hot of passion, death-dealing and life-affirming, but always dangerous; very, very dangerous.

Mallory entered the chamber with Lugh, Rhiannon and two other gods Caitlin didn't recognise. With each passing day, she found Mallory more impressive as he rose to the challenge of dealing with the responsibilities that had been thrust upon him. Yet she was troubled by the deep sadness that now suffused him. There appeared to be no cause for it, but it had gained such a powerful grip on him that it was almost as if he had decided that the best of his life now lay behind him, and only duty and sacrifice were ahead.

He was concerned about her too; it was visible in his face whenever they were together, and after their decision to travel to the Grim Lands it had become even more intense.

Mallory believed the Morrigan was a corruption that would eventually eat away the essence of the Caitlin he knew. How could she explain to him that she finally felt whole? With the Morrigan inside her, doubts faded like the morning mist. Her slowly creeping, black despair was now walled off. Her mind was clear and fresh, her thoughts sharp, and she fizzed with an energy and unshakable vision. It was almost like a drug. It was almost as if it was meant to be.

Mallory took her to one side. "Church and the others are getting a briefing from Decebalus on the gods and the readiness of the Army of Dragons, but he'll be along if you need him."

"I'm fine."

"You're sure?" he pressed.

"As a Sister of Dragons, they'd listen to me, but you know they've got a deep-seated prejudice against Fragile Creatures. With the Morrigan inside me, though, I'm one of them—they have to listen. Doubly so, because they're scared of the Morrigan, and a Sister of Dragons and the Morrigan combined is just too much for them to contemplate."

"If you can't win them over with rational argument, give them your spooky stare and terrify them into submission. Nice strategy." He squeezed her hand. "Good luck."

As Mallory left, Hunter sauntered up, seemingly oblivious to the weight of the historic occasion. "Still no sign of the last two courts," he noted.

"So we're missing the Unseelie Court and the Court of the Final Word."

"Yeah, I wouldn't hold my breath for that last one."

"Oh."

"We had a bit of a falling out."

"That's never stopped them before," Caitlin said, puzzled.

"They had a lot of big plans. But in the end they came to nothing." Hunter smiled tightly.

Caitlin shrugged. "Apparently the Unseelie Court hates everybody, and they've got a real grudge against the human race from hundreds of years ago."

"So this is it—eighteen of the twenty Great Courts." He looked around at the silent ranks glowing in the sun with a diffuse golden light. "All the arrogant bastards hanging on the words of one Fragile Creature." He surprised her with a kiss on the cheek. "Knock 'em dead. Literally, if possible."

Hunter joined Mallory, Lugh and Rhiannon on the edge of the floor and Caitlin immediately went to the Speaker's position.

"These are the End-Times," she said in a strong, clear voice. "You know it in your hearts. You can feel the ashes on the wind. And if you still doubt, you can look up into the sky and see the Burning Man looking back, ready to judge you. I know for a race like the Golden Ones it's easy to dismiss these signs. You have existed—and exerted your power—far beyond the time of Fragile Creatures, and all other beings in the Far Lands and the Fixed Lands. You have always believed this rule would continue for all time. Unshakable. Yet I know you understand the rules of Existence, and that you know the most important one, for the wiser ones amongst you have stated it many times— there is always something higher. What you now face is higher. And you have been expecting this time because it holds such a powerful place in your own stories and mythology: the time when the Devourer of All Things will return to end the days of gods and men, to wipe the board clean, and to set out its dark vision for a new age."

As she looked around the audience, Caitlin experienced a startling moment of clarity. Once again she was the small-town doctor whose only aim in life was to heal the people who came to her. And here she was addressing a congregation of gods. She was so out of her depth it was laughable. Yet, aston-ishingly, they were heeding her every word.

The power of the Tuatha Dé Danaan was so great she could feel the throb of it in the air. Some of the lower ranks had the plasticky features of shop dummies, as though they had been freshly minted. But the oldest were barely human in shape at all; some she perceived only as balls of brilliant light, and amongst those, she knew, was the one the others spoke of in reverent tones as the Dagda.

"This is an historic meeting," she continued. "The first time the Great Courts have joined for a council since you left the four cities of your homeland. You're all suspicious of each other, I know that. But above all you recognise that this is about the survival of your race."

Caitlin placed one hand on the Wish-Post. In the air above it, an image coalesced until everyone in the room felt as if they were standing amidst the scene they witnessed. There was the Enemy Fortress sprawling on a scale that took the breath away, the smell of rotting meat and burning, clouds of greasy smoke obscuring the sky, the constant beat of heavy machinery. Overhead, the Burning Man glowed through the billowing smoke. The image closed in on the shape until everyone could see the figures writhing within the conflagration.

"You always thought yourselves the most powerful things in Existence, but in the end that's all you are—fuel," Caitlin continued. "The Burning Man has been created to provide a space in which the Void can manifest some aspect of itself. Its power is normally diffuse across the entire universe, a faint background energy that keeps the whole mess running. It needs to focus that power in one place, at one time, to change the structure of things. It already has immeasurable power—enough to transform the Fixed Lands with the help of its agents, the Army of the Ten Billion Spiders. So why does it need to come here? Why is it intent on drawing itself into an overwhelming force? Because it knows its success is not guaranteed. It knows that somewhere in this land are the keys to a force that could stop it in its tracks, perhaps even destroy it."

The image above the Wish-Post changed to a view over the great megalithic structure at Callanish on the north-west coast of the Scottish Isle of Lewis. In the hazy pre-dawn, the standing stones shone like silver against the rolling green landscape shaped by the blasting Atlantic gales. As the golden rays from the rising sun touched one of the stones, lines of Blue Fire ran out in all directions, crossing, interlinking, until an intricate network blazed across the landscape. A communal intake of breath whispered around the chamber.

"The Blue Fire is the mark of Existence in our reality," Caitlin said. "It is the lifeblood, flowing through everything. Can you feel its power?"

The Wish-Post ensured the observers lived the image it revealed. An exhilarating feeling of rejuvenation, of hope and awe, connected everyone in the room.

"Existence is the equal and opposite of the Devourer of All Things. Life to the Void's Anti-Life. Hope to its despair. And small shards of Existence are embedded in all Fragile Creatures. We call it the Pendragon Spirit. The Brothers and Sisters of Dragons can access that power, but soon all Fragile Creatures will be able to bring it to life inside them. You call us Fragile Creatures, but we are not. We are gods, all of us."

Caitlin expected some resistance, but as she looked around the intense, beautiful faces, she saw the first signs of mute acceptance.

"The Pendragon Spirit was planted in Fragile Creatures at the very beginning, and it is there for a reason," she continued. "It's the secret weapon, ready to be unleashed when we need it most. And that time is now. The final battle with the Void, to decide our survival or destruction, to decide the shape of all reality to come. The biggest stakes of all."

Amidst the thunder of the blood in her head, she could hear the Morrigan urging her on.

"This is not the time for the Golden Ones to remain aloof, or to indulge in petty squabbles amongst yourselves. This is the time to reach your potential —to rise above your limitations, put aside your arrogance and recover humility. To reach out to those who can help you, and thereby help yourselves. Individually, we can achieve nothing. Together we can change reality."

Caitlin searched the faces for some sign that she was winning them over, but they all remained implacable.

"I hereby call upon the Great Courts of the Golden Ones to stand together as one, united for the first time since you left your homeland. I ask you to join with the other gods, your cousins from across the Great Dominions, to create the greatest force the Far Lands have ever seen. And I call on you to stand shoulder to shoulder with the Brothers and Sisters of Dragons, as allies in this great war.

"Stand now with the Kingdom of the Serpent, which symbolises the full force of Existence and the power of the Blue Fire. Together we can defeat the Kingdom of the Spider. Together we can win."

A long moment of silence followed her words, until Lugh said loudly, "The Court of Soul's Ease stands with the Brothers and Sisters of Dragons, as equals and allies."

One by one, the kings and queens of the Great Courts rose to announce their support in steady, if at times bemused, voices. Her heart pounding, Caitlin glanced towards Mallory who nodded in return. She felt warmed by the look of pride she saw in his eyes.

"This is an historic moment," she announced, when the final Golden Ones had returned to their seats. "We stand together, now and for evermore. A formidable partnership. Go back to your courts and celebrate what has been achieved this day. In the meantime, battle plans are being drawn up and we will shortly call your leaders together to discuss tactics."

As the Tuatha Dé Danaan began to drift away, Mallory came over. Caitlin could tell he wanted to hug her, but he restrained himself and clapped one tentative hand on her arm instead. "Now for the hard part," he said.

"Let's celebrate our little achievements, shall we?"

Before he could respond, a low-pitched hum rose up, growing louder until they were forced to cover their ears.

"That's the same sound that came when Jerzy fell sick," Mallory shouted.

All around, the Tuatha Dé Danaan were reeling. Some fell back into their seats while others clutched at the walls for support, rubbing their temples as if afflicted with acute headaches. There was a dimming of the faint golden glow that exuded from their skin so that they looked unaccountably sickly.

"What's wrong with them?" Caitlin said.

The sound appeared to emanate from every part of the vast chamber. As Caitlin prepared to scramble out of the room, she caught sight of Hunter pointing towards the upper tiers. Following his finger, she saw rapid movement across the highest row of Tuatha Dé Danaan, spreading to each row in turn.

"The Caraprix!" Mallory exclaimed.

The shape-shifting creatures that held a symbiotic relationship with the gods were separating from their hosts, where they had been disguised as clasps and amulets, buckles, jewellery and daggers. Silvery flashes caught the sunlight as they fluidly transformed into mercury eggs that slithered across golden bodies, down walls, onto the floor and away.

Beside Mallory, Rhiannon cried gently, one arm across her stomach as if gripped by a physical pain of loss, the cauterised wound of her missing hand reaching out with invisible fingers for the disappearing Caraprix.

"They are deserting us," she whispered, "our friends, our souls. They have been with us from the very beginning and now they are going."

"Is this the first sign that the end is near?" Lugh cried. "We are abandoned, here, when we need them most."

The Tuatha Dé Danaan collapsed into their seats at the devastating emotional loss of separation, but they also appeared to be physically weakened.

"Our luck is gone!" Lugh continued. "Our power!"

Mallory grabbed Caitlin's arm and with Hunter they escaped from the chamber and the teeth-jarring drone.

"Several questions spring to mind," Hunter said as they moved along the corridor. "Why now? Where are the Caraprix going? What power do they have? Are they a threat to us?"

74

"My instinct is to plan for the worst," Mallory replied. "We know they've been used to control people before."

"But we've never seen a sign that they've got any real kind of consciousness," Caitlin said. "They've always been pretty benign, changing shape and doing what they're told by the Golden Ones."

"The Tuatha Dé Danaan aren't telling them to scurry away," Hunter observed. "So who is?"

"I think I might be able to answer that." Mallory sprinted ahead.

It appeared he was right, for soon they intersected with a stream of Caraprix heading in one direction. Covering their ears, they joined the silvery flow until they arrived at Doctor Jay's chambers where the Caraprix massed around the door, seeking out every gap around the jamb to ooze inside.

"Jerzy has a Caraprix inside his head," Mallory said. "The Court of the Final Word put it there so they could control him."

"And these others are trying to get to it?" Caitlin asked.

"The droning came from Jerzy first," Mallory replied. "I think the Caraprix in his head was calling to the others."

"Why?" Caitlin said.

"Maybe they just want a big old shape-changing party." Hunter threw open the door. They had one brief glimpse of Jerzy standing in the centre of the chamber with the Caraprix forming a growing silver pool around him, and then the door slammed shut of its own accord. However much they tried, they could not get it open again.

3

Beyond the walls, the Great Plain stretched to the purple mountains on the horizon where the dark smudge of the Enemy gathered. Faint tremors already ran through the ground. The approaching threat was starkly contrasted with the peace of their surroundings, where only the gentle breeze stirred the long grass, accompanied by the sound of crickets.

"All right," Ruth said. "You got me. Where are they?"

Veitch continued to scan the grasslands before announcing, "Got to be some kind of magic. Hidden in plain sight kind of thing."

"Glamour," Church replied. "The Enemy won't see them till we want them to be seen. They won't be able to judge the scale of our forces, or make preparations for our secret weapons."

He led them forwards a few paces until they felt the sensation of passing through a heavy curtain. With a pop, they emerged into the same scenery now filled with more than a hundred Brothers and Sisters of Dragons standing in ranks. Decebalus's barking voice emerged from their midst.

"Blimey," Veitch said. "He's got some lungs on him. Mallory made a good choice for sergeant major."

"We are all going to die!" Decebalus bellowed as he marched through the Army of Dragons. "Enjoy your last moments, and take five of the enemy with you when you pass!"

Behind the Brothers and Sisters, a flag bearing a blue dragon on a white background fluttered above their small, hastily assembled camp.

"You may think you are few in number, but you are worth more than ten, more than twenty, more than a hundred of the Enemy!" Decebalus roared. "The Pendragon Spirit glows within our hearts, joining us together as one. One mind, one body. We care for each other, we protect each other and we strike as one weapon!"

Filled with pride, Church watched the brave, determined faces as Decebalus split the army up into groups of five to prepare for the tasks he had assigned them.

"Do you think they're up to it?" Ruth asked. "We learned on the job, and they've not been through a fraction of the things we've experienced."

"Look at them—they're great," Church replied.

Decebalus summoned the three of them over to a group of five strapping themselves into silver and blue armour. "Greet our brave," Decebalus said. "They have volunteered to scout the Enemy lines. A dangerous task."

Church felt uncomfortable when the Brothers and Sisters of Dragons looked at him with clear awe. "Who are you?" he asked.

"Sound off!" Decebalus shouted when the group simply gaped.

"Leon Corbett," the first said, with a strong Midlands accent. He towered over the others and had long, wavy hair and a tribal tattoo around his upper right arm.

"Kelly Broadbent," ventured the woman next to him. She had auburn hair and something of Ruth about her, Church thought.

"Adam Garrett." This one had spiky brown hair and dark-brown eyes. Hunter or Veitch, Church thought. He was still astonished how Existence played out the same archetypes through each team.

The fourth introduced herself with the lyrical name of Aurelia Verdin. She was in her early twenties. "I'm the horse expert," she said confidently. "The others won't be able to keep up."

"And I'm Richard Flynn." Church saw he was definitely the Shavi of the group, a gentle Glaswegian barely out of his teens, with green-grey eyes and a touch of the mystical about him.

"I'm proud of you all," Church said, shaking each of their hands in turn. "It's a dangerous mission, but the information you bring back will help us win."

Once the group had mounted their horses and were looking towards the horizon, Ruth said, "Decebalus introduced them to us because he thinks there's a good chance they're not coming back."

"They looked like a strong team. If any can get back, it's them."

"How many of these people are going to die, Church?" Ruth pressed. "You saved them all from being killed in their own times . . ." She flashed a glance at Veitch, who didn't meet her gaze. "Only for them to die now."

Veitch studied the groups as they put on their armour and inspected their weapons, a jarring combination of strength and innocence. "Nobody lives forever."

"That's a cliché."

"It's true. All of us, we're privileged. For a short space of time, we've been given something that no one else gets to have. That connection with something big. Knowing that we've got a part to play. That we mean something. That we're not just here to work and earn and eat and drink and die. That's a big thing." His eyes blazed. "There's a price for everything. That's one of those hidden rules you lot keep banging on about. And if the price for that is you give up your life, I reckon it's worth paying. And I bet that lot do too. Once you've tasted it, nothing else compares."

Tom waited on the edge of the Army of Dragons' camp, smoking furtively. "If you've finished with your morning constitutional, there's something you ought to see," he said. He gestured towards a vast expanse of rolling grassland.

"What?" Church said.

"Why isn't Shavi here?" Tom snapped. "He's the only one of you with any sense. Look!"

Church, Ruth and Veitch looked again, and this time they saw a faint wavering in the air over the plain, like a heat haze.

"More glamour?" Church said.

"Break out the cakes and ale." Tom strode ahead. "An additional layer of camouflage, as much to protect the delicate sensibilities of mortals as anything. Follow me."

The sensation of the heavy curtain passed again before they emerged into a cacophony of song and music, bellows, roaring laughter, incessant chatter and the clatter of weapons, followed a split second later by an exhilarating blaze of colour and movement.

Sprawling for several miles was a tent city comprising numerous camps merging into one chaotic mess. Banners flew above the largest tents, marked with runes or symbols—dragons, birds, lightning bolts.

Ruth involuntarily put her hands to her ears at the volume. They were all mesmerised by the sensory assault: the rich aromas of roasting meat and campfire smoke, spices and perfumes, the sulphurous blast of furnaces, oiled leather, mead.

Everywhere people surged, talking, wrestling, arguing, fighting, having sex, drinking, laughing, barking orders, calling for aid.

Not people, Church thought. Gods.

The camp nearest to them belonged to the Aesir. Now recovered from the wounds he had received in Norway, Tyr engaged Freyja in sexual banter before winking and moving on through a cascade of sparks where a blacksmith worked an axe-blade on an anvil in the entrance to a smoky tent.

"These are all the gods who've joined the fight?" Ruth asked.

"From every Great Dominion bar one—the Egyptians, which you appear to have decimated," Tom replied. "That Hunter has an annoyingly flamboyant personality, but he makes a convincing argument. These gods have barely communed since the beginning of this cycle of Existence, yet here they are, cheek by jowl. And more importantly, they are not killing each other, as one would expect. What you have achieved here is huge, and only the Brothers and Sisters of Dragons could have done it."

"I don't understand why they listened to us," Veitch said.

"That's because you're an idiot. They respect you, God knows why. They see things in you that you don't see yourself. They see in you themselves as infants."

"You mean humanity is going to end up like them?" Ruth said. "How depressing."

"No, you'll be better, because you've got the Pendragon Spirit. You're Existence's new, refined model."

A tremendous clamour drew them to a large tent filled with Aesir swigging from flagons of mead as they cheered and argued around a large oaken table where two men arm-wrestled, the veins on their foreheads standing out, faces like stone from the concentration, sinews bulging. Most were so drunk they could barely stand.

"They have been locked in struggle for two hours, neither of them gaining the slightest advantage." Freyja appeared beside them, her potent sexuality making their heads spin.

One of the men was Thor, his wild mane of hair a fiery red, his eyes as grey as the skies over the northern wastes. The other was Chinese, his body just as strong, his features marred by a ragged scar that necessitated a patch over his left eye. He was bald with a long, black ponytail. A silver axe etched with red Chinese characters rested against the table next to Thor's hammer, Mjolnir.

"Lei-Gong." Church recognised the figure from the assemblage of gods beneath the Forbidden Palace in Beijing.

"Stop now!" Freyja called. "We have honoured guests. Brothers and Sisters of Dragons."

Reluctantly, Thor and Lei-Gong broke their grip.

"This pretender lays claim to control of the storm and the lightning and the thunder," Thor bellowed.

"You are the pretender," Lei-Gong said.

"And so it begins." Tom sighed.

"Do not heed those two," Freyja said. "They are both hot-headed. The rest of my brothers and sisters, and my cousins, have experienced a revelation during our brief time here—"

"A rude awakening," Tom interjected.

"Do not diminish us, True Thomas. During all our time, we have—each family group—believed ourselves to be the pinnacle of Existence. To accept that we have equals is . . ." A shadow crossed her face. "Crushing."

"Tough," Veitch said sardonically.

"Yet also liberating," Freyja continued. "I have found much in common with my cousins, and a greater understanding of our place within Existence. We all, ultimately, seek wisdom, do we not, and that is its own reward?"

"Will that make you any less manipulative?" Church asked.

Freyja smiled. "It is the nature of all living things to have their own agenda. And to have their own flaws." She gently took Tom's hand, and the others were all surprised to see him flinch. "How I admire your ring, True Thomas. Andvarinaut. Why, is that not cursed to bring destruction to all who possess it?" Her smile felt like the wind across a frozen plain. She gave a slight, ironic bow, and left.

"What's going on with you two?" Church said. "When you said Freyja gave you that ring to help us find what we were looking for, you didn't say it was cursed."

"Though your arrogance tells you otherwise, I do not answer to you."

"What's the curse? What have you done, Tom?"

A terrible, haunted quality sparked briefly in Tom's eyes, and then he almost ran from the tent and lost himself in the throng outside.

4

Entranced, Church, Veitch and Ruth moved amongst the camps of the tent city, each one with its own particular flavour, each wild and untamed.

They avoided the gaze of a snake-haired woman and were mesmerised for almost half an hour by the mercurial tongue of Hermes, speaking what at first appeared to be nonsense as he addressed a small crowd. More snakes slithered in streams from a black tent where Damballah watched them with burning eyes. Birds flocked around the beak-faced Tangata-Manu. Ishtar ignited barely controllable erotic desires as she attempted to summon the three of them to her tent, and the Shichi-Fuku-Jin travelled in a boat that floated a foot above the ground, offering Church good fortune for the coming battle.

Finally, they could take no more. In the midst of the gods, every sense was forced to operate at its most heightened, and they began to feel queasy from the power that radiated off each of the beings. Despite the status of the Brothers and Sisters of Dragons, the sense of threat from many quarters was palpable, and on more than one occasion they remained unsure about the virtue of having the gods at their backs.

Emerging from the bubble of glamour, it felt as if they had escaped into a quiet room where they could finally catch their breath.

In the shadow of the walls, Etain and the other Brothers and Sisters of Spiders waited on their mounts, dead, unblinking eyes fixed on Veitch.

"Look, I'll catch you later," he said to Church and Ruth uncomfortably. "I'm just...you know...going to say a quick word." He went over to the group and, for the briefest moment, Etain's eyes snapped onto Church, and then Ruth.

"I don't trust her," Church said.

"I thought she was an old girlfriend of yours," Ruth said tartly. "Oh, wait...and what about Niamh, psychotic bitch and arch-manipulator? A lack of trustworthiness seems to be the defining factor. You certainly know how to pick the rotten apples in every barrel."

"I picked you, didn't I?"

"A brief lapse in your bad taste."

Acutely aware of the time for their departure drawing closer, Church led the way back to the city gates. "So, are things all right with us?" he asked hesitantly.

"This isn't the time to have that kind of conversation," Ruth replied, before adding, "We're fine."

"What about Veitch?"

"It's complicated."

"How?"

"He needs me. And I've got to help him, because we all need him."

Church set his jaw.

"I know that's not what you want to hear," Ruth continued. "Church, I don't want anyone else but you in my life. But I meant what I said to you in Norway."

"Is this where you give me the Casablanca talk?"

"We don't amount to anything compared to what's going on around us."

"I disagree with you so profoundly I can barely put it into words. You and me, what we have, is the entire reason why we do what we do. It's a symbol—"

"Don't start intellectualising just to win your argument."

"I can't help who I am, Ruth. I think deeply about everything. Including you and me...and Veitch. I know he's trying to win you over, and I'm not going to stand back and let it happen."

Her eyes flashed and Church felt as if he was looking into a deep well of Blue Fire. "Okay, let's get one thing straight," she said. "I am not a ball that bounces back and forth between you and Ryan. I am not here to be fought over. It is not my role to be 'the girlfriend.' You love your archetypes, but I'm not playing that one."

"I didn't mean that—"

"Accept that I love you. Deeply. And then give me space to find my own path to where you want me to be." She didn't wait for a reply, marching through the gates and up the winding, cobbled street towards the Palace of Glorious Light. In every word and every movement, he saw the strength and sensitivity that had first attracted him to her, undiminished.

She was right, he knew that. And he hated his own insecurity, but he was more afraid of losing her than anything else. He wanted to claim that he'd accepted the hero's role for the sake of humanity, and Existence, and all the good, decent reasons that the storybooks liked to claim. But it was for Ruth. Always Ruth. And while he could rise above that for most of the time and do the right thing, if he didn't have Ruth he was afraid of what he would do.

The depth of his feelings was not only the source of his strength, but also his greatest weakness, and in them he could hear the first seductive whispers of the Libertarian. Sickened and afraid, he hurried into the city.

5

The sun was at its height when Mallory slipped into the room in the most secluded part of the castle. In a mood of intense, brooding silence, Veitch, Laura, Shavi, Hunter and Caitlin waited. There were no windows, and the only light came from two small lanterns in opposite corners.

"All here, then," Mallory said, clearly expecting there to have been some non-arrivals.

"Ruth's a frosty cow, but I don't like it that she's not here. I feel like a back-stabber. I'm a lot of things, but I'm not that," Laura said.

"It would not be fair to place this burden on Ruth," Shavi said. "She cannot be expected to make rational choices."

"You're just afraid she might stop you before you go insane," Laura muttered.

"So you're opposed to it?" Caitlin pressed.

"Nobody's opposed to anything yet, because we haven't come to any conclusion." Mallory took a chair in one corner where he could keep an eye on the door.

"I've got an entire book of clichés just for this occasion." Hunter remained standing, arms folded. Laura was convinced he had chosen the position so the lamplight would illuminate the best aspect of his features. "But I'll select one or two choice ones to start us off. War demands that people do unpalatable things because war is all about winning, especially this one where the stakes are higher than anything I ever dreamed of back in my not-so-glory days."

"What about moral purity?" Shavi argued. "Our fight is meaningless if we are as bad as the Enemy."

"You think the moral high ground will look so pretty when your family and friends and . . . everybody . . . have been raped and slaughtered, and the bad guys win for all time?" Hunter responded. "If you don't win, nothing matters."

"The Morrigan is telling me this is the right thing to do, and not to be sentimental," Caitlin said, "but as a doctor, and having sworn the Hippocratic Oath, I can't condone hurting anyone."

"Which is rich coming from the psycho with the axe," Laura said. "But we're on the same side."

"You know why a lot of military and Security Service people haven't got any time for the protesters back home? Because they're like people who eat sausages, but don't want to know what goes into them," Hunter said firmly. "People have the luxury of arguing about the moral high ground because they don't have to make any of the hard choices at the sharp end. They pay people to do that, so they can sleep in their beds and put it all out of their pretty, civilised minds. But let's understand some of the realities of war here. It's nasty and brutish and thrives on the worst of human nature. Nobody loves it, nobody wants it, but we have to do it, or we die, and everything we believe in dies. Once again: are we prepared to say that we sacrificed all of humanity, but we played fair?"

"This isn't some hypothetical Officer Training debating point," Laura snapped. "It's personal. That makes it different."

"No, it doesn't," Hunter said.

"Okay, you seem to be arguing a very clear point here—" Mallory began.

"This goes against everything we stand for," Shavi pressed. His voice cracked and he was close to tears of frustration. In someone so placid, the sight was shocking.

"There's no black and white," Hunter said. "No good and evil choices, whatever thoughts you might like to comfort yourselves with. It's grey, it's messy. And that's my final cliché of the day."

"Moral relativism underpinned the Holocaust, and Apartheid," Shavi said sharply.

Hunter bristled, and Mallory stepped in before he lost his temper, a first that would have been just as shocking as Shavi's desperation. "Reviewing: events in the coming days are going to turn Church into the Libertarian. If that happens, Existence loses its champion and the Void wins. We all know that time, reality—everything is fluid. It shifts. New presents, subtle alterations to the past, anything to maintain the Void's control. If we can prevent the sequence of events that turns Church into our worst enemy, we stop the Libertarian existing and maybe . . . maybe . . . we win."

"Maybe!" Shavi interjected bitterly.

"And if we can't prevent it happening, we kill Church. The Libertarian doesn't exist. The Void loses its prime agent." Mallory looked around the faces slowly. "You know we don't have a choice. We can't let Church become the Libertarian."

Shavi looked away. Caitlin remained impassive. Laura nodded reluctantly.

"One of us has to be prepared to do it," Hunter said. "There's no point waiting until the crucial moment and then finding nobody is prepared to pull the trigger. So it looks like it's me. I've done it before. I can do it again." A brief glimmer of self-loathing burned in Hunter's mind.

"No." Veitch had remained so silent until now that the others had forgotten he was there, in the darkest part of the room between the two lamps. "It's not right you should have to live with it, however much it needs to be done," he said, stepping into the light. "You know it has to be me. I've got nothing to lose. I'll kill Church."

6

Mallory spent the rest of the afternoon preparing for that evening's ritual. An oppressive apprehension mounted with the fading of the light, and by the time night fell the feeling was so potent it appeared to have spread across the entire city. Fewer lights burned in the windows of the houses, and none of the familiar songs rose up from the inns and public squares. Beyond the walls, the war camps were silent. The Burning Man hung over all.

As Mallory looked out across the city from the window of his chamber, his attention was drawn by one particular light in the winding streets below. It was blue and moving from side to side in a manner that suggested it was signalling. After a moment or two, he became convinced it was signalling to him, although he knew how ridiculous that would have seemed to anyone else.

With little else to do until the ritual, he made his way down to the approach to the palace. To his surprise, the light still wavered gently in the street ahead. Intrigued, he headed towards it, only for the light to move away. He followed for a while, but when he stopped, the light stopped too, and that was when he realised it was leading him on. Remembering the Hortha in the palace loft, he let one hand fall to his sword and proceeded with caution.

Along winding streets, down alleys and across deserted courtyards, he pursued the light, always the same distance ahead. Just when he thought he really was taking an indiscriminate risk, he came to a part of the city he had never visited before, and an overgrown area in the centre of a square, fenced off by rusted, sagging iron railings. Stone monuments engulfed by ivy rose from the long, yellowing grass. It reminded Mallory of an abandoned Victorian cemetery. The gate hung open, and the blue light flickered amongst the statues and mausoleums.

"I've played the game this far. Time to own up," Mallory said as he stepped through the gate.

"Brother of Dragons. Draw nearer."

Mallory recognised the resonant voice. Relaxing, he pushed through the long grass until he encountered a towering figure waiting in the lee of a statue. A wild mane of black hair and a thick beard, coal eyes simmering beneath an overhanging brow. A belted shift of what appeared to be sackcloth. A thong fastened around his left forearm bore several cruel hooks. The blue light came from the dancing flame of a lantern.

"Caretaker," Mallory said. "You found your way to me again."

Mallory recalled the first time he had encountered the mysterious stranger in Salisbury, and discovered that he was, if not a friend, then a benign guide through the dark places.

"I will always be near you, Brother of Dragons."

"Why are you here, now?"

The Caretaker raised the lantern so the illumination picked out the strength in his features. "My lamp. The Wayfinder. With this, I walk the boundaries of this world and all worlds. A light burning brightly in the long watches of the night."

"I know the lamp. It's guided the Brothers and Sisters of Dragons on more than one occasion."

"And so it shall again." As the Caretaker lowered the Wayfinder, the flame moved with a life of its own. "All there has ever been has been leading towards this time. Millions upon millions of interlocking events, grains of sand, one bumping into another, shifting the course of a mighty river. And I have shepherded them all. But soon my work will come to an end."

"You work with the Puck?"

"The Oldest Things in the Land are agents of a higher purpose."

"How do I know you haven't been manipulating me?"

"I have been manipulating you." His eyes glowed. "But that does not mean that I do not look on you and the other Brothers and Sisters of Dragons with fondness. Your road has been long and hard and I have shone the light for you whenever you needed to see your way. But soon your journey will be over."

"I don't know if I like the sound of that."

After a moment of silence, the Caretaker said, "Remember, Brother of Dragons, that even terrible events, from one perspective, may lead to great good from another, greater perspective. The view across Existence is limitless, and within that all things have their place. Leave the deep sadness in your heart behind, and turn your attention to the distant horizon."

The Caretaker's words reminded Mallory of something Ogma had said to him in his great library and, as then, they touched him on a level he couldn't comprehend. "So you're here to show me the way?" Mallory asked.

"An old friend will show you the way." The Caretaker smiled, and as he raised the lantern even higher, the blue flame leaped and grew.

Mallory took a step back as the flame jumped from the Wayfinder and surged into the crackling shape of a man. "Hello, Mallory," it said.

Within the Blue Fire, features flickered. It was Hal, Mallory knew, the fourth member of his team, who had sacrificed himself to the currents of the Blue Fire to help and guide the Brothers and Sisters of Dragons across the ages.

"Hal. Everyone says you're hot stuff."

Laughter rose and fell as the flames danced. "I like you, Mallory. I've been keeping a particular eye on you from the depths of my blue home. Pity we couldn't have hung out, you know, when I had a body."

"Not exactly a bundle of laughs at the moment. Lot on my plate."

"Which is exactly why I'm here. You're going to the Grim Lands . . . or the Grey Lands . . . why does that place get two names? It's a big place, Mallory. Infinite, in fact. The chance of you just stumbling across the Extinction Shears is . . . well, it's not going to happen."

"We like our missions impossible."

"I bet you'd like some help more. Say, a lantern with a flame that will point relentlessly to the object you're searching for."

Mallory grinned. "That might come in handy."

"Thought you'd say that. Only one problem: the Blue Fire doesn't reach there. You couldn't have such a powerful force for life in a place of death, right? And that means the Wayfinder wouldn't work properly . . . unless you took your own powerhouse of Blue Fire with you."

"You?"

"Me. I have to detach myself from the flow, which will be a wrench. It's amazing in here, Mallory, like being in touch with everything, feeling everything, seeing how it's all interconnected, how it all means something. Can you imagine what that's like?"

The note of loss in his voice was powerful. "But you're still going to do it?" Mallory asked.

"Of course. How could I not?"

"And . . . what? You get to be the genie in the lamp?"

"Yeah, that's me. I'll be able to help you out in a much more personal and direct way than I can now. But you're going to have to look after me too. Once I cut myself off from the flow of the Blue Fire, I lose so much power. In that form, I can be . . . I hate to use the term 'killed' for a living flame, but that about sums it up. I die. I don't go back to the Blue Fire." Again, that palpable sense of loss in his voice.

"We'll look after you, Hal. You can count on us."

"Then it's done. Take the lantern, Mallory . . . and let's strike out for the great adventure."

The figure flickered, faded and disappeared back into the lantern. The Caretaker held it out for Mallory to take. "Be strong, Brother of Dragons, and trust the light to guide your way."

When Mallory's fingers closed around the Wayfinder there was an electric burst and a feeling of well-being rushed through him. The flame engulfed his whole vision, and when he finally looked around, he was alone.

7

On the roof of the Fortress of the Enemy, amidst the smell of rotting meat and the thick, greasy smoke, the Libertarian watched the stars.

"How I hate them." He sighed.

Niamh took his hand. "Not long now."

"Yes. Nearly there." He turned his attention to the crackling outline of the Burning Man, now half-filled with fire.

"Tell me how it happens," she said with a note of glee.

He cast a dismissive glance her way. "A bitter desire for revenge is not a very attractive quality, you know."

"You must feel it too. Hatred for him, for all of them, and everything they stand for."

"Actually, no. They're misguided. Poor lambs who have lost their way. Unfortunately, once they are back on the path, they become sheep to the slaughter."

"Tell me how it happens," she repeated.

"Only I get to know that. This whole business is . . . hmm, let me select a cliché for your enjoyment . . . a house of cards. So fragile. A mass of subtle, interconnecting events. Change one and the whole thing falls apart."

"Even now?"

"Especially now. As we approach the end, everything is in a state of flux.

So many variables. But do not worry, my bitter, twisted love. I intend to keep a firm hand on the tiller. If the currents try to push us away, I will steer us back into the flow of the blood-dimmed tides. Subtlety is the key. A shift in emotion can be just as effective as a slice across the jugular. More so, in fact."

"But you wait here?" Niamh said. "Why are you not influencing the Brothers and Sisters of Dragons?"

"Because," he said with a faint smile as he turned back to the stars, "all goes to plan."

8

After sharing the news about the Wayfinder, Mallory and Caitlin made their goodbyes in a bright manner that belied the nature of what they were about to endure.

They took themselves to Math's chamber where the sorcerer had already marked out a ritual space in the centre of the floor. He stood in one corner, quietly mouthing incantations that left the atmosphere charged. Veitch perched on the edge of a table, flexing his silver hand rhythmically.

"You ready?" he said.

"You're joking?" Mallory said. "Dying is the biggest human fear. You condition yourself to spend all your life running in the opposite direction."

"It's not an ending." Caitlin's axe was strapped in a harness across her back. "If anyone should know that, it's the Brothers and Sisters of Dragons."

"Easy for you to say, with the Morrigan riding you like a horse. This is home ground for her."

"If it makes it any easier, I've been through it," Veitch said.

"It doesn't."

"Why did you do it?" Caitlin asked.

"I wanted to break any control the spiders had over me," Veitch replied. "I wanted to be my own man again." He paused. "This is going to sound weird, but the Grim Lands are the only place I ever felt at home."

"That's sad," Caitlin said.

"No, it's weird." Mallory cast a suspicious eye towards Math, whose incantation had grown louder. "What's it like?" he added uneasily.

"Pain, just for a bit. Then it's like being on a roller coaster heading down the biggest dip. Queasy. And then . . . nothing. Next thing you know, you'll be waking up in the temple in the Grim Lands. Don't touch anything there, right? It's the Void's place. Get straight out."

"And the dead?" Caitlin asked.

"Don't expect them to be friendly. They welcomed me with open arms . . . I don't know why. But they're not usually so happy about the living trespassing on their ground."

"How do I know this isn't just one of your ploys to do me in?" Mallory asked.

"Look, mate, I know you don't trust me, and I know you don't like me, but honestly, if I wanted to do that, I'd just gut you in your room at night when you weren't looking."

"You could try."

"All right." Caitlin sighed. "Let's put the whole men thing behind us. This is serious."

"Just . . . don't worry," Veitch continued. "I wasn't going to take any risks with this. I went out of my way to find a ritual that could take me over the barrier in one piece. I was primed and fully charged when Church got me down in Cornwall. Half an hour after they carted my body off, I was in the Grim Lands. And here I am. I look okay to you?"

Mallory took a deep breath and looked to Caitlin. "Okay, then. We've got a job to do."

She took his hand and led him into the ritual circle.

"It's the ride of a lifetime, Mallory. Imagine how much more you're going to appreciate life when you've died and come out the other side."

"How do you know I haven't died and come back already?" Mallory said. Caitlin fixed him with a quizzical gaze, but he didn't respond.

Math's voice grew louder, the rhythmic chanting taking on a hypnotic quality. The atmosphere became more intense. Strange shadows flitted across the room.

"Here." Veitch handed them each a goblet of dark liquid. "So you won't feel a thing."

"How are you going to do it?" Mallory asked.

Veitch held up a long silver knife, the handle carved with symbols.

Mallory eyed it for a moment, then downed his drink in one. "Death, here we come," he said with as much bravado as he could muster.

9

Night was falling as the thick smudge of black moved across the entire span of the Great Plain. Storm clouds boiled above it, throwing out jagged bolts of lightning that turned the darkening sky white, and with it came the deep, resonant heartbeat in the ground. *Thoom. Thoom. Thoom.*

The Enemy had arrived.

With a mounting feeling of dread, Church watched from the battlements of the great wall. Even with the Army of the Ten Billion Spiders and the Burning Man, he had never really comprehended the true scale of what they faced. "How many of them are there?" he breathed.

"Perhaps a million." Beside him, Lugh remained phlegmatic. "Perhaps more."

"How can anyone survive this kind of battle?" Church said.

"We do what we can. As do you."

Lugh's faith was touching, but Church had a more immediate concern. "How are we going to get past the Enemy lines?"

"There may be another route." Math's eerie, echoing voice rose up behind Church, where the sorcerer had just arrived with Veitch and Tom.

"All done?" Church asked.

Veitch nodded, but wouldn't meet Church's eyes. The killing had clearly affected him.

"What other route?" Church asked.

"There are paths that cross lands and time and everything we know. One only needs to locate the correct door," Math replied. "Through Winter-side, which shimmers just a breath away from this land, stories tell of many routes."

"You can show us the way?"

Math shook his head. "There are only stories. One speaks of a door in the Halls of the Drakusa, which exists, like this Great Court, in both Summer-side and Winter-side."

"Then we could get into Winter-side here, and back out again there," Veitch said.

"How do we find it?" Church asked.

"There are only stories," Math repeated.

Tom sighed. "All you great heroes, and as usual, you're at a loss. It's a good job I'm here." He showed them the ring Freyja had given him. "One of its more pleasing abilities is to guide the owner to their heart's desire. That led us to Ruth, so you know it works. I suppose, if you ask me nicely, I can accompany you to Winter-side and show you the way."

"Woo hoo," Veitch said with weary sarcasm. "Us and the old git on the road again. Just like old times."

Thoom-thoom-thoom. The walls shook as the Enemy neared.

Night fell.

CHAPTER THREE
THE HALLS OF THE DRAKUSA

1

In the centre of an unremarkable cobbled square stood the Gateway to Winter, a stone arch marked with a leafless tree on the keystone. Around it, a still, black pool reflected the glittering stars so that it appeared as if what was above also lay below.

Gathered before the arch, Church and the others were dressed in thick furs despite the summery warmth.

"Winter-side has many dangers," Lugh said to Church, who was carrying out a last-minute check of provisions. "My people have always avoided its desolation, but the stories of the terrors that lurk there are rife. Some say it was the original home of the Fomorii, and anywhere that could birth that foul race cannot be a good land."

"We're not complacent," Church replied. "We know the Void is going to do everything it can to stop us reaching the Fortress of the Enemy. It's worried that we might be able to stop it, and that means we stand a chance."

"Despite all evidence to the contrary," Laura muttered as she passed, tugging with irritation at the furs.

On the fringes of the group, a tearful Mahalia quietly but intensely confronted Jack, but he remained resolute, if sad. Church was impressed by how the teenager had risen to the responsibility of being one of the Two Keys, as had Miller, who shuffled awkwardly nearby, trying to ignore the outpouring of emotion. Crowther watched the two with fatherly concern, but did not interfere.

"I can understand how Mahalia feels," Ruth said. "It's awful to feel so powerless when someone you love goes into danger."

"I bet you've never felt powerless in your life," Church said.

"That shows how much you know."

For the last ten minutes, Tom had been sitting on the low stone wall surrounding the pool, smoking and talking intently to Shavi. As it had been for several hours, most of the conversation was about the Caraprix and the meaning of their sudden evacuation from the Tuatha Dé Danaan to Doctor Jay's lab where Jerzy still lay. Since then, no one had been able to gain access to the room to find the reason for the light blazing under the door and the constant jarring noise.

Shavi saw Church looking and came over. "I have a question," he said to Rhiannon and Lugh. "We are searching for the Halls of the Drakusa. Who are the Drakusa? Tom has spent a lifetime amassing knowledge of the Far Lands and he has never heard tell of them."

"The Golden Ones do not talk of them," Rhiannon said. "We rarely acknowledge they existed, even amongst ourselves."

"The Golden Ones have survived and found strength in self-delusion," Lugh began cautiously. "That we are the first and that we are the last. That we are at the heart of Existence. That we are the strongest."

"We are not," Rhiannon said. "And we might have climbed higher on the ladder of Existence if we had found the wisdom to recognise the truth earlier."

"The Drakusa came before you?" Church asked.

"They, and others," Lugh replied.

"What happened to them?" Shavi queried.

"No one knows. The footprints of those lost civilisations can still be found across the Far Lands, if one looks carefully," Rhiannon admitted. "In ruins, so overgrown they have almost become part of the landscape, in artefacts, in rumours and prophecies and stories where their existence is clear in what is not said, rather than what is."

Veitch and Hunter arrived with Virginia Dare, who was wrapped in a cloak so thick there was only a hint of the pale moon of her face. Her head was bowed, her arms wrapped around her, locked so deeply within herself she appeared oblivious to her surroundings.

"I'm not sure she's up to this," Ruth whispered.

"We don't have a choice," Church said. "She's been traumatised. Her mind keeps shutting down to protect her from what she's been through and that's going to make her a burden for us when we hit danger." He paused. "And I know how cruel it is to take her back there. If I could think of any other way to do this, I would."

Within a quarter of an hour, they were ready to make the journey to

Winter-side. Shavi cast his eyes over the group. "Ten of us," he said. "Six Brothers and Sisters of Dragons, Tom, Miller, Jack and Virginia. Nine would have been better."

"Great. Nine potential sources of irritation," Laura said. "It was bad enough when there were only five of us."

A moment after Lugh and Rhiannon said their goodbyes, Church passed through the arch and found himself in the same square, only now foot-deep in snow. An unearthly stillness lay over the normally bustling city.

Once the others had joined him, they made their way along the winding cobbled streets, through the eerily deserted city, noting how the street-plan and the buildings echoed their counterparts on Summer-side, but were subtly different. A sense of menace pervaded the court, engrained in the distorted proportions of the architecture, or the odd way shadows fell, or the occasional sound that echoed through the stillness: a dog's howl, snow suddenly falling from a roof, something that sounded like a baby crying, but was clearly not.

The high buildings protected them from most of the elements, but when they ventured beyond the gates onto the Great Plain, they were blasted by a bitter gale that propelled snowflakes into their flesh like burning needles. Bowing their heads, they drove on through the knee-high snow, Tom guiding them with every subtle tug on his ring-finger.

When the pink glow of dawn finally warmed the horizon, their faces, fingers and toes were numb and snow encrusted the front of their furs. Laura complained vehemently and Tom, Miller and Jack found it hard going, but the others maintained the pace. Of all of them, Hunter appeared to be thriving on the hardship.

It took most of the day to cross the arc of the Plain that took them to the foothills. They made camp on the gentle slopes, in a hollow filled with spiky gorse bushes and rocky outcroppings. Hunter lit a fire with remarkable speed, and soon they had four tents pitched around it, with water boiling for a warm drink. They ate their dry biscuits in two of the tents, clustered together for warmth, and soon fell asleep from exhaustion.

Church woke in the middle of the night, unsettled without knowing why. Crawling out into the bitter darkness, he found that the snow had stopped falling and the stars glimmered icily. It was Veitch's watch, but something was wrong. Church could see him prowling the edge of the camp beyond the red embers of the fire, his sword drawn, occasional flickers of blue amongst darting black flames.

"What's up?" Church followed Veitch's gaze to the snow-covered lip of the hollow.

"Something out there."

"An animal? Or worse?"

"Dunno yet. I caught sight of it against the skyline, just a flash. It was big. Don't know if it was looking down here, or just prowling around. You'll be able to smell the smoke from the fire for miles."

"Maybe the campfire wasn't the smartest move."

"Nah, we needed to stay warm. Besides, we've not seen any sign of life since we got here. As far as we knew, this was a dead place."

"I see you didn't wander up there to investigate."

Veitch laughed quietly. "Right, 'cause I'm a total no-mark, stumbling into the night to investigate a noise. My big slasher-pic moment."

"There's two of us now."

"Still not a good idea. There's no cover. Best I just sit down here and keep an eye."

"I'll keep you company."

"You don't need to."

"Four eyes are better than two. And it gets lonely on your own."

Veitch eyed Church curiously for a moment and then nodded. They sat on the leather provision bags while Veitch stoked the fire until the flames licked up again. As they warmed, conversation came easily and after a while Church realised how much it was like the early days of their friendship. He could see that Veitch felt it too, but neither of them spoke of it.

When dawn broke, they roused the others, who emerged stamping their feet and complaining to fight for space around the fire. They ate a quick breakfast of more dry biscuits, and then Veitch and Church ventured up to the ridge. The snow was disturbed and large tracks led off across the landscape.

"What do you reckon?" Veitch said.

"I don't get it," Church replied. "The tracks change. See here—these look like some kind of animal print, these are more like a reptile and these . . ." He paused at a series of circular holes in the snow disappearing into the distance, unable to find the words. "Whatever, it looks like it was watching us."

Veitch peered towards the horizon. "It's not here now. Maybe it thought we were too much trouble for a snack."

"Those black clouds look full of snow," Church noted. "We'd better get moving before it hits. We're going to freeze to death out here if it gets any colder."

Church slid down the bank to the camp. Veitch inspected the tracks for a moment longer, casting his gaze across the expanse of snow, and then he followed Church, troubled without knowing why.

2

At noon, the storm struck with a ferocious force that battered them this way and that, making any progress difficult. The blizzard was so intense that the ground and sky merged into one sheet of white that left their senses reeling. Laura was worst hit by the white-out-induced vertigo and she pitched forwards into the deepening drifts at regular intervals, cursing loudly as her frustration and anger grew.

Each time Hunter helped her to her feet, only for her to shake him off furiously. "I'm a hothouse plant," she shouted. "I'm not meant for these conditions."

"Yeah, you're just a frail little flower," he said lightly, but he was worried about her. The strange state imposed upon her by Cernunnos was still a mystery and he had no idea how the cold would affect her, although he was concerned by the blue tinge growing around her mouth and eyes.

He struggled over to Church and said, "I'm worried about Laura. She's not coping well with this weather. We need to get to shelter."

Church pulled the scarf from his mouth and shouted over the gale, "Okay, if we can find somewhere, but it's impossible to see anything in this. At least we're moving uphill. There might be more shelter when we get into the mountains."

"If we do," Hunter yelled back. Frustrated, he turned towards Laura and noticed that he could now see only seven other black smudges in the swirling white. "Someone's missing," he called to Church. "Get everyone huddled together, now!"

Once the group had packed into a tight knot, they realised it was Jack who was missing. "He was right next to me a minute ago," Miller said as he hugged Virginia close to him.

"If he wanders off, we'll never find him," Tom snapped. "Why can't you organise things better?" He wiped the snow off his spectacles.

"If we all start looking for him, we'll never find our way back together," Hunter said. "Let me go. I've experienced worse than this in Nepal."

"How are you going to find your way back to us?" Church asked. "The footprints are filling up quickly."

"I'm like an animal—I have an unerring sense of direction."

"Don't be an idiot," Laura said, but before she could stop him, he disappeared into the blizzard.

Rapidly, he followed their footprints back and then searched for Jack's outlying track. Church was right—their trail was already becoming a ghost, and he guessed he would only have a few minutes before he lost his way back to the group.

He called Jack's name, but the wind stole his voice only a few feet from his mouth. After a moment, he came across a set of tracks that peeled off from the main body of the others. Keeping his head low, he pressed on into the face of the gale.

He hadn't gone far when his senses picked up movement nearby.

"Jack," he called again. Even as the name left his mouth, he realised any movement he might have perceived came from something much larger than a teenage boy.

Another shape loomed and was gone in the blink of an eye. This time he glimpsed something black, dense and powerful before the white folded around it.

A second shape, this time to his left, though blurred as if in a state of flux. Another, and another. They were all around, but they didn't appear to be circling him. Perhaps they were as snow-blind as he was.

How many? he thought.

Stock-still, he listened and watched for any sign of movement. But then his attention fell on Jack's rapidly blurring footprints, and he realised he would lose the trail if he waited too long. Without a second thought, he drove on, fast and low.

He'd barely gone twenty feet when the ground shook with a thunderous approach behind him. Without looking back, he threw himself to one side, burying himself deep in a drift. He had the impression of something almost eight feet tall crashing by, a glimpse of gleaming, oily black skin, and then it was gone.

Hunter moved quickly back onto the trail. More of the beasts converged upon the location, the ground shaking from their movement, their shapes passing through the intense whirl of white like massive ships in a sea fog.

One of them came out of the blizzard directly at him. A sword-like limb with a serrated edge slashed, but he ducked just beneath it and kept running. It turned rapidly and pursued—too late, for the snow had already swallowed him.

The footprints he was following were more defined: he was closing on Jack. If, by some slight chance, he was still alive. The rising ground crested a ridge and descended into a hollow filled with boulders. Scree shifted under the snow beneath his boots. The rocks allowed him some cover as he ducked and raced amongst them. Occasionally, the black creatures loomed over him, sparks flying as their limbs scraped against the stone. Each time he glimpsed one, his perception changed: he thought they were giant insects, then lizards, then something resembling a crab crossed with a piece of machinery.

And then the footprints ahead disappeared.

He ranged around, hearing the beasts crash closer amidst low, rumbling noises that he guessed was some form of communication. He had convinced himself that Jack had already been killed when he heard the boy's quiet voice: "Hunter."

Ducking down, Hunter found Jack pressed into a crevice in the rock wall, beneath an overhanging boulder. The boy's face was as white as the snow, his eyes ranging with a deep-seated fear. Hunter quickly pressed himself into the crevice, shielding Jack's shaking body from the roaming creatures.

"Nice spot—room with a view," he whispered. "Don't worry. We're going to be all right."

"What are they?" Jack said.

"Whatever they are, they're not the smartest or they'd have methodically tracked us down by now."

One of the beasts tore past their hiding pace. Jack flinched, then calmed himself. "I'm all right."

"I know you are." Delving into his pack, Hunter found the silver-scaled, brass-taloned Balor Claw.

"What's that?" Jack hissed.

"A weapon."

"You can't use it here! There are too many of them. You won't last a minute."

Hunter couldn't tell Jack he had it ready for a last stand, to take one or two of the creatures with them. "I'm just keeping it where I can see it," he said with a grin.

"I can't feel my feet," Jack said.

"Just a little while longer. They'll move away soon when they realise they can't find us." Hunter tried to sound reassuring, but he knew if they stayed in the crevice much longer they'd freeze to death; and they wouldn't stand a chance if they ventured out amongst the hunting creatures. Beyond that, the tracks back to the rest of the group would probably have been lost.

Jack's lips were already turning blue, and the familiar signs of hypothermia were evident in his skin and breathing. Hunter pulled the boy close to him and wrapped his arms around him. "Forget the whole 'men don't hug' thing," he said. "This is about staying warm. We'll be fine. We'll be out of here in no time."

3

The Court of the Soaring Spirit felt empty without Mallory, Caitlin and the others. Decebalus stood outside Doctor Jay's lab for long minutes, mulling over his new role as leader of the Army of Dragons, happy to accept the responsibility, although missing the camaraderie of his friends. He barely spared a thought for the gently pulsing light and the noise grinding out from the sealed room. The Caraprix were not a threat, he had decided, and so they were an irrelevance.

Weighing his strategy carefully, he sought out the sorcerer Math in his shadowy rooms.

"I have never met a sorcerer who has not deserved to be hacked into bloody chunks," the barbarian said as he watched the slowly turning mask. "You will be happy to know that in this matter I have learned some restraint from my good friends. But only some. So hear me out."

The mask turned. Math said nothing.

"The Enemy approaches. My forces are strong, but a good general always keeps something in reserve. I need . . . something. Possibly magickal. And I want it to be a response that will take their breath away to such a degree they will never return."

Math contemplated for a moment, and then said, "How far do you intend to go?"

Decebalus grinned.

4

"Should we go after Hunter?" Ruth ventured.

"There's no point doing anything until this blizzard lifts," Church replied. "We could be stamping around in circles and getting nowhere."

Laura's face was emotionless. "He'll be fine. He's tougher than you bunch of wimps." She turned away from them quickly.

Shavi suddenly became animated, involuntarily clutching at his alien eye.

"What's wrong?" Veitch asked.

"Hurry! We must leave this place immediately!" Shavi said urgently. "Something is coming!"

Church peered into the blizzard as faint tremors ran through the ground, growing stronger. "Okay, let's move on."

"What about Hunter?" Laura snapped. "If we leave here, he'll never find us."

"He'll find us. He's good."

Tom grabbed Church's arm as they struggled up the slope. "I don't like this. There have always been terrible things in this place." The words died in his throat as one of the beasts emerged from the snow behind them. Inky black, at first glance it resembled a giant spider, rising up above them on long, sharp legs that looked as if they were made of iron. It wavered for a second so they felt they were under the scrutiny of a cold, alien intellect, and then it began to change. Armoured plates resembling an insect's carapace unfolded out of the black body and locked into place. Spikes and a horned ridge emerged, along with other razor-sharp appendages.

"Bloody hell!" Veitch gasped. "Fomorii!"

The others scrambled up the incline as fast as they could, but Miller continued to gape. Veitch hit him like a runaway train and propelled him away. "Stand still, you're dead," Veitch hissed. "They're killing machines."

The way became much steeper, littered with outcropping rocks and huge boulders that made it difficult to advance. Behind them, the Fomor raced only feet away. Breath burned in their lungs as they wound around the obstacles.

Echoing through the howling gale came the sounds of more Fomorii joining the pursuit, a haunting, deep call and response that became more frenzied, as though the creatures recognised their prey.

They came up hard against a cliff rising high over their heads. A path wound around the foot of it, barely wide enough for one person, with the ground plummeting away steeply.

As Veitch and Miller passed the last boulder before the path began, they caught a glimpse of someone crouching out of sight. When the Fomor pounded up behind them, Church jumped out at the last and swung Caledfwlch in an arc, a trail of Blue Fire sizzling through the snow. Sparks flew as the blade hacked into one of the creature's front legs. As the creature half-rounded on Church, it lost its balance. With a roar, Church rammed into it with the sword, bracing against the boulder and levering it onto the slippery, snow-covered slope. The Fomor hovered for a second and then went crashing down until it was lost in the swirling snow.

"Nice one, mate!" Veitch called as Church caught up with the group.

"Let's not start cheering yet," Church shouted back. "The others are coming up fast behind."

With the wind lashing them, they pressed their backs against the cliff face and edged around the path. "We're still going in the right direction," Tom said, "as long as we don't fall to our doom. This path, in such a deserted landscape, is here for a reason."

"What are they?" Miller asked again, struggling to cope with the terror surging through his system.

"Race enemies of those golden-skinned bastards." The flickering black flames of Veitch's sword were a stark contrast to the snow. "We fought them before. Beat 'em, too, at the Battle of London."

Miller glanced back and almost lost his balance. "It changed shape."

"They do that a lot." Veitch looked to Church. "You think there's just a handful of 'em?"

"All of them disappeared after the Battle of London. What if they came here, to lick their wounds?" Church paused. "What if this is the Void's secret army, just like we have the Army of Dragons and the gods?"

"You stopped them once, right?" Miller said hopefully. "You can do it again."

Looking out into the blizzard, Veitch had the odd sensation of a sea of white in which they could float.

"They're coming!" Church said. "Let's move this along!"

Behind them, the call of the Fomorii echoed off the cliff-side; it contained a note of jubilance, perhaps that their old enemies were finally in their grasp, and it was followed by a metallic grinding that set their teeth on edge—the beasts' limbs dragging on the rock-face.

From the rear, Church urged them to move faster, but the path soon became more precarious as it crawled up and around the lower stage of the mountain they knew was hidden above their heads in the blizzard. As they rounded a bluff, they became more sheltered from the buffeting gale and visibility improved. They could see the path dropping down towards a horseshoe-shaped area enclosed by the towering rock. A single, twisted, ancient hawthorn stood in the centre.

"Bleedin' great," Veitch said. "No way out. We can't go back. You old bastard—you've led us to the perfect place for a slaughter."

"Shut up!" Tom snapped. He examined his ring and Church could see from his face that he feared Freyja had planned this all along.

The hunting cries of the Fomorii rang out through the blizzard, ten joining twenty, more each second, echoing from out across the Great Plain as they converged on the mountains.

"You know what—I'm starting to think you're right," Veitch said. "All the Fomorii are here in Winter-side. We're screwed."

After they'd skidded down the path into the horseshoe-shaped area, Church and Veitch moved quickly around the rock walls looking for any sign of a hidden passage or footholds that would help them climb to safety.

"Do you see anything here?" Ruth asked Shavi. He turned in a slow arc, letting his alien eye focus on everything. After a moment, he shook his head.

"Fucking brilliant!" Laura blazed. "First you lose Hunter, now this!" Tears stung her eyes.

The low hunting calls grew louder. From out of the blizzard emerged the Fomorii, some descending the winding path, others clinging to the rock-face, still more rising up on the edge of the horseshoe-shaped area from where the land fell away precipitously.

Church and Veitch faced them, drawing their swords so that blue and black energy sparked between them. Ruth joined them, Blue Fire crackling around the tip of the Spear of Lugh.

Laura brushed away her tears to take a flank, but when she saw Shavi joining them, she urged him back. "Let's face it, Shavster, you're about as useful as a wet towel in a fight like this. Go help Team Loser find a way out of here."

"We have travelled the worlds together and you are all more dear to me than anyone else in my life. We have truly lived together and we should die together," he replied.

She set her jaw. "We're not about to die, because Hunter's going to come over that hill with the cavalry and crush these bastards dead. Now, go!"

In Shavi's look of sad fondness, they both accepted the lie in Laura's words, and then he turned and hurried to Tom and Miller who were scrambling around the foot of the cliffs. Virginia watched them blankly.

An oily flow of Fomorii washed into the horseshoe area until they stood ranged from cliff to cliff. It was like looking into a haze as their edges blurred with the constant shape-changing: armour plates snapping into place, human forms becoming insectile, cruel spikes and horns bursting from the hard skin.

"I've not missed them," Church said.

"You know what makes me sick?" Veitch said. "There's nobody here to write about how bleedin' brilliant we'll be when we go down fighting."

Ruth smiled to herself. "That's all you've ever wanted, isn't it? To be seen as one of the heroes."

"Yeah, I want my name up in lights, why not?"

"Not going to happen, you tattooed psycho." Laura crouched down and buried one hand in the snow until she was touching the ground. Concentration darkened her face, and after a second a row of bramble crawled slowly from the frozen ground along the ranks of Fomorii. With a gasp, Laura sagged back onto her behind. "God, this place is too frozen. I'm as useless as Shavi."

"You tried," Church said. "Drop back with the others."

The Fomorii held back for a second, and then they broke like a wave at the shore.

"No," Ruth whispered defiantly.

A sound thundered at the base of Church and Veitch's skulls. Ruth had uttered a word of power, her eyes rolling back to reveal the whites. She appeared greater than the mere dimensions of her form, magnificent, and with each passing second, more terrifying.

The wind roiled into a fist and slammed into the approaching line of Fomorii, smashing them back. Bullets of snow and ice tore into them and lightning crashed from the sky, leaving charred circles in the snow and the twisted remnants of bodies. In a trance, she levelled the Spear of Lugh, and Blue Fire surged from the tip. The Fomorii recoiled from contact with it.

Only one of the creatures made it through Ruth's assault, but Church and Veitch were ready for it. They attacked from either side, hacking and thrusting. Screeching, the Fomor lashed out, its limbs changing shape as it moved to find the most lethal aspect. One glancing blow sent Church sprawling, but Veitch was already in the space Church had occupied before he hit the ground, preventing the Fomor from delivering a killing blow.

At the cliff wall, Miller and Shavi were drawn by the furious battle, but Tom continued to search furiously, Virginia observing him. With angry frustration, he took a step back and shouted at Shavi, "Something's here. You're supposed to be a saviour of the universe. Find it."

"I see nothing," Shavi responded. "No hidden door or path—"

"Wait." Miller pointed hesitantly to the lifeless tree. "That stands in such a perfect position in this space . . . is it natural?"

Shavi ran his hands over the bark.

"Yes," Tom said. "Yes! Symbolic. It's a sign. A message—"

"Here, in this desolate, frozen, rocky place," Shavi continued with a smile, "is life."

As he moved his hands over the rough bark, he felt the faintest pulse deep within. Resting his forehead against the trunk, eyes closed, he held it, fanned it, drew it out from the sleeping core. Miller's hand went to his stomach where he felt an involuntary connective warmth.

A faint blue light appeared on the trunk. Breathing in the smell of burned iron, Shavi concentrated, forcing the long-dormant power to grow stronger. The light became a single flame that appeared to die in the cold breeze, until suddenly it erupted along the length of the trunk and the entire tree blazed with the Blue Fire, each shimmering finger now a leaf on the once-dead branches.

At the foot of the tree, the earth energy crackled into the snow, moving in a rapid, dizzying spiral until it sizzled in a direct line towards the cliff wall and up the rock face where it illuminated the sign of a dragon eating its tail.

"Here!" Tom yelled. "Here, now!"

Shavi raced towards it and slammed his hand into the centre of the symbol. A flash dazzled them all for a second, and then with a judder that threw them from their feet, the rock tore itself open to reveal a door into a dark space.

"Church! Ryan! Ruth! Come, now!" Shavi called.

Church and Veitch continued to whirl around the remaining Fomor, their swords leaving fiery trails in the air. They were both covered with cuts that spattered blood onto the snow. But Ruth was almost unrecognisable. She hovered six inches above the ground, arms outstretched, head back, the blue light from the Spear washing around before driving out intermittently at the storm-tossed ranks of Fomorii still closing in. She held them back, though just barely. To Shavi, she looked like one of the gods, as frightening and enig-matic as a force of nature.

He ran to her, but when he placed his hand on her side, her head snapped around, her face filled with fury and he was thrown ten feet back with a blast that left him close to unconsciousness.

Church's cry shocked Ruth from her trance, and she crashed to the ground. Still dazed, she was at first unable to comprehend Shavi's smoking form as he staggered to his feet, but gradually realisation dawned on her. Her devastation was clear in her face.

"Ruth!" Church called urgently.

The lines of Fomorii gradually recovered and prepared to attack. Although they held their enemy at bay, Church and Veitch could not find an opening to escape towards Shavi. Gathering herself, Ruth dived beneath the attacking beast and rammed the Spear of Lugh up into the creature's belly. Amidst a burst of blue light, the Fomor exploded. As the body parts rained down, Church and Veitch grabbed Ruth and half-dragged her towards the gaping hole in the cliff-face where Shavi beckoned urgently. Behind them, the howls of the approaching Fomorii echoed.

Diving through the open doorway, they had one last look at the horde of shape-shifting beasts bearing down on them before the door slid shut and they were plunged into darkness.

As they caught their breath, Tom struck his flint and found a cobweb-festooned lantern hanging on a hook next to the door. The flame guttered, then leaped. They stood in a vast entrance hall amidst blocks of fallen masonry and discarded swords, spears and shields as if a final battle had been fought there. Columns soared up into the dark and ahead of them a few cracked steps led up to a towering archway beyond which lay only shadows.

Tearfully, Ruth hugged Shavi. "I'm so sorry. I could have killed you."

"A slight singe here and there, but I am fine."

"We'd all be dead if not for you," Church said.

"You're a scary woman," Veitch added. "Where did all that come from?"

"The power's been growing in me for a long time." She ran a shaking hand through her hair. "Back on our world, I could feel it, but didn't really know how to get to it. Here . . ." She chewed her lip. "I'm afraid I might not be able to control it."

"It's always about you," Laura snapped. "Hunter's still out there. And Jack. We can't leave them."

"We can't go back out," Veitch said sharply.

Sensing the mounting tension, Church stepped between the two of them. "Hunter's one of us and we don't abandon anyone. And we can't go on without Jack. We need him. Maybe if we wait until the Fomorii have dispersed—"

Shavi shook his head. "I can find no way to open this door from the inside."

"There's got to be," Laura insisted.

"You are right," Shavi replied, "but there is no source of Blue Fire in here. There must be a different mechanism for opening it."

Cursing loudly, Laura booted a rock furiously into the shadows where it bounced off walls with a series of echoes that was unnerving in the stillness.

"What is this place?" Miller scraped his boot through the thick, white dust on the floor. "It doesn't look like anyone's been here in centuries."

"These," Tom replied, "are the Halls of the Drakusa."

5

In the narrow view of snowy ground from the crevice, Hunter counted the passing Fomorii as they ranged by, their resonant call and response rumbling through the rock itself. He estimated at least twenty were still hunting for him and Jack, and they were drawing close to their hiding place. Even with the Balor Claw, he guessed he wouldn't last more than a moment or two out there. Beside him, Jack shook violently from the cold and Hunter could barely feel his own feet. As far as he could assess, he had only two options: freeze to death or get torn apart by the beasts.

As he turned his head away from the opening to whisper more words of encouragement to Jack, he felt a current of air move across his face. Instantly, he registered that it had come from within the crevice.

He urged Jack to move to one side so he could crawl to the back of the crevice, where he found a dark hole leading in and down, barely big enough for him to squeeze inside. He motioned to Jack and said quietly, "There's a draught. That means it leads to a cave system with some kind of egress."

"You're insane," Jack hissed. "Look how small it is! We'll get stuck in there and die. Horribly."

"We're going to die horribly if we stay here and that's the truth. You need to take my lead on this, Jack."

Jack examined the hole anxiously. "Look at it, Hunter. If we get in there and find it's too small to go on, we're not going to be able to back out. We'll be trapped in a space about as big as a coffin. I think I might go mad."

"I know I'm asking a lot of you, Jack, but this whole business is asking a lot of all of us. We've got to rise above our fears, because everyone is depending on us. If you die here, the hope that Church is fighting for dies with you."

"Have you done anything like this before?"

Without missing a beat, Hunter replied, "In the former Yugoslavia, I was buried alive in a mass grave. About one hundred dead Muslim villagers on top of me. I had to work my way through the bodies and then dig myself out with my bare hands. I rate this as slightly better odds."

Jack's terrible fears fought on his face. After one brief glance back at the Fomorii, he nodded. "All right."

"Good lad. I'll go first. It's going to be pitch black in there, but if you can feel my boots ahead of you, you'll be okay."

Hunter manoeuvred himself and then wriggled his head into the hole. The air smelled of deep, wet places. He forced his shoulders in. The granite above dug deep into his back, and for a moment he feared he was wedged. Jack was right: there would be no coming back out the same way. Pressing hard, he constricted his breathing and ignored the burning compression in his back and chest. After a second, he had forced his way under the lip of rock into an area that allowed him little more than an inch on every side. Jack wriggled in close behind him, occasionally reaching out to his boot-heel for reassurance. Hunter was overwhelmed by the boy's bravery; few others would have been able to suppress such a basic human fear for the greater good.

There was only room to reach out ahead and use his fingers to drag him down the slight incline, with a gentle push from his boot-tips for a little extra thrust; it was going to take a long time to get wherever they were going—and he refused to entertain any other thought than that there was a definite destination ahead.

Breathing was difficult and increasingly painful. He had to take small, regulated gasps to prevent hyperventilation; in between gulps, he instructed Jack to do the same. His fingers were numb, but he was convinced they were tearing from the exertion against the hard rock; he was sure he could smell blood.

The fissure continued down a little steeper. Their body heat in the confined space eased the freezing temperatures, but water regularly dripped and ran under their fingers. Another fear: drowning in an enclosed space.

Hunter came to a halt at a sharp right turn. Jack called out in a panicked voice, worrying that Hunter had reached a dead end. It took several moments to calm him, and then a further fifteen minutes for Hunter to edge, squeeze and twist halfway around the bend. Once again he was convinced he was wedged in place, twisted at right angles, in complete darkness, with barely a chance to breathe and listening to the whimpering of a traumatised boy behind him. Heart pounding, the blood thundering through his head, he closed his eyes, thinking of Laura and the last night they had spent together. Gradually, his breathing regulated and he eased and pressed forwards a fraction of an inch at a time.

Once around the turn, the fissure broadened and the incline became steeper so he could drag himself faster, which eased Jack's anxiety. Ten minutes later it became steeper still, and before he had time to think the slope was so sheer he began to slide. He called out to Jack to hold fast, but by that time he was speeding out of control, cracking bones and tearing skin. He went over an edge and into free fall for a split second before hitting icy water. It was barely five feet deep, and his arms protected him from the worst of the impact, but he sucked in a mouthful of water before he managed to surface.

Feeling around, he discovered that the fissure continued horizontally again, but most of it was filled with water. Only a tiny air space remained, and he had no idea how long that continued in any useable form.

Jack was calling his name frantically. "It's all right—I'm here," he called back. "It's only a short drop, and there's water at the bottom. Yell when you're coming and I'll try to catch you—or at least try to stop getting brained."

When Jack was next to him, relieved at the prospect of standing upright with room to breathe, Hunter broached the news about the almost-submerged tunnel. Jack's mood changed instantly and he released a couple of wracking sobs before he calmed.

"I can't do it," he whimpered.

"You said that about the crawling and the squeezing, but look at what you did there."

Distantly, but unmistakably within the fissure, came the teeth-jarring rumble of the Fomorii.

"Sounds like they've found out where we went," Hunter said. "We can't hang around here."

Echoes of scrabbling in the fissure, drawing rapidly closer. Hunter was unnerved by how speedily the Fomorii moved.

"You've got to trust me, Jack. We'll get through this."

"I do trust you, Hunter."

Hunter flinched, unsettled yet oddly moved by this new experience. "Hold on to my jacket, and give a tug if anything's wrong."

Taking a deep breath, he ducked under the water. Jack followed closely. In the floating dark, the claustrophobia and fear of suffocation were even more intense. Hunter measured his pace to Jack's endurance, pausing regularly to grab a breath from the tiny gap against the tunnel roof.

At one point Jack began to thrash as if he were drowning, and Hunter was forced to grab him and hold his head up tightly. In Hunter's arms, Jack relaxed, still trusting.

The journey felt as if it was taking an age, and just at the point when Hunter started to fear hypothermia would set in, they emerged from the tunnel into what felt from the air currents and echoes like a large cavern. Hunter dragged Jack from the water onto a flat rock surface and held him tightly until he had warmed.

"I never knew my father," Jack said after a moment.

Hunter didn't know how to respond.

"The Tuatha Dé Danaan stole me from my mother when I was a baby and took me to the Court of the Final Word where they put the Wish-Hex inside me. They made me into a weapon. Then they kept me prisoner till Caitlin and Mahalia set me free." He wiped the snot from his dripping nose with the back of his hand.

"Doesn't sound like you've had much of a life, mate."

"That just makes me want to fight for it even more."

Hunter was impressed by the determination in Jack's voice; it reminded him of himself, before the sourness took hold of his life. "Keep hold of that thought, kid, because now we need to find a way out of here before those things pop up out of the water."

Following the air current, they moved tentatively away from their resting place, feeling into the dark ahead of them in case there were any gaping pits or more sudden inclines. Hunter put out of his head the possibility that the breeze came from a tiny fissure and that there might be no way out of the cavern.

Progress was slow and the fear of the Fomorii emerging from the water behind them grew. But then the texture underfoot changed from hard rock to smaller items that rolled and crunched, in some areas several inches deep. Harder objects lay amongst them.

"What is that? Dry wood?" Jack asked.

"Down here?" Hunter knelt to investigate. His fingers ran over dry, fragile things, some tubular, some sharp, some curved, and what were clearly metal artefacts scattered amongst them. "I think there's a sword here. And a . . . shield?" he ventured. "A helmet?"

They continued treading tentatively over the cracking, shifting surface for several more minutes until Jack's foot caught something that clanged and bounced. He felt around for it in the dark and raised it, letting his fingers see the surface. "A lantern!" he said.

With his flint, Hunter lit the wick. The flame was weak, but held on to life. The shadows rushed away, dancing back menacingly with each flicker of the light.

"Oh," Jack said as he looked around with mounting uneasiness.

Hunter followed his gaze in a wide arc across the cavern. "You can say that again."

Human bones lay everywhere. The vast sea of dirty yellow and brown was a civilisation in essence, skulls smashed, limbs torn apart, ribs broken, the clothes that had contained them long since rotted away with only the metal remnants of weapons and armour still remaining.

"What the hell happened here?" Hunter said.

6

The scale of the Halls of the Drakusa spoke of grandeur. Ceilings soared cathedral-like overhead and huge chambers that could have accommodated a small army rang with their hesitant footsteps. Church led his group past pillars of marble and extensive murals that must once have gleamed with colour, but were now faded and barely visible, the most obvious symbol of the decay and great age that shrouded the Halls. A desert of white dust interspersed with piles of shattered masonry and discarded everyday objects covered the stone flags. Only darkness and shadows remained in a place that had once thronged with life.

Shavi examined some of the murals as they passed. "Who were the Drakusa?" he asked.

"Every race has the arrogance to believe they were the first and best," Tom said, joining him. "The old stories hint at others who came before. Races that rose up, established civilisations and were then wiped clean and forgotten, through their own hubris or at the whims of angry gods."

"You don't really think that could happen to us?" Ruth said. "With all our technology, our learning—"

"You think these people didn't have their own technology, different from ours, maybe more powerful, their own wisdom?" Intrigued, Tom brushed away some of the dust and cobwebs that obscured the mural.

Shavi saw what Tom was seeing, and joined him. From beneath the grime of ages, faint images emerged of oval shapes, giant in scale compared to the human figures prostrate before them. Some of the egg shapes appeared to be spouting tentacles, or were in the process of becoming something else.

"Those," Shavi said, puzzled, "are Caraprix."

His expression troubled, Tom studied the mural.

"Never seen any that big," Laura said.

"It's symbolic," Tom muttered.

"So the Drakusa knew of the Caraprix, long before the Tuatha Dé Danaan." Raising the lantern, Church looked around the walls in a new light. Images of Caraprix were visible everywhere, on the walls behind the dust, in mosaics on the floor and carvings on the marble pillars, emerging in part here and there, barely recognisable in isolation but taken together presenting a temple to the shape-shifting creatures. "This place implies that they're gods or something."

"Whoever did all these pictures. . . why are they making such a big deal out of them?" Veitch asked. "The Caraprix are just pets, right? Those golden-skinned bastards have them around for entertainment."

"I think we have been a little blind and stupid," Tom began. "All the time the Caraprix have been before our eyes, and we have misjudged them. We have not seen their true nature."

A flicker of Blue Fire sizzled randomly at the tip of Ruth's spear and they all jumped. "What do you mean?" Ruth asked.

"We have been told many, many times that the closer things are to the heart of Existence, the more fluid they are," Tom replied. "And these are the most fluid things of all. They have no fixed shape, no definable purpose. They can be anything they want. What, I wonder, are the limits of that? What could they really be?"

Church indicated another image, a figure with arms outstretched, strings connecting his fingers to a row of dancing marionettes. "The Puppeteer," he said. "I've seen him before. In Venice, back in Elizabethan times. And in the court. So he existed before the current Age, before the Tuatha Dé Danaan? Why would he be painted here?"

"It's not that I don't find your noodling and navel-gazing so, so fascinating," Laura snapped, "but what say we forget all this and move on before those Fomorii find a way in here and hunt us down like rabbits."

"She's right," Veitch said. "This isn't important. We need to find the gate to Summer-side, and this place is so big we could be searching for years."

Tom glared at Veitch, about to launch an angry comment, when Church dropped a hand on his shoulder. "This isn't the place for a fight." He nodded towards Miller and Virginia, who were sitting together on a piece of fallen pillar. Miller had a reassuring arm around the frightened girl's shoulders, but his fixed expression revealed his own repressed terror. "We forget they're not like us," Church continued. "They've not seen the things we've seen, and they're not built to deal with what they've found here."

"They're not like you," Tom said pointedly.

Their unease mounted as they continued through the empty, ringing halls. The scale of the place, the silence, the darkness, the decay combined to create a thick, oppressive atmosphere that was profoundly unsettling. Though none of them gave voice to it, they all felt as if they were being watched by hateful eyes from the shadows just beyond the extent of the thin lantern light.

The stillness was so intense that even the slightest sound was magnified, and all their senses were heightened. After an hour, they heard a short, dull grind that could have been a door opening. It was so faint and distant that they would have dismissed it at any other time, but in that place it sounded like a tolling bell.

"I don't think we're alone in here," Church said.

"They're coming."

They all turned to look at Virginia, who had thrown off her hood and was smiling. It added a macabre cast to the desperate terror glittering in her eyes.

"The Fomorii?" Church asked.

Virginia shook her head. "Worse than that."

7

Claustrophobic darkness, and hard stone all around. The ragged heat of his breath. Pain, fading quickly, flashes of images in his memory so terrifying that his consciousness recoiled at their touch. Thankfully, the images subsided as Mallory came round.

He choked back bile at the abiding recollection of the touch of hard steel at his throat, the sensation of what followed and the scream of his mind as it wound down into darkness, and knew that it would haunt him for as long as he lived.

But he was alive. The ritual had worked. Everything was subsumed beneath the rush of wonder and relief, and he began frantically to feel around his environment. He was in a stone box, as Veitch had told him to expect.

Pressing his hands against the lid, he lifted. The lid ground to one side and flickering torchlight added another level of relief. Dank air rushed into the dry, dusty interior of the box.

Once he had clambered out, he found another stone box on a plinth next to him. Scuffling sounds came from within. He eased the lid off and helped Caitlin out. She clutched the Wayfinder to her chest, the blue flame providing welcome relief in that gloomy place.

"Look after me," Caitlin said in the fragile voice of her Amy personality.

Mallory hugged her to him. "Course I will."

He held her until she released herself. "It's okay—she's gone back to Brigid and Briony now." She forced a wan smile, her eyes dark and limpid.

"The Morrigan?"

"Is waiting." She stared into his eyes for a moment longer, and her gaze was briefly filled with all the powerful emotions she kept repressed. She broke off when she realised what she was revealing, although she knew he understood. "Come on—we've got a job to do."

When she held the lantern aloft, it revealed a huge chamber built from cyclopean stone blocks beyond the ability of any human to carve or move. Wall paintings also beyond human scale soared up into the shadows, incomprehensible and troubling, and here and there were effigies of squat, misshapen figures or tall, spindly beings. Not human.

"A temple," Mallory said.

"Here? What do the dead worship?"

Mallory couldn't answer.

With a shudder, Caitlin turned her attention to the lamp's flame, which was bending unnaturally to point away from them. "So Hal's in there somewhere? How do we talk to him?"

"If we call on him, he'll come," Mallory said. "But we've got to protect that lamp with our lives. Hal can die here, though die might not be the right word."

"He'll be fine. We just put our heads down, follow the flame and we'll be at the Market in no time."

"I like your optimism."

As they searched for an exit, they found an area where a foot-high egg of swirling sapphire and emerald stood on a waist-high stone column. Every instinct told them to move on, but it drew them in nonetheless.

"What is that?" Caitlin said. "It feels electric. Is it pulsing?"

Mesmerised, they stepped onto the dais surrounding the column; when they got within three feet of the egg they passed through some invisible boundary where everything became green-tinged and all sounds from the chamber beyond were muffled.

Cautiously, Caitlin reached out towards the egg, every warning instinct suppressed. When her fingers came within an inch of its surface, there was a shimmer and they found themselves standing in a three-dimensional view of a dark hall where Church and the others stood around Virginia.

"It's some kind of viewing thing, like the Wish-Post in the Great Courts," Mallory said. He paused. "Where's Hunter and Jack?"

The scene shifted to reveal the cavern of bones. "Now why are they not with the others?" Caitlin asked.

The scene shifted again, this time unprompted. Mallory looking younger, happier, standing in Salisbury Cathedral. Caitlin standing in the rain, crying, covered in clay. Stonehenge in the morning sun, Blue Fire flickering above each trilithon. Church on his knees before the Libertarian, covered in blood. Someone reading a book, looking directly at Mallory and Caitlin.

A bolt of pain struck Mallory between the eyes, and instead of looking into the egg, something was looking out at him. He had the overwhelming sensation of a crushing consciousness focusing the full extent of its power upon him. It sizzled into his brain, crawling into his thoughts, turning over every aspect of who he was and what he wanted. Flames flickered around his perception and the image of the Burning Man began to fall into relief around them.

Caitlin grabbed Mallory and propelled him out of the active zone around the egg. He cried out as the consciousness was painfully torn from his mind. "The Void," he gasped. "It was looking into me. It recognised me." He sucked in a breath of air. "It knows who all of us are, every human. It knows our strengths, and our weaknesses. Our desires."

"I think we make a vow not to touch anything else in this world," Caitlin said, helping Mallory to his feet. "Nothing good's going to come out of anything here."

As Mallory recovered, they heard a noise coming from the direction of the two Rebirth Boxes. Creeping back to the chamber, they saw an arm of twisted blackthorn rise from one of the boxes, and then another. The Hortha rose up and turned its crumpled-paper face towards them.

In that briefest contact, Mallory had a premonition of his own death. Chilled, he guided Caitlin quickly away. While the Hortha adjusted to the transition to the Grim Lands, they moved quickly through the dark chambers until they found the exit tunnel that Veitch had described. It led out into a fissure in the rock in which the temple had been carved. Overhead, a slate-grey sky was occasionally revealed by gaps in the constantly drifting mist. Black shapes moved across it; birds, they guessed, although the perspective suggested something much larger. Every sound was dampened, the rattle of a kicked stone so muffled it could barely be heard six feet away.

They scrambled up a scree-slope onto a bleak, featureless terrain of hard rock and shale, though the mist made it impossible to see too far ahead. Although there was no breeze, the mist continued to fold and twist, licking at them, enswathing them until they moved on rapidly to leave it behind.

"Nice place," Mallory said. "Reminds me of a day I spent in Harlow."

"I guess the dead don't need much in the way of scenery."

The timbre of Caitlin's voice had changed subtly. Most people wouldn't have noticed, but Mallory was always struck by the slight physical alterations that came over her when one of her personalities took over. This one he recognised as the Morrigan, not in full control, but far back in her head, slackly taking the reins.

"We got out of that temple just in time," he said. "We're not leaving a trail here. That should make it difficult for the Hortha to follow us."

"No trail you can see," Caitlin corrected.

"You're not going to let me hide away in my all-is-right-with-the-world fantasies, are you?"

"That won't benefit us. We need to be aware, to keep moving. If that thing crossed the barrier into the Grim Lands, it's not going to give up easily."

"The worst thing about that lantern is that it gives no indication of distance. What happens if we've got to follow that flame for thousands of miles?"

"I'm not sure distance or time mean much here. It just. . . is . . ."

Caitlin's voice dried up as the first feature emerged from the mist: a pair of iron gates in a Victorian style, one of them hanging askew from a broken hinge. They were supported by two stone columns on which black gargoyles perched. In the centre of the wrought-iron arch above the gate was a skull resting on crossed bones. On either side, rusted iron railings stretched out until they were lost in the shifting mist. Beyond sprawled a graveyard: markers, mausoleums, tombs, statues of weeping angels, some of them sagging at angles or broken, suggesting great age. The lichen-covered stone glowed spectrally in the strange, diffuse light. Ivy grew up some of the monuments, obscuring their meaning, and long, yellowing grass grew amongst the graves, along with wild flowers that were splashes of queasy colour in the grey.

Apprehensively, Mallory and Caitlin halted at the gate, but the Wayfinder continued to point directly ahead.

"You're just asking for trouble going through a place like that in a place like this," Mallory said.

Caitlin followed the line of the railings into the mist. "I have a horrible feeling this graveyard goes on a long, long way. I don't think we'll be able to go around it."

Mallory sighed. "Yep. Makes perfect sense."

Standing before the gate, he glanced up at the arch and briefly thought he saw his own face on the skull. The illusion passed quickly and he took hold of the sagging gate, which emitted a protesting, resonant scream from its rusted, long-unused hinges. It was the only sound that carried any distance, and seemed to go on and on and on into the mist.

"I'm living in a really bad horror movie," he said, his palms unbearably sweaty. If the Hortha was on the move, it would have heard that metallic wrenching.

Once again they came to a halt, on the threshold. Every sense told them not to enter the graveyard, but the Wayfinder continued to urge them on.

"Come on—don't be scared!"

The voice startled them. Mallory exchanged a glance with Caitlin and then drew his sword. The Blue Fire around the blade was barely evident. Caitlin reached behind and removed her axe from its harness.

"What fine weapons! What a sword! What an axe! But that sword . . . yes!

One of the Three Great Swords of Existence, if I am not mistaken. And I am rarely mistaken, unless I am in my cups, which, admittedly, has not been much of an option in recent times."

The deeply theatrical voice hid any true emotion. Mallory had an impression of some old stage ham, living on past glories. "Who's there?" he called.

"A friend. Nothing more."

"Somehow I doubt that."

As Mallory and Caitlin crossed the threshold, they felt a sudden tingle of uneasiness as if the barrier had been real and not just imaginary. Whoever was there was hidden amongst the clutter of mausoleums and grave markers.

"Don't worry! I won't bite! Indeed, I am utterly desperate for invigorating human conversation. Why, we are social beings. We are not meant for this dreary, unstimulating place—where, I might add, I should not be. But enough about that travesty for now, lest I find myself carried away on a wave of bitterness, which will only wash me up on the bleak shores of despair."

Mallory pushed through the long grass, searching all around. The mist hid objects, then revealed them, then hid them again, so they quickly lost all sense of direction. They could no longer see the gate, although they had not gone far.

"But as the great Shelley said," the speaker continued, "'Some say that gleams of a remoter world visit the soul in sleep—that death is slumber.' So perhaps I . . . perhaps all of us happy breed . . . are only sleeping."

As Mallory and Caitlin rounded an ivy-clustered mausoleum they finally found the speaker, sitting cross-legged on a tomb. He was a strange figure. Though in his mid-forties, he had long, silver hair and a gaunt face. He wore a black suit, shiny from wear, offset by a flamboyant red brocade waistcoat. His boots were worn and holed on the soles.

"What are you doing here?" Caitlin asked.

"Just resting my old bones." He chuckled, revealing a gap between nicotine-stained teeth.

"Who are you?" Mallory asked.

"Who am I? The great existential question. Who. Am. I. There are many possible answers—"

"Who are you?" Mallory repeated fiercely.

"I am the bard of the hedgerows, the king of the open road, alley sloper, gourmand and wit." He held his arms wide. "My name is Callow."

CHAPTER FOUR
DEATH AT THE GROGHAAN GATE

1

The Halls of the Drakusa were endless, and silent. The tip of the Spear of Lugh burning with Blue Fire to light her path, Ruth led the way through chamber after chamber where the shadows pressed hard against them and the oppressive sense of threat grew by the moment. More energy burned at the rear of the column where Church and Veitch had their swords drawn to defend the group from any attack.

"This place is a bleedin' maze," Veitch hissed. "We could be going round and round in circles."

"Shavi seems to have his bearings, or at least his eye does." Church paused to listen intently as he had done so many times since Virginia had warned them that they were being pursued.

"Anything?" Veitch asked.

Church shook his head.

"Maybe she was just spooked by the dark. She's only a kid."

"The noise—"

"Echoes. Stones." He wasn't even convincing himself. "Let's close the door on this room. Barricade it. If there is anything behind us, it might slow them down."

Church agreed, and they called on Ruth to stop the column while they ran the length of the huge chamber. The doors closed easily and quietly, and there was a heavy oaken bar to lock them in place. Then they dragged numerous chunks of shattered masonry against the doors to add to the barricade.

Veitch wasn't impressed. "Wish we could booby trap it as well. Blow the bastards up."

Church laughed. "I don't know how I survived without you, Ryan."

"Neither do I." He grinned to himself before growing serious once more. "We're doing all right, aren't we?"

"We've not killed each other yet."

"Yeah. After recent times, that's a definite success story."

Halfway across the chamber, Church's eye was caught by a disturbance in the dust off to one side of the path they had taken. They'd been careful to obscure their tracks as much as possible, but here an arrow had been drawn with a symbol he didn't understand, and a serpentine squiggle that he guessed was meant to signify a dragon.

"Ryan," he called quietly.

Veitch skidded to a halt and ran back. When he saw the mark in the dust, he snarled, "We've got a snake in the group. Or a spider."

Church nodded. "They're marking the way for whatever's coming up behind. I didn't see anybody do this, but then we were always looking back." He glanced towards the group, who were all looking his way. "And now they know we're on to them."

Veitch scrubbed out the sign. "Bollocks. I'm going to carve it out of them."

"We can't torture everyone until we find out who it is."

Veitch still appeared to consider this a viable option.

"We might be able to use it in our favour," Church said.

"Play it cool, screw with their heads a bit?"

"Something like that."

Veitch nodded. "Works for me."

Church looked back at his friends' faces. "I know we were warned there was a traitor in the group. I just can't believe it."

"It's the girl—Virginia," Veitch whispered. "Got to be. Look at it logically. How the hell did someone that young get away from the Enemy Fortress? Come on—millions of the worst things there are all around and she manages to wriggle out, travel God knows how many miles and then just hooks up with Decebalus?"

Church eyed the fragile girl. "They let her out?"

"Sent her back, primed to explode right in the middle of us."

"I've spoken to her, Ryan. I believe what she's saying."

"She believes it—that's the point. You know how clever all these bastards are at manipulating us poor humans. She doesn't know she's set up to do us all in." He paused. "Same as I didn't know back in the Battle of London."

A moment of tension passed quickly, dismissed by Veitch with a quick smile. "Don't blame you, though. Not any more. Nobody could have known." A pause. "You couldn't have saved me."

When they returned to the group, Ruth asked what they had been inspecting, but they brushed her off with a comment about feeling for vibrations of pursuit in the floor. She didn't believe them, but said nothing. Church carefully watched the others' faces, but no one showed any suspicious sign.

Two chambers on and Shavi brought them to a halt. He was rubbing his eye as if it was causing him some discomfort. "There is something around here," he said hesitantly, before pointing tentatively to a room off to their left that they had all missed.

"What's in there?" Laura asked.

"I see . . . connections," Shavi began. "Places where the Invisible World interacts with our own. Something in that room calls to me."

They all hesitated until Ruth pushed her way through them to the chamber's door. "We can't ignore anything that might help us," she said.

"And we can't ignore anything that might, like, kill us," Laura added tartly.

The chamber was more intimate than the others, with a series of runic symbols painted on the walls in an oily black that had not become obscured by dust like the many murals they had passed. As Shavi ventured into the chamber, one of the symbols began to glow faintly. Virginia buried her face in Miller's chest. Shavi looked back and forth with urgency, seeing things that no one else could.

"Shadows," he whispered. "Rising from the stones. Locked here for an age."

Suddenly he grew stock still, his eyes fixed on a place far beyond the four walls. A droplet of blood trickled from his nose. His mouth opened and his lips moved, but no sound issued for a full five seconds, and then it came with a boom that made their ears ring: a word of power.

Gradually, the shadows became visible, faint smudges in the air coalescing on one form standing in a proscribed circle etched into the stone flags. In the shimmering air, a bearded, long-haired man appeared, more than six feet tall, wearing furs and chain mail, a shield strapped to his back, swords and axes hanging from him, and a spear with a silver tip clutched in his right hand.

He wore a horned helmet of black and silver that protected his cheekbones and nose, so that his eyes lay deep in shadow. He appeared grainy, not wholly there, like a bad hologram.

"The Age of Warriors has passed," he said in a deep, rasping voice that did not sound human. Behind him, in the air itself, images of what he described played out in vivid colour. "Since time before time, the Drakusa have been the greatest race. Our forges produced weapons that could bring the stars down from the heavens. Our armies scourged the Far Lands and the fields and hills ran red with blood. No one could stand before us, and our battles became legends, sung over fires in the long nights, reducing the women to tears at the wonder of our courage. And yet the Drakusa are no more.

"From our victories we forged a peace based on blood and iron—a warrior's peace, in which no man or woman lived in fear, a golden age of prosperity for all. And yet the Drakusa are no more.

"How could we fall so far, so hard? Here, then, is a cautionary tale, people-yet-to-come. Here is our gift to you, the race of warriors that lies beyond the sun. Know your enemies. Do not look for the iron raised against you, the sword or the axe or the spear. Do not seek out eyes that promise hatred and death. The true enemies are cleverer. They pose as friends. They pretend to be part of your dreams, and to offer you your heart's desire. They stand at your side, and then move to your back when the time comes."

In the air around him, the shifting scenes of carnage and warfare became mellower. Autumnal hues painted deep forests and a low sun behind mountaintops.

"Seasons turn. Nothing abides forever. Even the greatest can be laid low in the blink of an eye."

Across the image, shadows flitted, their shape changing as they moved. Familiar glints of silver flashed like the sun.

"Caraprix," Church said.

"The Drakusa were torn down by the ones we raised highest," the warrior continued. "Know this: the Caraprix cannot be trusted. They are the enemy of all there is. Their purpose is to wipe clean, like the maggots in a corpse leaving only bones behind. When they turned on us, we could do nothing. Our weapons meant nothing. Our courage meant nothing. One thing we created in the final days to prevent our destruction, but time slipped through our fingers like the sands of Far-el-Quah. It waits here still. In the end, every-thing we had achieved in our great age was wiped away. Nothing remains. Know the terrible sadness of the Drakusa, warriors-yet-to-be, and despair."

The warrior bowed his head silently for a moment. The flickering images behind him died away.

When he looked back up, he spoke quietly, but his voice was filled with emotion. "If the Caraprix still infest this place, flee. Now. Go to the Groghaan Gate. Return to the Land of Always Summer and fill your heart with hope that you can run far enough and fast enough. Go to the Groghaan Gate and seek the Heart of the Drakusa. But beware: the way has been made treacherous to slow the vile beasts. Courage will prevail." A pause. "The Age of Warriors has passed."

The warrior winked out and the room returned to normal. Reeling from his trance, Shavi staggered back until he was caught by Church.

"Bloody hell," Veitch said. "The Caraprix...back at the court."

"So...what? They're just going to wipe us out?" Laura said.

"Like the spiders did on Earth," Church said. "Wipe everything out and start again."

"What can we do?" Shavi asked.

"You can't do anything," Tom snapped. "This is bigger than you! You're just little cogs in a vast machine, turning slowly, not even knowing what you're doing. Following the pattern someone else has set for you." He gnawed on a knuckle, long-stifled desperation breaking through his carefully devised exterior.

"Did you know the Caraprix were a threat?" Church asked.

"I don't know anything either, you idiot! I just see flashes of what's to come. Do I have to explain it to you again?" he said with bitter sarcasm. "Disconnected images like the views from windows as you climb a tower. Who knows how they all link together? Who knows what it all means? Meaning can only be divined by a true perspective, and neither you nor I have that. We live in ignorance, and do our best as we fumble around in the dark."

"What are the Caraprix?" Church pressed. "Are they just the equivalent of the spiders—"

"I don't know!" Tom marched out of the chamber, a forlorn figure.

"I thought he was supposed to be our guide," Laura said.

"He does his best," Church said. "We just don't do our best for him."

The warrior's message hung heavily over them as they continued their journey, worming its way into their thoughts and infecting them with a mood of hopelessness.

"I thought the Caraprix were supposed to be close to Existence," Ruth said to Church. "Does this mean we've been lying to ourselves all along? That we're on the wrong side? Maybe the Libertarian is right—people don't want the torment of trying to be better than they are. All that insecurity and worry and struggle and pain. The things we've had to face. They just want to live in stability, with as much happiness as they can grasp before it all falls apart. The Mundane Spell might actually have been a blessing."

Church had no answers for her questions, but her words struck a chord and he pondered them in silence as they continued through the gloomy halls.

2

Decebalus had risen with the sun, climbing the highest tower of the Court of the Soaring Spirit to get the clearest view across the Great Plain to the mountains and the sprawling Forest of the Night that bordered it. What he saw left him with a chill that even the warmth of the sun couldn't lift. Only the white-streaked mountaintops were visible, the forest not at all. The army surrounding the city was so large he had the impression of standing on a lighthouse on an island in the centre of a black, turbulent ocean. War machines belched out thick black smoke to fill the sky, mingling with the odd purple mist clinging to some of the enemy. Three Riot-Beasts came and went, their roving eyes revealing their idiot power that blasted out in a directionless fury that occasionally hit their own forces. It was like no army Decebalus had ever faced in his lifetime of battle. In his mind, he felt as if he was looking at a seething anthill, but what his eyes saw was even worse and his consciousness squirmed and skittered across it, refusing to accept the reality.

"They know we are not defenceless." Lugh had joined him silently. "They fear the Brothers and Sisters of Dragons in our midst, and they wonder what other powers we have at our disposal. As well they should. But they will attack soon enough."

"What makes my blood boil is that this is no true battle. Its outcome is meaningless to the Enemy. It is simply a way of harrying and distracting the Brothers and Sisters of Dragons until the Void has claimed its place in this world. And yet we must fight, and we must die. And what do we gain?"

"Survival." Lugh's face was drawn, yet to Decebalus he appeared to have grown in stature since the barbarian had first encountered him. "All things under Existence are in peril. Extinction waits for Fragile Creatures and for gods. When the Void remakes this place, we will no longer be in it, replaced by supine peoples who will live in peace within the Mundane Spell, and never challenge the will of the Devourer of All Things."

Decebalus nodded. "You make sense, for a slippery manipulator of men. For all time, until this time, there was always a chance the Void could be deposed, however slim that chance might be. If this war is lost, there will never be a chance again. The Void rules, for all time."

"And we play our part here, by distracting the Enemy and deflecting the bulk of its forces from hunting Jack Giant-Killer and his fellows. There is little glory in any victory here." He smiled wryly. "But we play a part, and sometimes that is enough."

They were interrupted by a Sister of Dragons with dyed red hair. Her name was Sarah Mazzarella, a thoughtful and intuitive woman to whom Decebalus had given the onerous task of liaising with the gods. "They're ready," she said, her voice weary. "They've agreed to accept your orders in the battle." She glanced at Lugh. "But no other."

"As it should be," Lugh said. "We would only fight amongst each other if one of us tried to gain ascendancy."

"You are an irritating and troublesome kind." Decebalus sighed. "It would be easier to herd cats with a stick and a flute." He nodded to Sarah. "Tell them we march onto the field of slaughter within the hour."

"I may reword that," she said as she left.

"You have a strategy in place?" Lugh asked.

"Yes. Run hard at the enemy and see if they fall down."

Lugh eyed Decebalus, unsure if he was joking.

"I have a plan," the barbarian said with a grin. He glanced towards the tower where smoke belched from the windows and lights flashed mysteriously. Math was hard at work.

As they made their way down towards their troops, there was a loud disturbance at the gate. Soon after, the chief of the guards ran breathlessly to them. "The Enemy has sent an emissary to talk," he gasped.

"We are not going to surrender!" Decebalus said.

Lugh caught his arm. "Let us listen to what he has to say."

At the gate, a skeletal figure in black robes with a sly smile and staring yellow eyes waited with three Redcaps who could barely contain their blood-lust. They all stank of rotting meat.

"Perhaps I should cut you down here, and save time," Decebalus mused.

"What would it profit you?" The skeletal man nodded mockingly. "I am Lorca, charged to speak for the one your kind knows as Seth, sole survivor of the Great Dominion of the desert lands, who commands this mighty force."

"Ah. He seeks revenge."

Lorca gave a chittering laugh. "Revenge is for equals, Fragile Creature. We come here to . . ." With a wry expression, Lorca searched for words that Decebalus might understand and finally settled on, "Save trouble."

"Save trouble? Why, I have been looking forward to this fight for a long time. I have organised my week around it."

"You wish to die so soon?"

"If needs must. But I have a bet on with the drinkers down at the Hunter's Moon. How many of you will I take with me? That is the question."

Lorca nodded, patronisingly.

"Say your piece and then we can get down to the sport," Decebalus said.

"Give up the Caraprix."

Taken aback, Decebalus shared a glance with Lugh.

"Give them up now, and we will leave you in peace here to live out the rest of your days, however long that may be," Lorca continued.

"Why would you want those silver rats?"

"Why would you? They are no use to Fragile Creatures."

"They were no use. Now that you have raised the matter, I think they may well be of great use indeed."

"Then you do not know their true nature. You harbour the seeds of your own destruction, Fragile Creature. The Caraprix are not benign. They are a force of destruction."

"Ah. So you are doing us a favour by taking them off our hands. I had the same proposition in the market this very morning. A ducat for my axe. To save me from cutting myself."

Lorca nodded and smiled, but his eyes were filled with a deathly cold. "Understand that you may make a gift of the Caraprix, or we will take them. The only difference is the life or death of everyone in this city."

"Run along now. I am tired of talking."

Lorca held Decebalus's gaze for a moment, before giving another contemptuous nod and retreating with the Redcaps.

"An interesting development," Decebalus mused.

"Then the Enemy has a reason to be here," Lugh said.

"There is a reason for everything. The question, then, is of what use are those shape-shifting rats to the Army of Ultimate Destruction?"

"They must be of great value indeed." Lugh pondered for a moment and then said, "And why did the Enemy not simply crush us and take the Caraprix? There is something here, I think."

"There is something, indeed!" Decebalus gave a pleased grin. "If the Enemy wants the Caraprix so badly that they are prepared to wheedle for them, our course of action is decided. They shall not have them!"

3

Hunter and Jack spent the better part of an hour searching the reaches of the cavern for an exit. Far behind them in the dark, the Fomorii hunted through the field of bones, drawing closer with every passing minute.

The sign would have been easy to miss if Jack had not been resting his forehead against the rock to calm his mounting panic. Faint vibrations rippled through the wall, a steady, rhythmic beat. He called Hunter over, who pressed his ear to the damp rock.

"You can hear it," he whispered. "Boom-boom-boom, like machinery."

"In here? What could it be?"

When Hunter edged along the wall in a particular direction, the beat grew fractionally louder, until he could hear it clearly. At that point, he spied handholds in the rock leading up to a small, dark opening about ten feet off the ground. Boosting Jack up, he followed him into a tunnel large enough for them to stand upright, cut through the rock. The beat emanated from some-where ahead.

The tunnel wound steadily upwards, presenting occasional rough-hewn steps for them to climb, the beat growing louder the closer they drew to the source. Soon it was ringing off the stone walls and vibrating beneath their feet.

BOOM-BOOM-BOOM.

They entered a large hall that smelled of sulphur and coal, with enormous furnaces along opposite walls, still black with soot, the tools of the smiths protruding from the dead cores. Half-completed swords and chain mail rusted on the ground amidst anvils and scattered hammers.

"Looks like we've found the back door into the Halls of the Drakusa," Hunter said.

"If the others got in, we could meet up with them." Jack's eyes gleamed with hope. "I was afraid we might have to go back the way we came."

Beyond, another chamber was given over to industrial production, but here its purpose was less clear: a faint chemical smell hung over benches covered with glass bottles and jars. Bones had been swept into the corners. Mysterious implements lay abandoned on the floor and on the benches, as if the occupants had been rudely disturbed.

The floor of the following chamber was covered with runes and ritual marks, and contained an overwhelming atmosphere of threat. Hunter and Jack couldn't bear to tarry in it for too long.

Finally the booming was so painful they had to cover their ears. The source was a huge iron door set in the wall of a long corridor, but the moment Hunter grabbed the handle with both hands and dragged the door open, silence fell.

Jack futilely urged his friend not to venture into the room, but Hunter's curiosity had got the better of him.

The chamber was lit by a shaft of natural sunlight falling from an incred-ible height overhead. Stone steps wound around the walls up the dizzying stretch to whatever lay in the dim upper reaches. The floor of the chamber was occupied by a giant with a brutish, bare, heavily scarred torso, its head covered with a leather hood, its arms outstretched and fastened to the floor by shackles. It was stock-still, head cocked, listening.

"How long has it been here?" Jack whispered.

"The Drakusa disappeared long before the Tuatha Dé Danaan arrived on the scene. . . an age ago."

"All that time? What does it feed on?"

"What does it feed on?" the giant repeated.

Jack started. "It heard me. It can speak."

Hunter pushed Jack back towards the door. As they stepped out of the chamber, the giant wrenched at its chains again and again, creating the deafening booming sound they had followed.

Hunter took them back into the chamber and it stopped, waiting.

"It's been trying to break free all this time," Hunter observed.

"It's been trying to break free," the giant repeated.

"Why is it mimicking what we say?" Jack asked.

"I don't think it is," Hunter replied thoughtfully. "Let's forget how it survived all this time. Why did the Drakusa imprison it here?"

The giant continued to listen intently.

"I don't like it," Jack decided.

"One hundred and ninety-three cried like a baby," the giant said.

"What's it talking about?" Jack asked before he saw Hunter staring, mouth open.

"Sixty-seven spilled blood and urine on the tiles," the giant continued.

"Get out of my head!" Hunter shouted.

"What's it saying?" Jack asked. "What's one hundred and ninety-three and sixty-seven?"

"Never you mind. Let's get out of here."

The door slammed shut. A lock fell into place.

"You're here now," the giant said.

4

The thunder of the barricaded door being torn open echoed through the halls, and was followed by a grinding, metallic sound of something being dragged over the stone flags.

"Dammit," Church said under his breath. They were only three halls away from where he and Veitch had discovered the sign in the dust.

"Did you really think you'd be given a free run right up to the gates of the Enemy?" Tom mocked. "They're going to be hunting and harrying you at every turn. The Void won't want to risk you getting anywhere near enough to do any damage. Everything at their disposal will have been put in place long ago to keep you away—spies, traitors, hunting parties, the kind of sentinels that can't be avoided, that never stop."

"Why didn't you say this before?" Church said sharply.

"What was the point? You never had any chance of getting through. Better to let you keep your hopes up to the last."

"And now you've decided to get my hopes down?"

Refusing to answer any further questions, Tom moved away, but Church was already wondering if he'd made the wrong decision to suspect Virginia. Was Tom's comment about spies and traitors a cry for help?

The grinding metallic sound drew closer. "They're outpacing us," Veitch said, glancing back. "We could barricade each door we pass through, but I don't reckon it'll do us much good."

"Better hope we get to the gate back to Summer-side pretty quick, then."

"You think they're going to stop at the gate? We've lost any advantage we had crossing through this God-forsaken place. They're going to be straight on us the minute we crash back into the Far Lands."

Ruth had overheard their conversation as she helped Miller and Virginia, who were flagging. "We have to stop them here. It's the only way."

Ahead, Tom and Shavi conferred intensely. "We both feel we are near to the gate," Shavi said, "but we cannot find the way."

"The warrior said we had to find the Heart of the Drakusa if we wanted to get to the Groghaan Gate." Church peered around the gloomy chamber, but it appeared to be as bare and forlorn as all the others.

The line of sight through the great doors of the chambers revealed flickering lights in the distant dark.

"Now would be a good time for inspiration," Laura said.

Everyone except Church rushed to search the chamber with urgency, dragging blocks of masonry aside, brushing the thick grime and cobwebs from crumbling murals, sweeping away the dust covering the flags. The echoes of the metallic grinding filled the room.

"The heart of a warrior," Church mused aloud. "The heart. Brave. Fearless.

Aspiring . . . no, no, reaching . . . for greatness . . ." A connection was made. Quickly, but methodically, Church began to investigate the walls, trying to see into the shadows that clustered overhead.

As Church moved the lantern, it brought a subtle shift in slivers of shadow on the stone near him: revealing protrusions only a few inches wide. Broadly spaced footholds wound up into the dark, invisible to the casual eye. He called the others over as the lights drew into the adjoining chamber.

"I'll go," Ruth said, handing her spear to Church.

"No, you'll break your neck." Veitch tried to pull her back. "No one's gonna get up there."

Ruth threw him off. "I'll go," she said fiercely. "I'm lighter, more agile—"

"And if anyone's going to break their neck it ought to be her," Laura said.

Pressed flat against the wall, Ruth put one foot on the lowest step and reached for the next. She had to stretch her fingers to find even the flimsiest handhold, and then, with a shaky, precarious step, she leaped to the next stone. When she almost fell from the fifth step, now well above their heads, Veitch had to look away.

"Get underneath to break her fall," he said to Laura as he turned to join Church facing the approaching lights. "We're going to have to fight."

"If we can hold them off, at least the others can get through."

"We're doing this all the way to the Enemy?"

"Probably."

From the shadows emerged a figure, eight feet tall with rusty iron plates on chains at the front and back of his body, muscular arms smeared with blood. He wore a helmet of smaller iron plates bolted together haphazardly. The now-deafening grating came from an enormous sword that he dragged behind him. Church and Veitch recognised the Iron Slaughterman from the description Mallory had given them of his encounter with the being in Ogma's library.

In the flickering torchlight, twenty figures swarmed around him, keeping low. They had the heads of wolves and rats but the bodies of men, snapping at the air in a hunting frenzy. Behind them, Church could just make out further movement, like clouds of smoke unfolding towards him.

"How are you doing?" Church called out.

"Still clinging on, if that's what you mean," Ruth shouted back.

Without slowing his step, the Iron Slaughterman began to swing the sword, which was as big as he was. Veins bulged on his straining sinews and the rusty, bloodstained sword began to gather speed in an arc.

"He's never going to hit us with that big bleedin' thing," Veitch mocked.

The sword swung round and round over the Iron Slaughterman's head as he ran. At the last he lowered the angle so it drove towards Church and Veitch, who leaped out of the way. The sword hit the flags with such explosive force that chunks of stone hurtled through the air. Church and Veitch were thrown from their feet, and a massive fissure opened in the floor.

Snapping and snarling, the wolves and rats attacked. Church rolled back to his feet, bringing Caledfwlch up sharply to bisect one from groin to shoulder, and then taking the head off another. Veitch had already despatched three, but the others were darting and retreating, trying to get past Church and Veitch to their more vulnerable companions.

Heaving his sword off the ground and whirling it in another slow, powerful arc, the Iron Slaughterman attacked again. Church ducked beneath the whistling blade at the last second and it crashed through a marble pillar, bringing down part of the ceiling in a cloud of billowing dust.

"Bastard's going to bring this place down around us." Veitch coughed as he and Church took the opportunity to retreat a few paces, unseen. When the dust cleared, Church saw a figure floating a foot in the air behind the attackers. Bone-white skin framed by black hair, becoming black skin and white hair, and back. Janus, the god of doorways and new beginnings, raised his golden key and ironwood stick, one to open the path, the other to drive away those who had no right to cross the threshold.

"Brothers of Dragons," he said in a scraping voice. "Your doors shall be closed forever."

Above them, they heard a cry of exultation from Ruth, and then a door ground open in the wall behind them.

"You see, that's irony," Church said to Janus.

"This place is winding down, and all places joined to it," Janus continued. "The lamps are going out. The doors are closing one by one by one. You cannot hold back the dark."

"We're the ones who carry the light," Veitch said defiantly. "A little blue spark, and that'll never go out."

As the rats and wolves circled, Church said to Janus, "You're a god. You're not controlled by the Anubis Box—you've still got free will. Why did you choose to side with the Void and the Army of the Ten Billion Spiders?"

"I am not just a god. I am Divom Deus, the gods' God. The first. I am one of the Oldest Things in the Land."

Before Church had a moment to reflect on what Janus had said, one of the rat creatures darted under his guard and flung itself into the newly opened doorway to block their retreat. It had only backed a few paces into the space beyond the door when the tubular corridor began to revolve and axes swung like pendulums at intermittent spaces along the way. One blade planted itself firmly in the rat creature's chest. With a strangled, bestial cry, it fell to the floor in a gout of blood and began to revolve and fall, revolve and fall.

"That was a spot of luck," Veitch said.

"The warrior told us the path to the gate had been booby-trapped." Church retreated with Veitch to the door. "This might only be a part of it."

Ruth joined them in the entrance to the revolving corridor as the Iron Slaughterman launched another attack. The sword ripped through wall and floor, bringing another deluge of masonry from the precarious ceiling.

"Let me go first! Follow my steps!" Ruth shouted above the roar of falling stonework. Darting into the revolving corridor, she performed intricate steps to dodge and duck the pendulum axes while fighting to keep her balance. Church held his breath as more than one came within a hair's breadth of her, but then she was through to the other side, urging Shavi, then Laura to follow.

The rat and wolf creatures leaped, snarling, only to be cut down by Church and Veitch. Another assault by the Iron Slaughterman tore through the walls on either side of the door, forcing Miller and Virginia to fall to their knees screaming as Tom dived into the revolving corridor.

Resonant creaks and groans warned them that the entire stone ceiling was about to come down. Once Tom, Miller and Virginia had made it through the axes, Church and Veitch followed, dancing amongst the blades with such balletic skill that they made it appear effortless.

Ruth waited at the foot of a winding stone staircase. She held up a hand to halt Church and Veitch, then jabbed her spear up the stairs. Blades shot out from both walls and snapped back into place; they would have sliced off the legs of anyone climbing them.

With the sounds of pursuit drawing closer along the revolving corridor, Ruth yelled, "See the gaps in the walls from which the blades extend? If you're careful, you can go over and under."

"We haven't got time to be careful," Veitch barked. "Move!"

Almost rigid with fear, Virginia was helped by Ruth and Miller. The others followed as quickly as they could. The ka-ching of the blades became a steady, terrifying beat as they worked their way up the steps. A cry rang out as one clipped Tom's boot and he sprawled, narrowly missing another blade. His stream of abuse told everyone he was all right.

A quaking at the foot of the steps warned Church that the Iron Slaughterman was close behind, the sound of shattering blades revealing how he was putting his sword to good use.

Freezing air, brilliant white light and the dying blizzard greeted them as they stumbled from the top of the steps onto a stone terrace on the side of the mountain. Across a dizzying gulf, on another rocky slope of the range, they could just make out what had to be the Groghaan Gate, a soaring arch of gleaming gold. A bridge had once spanned the gulf between the two peaks, but it had been shattered at intervals so that sections were suspended on either side of columns that dropped down into the white wastes below.

"We're never going to get across there," Veitch said, peering over the lip of the first section of bridge. Vertigo made him wobble and he took a step back from the edge.

"Then we make our stand here," Church said.

5

In the chamber in the depths of the Halls of the Drakusa, Jack frantically wrenched at the door handle, but it remained resolutely closed.

Standing his ground before the chained giant, Hunter's face revealed the strain of keeping the creature out of his thoughts.

"Who are you?" Hunter asked.

"Who are you?" the giant said.

"Okay, we could keep doing this all day, but it's already getting old."

"Getting old."

Wiping away a dribble of blood from his left nostril, Hunter continued, "Clearly the Drakusa saw you as too much of a threat to leave you wandering around. Are you responsible for all the bones in the basement?"

"Bones."

"Of course, if that's what remains of the Drakusa, it doesn't explain who chained you up here."

Hunter became aware that Jack was no longer rattling at the door in panic. The boy now watched Hunter with hooded eyes, his body held in an odd posture with one shoulder slumped. Before Hunter could ask what was wrong, Jack attacked in a murderous rage, screaming and attempting to tear at Hunter's flesh, throat, eyes.

It was an effort even for Hunter to hold him off, but as he wrestled Jack back, an insidious darkness crept into the back of his head. He saw himself pressing his thumbs into Jack's throat and squeezing the life from him before tearing off his skin, ripping out his eyes, brutalising his body beyond all recognition. His head swam with the last, desperate expressions of all the people he had killed, their fear of what was to come on the other side of death, their grief for the ones they were leaving behind, the terrible sight of the intelligence winking out in their eyes. And then he was hanging himself from a short rope in the corner of the room, his face turning black, the skin decaying, the insects moving in.

For anyone else, the creeping infection of morbidity would have destroyed them, but death had been Hunter's companion for too long. He wasn't scared of it; nor did it revolt him. It was simply a necessary if distasteful part of life. He snapped himself back from the flood of oppressive images and forced his thoughts to right themselves.

Jack rolled on the floor, gasping for air, his throat still bearing the red marks of Hunter's fingers. The death-images assaulted his mind, driving him slowly insane.

The giant cocked his hooded head towards Hunter. "I am El-Di-Gah-Wis-Lor, the final judgement of the Drakusa, the dark at the end, the breath of the grave," he began. "I am death, and I bring death. Brought into being for one purpose, to end the plague of the Caraprix, I was not allowed to fulfil my destiny. And so I have waited, and waited, and my urge for death has risen with each season. And now you are here, and I will have my way."

Blood flew in droplets as Hunter shook his head to clear his mind. "All well and good, except you're unfortunate to have the wrong person in here. You see, I am death, and I'm a bigger, badder death than you."

Hunter tore open his bag and rammed his hand into the Balor Claw. It sang eagerly when it bonded with its master. "Now we'll see. Skull for skull and bone for bone."

From beyond the door, he could hear the low, rumbling sound of the approaching Fomorii. Jack whined, spat blood, drawing them closer.

Bounding at the giant, Hunter tore off the hood. Red eyes that had not seen in an age rolled in a devastated face that resembled a melted candle. When they fixed on Hunter, he saw within a monstrous intellect, unknowable, uncaring, whose sole purpose was to destroy him, destroy every living thing. For the first time in his monstrous, debased life, he shuddered.

And then he brandished the Balor Claw in front of the giant's face and said, "This is worse than death. It can reduce you to nothing in an instant. Do you understand?"

Hunter wanted to look away when those hideous eyes revolved back to him. "I have learned your words. I know your mind. We are death."

Despair washed through Hunter when he heard his worst fears given voice. "Leave the boy alone," he said.

The red, staring eyes focused on Jack, then snapped away as if they were removing a hook and line. Jack rolled onto his back, gasping and crying.

The door throbbed with a ferocious pounding that would rend it open within seconds. Hunter glanced at the stone steps winding around the chamber walls, but then a notion struck him.

"You can control minds," he said. "Can you control them?"

"The Nightwalkers. They nested here in recent times. I have felt them scurrying and searching. Directionless. Hopeless."

"Can you control them?"

The answer was clear in the giant's red eyes.

"Then open the door."

6

The blizzard blasted across the terrace again, limiting visibility to one little world of brutality and strife. Bodies of the rat and wolf creatures were scattered all around in shocking Rorschach blots of colour on the blank canvas, but the Iron Slaughterman remained impervious to Church, Veitch and Ruth's attacks. His skill and speed with the sword belied his enormous size, a wall of iron that deflected their attacks and forced them on the defensive. Only the limited space on the terrace prevented the Iron Slaughterman from destroying them, but they all knew it was only a matter of time.

"Find a way to get across to the next part of the bridge!" Church yelled to the others as they shielded their heads from the raining chunks of rock in the far corner of the terrace.

"Does he expect us to fly?" Tom snapped.

"At least Janus has not ventured this far," Shavi said. Peering over the edge of the terrace, he could just make out the next section of shattered bridge through the blizzard. "If only we had a rope," he said.

"If we don't hurry we won't even be able to see where it is," Miller whined.

"I might be able to help." Her voice filled with uncertainty, Laura joined Shavi at the edge and showed him a handful of seeds she had retrieved from her pocket. "I brought these from the court. Thought they might come in handy some time, you know, with my freakish ability to make things grow."

Shavi smiled at her. "That shows excellent foresight."

"Yeah, well, I only did it so I could hear that lovely patronising tone in your voice—"

A boulder dislodged from the cliff face by the Iron Slaughterman's sword crashed so near it almost flung them over the edge. With a scream, Virginia buried her head into Miller's chest.

Laura cursed loudly. "We've got to try this now. But here's the deal—it's too cold. I can't keep things alive here for more than a minute or two. I might be able to get something to reach across the gap, but there's no guarantee it won't wither when you're halfway across. And . . . especially with all this . . ." She glanced anxiously at the furious battle. "I don't know if I can keep my concentration. If that goes . . . you go."

Shavi took Laura's hand. "I trust you. We all do."

Laura's face fell, but she quickly hid it behind a mocking smile. "God, you're such an idiot loser, Shavster."

Placing one of the seeds in a crack in the edge of the terrace, she closed her eyes and bowed her head. The sight of the seed bursting into green life, unfolding and extending rapidly, still left her breathless with disbelief and excitement. Who was she to have these kinds of abilities? She restrained the part of her that didn't believe she deserved to be special, and concentrated so that the strand of dense, twisting vine thickened and spread across the gap.

"Go, Shavi, go!" she urged.

Without a second thought, Shavi leaped onto the vine, wrapped his legs and arms around it and shimmied across. It swung wildly with his exertions, the wind threatening to tear him off. Fighting to maintain her concentration, Laura held the vine together, but in the bitter cold the leaves were already blackening as fast as they had grown and the strand began to unravel and die. Through the wall of snow, Laura glimpsed Shavi scrambling onto the shattered edge of the next section of bridge. Grinning, he gave her the thumbs-up before the snow obscured him.

Sagging back with a gasp, Laura let the vine fall away. The strain was already telling on her, but she was determined not to let them down. Ignoring the rocks falling around her, she placed another seed in the crack and grew it quickly. "Go on, old man—you're next," she said. "I just hope your arthritic joints hold out."

"If I fall, let it be known she did it on purpose," Tom said to Miller.

With surprising agility, he shimmied across the vine and disappeared into the blizzard. When Laura felt the vine grow less taut, she let it fall away.

"Your turn, Miller," she said.

"I'll carry Virginia. She can wrap her arms and legs around me."

"It'll be too much for you."

"Laura, she'll never make it on her own."

The girl kept glancing at the dizzying drop, her face as white as the snow. Laura's heart went out to her. "Okay," she said hesitantly. "I'll try to make the vine stronger. Just . . . just be quick."

But before she could use the third seed, a cry rang out. The Iron Slaughterman had struck Ruth a glancing blow, propelling her into the mountainside where she slumped, unconscious. Her injury had distracted both Church and Veitch. Laura called out as the great sword hurtled towards Veitch and while her warning came in time for him to take one brief step back, the blade still ripped across his chest, releasing a spurt of blood. Veitch staggered backwards into the snow.

"Miller, you're going to have to heal him," Laura shouted.

The Iron Slaughterman drove Church back against the wall where Veitch lay. When the giant sword pounded into the rock near where his head had been, the resultant explosion of shards of stone laid him flat.

Despite the threat, Miller scrambled towards Church and Veitch, but the Iron Slaughterman rounded on him instantly.

"This is it," Laura gasped.

So fast was the attack on the Iron Slaughterman that Laura barely saw it. A second or two had passed before she realised he was battling furiously with a pair of Fomorii, their oily black shapes snapping and changing, claws and spikes and horns tearing through the Iron Slaughterman's defences before they clung onto him, their snapping jaws darting. His arm fell away, and in his frenzy to throw off the Fomorii, he careered to the edge, and over, taking both beasts with him.

As Miller ran to help Veitch, Laura scrambled to the edge, but the Iron Slaughterman had already been lost in the swirling blizzard.

"I hope you were expecting me."

Laura whirled at the familiar voice. Hunter sauntered up jauntily, Jack creeping out from the top of the stairs behind him. For once, Laura gave in to honest emotion and threw her arms around Hunter, kissing him passionately on the edge of the precipice, oblivious to the drop, the cold, the wind.

"I take it from that greeting that you weren't expecting me," Hunter said with a grin. Behind him, a soft blue glow rose up as Miller healed Veitch, who was unconscious from the shock of his wound and the blood loss.

"You're always full of surprises," she said.

"Here's another one: I've got my own giant. He's roaming around in the hall down there. Turns out he can control those shape-shifting things." His grin was swaggering, but his eyes told of a deeper emotion that made her ache. "So, did you miss me?" he asked.

"I'm sorry," she said.

He pulled back, puzzled. "For what?"

Laura placed her hands firmly on his chest and pushed. For only the briefest moment she had to bear the searing look of betrayal in his face before Hunter went over the edge and was lost to the snowstorm.

"Laura!" His face torn with horror, Miller raced towards her. "What have you done?"

With a flourish, Laura flicked one of the seeds into the air. Green shoots burst from it, rippling and extending rapidly until they lashed around Miller, holding him fast. Laura grabbed the other end of the vine and yanked him towards her. Aghast, he tried to force out a question that would make sense of her devastating actions, but she elbowed him sharply in the face, and as he reeled in a daze, she propelled him over the edge after Hunter.

Jack and Virginia were rooted and though they struggled briefly, she was too strong and too determined.

Church and Ruth came round as Laura returned from the edge of the terrace. Dazed, they struggled to their feet, not yet noticing who was missing. Laura helped Veitch up, his wound already healed, thanks to Miller. Although still weak, the Pendragon Spirit would soon have him back to full strength.

"Church, it's terrible," Laura said when she saw the questions start to surface in his face. "That bastard with the sword . . ." She choked back a sob. "He killed Hunter. And . . . and he took Miller, Jack and Virginia over the edge with him." Tears streamed down her face.

The others stared in abject shock until Ruth stepped forwards to comfort Laura with a hug.

"Hunter? Shit." Veitch looked to Church, who already understood the implications.

"Not just Hunter. We've lost the Two Keys, and our way into the Enemy Fortress," Church said. "It's all over."

7

In the timeless Grim Lands, only seconds had passed. Mallory and Caitlin watched as the flamboyant Callow did a little jig on top of the tomb.

"You've got a lot of energy for a dead man," Mallory said.

"Ah, but then I am not like others you will find in this dismal place.

When I walked the world, I was filled with more life than any of the grey, workaday drudges I encountered on their morose treks into the coffin they called the office. I drank deeply of the heady cup of life! I imbibed all there was to offer. And more!"

Mallory and Caitlin exchanged a glance, but if Callow noticed, he didn't appear to care.

"And then it was all so cruelly snatched away!" Callow added.

"I'm betting one or two others here would say the same thing," Mallory said.

"No! I was not meant to die. It was an error of cosmic proportions. And if proof you need, it is the simple fact that I am still here."

Caitlin eyed him curiously. "What do you mean?"

"I am not allowed to continue. The Grey Lands is simply a waiting room. The vast majority of shades you find here are in the process of moving on. To where, I do not know. Heaven? Hell? Why this is hell, nor am I out of it. Perhaps back into the innocent foetus, with all the possibilities once again lying ahead, to do right, or wrong, learn, or not, and find their way . . . where? Back here!"

Mallory began to grow weary of Callow's chatter and prepared to head off. Callow instantly read the signs and leaped in front of him.

"Some of the shades get trapped here, true, for reasons I have not yet discerned. But you can tell their type instantly. Consumed by bitterness, infected with despair, none of them exhibit the joy you see here in my humble form. No, I am a true anomaly—neither dead nor alive. Caught in a web not of my own making, and no one prepared to throw up their arms and admit to their mistake."

"We can't waste time here," Caitlin said with irritation.

"Take me with you!" Callow pleaded, grabbing hold of Mallory's jacket.

Prising him off, Mallory said, "Nice story, but I'm pretty sure you're meant to be here, and I wouldn't want to get on the wrong side of whoever sets the rules in this place."

"Please!" Callow started to cry. "You don't know what it's like here!"

"Mallory," Caitlin pressed. When she held up the Wayfinder to examine the direction of the blue flame, Callow stopped crying instantly and his eyes narrowed.

Mallory noticed the sudden change in his demeanour and asked, "What's wrong?"

"That lantern. I have seen it before. In the possession of my very good friends." Callow slyly watched Mallory's interest grow. "The remarkable, the astonishing Jack Churchill. And Ruth Gallagher. And the lovely Laura. Shavi. And the other one."

"You know Church and the others?" Caitlin asked.

"We were travelling partners for a time, during that age of upheaval, that Age of Misrule. Oh, how they mourned my passing! Oh, how they would celebrate joyously if I returned to the land of the quick!"

The resonant creak of the cemetery gate echoed through the mist. Callow started, and ran to the edge of a mausoleum to peer uneasily into the grey, where he plucked at the fraying sleeve of his jacket. Mallory and Caitlin left him there and tried to pick a path through the cluttered mass of monuments to the dead, but within a moment he had joined them again.

"Let me guide you," he said. "You'll never find your way through this sprawling city of the departed without my help. There are many hidden dangers, and sometimes a slight detour could save you a limb or a life. You really would not want to be permanent residents here."

From behind them came the dull sound of something dry and scratchy being drawn across stone. "Who's there?" Mallory asked.

"I saw no one. I would not expect the dead to be passing through here at this time; unless, of course, they have learned of your arrival. Then it would be a time to beware. They are jealous of the living, and their bitterness drives them to extremes. And unpleasantness."

"Bring him along," Caitlin said. "It won't hurt."

"All right. But any sign of deceit and you'll wish you'd stayed in your tomb," Mallory said bluntly. "And don't get any ideas about coming back with us. This is a short-term deal through this God-forsaken place."

"Of course, of course," Callow said slyly, "but once we are firm friends on the road of life . . . or death . . . who knows?"

"I know," Mallory said firmly. "Move."

With a bow, Callow swung one arm out flamboyantly to guide them on their way. They were soon lost amongst the mausoleums and grave markers and leaning, ivy-covered statues, and though Callow whistled jauntily a few yards ahead of them, they were left uneasy by the constant morbidity of their surroundings.

"Is this what death is," Caitlin asked, "one never-changing bleak landscape that goes on forever?" Hugging her arms around her, she fought off the creeping desolation imposed by their surroundings.

"Don't start asking me about the afterlife," Mallory said. "I never used to think there was one. For me, life itself was enough of a purgatory."

"You too?"

"I didn't use to think that. I was arrogant. Everything was just a big sweet-store where I could pick and choose until I grew fat. Then life slaps you around the face and shows you what it's really like." He caught himself. "Now I sound like a pathetic, self-pitying loser. I don't really believe that. There's a lot of good. It's just that once you've experienced the worst there is, it's impossible to see the world in that totally innocent way any more."

"But we still have hope, don't we? That's what keeps us going. It would have been so easy to give in when Grant and Liam died, but if I had I'd never have met you." It was Caitlin's turn to catch herself, afraid she'd said too much. She added hastily, "What happened to you?"

"In my arrogance, I attracted the attention of a particularly nasty bunch of people. I thought I could control them, beat them, until I realised there are people in this world who are capable of harder, more terrible things than you can ever dream, and if you come up against them, you can't match them. You always lose. They gave me a choice that no person should ever have to make. I killed someone, and it destroyed me. I couldn't live with it. And then I tried to kill myself." He paused. "I did kill myself. Don't ask me how I ended up here. Maybe there are just a whole load of successive lives. You die in one, you get bumped up to the next."

"But there's a reason you came here," Caitlin pressed. "If you hadn't killed yourself, you wouldn't have been here to try to save this world and we'd have lost long ago. Out of that awful thing, something good is happening."

"It'd be nice to believe that." Mallory clearly did not believe. "But it still sounds naïve to me."

"It's like Shavi kept saying—the pattern, the hidden pattern," she said. "It's all too complex, so everything seems random and punctuated with all these bleak, horrible events, but the big picture...it could be something beyond our dreams."

"I can see the pattern here. You've been sent to make sure I don't turn into a miserable, grumpy old git that the children throw stones at in the street."

"It's mutual, Mallory."

With a sudden urgency, he caught her arm. "There's someone here." He tried to pinpoint the direction of the noise he had heard, but with the deadened sound of the cemetery, it was impossible. Oblivious, Callow punctuated his progress with bursts of whistling.

Caitlin became darker, her posture more aggressive. The Morrigan drew forwards.

A faint rasp away to his left. Mallory turned, sword drawn, but there was nothing to see. Then a whisper of movement ahead, just beyond the visibility the mist allowed him.

Circling, he thought. Looking for an opening.

Though they were both on their guard, neither were prepared for the silent figure rising up beside a tomb they had just passed. The Hortha gripped Caitlin across the mouth with a twisted blackthorn hand, spun her around and extended the index finger of its right hand to drive it between her eyes and into her brain.

With a muffled snarl, Caitlin drove her axe down into the Hortha's thigh. Dry blackthorn shattered as the blade almost severed the limb. As the Hortha lurched to one side, his attack was thrown off-balance, and the finger-spear tore open the flesh along the side of her temple.

Wriggling free, Caitlin flipped back to land on her feet, axe ready to attack, pausing only to watch with disgust as the Hortha raised its finger to drop a minute amount of her blood into its paper mouth.

The axe crashed into the Hortha's torso, but as soon as Caitlin withdrew it, the blackthorn was already growing back into place with a snap and a pop.

"I taste your thoughts," it said. "There is nowhere to run now."

Caitlin and Mallory attacked together, but the Hortha evaded them with a speed that made it a blur. It used the folding mist to hide itself before coming at them rapidly from another direction. They cut off chunks here and there, a hand, half a leg, but it regrew just as quickly, and their sense of futility mounted with their unease.

Hailing them from the cover of a mausoleum, Callow beckoned frantically. Mallory signalled to Caitlin with his eyes, and when the Hortha withdrew into the mist, they both ran.

"We're just wasting our time," Mallory said breathlessly as they moved away through the cemetery. "We're never going to stop him like that."

"How did he follow us here from the temple?" Caitlin said. "We left no trail."

"No time for that now," Callow said. "The great Lord gave us brains to use in situations like this. Brute strength is all well and good, but it pales behind the advantages of the grey matter, used well and wisely."

He led them on a fast, winding path through the grave markers until he came to a mausoleum that had been marked with a red cross on the door.

"What's so special about this one?" Mallory asked.

"These are all houses of the dead," Callow replied, "but some are home to worse things than the dearly departed. Once I open the door, venture no further than the light reaches into the dark. Stand on either side of the door, and when your friend enters, emerge victorious!"

At first Mallory wasn't convinced, but when he read the repressed fear in Callow's face as he wrenched the stone door open, he stepped in with Caitlin right behind.

Callow had been right. The light died unnaturally quickly and sound was deadened close to the source. Beyond the few inches of grey illumination around the doorway, the darkness swam like oil. It had dimension, and texture, and gave off a quality that made them feel dread.

As they stood on either side of the door looking into the dark, their skin prickled and they had the unmistakable sense of something looking back at them. Their fears were confirmed when a faint voice whispered, "Closer." There was nothing inherently threatening in the tone, but it chilled them nonetheless.

The Hortha was in the mausoleum before they realised, moving low like an animal, rapidly searching the dark depths. Caitlin planted her axe in its back to disable it while they both darted out. Callow slammed the door shut the moment they were in the light.

The sounds that emanated from the mausoleum were chilling: a high-pitched shriek, a frantic rustling, something crashing from wall to wall and a wild thrashing noise. Then an unnerving silence.

Callow gave a deep bow. "No more will your enemy trouble you."

"What was in there?" Caitlin asked.

Callow blanched and held up a hand. "Speak of the devil and he will appear. In some aphorisms, there is a deeper truth. Trust the wisdom I have learned in hedgerow, field and forest: there are times when it is best to speak, and times when silence must rule. Shall we?" He swept an arm to guide their way. "And, perhaps, a word of thanks?"

Caitlin, who had once again lost the dark sheen of the Morrigan, said with a smile, "Thank you, Mr Callow, you were a great help."

"And I intend to carry on in that manner. Indeed, it is my hope to make myself indispensable to you, my travelling companions. Oh, the joys of being part of a band once more! Let us walk on and not look back!"

But Mallory couldn't resist one final glance at the silent mausoleum, and at the others that lay all around, and wondered what other threats lay hidden in the mist.

8

The blizzard continued to tear its bitter path between the mountain peaks as Laura became the final surviving member of their band to make the precarious journey from the last section of the shattered bridge to the terrace that lay before the Groghaan Gate. The mood was desperate. Church, Veitch, Ruth and Shavi stared into the middle distance, while Tom sat in a nook in the rocks, smoking.

Veitch extended a hand to help Laura up onto the terrace. "I know we've given each other a hard time," he said awkwardly, "but you saved us here. And I wanted to say, you know, thanks."

"All right, tattoo-boy—don't get all misty on me. Just doing my job."

They exchanged a moment of silent communication before Shavi came over. "I am concerned about Church," he whispered. "The loss of the Two Keys, Virginia and Hunter has hit him hard." He glanced back at Church, who had one hand on his forehead, deep in thought. "I am afraid that despair might be setting in. He fears the mission is already lost. And—"

"And you're worried this might be the point when he stops being Church and starts becoming the Libertarian," Veitch continued.

Shavi nodded.

"That's awful," Laura said. "I mean, if one thing had to tip him over the edge, it would be this, right? But still...God." She looked away, chewing a lip.

"I'll keep an eye on him," Veitch said, "and if I see anything dodgy . . ." He steeled himself. "I'll do what I have to do."

Hugging her arms around her for warmth, Ruth called them over. "We can't stand around here talking—we'll freeze to death."

"Mate, you want to carry on?" Veitch said to Church.

Church inspected the Groghaan Gate arching up at least twenty feet above their heads, the top lost in the snowstorm. It was constructed of some unknown material that sparkled like the sun, and from it came a feeling of electricity. "What else can we do? Go back and die? Go on and die?"

Behind him, Shavi, Veitch and Laura looked at each other uneasily.

Church reached out to the shimmering arch, his fingers tingling as they brushed the warm surface. "This is marvellous. The Drakusa must have passed through here every day, between Winter-side and Summer-side. Such an amazing thing to do, moving between worlds. They must have thought they owned everything. Kings of the world. And now they're gone." He turned back to the others defiantly. "We might not be able to win, but that doesn't mean we give up. We're going to make life a misery for the Enemy. We're going to show it what it means to stand for Existence. What it means to have the Pendragon Spirit. What it means to be a Fragile Creature. We're going to tear the whole damned thing down. From this point on, this is a suicide mission. As long as we know that, we're not going to be disappointed how it turns out."

The others nodded without a moment's thought.

"No happy endings," he said, before turning back to the gate. "Let's go." He stepped through the arch and with a shimmer he was gone.

CHAPTER FIVE
DIASPORA

1

In the blistering morning sun, the sands beyond the jungle's edge shimmered in a heat haze that gave an illusory quality to the rolling, golden world. From the shade of a canopy on the terrace, Church watched the barrens, deep in thought, smelling the dry desert wind as he sipped the hot, spicy drink brought to him by the scaled café owner.

Through the haze, the figure of the Burning Man glowed like coals in smoke, still there, always there, but closer now, looming so large Church was convinced he would soon be able to feel the heat.

From the moment they had stepped through the Groghaan Gate, the journey had been hard, but at least the exhaustion and the strife had left little space for black thoughts. The Halls of the Drakusa on Summer-side had been reclaimed by the landscape an age ago. They rested beneath a grassy mound in the northlands beyond the foothills of the mountains, a few crumbling stones all that remained on the surface to mark the glory of the once-mighty Drakusa, and even they were so weathered that they were easily mistaken for an outcropping of natural rock.

They spent an hour in the halls mourning their dead. Though she tried to hide it behind her flinty exterior, Laura's devastation at the loss of Hunter was clear, and she had to be persuaded by all to continue, in Hunter's name. Never once did she cry, though for a while she disappeared into an antechamber to be alone with her emotions; she sat silently in the centre of the room, her head bowed, her features hidden.

All of them felt grief for the deaths of Miller, Jack and Virginia, far beyond what their loss meant for the mission. The others were surprised to see that even Veitch was touched, particularly by the passing of Miller, whom he considered a friend, he said, even though he had never expressed it. At the end of the hour, their hearts were still heavy, but they found the strength to go on.

Following the deep, lush river valleys that offered dense tree-cover and deep shadow, they moved steadily north, across the stinking, haunted marshlands where the insects were bigger than fists and carried a poisonous punch that could paralyse and kill; into the tropical jungle where the night was filled with drums and the howls of hunting beasts. They avoided the mysterious tribes who worshipped brutish idols and came and went from the dense interior like ghosts, just as they had avoided the war-bands of the Enemy that roamed across every part of the land, harrying and slaughtering. After the death of the Iron Slaughterman, they knew Janus would have despatched others with the specific task of tracking them down and destroying them, and on one occasion they had seen something terrible silhouetted against the moon on a ridge, but nothing had located them. It was only a matter of time.

And finally they had come to the Court of Endless Horizons, abandoned by the Tuatha Dé Danaan as they raced towards sanctuary at the Court of the Soaring Spirit. Now it was filled with hundreds of thousands of refugees from every part of the Far Lands, dwarfish mountain-dwellers and the willowy, silver-eyed hunters of the western plains, the lizard-skinned people from the river deltas, and other, stranger beings that rarely ventured from the shadows. All swarmed on the streets, or crammed into buildings in the sweltering heat, race upon race sharing the same space, begging for food, sweating, fighting, haggling for transport or the promise of safe passage; all of them united by their fear of an Enemy that was alien to them in every aspect, a threat that exhibited no compassion, not even the slightest empathy, who could not be cajoled, or pleaded with, or flattered; who slaughtered with a devastating dispassion. Even in the Far Lands with its extremes of emotion and distorted motivations, this was an anomaly.

The city itself was a gleaming monument to the glory of the Tuatha Dé Danaan. Soaring towers of brass and gold reached far above the steaming jungle that surrounded it on three sides, kept at bay by walls of beaten copper and steel, a sculpture of grace and beauty in the heart of a primal setting. A sleek futurism in the materials and design of the buildings was set against an almost medieval confusion of tiny, twisting streets and alleys leading off the broad, leafy main thoroughfares, yet somehow the incongruity worked. The quarter nearest the gate through which they had entered was still rich with the scents of the spices that used to be stored in the warehouses along the wall, and the heavy, ornate incense-burners that swung from the lamps along the streets suggested the entire court would once have been filled with beautiful aromas.

In its time, it must have been a breathtaking place, Church guessed; now it stank and seethed, filled with the hollow hopes of desperate people who knew death was always a step or two away.

After struggling to live off the land for so many weeks, they thought they would have even more trouble obtaining food in the overpopulated city, but they encountered enough people who were aware of the growing legend of the Brothers and Sisters of Dragons to guide them to a place of shelter. Veitch was stunned that their reputation could earn them free food and drink in the rooftop café when so many were starving, everything they required given freely, and without obligation.

Irritable in the heat, Tom joined Church and was instantly presented with a cup of the hot, spicy drink. The waitress, a tall, willowy woman with a forked snake-tongue, bowed. "True Thomas," she lisped. "Your presence here is recognised and welcomed."

Tom nodded grumpily. "It grates on me to be treated like an elite," he said when the waitress had gone. "All those people out there suffering and we get free drinks."

"It makes them happy," Church replied. "They believe in us, and want to hope that we can make things better for them. If that's the least we can do, then it's something. Everyone deserves a little hope to make them happier."

Tom snorted. "Hope is meaningless if there's no chance of it being effected. Otherwise it's just delusion." He fixed a cold eye on Church. "Are you losing hope?"

"I'm not planning the victory party, if that's what you mean. I'm waiting for a sign that there's still some way we can make a difference. The Puck has helped me more than once. Why hasn't he appeared since Winter-side? Because there's nothing we can do?"

"The universe gives you a helping hand when you put some energy into the process yourself, not when you're sitting back hoping something will just turn up."

"We are doing something. The others are out gathering information about the Enemy, the Fortress—they call it the House of Pain around here. What we need right now is a way into it."

"And what are you doing?"

"Thinking."

The Morvren had gathered on every treetop around the city; often silent, they were now cawing as if filled with an insatiable hunger. Their number had increased rapidly, and Church didn't know if it was because they were breeding, if the possibility of death that attracted them had grown more intense, or if it was symbolic of the level of threat now facing him. From the rooftop, it looked as if a black shroud had been laid across the steaming jungle.

"My mistake," Tom said, blowing on his drink. "I thought you were doing nothing."

"Why hasn't the Libertarian been hounding us?" Church asked.

"We have been a little elusive."

"He's me. He must know what I've done, where I've been. So why doesn't he just turn up out of the blue, slit everyone's throats, dump me in a cell and be done with it?"

"Time and memory are slippery things," Tom began edgily. "We can't trust ourselves. We never quite remember things how they actually were. And time itself is not fixed, you know that. On every occasion you go back, something subtle alters. It might not be enough to change the big events ranged through history like tent-poles supporting the whole damn canvas of everything. Or it might. The Libertarian has to be extremely cautious. He won't want to risk doing anything that might stop him coming into being, so that he winks out like a star at dawn."

"It makes my head hurt thinking about it," Church grumbled.

"That's because you see things in a linear way, and in terms of simple cause and effect. I've lived with my ragged view of the future for a long time, and I can tell you that nothing is clear, everything shifts and changes like the grains of sand on the beach, and you can never predict which way one will go."

"He must think like me, so I've been trying to put myself in his head," Church continued. "What does he want? For me to change and become him, I presume. If I don't, he doesn't get to exist. You're right—this whole screwed-up timeline thing is a mess, but if the Libertarian is still around, then what lies ahead guarantees I become him. Things are panning out just as they should, from the Libertarian's point of view, like clockwork. But he's not going to take any chance that I might change events, or that the Puck might push me down another path or something, so he's going to keep manipulating me into situations that will make me become him. Basically, if he's not around, things are going badly. If he is, there's a chance I might be able to put things right."

"I don't think it's wholly wise to put yourself into the Libertarian's thought processes. That alone may be leading you towards that destiny."

Church sipped his hot drink thoughtfully. "Another thing: the Blue Fire exists all over our world, if you look closely enough. It's here in the Far Lands, certainly, but not to the same degree. And why isn't this place swarming with Fabulous Beasts? You'd have thought of all places, here would be their true home, where they'd thrive."

A hint of a smile flickered on Tom's lips before he wiped it away. "Yes, I wonder why that is."

"I suppose you're not going to tell me."

"Where would be the fun in that? Especially when you're doing so well with your thinking," Tom added caustically.

"When did things become so difficult?" Church asked after a moment's reflection. "It used to be so easy, in our world, with the Blue Fire everywhere. Seeing the magic in the world. The choices were clear."

Tom's brief glance revealed an unusual hint of tenderness. "If the choices are clear they are usually false choices. Life is muddy and complex, without any easy answers."

"But these days I'm not even sure we're on the right side. I don't know what I'm fighting for any more. I don't know why I'm having to make all these sacrifices."

"You've been on the road a long time. You're weary—"

"It's beyond that. What if the Libertarian is right? People aren't in the world for long. They just want a little security, a few home comforts, time to spend with their loved ones. Is that so bad? All I want is some time with Ruth, to enjoy what we have. Why should I give that up to keep fighting for something I don't understand any more?"

Tom made to speak, then caught himself, his expression registering a deep concern. Church was distracted by the sight of the Morvren suddenly taking wing as one, a black cloud that blocked out the sun and cast the whole city into shade.

What's disturbed them? he wondered.

2

The crowd smelled of lime and vinegar and allspice, woodsmoke, bitumen and sulphur, and the hot odour that came off skin on a summer's day. From a feverish dream or a nightmare drawn from nursery storybooks, the inhabitants of the court came in a vast wave, sweeping in eddies around obstacles, fallen bodies, sleeping beasts, surging off each other, too-fast, too-slow, with everywhere and nowhere to go. It was impossible to see more than a couple of feet on any side. Some begged for food, or board, or information, others ran with the hope of a destination or fled some unrevealed threat, fear burning in their faces. Some had murder in their eyes, or the sly desire to make gain from misfortune.

"Jesus Christ, this is worse than Oxford Street just before Christmas," Veitch complained as he and Shavi pushed through the throng. Overhead, people hung from windows, two or three crammed into the gap, wailing or yelling to people across the way. The din made his ears hurt.

"You can almost smell the desperation. These beings have known nothing but always-summer, and now they sense the twilight coming in."

"There you go again, feeling sorry for a bunch of people you don't know." Veitch roughly thrust aside a man rippling with rolls of fat, his clothes sodden with sweat. "I've missed you. You're my conscience."

"And I have missed you, my friend. More than you might know. We were all bereft when we thought you dead after the Battle of London, but I felt as if I had truly lost a brother. A brother more than the brothers of my own family, who disowned me when I failed to follow their path."

"Don't go getting sentimental on me. I can't be doing with that . . . Hey, what the bleedin' hell's that?"

Veitch pushed through the dense flow to one side where a puppeteer was performing a show in the shade of an inn. He was at least eight feet tall, with long, black robes that Veitch presumed obscured his stilts, and he wore a white mask with a curving nose like a bird's beak. He looked like the wall painting in the Halls of the Drakusa. But it was the dancing puppets that caught Veitch's eye: they resembled Church, Shavi, Ruth, Laura and himself. The Church and Ruth puppets were hugging, while the Veitch one stood off to one side, holding a sword, before turning to attack. Veitch experienced a brief burst of anger moderated by the knowledge that he was surely imagining the resemblances. He took one step towards the puppet-master, and was sent flying by a woman weaving frantically through the crowd.

Cursing underneath the figure sprawling on top of him, Veitch was shocked to see she was human, wearing modern clothes, and gripped by such terror that her eyes barely saw him.

"Calm down." He caught her shoulders as she prepared to throw herself off him to run again. "Where the hell did you come from?"

His words cut through her fear and she gradually focused on him. "You're from Earth? Oh God, oh God, what's happening to me? Where is this place?" Sobbing fitfully, she collapsed into him.

Veitch helped her to her feet. After her fugue, she was now shaking uncontrollably. Awkwardly, Veitch tried to calm her. "I'm Ryan. What's your name?"

"R-R-Rachel," she stuttered. "Something was chasing me! Making me come this way. I-I remember . . . a grin, like it couldn't decide if it wanted to eat me up or kiss me . . . and those eyes . . . and . . . and . . ." The memory slipped from her and she shook her head in frustration.

"How did you get here?"

Before she could answer, a column of smoke soared up above the rooftops accompanied by a boom that echoed off the metallic walls. Sizzling, coloured lights arced out from the direction of the explosion.

The crowd responded with panic, and in the mêlée Veitch and Rachel were torn apart. Already forgetting her, Veitch fought his way to Shavi and said, "Let's get back to Church till we know what's going on."

"No. If we can help, we should."

Veitch set his jaw. "I bloody hate you, Shavi."

3

When the blast happened, Ruth and Laura had been quietly questioning the occupants of one of the overcrowded inns, but few had any knowledge of the Enemy Fortress itself, and those that did were too afraid to discuss it. Only one street away, the explosion shook the building so furiously that tankards flew from tables, spilling ale and wine across the sawdust-covered boards. Fearing the worst, the anxious drinkers flooded from the inn into the screaming mob outside, leaving Ruth and Laura to edge through one of the vermin-infested alleys to find a view of the blast site.

"I can do the reconnaissance," Ruth suggested. "Why don't you head back?"

"You don't have to keep treating me like I'm a baby," Laura responded with undue harshness. "Hunter's gone. I'm dealing with it. I'm not going to collapse in tears at the first sign of trouble."

"Sorry for thinking of you." Ruth bristled.

At the end of the alley, rubble and twisted metal were strewn across the street along with the bodies of several passers-by caught in the blast. Flickers of flame and thick, acrid smoke rose up from the ruins of a demolished building.

As the smoke shifted, they caught glimpses of a giant figure strapped to an X-frame in the wreckage of the building.

"He couldn't have been there before," Ruth said. "There'd be nothing left of him. He must have been brought in after the explosion. Why?"

"Maybe it's his place, and someone wants to make an example of him," Laura replied. "You know, like tar-and-feathering. He probably sold some gangster a knock-off watch."

The shifting smoke revealed wild black hair and a beard. Ruth's tart response to Laura died in her throat. "I know him! I saw him, back in London, when the Void had me living that fake life. He's the one Mallory said gave him the lantern . . . the Caretaker."

"What's he doing here? And . . . who did that to him?"

As the smoke finally cleared, the extent of the Caretaker's plight was revealed. Wounds gaped on his arms, his head sagged and more ragged cuts marred what skin was visible on his face. Jagged twists of barbed wire held his wrists and legs to the X-frame, and another had been fastened around his neck.

"Poor man!" Ruth said. "It looks like he's been tortured."

"He's not a man, is he, though?" Laura replied. "He's . . . something else."

"That doesn't mean he can't feel pain." Ruth brushed away a stray tear. "We have to help him. He's going to die there."

Wrenching his head back painfully, the Caretaker said in a booming voice that would have carried three streets away, "Brothers and Sisters of Dragons! If you can hear me, stay away! My time here is nearly done, and there is nothing you can do to aid me!"

"Did he hear me?" Ruth whispered, before realising, "The Enemy must be nearby. He's saying it so loudly so they won't realise how close we are."

The Caretaker sucked in a juddering breath of air. "The Enemy knows you are here," he continued. "They wish to draw you out. You will not be allowed to get any closer to your destination. They fear you, Brothers and Sisters of Dragons. They fear the power that burns in your hearts."

Ruth began to cry silently at the Caretaker's suffering. "He needs our help," she said desperately. "We can't just leave him to die."

"You must forget me," he continued. "The Oldest Things in the Land have attempted to help you as best we could during your long struggle. But that aid may well be coming to an end. We face our own battles, with our own kind, and now, as the great plans fragment on both sides, only chaos beckons. The outcome is uncertain." Wincing, he took another deep breath. "Your lessons are not yet complete, but this desperate time has brought the teaching to an end. We must all hope that you have learned enough to defeat the Enemy." He paused, then repeated wearily, "The outcome is uncertain."

"You think we should risk it?" Laura asked. "Whip out there quick, drag him down and bring him back? We might be able to get away with it."

"We have to listen to him," Ruth said dismally. "He's right—there's too much at stake."

A deep shadow fell across the ruined building, though the source was not visible from Ruth and Laura's vantage point. As they craned to see, a noise behind them alerted them to the approach of Veitch and Shavi.

"The lights are going out all across the lands," the Caretaker intoned, "and I will no longer be there to keep the last lamp lit." His eyes flickered, and his head slumped forwards onto his chest.

As Ruth stifled a cry, Veitch put his arms around her to comfort her. "If even they're dying . . ." he began, before catching himself.

An intense blue light burned where the Caretaker had hung from the X-frame, and when it finally cleared his body had gone.

The deep shadow remained, however, and grew stronger. Across the rooftops, something feline darted, its shape altering as it moved into an almost-human form. A mirror glinted in its hand. As they tried to perceive what it truly was, darkness folded around it and briefly blocked out the sun. Cold fingers of dread touched them all.

"I do not think it wise to stay here any longer," Shavi said.

4

Although none of them knew the Caretaker, they all felt a deep grief at his death. Instinctively, they recognised that something good had passed and the universe was a worse place for it.

For a long hour, they had sat in a shady spot on the café terrace where they could not be seen by the other clientele, drinking cups of the hot, spicy drink and trying to make sense of what had just occurred. Ahead of them, the setting sun turned the desert the colour of blood.

"This is a right bleedin' mess. You don't know who to trust," Veitch said.

Laura fixed a knowing eye on him. "Very true."

Veitch glared at her.

"I can't believe the Caretaker's dead." Ruth's knuckles were white on her spear. "Something so powerful, destroyed by the Enemy."

"Janus is one of the Oldest Things in the Land," Tom reminded her, "and he has joined the Void."

"So . . . what? This is a civil war?" Laura said.

"Could be." As Church listened to the soaring dusk song of one of the many sects now occupying the city, he remembered a similar moment in Cairo, sitting on the edge of mystery in a hot, sprawling city, looking into the night and wondering what the future held for them. Would there ever be a chance for rest, or was this as good as it got—a brief interlude in the chaos of life before it wound down to failure and death? "The Caretaker said the Enemy knew we were here. How?" He looked around the group carefully.

"The most obvious answer would be that someone told them," Tom said.

Veitch sneered. "You're saying one of us? Nah."

"You would say that," Laura said.

Church saw Veitch bristle and stepped in quickly. "I'm not saying anything, except it's something we need to keep at the back of our minds."

"That we can't trust one of us?" Veitch continued, growing more incensed.

"That defeats the whole point of the Five. A team, all together when it's backs-to-the-wall time."

"That didn't stop you when you sold us out first time around," Laura said.

"That wasn't me!"

"Will you two stop it?" Ruth snapped. "Don't you get it? The Enemy knows we're here—they're not going to sit back, they're going to come looking for us...with something powerful enough to kill the Caretaker."

Accepting the magnitude of Ruth's words, Veitch and Laura fell silent.

"So, should we leave the city tonight?" Shavi asked.

"And go where?" Church said. "We came here to try to find a way into the House of Pain. We shouldn't leave till we've got the information we need. And it's a big, crowded city—the Enemy's going to take some time to find us. If we're smart."

"I agree with Church," Tom said.

"You don't get a vote, old man." Laura swung one booted foot onto the table and stretched out, hands behind her head. The others remained tense.

Veitch sat up sharply, remembering. "I forgot...I met a girl."

"Did you hold hands and skip?" Laura asked.

"A girl from Earth."

"You're sure?" Church asked.

"Looked like she'd just arrived. She was in a right panic. Being chased by something, she said."

"Impossible," Tom snorted. "You know all the gateways to the Fixed Lands were closed by the Army of the Ten Billion Spiders."

"She just got here, I tell you."

Church thought for a moment, trying to contain his mounting excitement. "That means there's another path back to Earth that we don't know about. We can go home."

Ruth couldn't hide her concern. "You're thinking about running away?"

His mind racing, Church ignored her, and the uneasiness the others were starting to exhibit. "Drop everything else and turn this city upside down. We need to find that woman."

The song of the cult reached a crescendo as darkness fell across the over-crowded city, stinking of sweat and misery and desperation, and filled with voices that never stopped. But with the fading of the light a new degree of misery was added. From the shadows, where nothing had been, shapes moved out into the population. No one saw them pass, but they felt them in their hearts, and the fear began to rise.

5

"Stand firm!" Decebalus bellowed as the Army of Dragons faced into a ferocious wind beneath a darkening sky. Amongst the roiling black clouds, the Riot-Beasts advanced, their eyes roving insanely. Bolts of lightning crashed randomly from them to sear the green plain.

"Sir. How are we supposed to get a bead on those things, if you don't mind me asking, sir?" Ronnie shouted above the gale. He'd polished the buttons of his army uniform ready for the battle and now wore the tin hat that had seen activity in Flanders.

"The Enemy hope to break our ranks with their war engines. They do not yet realise what weapons we wield, and neither do you. Watch."

Decebalus raised his eyes to the heavens, ignoring the heavy rain. Despite numbering almost a hundred and fifty, the Army of Dragons was a small knot of resistance compared to the seemingly never-ending ranks of the Enemy. The Dacian barbarian was proud of his troops, huddled together in the face of such overwhelming opposition. They came from more civilised times than he knew, and he had feared their softness of muscle would hamper them in the coming struggle, but they had shown a deeper seam of hardness than he could ever have hoped. Warriors, tacticians, mystics and magicians, they were individuals with a group mind and a spirit that could never be broken. In their eyes, he could see their fear, but still they stood firm. Heroes, he thought. No wonder the Devourer of All Things was afraid of what they could achieve.

Under the clouds, the day became like night. Forty feet away, a bolt of lightning raised a shower of burned earth, and although he could feel its heat, he did not flinch. Instead, he started to laugh heartily, celebrating the storm.

"Pardon me, sir," Ronnie said, "but the boys and girls will probably think you've gone mad. Madder."

"Let them! Mad, yes! Mad with joy at the horror the Enemy will feel when they see how they have underestimated us! See!"

As if on cue, the glamour disappeared and the ranks of the gods were revealed. All around the small clump of Brothers and Sisters of Dragons, like a sunlit mirror at the heart of the storm, the powerful beings dazzled their mortal comrades.

"Crikey!" Ronnie exclaimed. "Is that why you wouldn't let us see them before?"

"The gods exist to make mortals mad," Decebalus replied. "The less you have to do with them, the better it is for you."

Two gleaming figures ran from the ranks at speed, arching their backs as they threw themselves into a glide just above the ground before soaring up on the air currents. One appeared to Ronnie to be flipping back and forth between two forms: a man with an ornate gold helmet and a coiled beast that appeared simultaneously to be bird, serpent and something constructed of lush foliage.

"That one goes by the name of Quetzalcóatl." Decebalus rolled his tongue around the syllables as though it had taken him a long time to learn the word. "All those gods are strange, but he was the strangest of all. Until the last, I could not tell if he even understood me."

The other figure began to glow like the sun as he flew upwards. His hair was wild, like a beggar's, but he wore golden armour that gave him majesty.

"And that one also hails from the Great Dominion of the southern Americas. His name is Viracocha," Decebalus continued. "His melancholy is breathtaking to see. And also irritating. He claims that his tears will wash away the world. But then they all say something like that."

Caught in the turbulence near the Riot-Beasts, the two gods fought to maintain their stability. Lightning flashed around them as the three monstrous creatures drifted towards the figures they dwarfed.

"They won't stand a chance!" Ronnie said.

When a lightning bolt finally found its way to Viracocha, he lit up like a star. It took Ronnie a second or two to realise that the flash had actually invigorated the god. Sparks fizzed from his fingertips and every follicle of hair until a corona surrounded him. From nowhere, he summoned a micro-weather system. Rain lashed like bullets at the nearest Riot-Beast, and winds buffeted it so it drifted untethered across the plain; and yet still Viracocha burned like a sun, the light growing more intense with each passing moment.

In contrast, Quetzalcóatl swooped like a raptor on a Riot-Beast, raking with claws and beak that came and went every time Ronnie could see him past the glare of Viracocha. Finally, with a sound like shattering glass, the Riot-Beast careered into another before crashing down, those dumb eyes rolling upwards one final time.

Before the creature fell onto the plain, the blazing sun that had been Viracocha threw back its arms and a blast of the purest, hottest light seared the Riot-Beast that had been throwing lightning at him in a ceaseless rain of crackling energy. The light tore through the Beast and continued across the plain to explode in a starburst over the heads of the Enemy, for the first time illuminating their dark ranks. Burning chunks of the Riot-Beast rained down onto the plain, setting the grass ablaze.

"Holy Mary, Mother of God," Ronnie gasped. "If we'd only had those at Flanders, sir, the world would be a happier place."

At an unheard summons, the third Riot-Beast turned and drifted back towards the Enemy lines. Their energies spent, Viracocha and Quetzalcóatl swooped down to the gods, amidst the cheers of the Army of Dragons and a tumultuous welcome from their fellows.

"And that is what two of the gods can achieve," Decebalus said with a grim smile. "At our backs we have more than a hundred. The odds have evened considerably."

6

On a day hotter than any they had experienced so far, the Court of Endless Horizons reflected a brassy light that made eyes ache and turned the streets into furnaces. The sluggish diaspora sought out the shade of alleys and porches, fanning themselves with the fronds of jungle trees, praying for dusk to fall but dreading it just as much. In the inns and markets, there had been talk of several slayings during the course of the night, beyond the usual bloody results of arguments caused by too many people with too little in too hot a place. Some of the bodies looked as if they had been mauled by a jungle beast; others wore expressions of outright terror frozen into their features at the final moment. Most agreed that something had arrived in the city that would only heap more misery on their suffering.

Aware of the rising tension, the Brothers and Sisters of Dragons moved efficiently from group to clump, beggar to prince, quietly asking about the female Fragile Creature who had last been seen racing through the streets in fear.

In the marketplace, amidst the smell of dried fish and charcoal-grilled meat and the din of people haggling for supplies from dawn to twilight, Church and Ruth debated leaving a note on the enormous wooden post where refugees separated from their loved ones tacked pleas for information regarding their whereabouts, or notes for clandestine meetings that were rarely attended.

"We could search this city for weeks and never stumble across this woman," Ruth said. She was uncomfortable in the heat and wore a white cotton scarf on her head fastened in a Middle Eastern style with a gold band, which served the dual purpose of keeping her cool and obscuring her identity to casual eyes. "If you really want to find her, we have to make some waves."

"If we do that, we're going to draw the Enemy straight to us."

"I don't understand why they haven't just descended on the city in force, anyway, if they know we're here."

"This has the Libertarian's fingerprints all over it. He has to play a careful game. He can't risk me getting killed, or badly hurt, but he has to stop us doing anything that might change the established pattern."

"He's not going to be so concerned about killing the rest of us."

"No."

"You know, it's weird how you talk about the Libertarian as if he's a completely different person."

"He is." The fleeting disbelief in Ruth's face stung him. "All right," he accepted, "there's a continuity. But something's broken in him, and until I know what it is I can't do anything to prevent it."

"But you think it's something to do with you and me."

"In that flash of precognition I had in the Forbidden City in Beijing, the Libertarian suggested I threw everything away because of my 'pathetic, doomed love.'"

"Why would you do that?"

"If you died—"

She rolled her eyes and grabbed his arm tightly. "Sometimes you need a shaking. All this is bigger than you and me—"

"I'm not so sure it is."

"It is. Love is a weakness, Church . . . all right, maybe not a weakness, but a luxury for people like us. We've got a terrifying responsibility. Everybody, literally everybody, is depending on us." She saw the touch of hurt in his face and softened. "You know how much I love you. You and me . . . we were always meant to be together. But we're expected to make sacrifices."

"That's all we do. Sacrifice our lives, our homes, our friends who die. We deserve something."

"No, we don't," she said gently. "And that's the awful thing. We have to do the job we've been given without the hope of any reward." She kissed him, and that made her words feel even harsher. "Everybody says men are tougher than women, but they're not, certainly not when it comes to emotions. Men spend all their lives putting them on one side and when they rear their ugly heads, men can't cope with them. They sting you harder than us. We're used to the pain. We can feel it and put the emotion to one side, get on with the job we've got to do. I'm sorry. I know how this must feel to you. But you've got to listen to me: if I die, you've got to carry on and finish this. If we're torn apart, like we were before, you mustn't give in to despair. All right?"

He gave a convincing nod, but he couldn't tell her his biggest fear: that the failure of their love was a fait accompli. As Ruth searched for the roots of the Libertarian within him, her fears of what he would become would drive her away from him and towards Veitch, thus pushing Church further down the path towards becoming the Libertarian. How could he break that cycle?

"I've seen things inside myself I'm not happy about," he admitted. "There's a darkness."

"There is in all of us." A shadow crossed Ruth's face.

"That's one of the reasons why I accepted Ryan back so readily. I understand him more now. I'm not sure that's a good thing."

"We're not pure," she pressed. "We're not heroes. We're just trying to do the best we can. It's because we're all friends that we can count on each other to get past our flaws." She hesitated, then added, "If people start going off on their own, we're lost. We're Five for a reason—a whole that's bigger and better than the individual parts."

The market suddenly felt too crowded and too noisy, and Church longed for the intimacy that had been missing since they had left Earth behind;

longer; it felt like an age since he and Ruth had been alone in the hotel room in Norway.

But the moment had passed, and Ruth was already moving to question a likely stallholder who was gossiping with every person within feet of his pitch. The explosion hit a second later. Deep in the centre of the sprawling marketplace, a column of black flame sent stalls, produce and bodies hurtling upwards with a boom that would have been heard across the entire city.

Thrown wildly by the blast wave, his head ringing and his hearing momentarily gone, Church was buried beneath a rain of vegetables, jewellery, votive ornaments and the heavy tarpaulin stall covers. His first thoughts were for Ruth and he quickly clawed his way out, only to find her helping badly injured survivors; some had lost limbs, others were so severely burned it was clear they would not last long. But Ruth moved quickly amongst them, helping to staunch the blood, bowing her head and muttering words of her Craft where they would help, offering a simple prayer where nothing would.

Church joined in, but the trickle of victims from the centre of the market had become a torrent, and the latest arrivals were consumed by a more immediate panic, glancing over their shoulders in fear as they staggered away from the blast zone.

Behind them lurched survivors who had been transformed by whatever magic lay within the explosion. The flesh had been ripped from their heads to leave bloodstained skulls, the eyes still intact and roving crazily as they attacked anyone who came near them, snapping and snarling with the ferocity of cornered wolves. One badly wounded man moved too slowly, his throat torn open by the bite of one of the skull-faced pursuers.

As others fell and the panic spiralled out of control, Church rushed to help. Blue Fire sizzled from Caledfwlch as he attacked. He could see there was no hope of the skull-faced victims recovering; indeed, there appeared to be nothing left of their personalities in their insane eyes. They had been turned into weapons and Church had no choice but to meet them head on to save the lives of others.

The primal savagery of the skull-faces slowed him a little, but his athleticism and skill with the sword served him in cutting them down before they could harm anyone else. When the last one had fallen, he ran back to Ruth and pulled her away from the survivors. She resisted, insisting on helping the wounded until Church said forcefully, "The Enemy did this to draw us out. They'll be here soon, and if we hang around more innocent people are going to get hurt."

Reluctantly, Ruth allowed him to lead her into the maze of alleys that led away from the market. When they were sure they had put enough space behind them, they rested and allowed themselves to contemplate the horror of the blast.

"They killed and injured all those people to get at us?" Ruth said.

"Come on—are you surprised? They know we're not going to sit back while innocents get hurt, so they'll keep attacking them until we act. And then they've got us."

"Terror, pure and simple. And if we try to resist, the people will give us up sooner or later. This is the Libertarian, isn't it?"

Church nodded uncomfortably. Ruth wouldn't meet his eye.

"And you're convinced we need to find this woman?"

"Yes."

"So we can run away?"

"Do you really think I want to run away?"

"No," she replied, unconvincingly. "It's just hard to see where this is going."

Another blast punctured the silence that followed her comment, somewhere on the far side of the city. Screams followed, distant but not diminished, followed by the shrill, dismal cries of the Morvren as they took flight, the portents of death they carried with them now inescapable.

7

On the eastern side of the city, in the shade of the great brass wall, Veitch and Shavi kept their heads down to avoid recognition as they pushed through the crowd. In the stifling heat, the smell was choking: excrement baked in the gutters and the bitter reek of urine mingled with the vinegary sweat that rose from every too-hot body jostling for space in the slow-moving flow. Occasionally, from some darkened space drifted the sour-apples stink of decomposition.

The only breathing space came where people had fallen, overcome by the heat, hunger, thirst or illness, sprawled on the burning cobbles, their chests rising and falling too slow, and slowing. Shavi attempted to help the first three they encountered, but without water or food or medical supplies, there was little he could do; and the simple act of stopping to offer comfort halted other passers-by who wondered if there was a chance of aid. The desperation in their eyes was almost too much to bear. Now Shavi and Veitch stepped over the prone forms like all the other people, but Veitch could see the tears glistening in Shavi's eyes.

As they edged into a narrow street filled with the shops of silversmiths and jewellery-makers, a gang of dirty children in torn clothes and blankets scrambled forwards and began to beg. Some were human in form, though their faces contained the familiar, sly touch of the Far Lands, but others were covered with thick hair, or had golden triple-lidded eyes or facial contusions that could have been natural or caused by malnutrition and the constant filth. Swarming around Shavi and Veitch's legs, they tugged at their clothes, some surreptitiously trying to slip their hands into pockets until Veitch slapped them away.

"Food, please," one of them said. "Just a crumb. My mother is dying. A crumb will keep her spark alight for another hour." It sounded like a line to elicit sympathy, but the savage emotion in his face offered an unbearable proof.

"We haven't got any food," Veitch said too harshly. "Clear off and bother someone else."

"A coin, then. It does not matter what kind. One coin will buy us a day more in the Far Lands."

"I am sorry," Shavi said. "We do not carry money."

"Don't bleedin' engage them in conversation. We'll never get rid of them," Veitch said with frustration.

His feelings already rubbed raw by the misery he had witnessed, Shavi was touched by the children's plight. Bending down, he tried to offer words of advice and support, but it only encouraged more children to cluster around, hands grasping the air for any sustenance he might be offering, and that brought the attention of passing adults who kicked at the children and rolled them into the gutters to get first chance at any offerings, the crowd pressing harder and harder so that Veitch and Shavi were trapped at its core.

"From now on, you do nothing until I say so," Veitch grumbled. "You're a bloody liability."

A man who towered a good two feet above everyone else, his barrel chest bare, thrust his way through the cluster with arms so muscular they appeared to be made of wood. He loomed over Veitch and Shavi, peering at them with blinking, piggy eyes.

"It is!" he exclaimed. "Two Brothers of Dragons!"

"Bleedin' great," Veitch said, trying to push through the tight knot without much luck.

"Here, here!" the ox-like man announced to the entire street, beckoning wildly. "We are saved! The Brothers and Sisters of Dragons are here, in the Court of Endless Horizons!"

Veitch's protests only drew more attention. The crowd around them swelled from one side of the street to the other, and the words Brothers of Dragons could be heard rising from awed whispers to jubilant shouts.

A woman in a black headdress with a third eye in the centre of her forehead clutched Shavi passionately. "Brother of Dragons. You will free us from the yoke of the Enemy. You will deliver us to salvation."

"You will ensure that the prophecy of these Last Days does not come to pass," another woman cried.

Veitch was stunned into silence by the sudden ignition of hope he saw in the faces gathered around him. Fingers brushed his clothes with the awe one would reserve for a great leader or a religious figure. Struggling to comprehend, he stared blankly at one outstretched hand wavering before him, and then gently took it. Someone else took his other hand, and within a moment he was forced to reach out and touch hand after hand, shocked by the relief he saw rise up in everyone he graced with a fleeting contact.

"We will do what we can," Shavi began, to try to curb expectations, but the cries only rose up louder: "They will help." "The Enemy is doomed." "We are saved!"

"How do they know about us?" Veitch asked Shavi.

A bearded man in white robes answered. "We have always known of the Brothers and Sisters of Dragons, in the oldest stories of the Far Lands, in the tales of all peoples from all places. The champions of Existence who will rise up to become the greatest heroes of all-time, all-place. In the earliest

days, they were whispered by mystics, and then told to children for the entertainment of young minds, but few truly believed. And then. . .oh, wonder
of wonders!. . .Jack, Giant-Killer, stepped into the Far Lands and began his
exploits, and the truth became known, and the legend of the Brothers and
Sisters of Dragons spread from mouth to mouth." His voice grew shriller as
his passion grew. "And the tales of other Brothers and Sisters of Dragons in
the Fixed Lands reached our ears, and we realised there was hope for us. . .the
great prophecy of the Devourer of All Things could be averted."

Caught up in his passion, the three-eyed woman continued, "And so when
the shadow of the Enemy began to spread across the Far Lands, we offered up
our prayers, and our incantations, and we wished. . .oh, how we wished. . .for
the Brothers and Sisters of Dragons to be sent to us to help us in our darkest
hour. And our calls have been answered. You are here! We are saved!"

Veitch was dragged from the adoration by a glimpse of Shavi's shattered
expression. "All right, we're trying to keep a low profile here!" he shouted.
"This isn't helping."

But his words were drowned out by the cries, which were growing louder
by the moment as more people herded into the street. Soon the commotion
would attract more unwanted attention.

Finally, Veitch put his head down and rammed a path through the crowd,
no longer caring if he bowled people over. Shavi followed in his wake, the wave
closing behind them, attempting to turn in their direction. For a moment, it
appeared they would be dragged down, but then Veitch broke through the
ranks of those who had recognised them and they were running and dodging
back through the flow, not slowing until they were two streets away.

In the shade of a warehouse that smelled of beer, Veitch gripped Shavi's
shoulders tightly, desperately wanting to drive away the upset expression on
his friend's face.

"Look, mate, so they trust us to do the job, so what?" he said.

"How can we meet those expectations?" Shavi replied. "Destroy the
Devourer of All Things? Change a prophecy of final destruction that has been
around since the beginning of time? They are treating us like some kind of
messiahs, but we are only human." He shook his head. "So much hope invested
in us. They offer up their lives to us, to save, because they know they cannot
save themselves."

"Of all of us, I never expected you to give in to despair."

"I am not giving in to despair," Shavi said adamantly. "But I am pragmatic, Ryan. All our plans have failed. The chances of progressing are slim, and even then . . ." His voice trailed off.

Veitch gave Shavi's shoulders a brief, firm shake. Deep inside he felt something swell, growing stronger, bright with the energy of the Pendragon Spirit; he had never felt its like before, but he knew it was something he had wanted all his life. "Listen to me—we're going to be the heroes they want us to be. We can't let them down. We don't have the luxury to be soft." He planted his thumb and forefinger in an L on his forehead. "To be losers. We've got to be hard, whatever the cost. And we've got to win, not for us, but for them, because that's the job we've been given. All right?"

Shavi smiled, but in his eyes Veitch caught a hint of pity at Veitch's naïvety. That only made Veitch more determined, and for the first time he had a clear vision of his own role. Despair was starting to infect all of them, unsurprising given the scale of the threat they faced. It was down to him to stop that despair spreading, to turn them around and show them the right direction. This was where he could finally transcend the person he had been all his life. The swelling emotions grew so strongly, he thought he might burst.

A hubbub rose up from the end of the street and they realised word was spreading rapidly about the Brothers and Sisters of Dragons in the city. "They want us to save them, but they're going to end up getting us killed. That's . . . what? . . . irony, right?" he said with a note of pride at his use of the term. "Come on, let's get out of here before we're hanging from a lamp post."

With the shouts and cries drawing closer, they hurried down a deserted alley until they came to a secluded inn few would have known was there. The sign above the entrance to the Wolf's Surprise showed a man's face with unmistakable lupine qualities. Out of place amongst the sleek metallic lines, it was a squat building with a corbelled flint wall and small bottle-glass windows that caught flickers of lamplight within, but reflected only darkness. Veitch and Shavi ducked into an atmosphere of ale and smoke, sweat and damp, but the coolness of the interior was inviting. They kept their heads down and averted their eyes until they found an obscure spot at the end of a curving bar.

After a pause to take in the new arrivals, the clientele returned to their drinks, as sullen and dispirited as the crowds filling the streets. A few surveyed

Veitch and Shavi as potential opportunities, but the glint in Veitch's eye and the hand on his sword deterred any advance.

Veitch looked around at the array of bizarre figures. "Used to drink in a boozer in Camberwell just like this," he muttered. "Still, better than being out there with all those bombs going off. What do you want?"

"Fruit juice."

"There's an old joke there somewhere." Veitch grinned. "God, I've missed winding you up."

"You have missed trying."

As Veitch ordered the drinks, the door crashed open and a voice boomed, "There! I told you. Brothers of Dragons!"

"Not a-bleedin'-gain." Veitch sighed.

Striding next to the bar was a man wearing furs despite the heat, with a wide-brimmed hat that had seen better days and a string of lizards round his neck. A blunderbuss hung from his belt. Behind him strode a painfully thin, extremely tall man in a dark suit, a huge stovepipe hat threatening to topple from his head, with darting eyes that had a silvery glint.

The hunter clapped a hand on Shavi's shoulder. "I knew it! Even in the middle of a crowd I can recognise a Brother of Dragons. What do you say, Shadow John?"

Leaning down to examine Shavi and Veitch, the man in the stovepipe hat exclaimed, "Bless my soul, you're right, Bearskin." He pumped their hands furiously. "How very wonderful to meet you both. We had the honour of making the acquaintance of one of your colleagues, young Hal of Oxford. A fine, upstanding fellow in the long tradition of your line. Mallory and Caitlin, too. The legend lives on."

"All right, all right, nice to meet you and all that. Now clear off. We're actually trying to be incognito," Veitch said.

"Very wise," Bearskin noted, ignoring Veitch's urgings. "This is not a time to be a Brother of Dragons. The Enemy must be hunting and harrying you."

"We are hunting and harrying the Enemy," Shavi said.

The clap of Bearskin's arm across Shavi's shoulders almost pitched him into the bar. "That's the spirit, good Brother!"

Shadow John grew lachrymose. "This is not a good time to be any living thing. How I regret fleeing the Court of the Soaring Spirit to seek sanctuary in a safer part of the Far Lands."

"There is no safety anywhere," Bearskin agreed.

"How I miss the Hunter's Moon." Deep in maudlin recollection, Shadow John rested his hands on his silver-topped cane, rocking gently from side to side.

"Best inn in all of the Far Lands."

"I miss that place like the Golden Ones miss their long-lost homeland," Shadow John cried.

Veitch saw Shavi scrutinising the new arrivals closely and recognised the light of an idea appear in his face. "You are a hunter?" Shavi said to Bearskin.

Bearskin tapped the edge of his right eye. "Never miss a thing. I track through the thickest parts of the Forest of the Night, or across the desert out there. I can see a blade of grass move on a hillside on the distant horizon."

"Then you could perhaps help us locate someone, in the heaving mass of this city? A woman?"

"A Fragile Creature?" Bearskin laughed heartily. "Fragile Creatures are the easiest to locate. Why, I have tracked them across . . ." His words dried up when he caught Shadow John's anxious expression. "Well, enough to say that I could sniff out a Fragile Creature anywhere in this forsaken place."

As the barman laid a tankard of ale on the bar, Veitch eyed it longingly and sighed. "Okay, let's go."

8

Along the western wall of the city—though directions meant little in the Far Lands where west could become north in the blink of an eye—lay a walled-off garden containing rows of monuments: statues commemorating some great moment from the long history of the Tuatha Dé Danaan, pyramids and spires of less-obvious meaning, sculptures that contained some unobtrusive element that was alien to the human sense of proportion and which caused an involuntary increase in anxiety and flutter of the heartbeat, gargoyles, beasts, spheres that glowed with an inner light though made of stone, and other, more abstract designs. Some areas of the garden would have been a peaceful oasis in the crowded city, with works of great beauty dappled by the sun through a canvas of willow or yew. Tropical plants with long, spiky leaves grew here and there, some sporting strong, sweetly perfumed pink flowers, and stone benches were placed intermittently in the cool shade along the gravelled paths.

Laura scrambled over the spike-topped wall only to discover that she was not the first to gain access. Several men, women and children had managed to haul themselves in, hoping to find a cool refuge from the seething madness of the city. They had all died where they sat, huddled in blankets against the chill of the night, or fiercely protecting a morsel of food with a knife. Under the shade of one tree, a mother and two children lay as if asleep, their faces peaceful, no marks on their bodies.

Laura was not deterred by this macabre sight. She gave the bodies a cursory glance as she crunched along the path, her well-honed ability not to accept anything with which she did not agree coming into play; her ego defined her world-view specifically, a pleasant place that was always Laura-centric. She didn't even think of Hunter when she saw the images of death all around; she couldn't, for that left her mind recoiling and placed her at risk from the rising tide of guilt and self-loathing.

The sun was high overhead when she came to a quiet grove at the heart of the garden where she had been summoned. The trees were densely packed and it was impossible to see into their dark heart, but she knew instinctively that a presence waited there. Her heart beat faster as she approached, and a deep dread enveloped her so that she had to fight not to flee back to the comfort of people in the crowded streets.

Ten feet from the grove, she realised she could barely hear the once-deafening sounds of the city that droned constantly in the background from morning to night. It was as if an invisible cloak had been thrown over that part of the garden. The silence was so intense in her mind that it had a texture, soft and gluey, almost liquid. It was unpleasant and unnerving, and felt, in its own unnatural way, as if it was waiting to be filled by something terrible.

"All right," she said, forcing the bravado into her voice as she had so many times, "I'm here."

There was no response. She could feel the pulse of her blood, so strong she was sure she could hear her own heartbeat growing steadily faster. Her stomach flipped queasily, the instinctive response to a hidden gaze moving slowly across her. The presence was so powerful it felt even larger than the grove hiding it, the electrical cloud of its inhuman intellect enveloping her, holding her fast. She had a mental flash of teeth, of talons, of being consumed, and she couldn't prevent a shudder.

For a long moment, she waited, too afraid to run away for fear it would pursue her, too scared to take a step closer in case it dragged her into the grove to a fate that she feared would be worse than anything she could imagine. And then, with such unbearable slowness that she felt she would faint with the dread of anticipation, a hand extended from the trees. At first she thought it was the paw of a big cat, sleek with black spots on white and orange fur, but within a flicker of her eye it changed to a desiccated, grey-skinned human hand clutching a rectangular hand mirror edged in silver with horns on each corner.

For some reason she couldn't explain, the mirror increased Laura's feelings of dread, pulling in her gaze until she couldn't tear her eyes away from it. The mirror glass didn't appear to be glass at all, but rather some kind of liquid with the silvery quality of mercury turning slowly to black as she watched; she was convinced she could plunge her hand into its depths. After a second, the mirror began to smoke.

"Sister of Dragons." The voice rang clearly in the zone of silence, but it sounded unused to human words, each syllable ending with a hint of an animalistic growl.

Laura forced herself not to faint; hidden within the voice were hints of blood and torn, decomposing flesh, of graveyards and inhuman savagery. "What do you want me to do?" she asked haltingly.

"The time has come for another to die," the voice growled.

After the presence in the grove had issued its order, Laura muttered a feeble response, but her thoughts screamed in the echoing halls of her head. Before she knew it she was running back through the garden in blind terror, throwing herself at the wall, kicking and scrambling over and losing herself in the sweaty throng, desperate for human contact, devastated by what she had given up, appalled by what she would do next.

9

Whistling a jaunty tune, the Libertarian wiped the blood from his fingers on the clothes of the young man who had offered him a hand of friendship and the promise of shelter, and then slowly climbed the steps in the tallest tower of the Court of Endless Horizons.

Through his lidless eyes, the world always looked blood-red. He wore sunglasses as an affectation, one of the many he had adopted for the theatrical style he had chosen to present to the world, but they had increasingly become a necessity to prevent the unpleasant psychological side effects engendered by the constantly swimming colour. At times it was almost hallucinogenic, plundering half-memories from the never-touched depths of his mind, twisting them into what-might-have-beens, conjuring distorted faces of old friends, long-slaughtered, old emotions, long-crushed. He could not be the person he was if he was reminded of the person he had been. That was why he had created such a ludicrous public persona, pieced together from silent movies, vaudeville and comic books. He had never been theatrical in his old life, and now he was somebody else, somebody so completely different that he could believe in it implicitly.

But still the fragmentary locked-off recollections haunted him.

When they became too intense, he killed, for that was the ultimate denial of his past-life; enemies, random strangers, even those who dwelled in the daily sphere of his existence; he couldn't really call them friends for there was no room for warm emotions in his sleek, secure, granite world.

And he loved who he was with a manic desperation. There were no circumstances in which he would choose to go back. In the restrictions of his life, he was free, as were all who believed in what he believed. There was not the tyranny of choice, the sickening insecurity of hope, all the striving and failing, the never-being-content. The world under the Void was the best possible world under the circumstances of existence. Everyone had the peace to live out their brief lives as best they could, slotting into a familiar mundane rhythm that asked nothing of them; and so they too were free. And when death finally came, it made them freer still. He couldn't understand how the person he once was had never recognised the stark, comforting simplicity of that life.

Throwing open the door at the top of the tower, he stepped out into the baking midday heat. A small balcony ran around the tower providing him with a three-hundred-and-sixty-degree vista of the entire city. The noise and the stink rose up from below in a sickening wave, but he found it rather comforting. Distress was part of the Void's way of letting people know they were alive. How could they possibly appreciate the tiny jewels they were allowed to discover if they were not surrounded by a field of ordure?

Yet for all the reassuring things he told himself, he felt increasingly uneasy, and he hated his old self for ruining the clean lines of his existence. As the time neared the point of transformation when he—and the Void—would finally be secure forever, there were too many potential vagaries, shifting nodes of possibilities and blank spots in his memory. Events were reaching a point of flux. It was a desperate time, and as he always told himself, desperate times bred desperate men.

He'd waited long enough, a touch on the rudder here, another there, subtle manipulations and nuance to guide his sheep to the place he needed them to be. Now it was time for grandiose actions, hardness, brutality and blood. He could not risk any further deviation from the true line. It was time to be bold.

Gripping the rail, he peered into the dizzying drop, hawked up a glob of phlegm and spat before looking out across the gleaming city. His heart beat harder with anticipation.

And then it came, at first feeling like a brief shadow across the eye, growing more intense by the second. The high sun, brilliant white, dimmed as though a cloud was passing before it. The temperature dropped a degree, and a wind rushed across the rooftops.

Down below, the din reduced a level, and as the city darkened, it faded to an eerie silence, stark and unsettling. How long had it been since this vile place was quiet? he wondered. In every street, heads turned up to examine the dimming sun. People hung from windows, craning their necks to search for clouds or flocks of birds. There were none.

Darker and darker still, until finally a deep, abiding gloom settled across the entire city. No sun was visible, no moon or stars. Fearful cries rose up as the inhabitants tried to make sense of the night coming down at noon. Frantically, torches and lamps were lit, but the quality of the dark was strange and intense, and their illumination only reached a fraction of its usual distance.

Then the shadows moved, and all across the great city, people began to die. Screams rose up. Panic swept through the streets as vast crowds stampeded for safety, crushing underfoot all who fell, desperately forcing their way into buildings to barricade the doors, killing anyone who impeded them.

The Libertarian smiled and nodded.

There was terror and there was blood and there was a night that would never end.

CHAPTER SIX
NIGHT COMES DOWN

1

In the alleys and winding streets of the Court of Endless Horizons, the dark was impenetrable. Ruth and Tom were en route from a false lead of a *distressed Fragile Creature* hiding in the grand marble interior of the Hall of Records when the gloom descended on the city. As the temperature plunged and the sun disappeared from view, Tom dragged Ruth into one of the deserted side alleys that, from the vile stench, had clearly been used as a toilet. His quick thinking saved them both from the frenzied crush that thundered down the street. People crashed through windows or had the life squeezed from them against the walls or underfoot.

Ruth covered her ears to block out the agonised screams and dying calls of the victims, which somehow stood out from the panicked roar of the crowd.

Although Tom stood next to her, she couldn't see him until she brought up her spear—the Blue Fire limning the head was just enough to illuminate the Rhymer's worried features.

"What have they done?" she said.

"The Enemy decided killing the Caretaker and blowing up huge chunks of the city wasn't enough. They've made it their place now."

Faint lights appeared in the main street, but they were so dim it took Ruth and Tom a moment to realise that their illumination was being smothered almost as much as the sun's rays. Figures felt their way hesitantly along the now-deserted street, searching for the path back to the place where they laid their heads. As the thin lights passed, Ruth occasionally glimpsed the outlines of those who had fallen.

"We should get back to Church," Ruth began. "Regroup, decide what we're going to do now—"

Tom silenced her with a sharp squeeze on her arm. "Do you hear something?"

Feeling along the wall, they came to the end of the alley. Across the way someone was trying to light one of the streetlamps. In the silence that had not existed in the street for many months, the hiss of the oil resonated, but from beyond it came the measured step of several feet on the cobbles and the ring of metal catching against walls.

Unable to pierce the darkness that lay at the end of the street, Ruth and Tom watched, neither realising they were holding their breath in anticipation. In the distance, tiny lights bobbed like fireflies, the dim torches of people stumbling home. When one winked out, Ruth thought her eyes were tricking her. But then a second and a third disappeared, and when the fourth extinguished it was accompanied by a faint cry.

"The Enemy is coming," Tom said redundantly.

He tried to pull Ruth back into the alley, but she resisted. "I want to see what we're up against."

The soupy darkness didn't give up its ghosts until they were almost upon Ruth and Tom's hiding place. Emerging from the unfolding black were figures that echoed the transformed victims of the blast Ruth had seen in the marketplace: the flesh had been stripped from their skulls, though the roving eyes remained, and into the bone had been embedded studs that created a mosaic effect; red and green feathers tufted from the back of a simple circlet headdress. They wore only a metal band across their shoulders that ended in a gold amulet, and a scarlet and orange cloth bound around their loins and fastened by a thick gold belt. A round shield fringed with feathers was strapped to their left forearm and in that hand they carried a wooden club. In their right hand they gripped a wooden spear with an obsidian blade.

"What are they—Aztec? Mayan? Incan?" Ruth whispered.

Though her voice was barely audible, the head of the nearest warrior cranked around in her direction. Tom pulled her back into the alley. Pressed against the wall and listening, Ruth could tell the warrior was poised to investigate. Before it could make any move, however, it was distracted by a man staggering towards the single flickering streetlamp. Instantly, the warrior ran forwards, driving his spear into the man's gut and up so that the shocked victim didn't even have time to cry out as he was lifted aloft. Thrashing wildly, he expired within a moment. The warrior dumped the body and continued after his comrades, the tip of his spear rattling across the cobbles.

Across the street others from the small band entered the buildings and brought screams within seconds. Though the warriors' numbers were small, their slaughter was systematic.

Levelling her spear, Ruth prepared to run across the street until Tom grabbed her forcefully. "Take a break from being an idiot," he snapped. "There's one of you, and however good you are with that spear and your Craft, you won't last long out there."

Ruth hesitated, then nodded. "Let's find the others."

As they set off down the alley, Ruth glanced back once, but the dark had already swallowed the street. The screams lingered, though, joining together to become one devastating cry of terror.

2

Church jerked awake from another searing image of himself lying on a table, as pale as death, ghostly faces moving around him. He had started to believe that the recurring dream was not a dream at all, but he refused to examine his nascent suspicions of what it really was. Every time he skirted it, he felt sick to the pit of his stomach; a part of him knew the truth, he was convinced. A part of him was truly afraid.

Exhaustion had left his head nodding as he waited in the rooftop café, but now he could see that the planned rendezvous would not be happening. He was alone in the chill dark with only the poor light from his sword for comfort. The sticky jungle smells and the dry desert wind still reached him, but he could see nothing beyond the edge of the roof. The constant screams and panicked cries rising up from the street made him feel queasy. All he could think of was Ruth still out there, trapped in the dark with the mob and, he feared from some of the sounds he heard, something deadlier.

It would have been more sensible to wait there for the others to find their way back to him, but his concern for Ruth overrode logic, and after a while pacing around the table anxiously, he made his way cautiously to the door.

His sword's Blue Fire gave him barely two feet of visibility. He was little better than blind in a sprawling city filled with danger.

Inside the building it was still stifling despite the temperature drop, and deafening with the cacophony of the many, many people crowded into every square foot of the ten floors, with only the café level kept out of bounds by the brutal guardians employed by the owner.

Trailing his left hand down the dry plaster, Church slowly descended the stairs to the next level, the stink of sweat and other bodily fluids increasing with every step. Each floor was a single room, used for some public function —a library, a meeting place—but their previous purpose had been almost obscured by makeshift beds and ramshackle tent-homes. The disturbed-hive drone of voices had increased considerably from the last time Church had passed through, the result, he guessed, of news of the descending darkness being passed on to those who were inside when it fell.

Reaching the next floor, he steeled himself for the arduous task of picking his way through the cluttered mass to the next flight of stairs against the opposite wall. Tiny lights bobbed here and there—candles, lanterns—small comfort to their owners but no use to him.

His very first step brought a squeal from someone underfoot, igniting a ripple of panic across the room and cries of, "What's wrong?" and, "Who is there?" Holding Caledfwlch before him like a torch, Church picked out his steps carefully, but the flickering blue light was a beacon of hope to any it fell upon. Soon pale faces caught in its glare were drawing up and moving in, curious and desperate. And as hands grasped him and pleas for assistance were issued, the desperate yearning for help swept across the room like fire.

Within minutes, bodies pressed against Church on every side, spinning him around, shaking his sense of direction. Fingers tore at his clothes and his skin, growing harder and angrier when they received no response. At first, he entreated people to allow him passage, but it proved hopeless and he quickly realised his only option was to put his head down and drive himself through the dense wall of bodies.

The next flight of stairs was located more by luck than judgement. Careering down them two steps at a time, he almost fell out of control in the dark, landing roughly on the next floor. The crush of people drawn to him began almost immediately.

Choking with the smell of bodies and the heat, Church continued to drive his way through the mass. Halfway across the room, amidst the pleadings and cries, a familiar, ironic voice broke through at his left ear: "Don't you just hate them? Stupid, witless sheep."

Church whirled, but all he saw were troubled, pale faces and grasping hands. The Libertarian had retreated back into the dark.

His heart pounding, Church renewed his efforts to press through the crowd. Faces came and went in the tight circle around him. Rough hands at his back became threatening. However fast he searched around the constantly looming bodies in the limited area of visibility, he knew he would never be able to see the Libertarian until the killer was on top of him.

He resorted to throwing people roughly out of his way, but that only increased the crowd's anger and made his passage even more difficult. Soon they would be attacking him instead of pleading for help. He forced himself to calm down.

The next two floors passed in a blur of tension. Church knew the Libertarian would not have departed; he was sickened to realise he was starting to know him as well as he knew himself. There was a thick vein of sadism in the pacing of his torment: how long could the Libertarian hold off before moving in to strike?

"Why don't you kill them?" The sly voice appeared at his right ear.

Church whirled again. A glimpse of red eyes disappearing into the dark. "Come closer and see what you get, you bastard!" Church yelled.

The crowd grew more agitated. As he pushed forwards, the flat of his blade clipped a woman's head and she shrieked as if he had stabbed her. Angry shouts deafened him. Someone punched his back; another tried to grab Caledfwlch and he had to throw the man to one side, brandishing the sword as a threat. It only maddened the crowd further.

Stay calm, he told himself. Any more and they'll rip you limb from limb.

Buying time, he apologised to the woman and placated those near to him, before moving on. Three more floors passed slowly, but as he entered the eighth floor down he caught a wisp of smoke.

You bastard. It was all Church had time to think before the panic started. Off to his left a dim light flickered, growing larger by the second as the blaze spread swiftly through the tinder-dry building, the jumble of possessions, bedding and shelters. Deafening shrieks became one voice as the entire floor moved as a single entity towards the stairs, crushing and trampling. Church was carried along in the flow, choking from the thick, acrid smoke as the temperature in the room intensified rapidly.

Soon even the supernatural darkness could not contain the inferno, and it blazed brightly as it raced across the room, consuming people, bringing down roof timbers in a cascade of sparks, raising a wall of heat that felled the young and the old as soon as it touched them.

"You don't have to kill them all!" Church raged impotently, torn between fury and bitter guilt that an entire building filled with people was being slaughtered just to get at him.

"Oh, but I do."

Church turned, and there was the Libertarian, his eyes as red as the flames that formed an infernal halo around him.

"Almost like looking in a mirror, isn't it?"

Before Church could raise Caledfwlch, the Libertarian jabbed a finger into a pressure point on Church's neck and he slumped to the floor, unconscious.

3

For once the streets of the Court of Endless Horizons were empty. Through the maze of dark alleys, side streets, squares and gardens, Bearskin and Shadow John led Veitch and Shavi at a breathless pace. Occasionally, Bearskin would stop to sniff the air or examine the dusty ground. To Shavi, there was never anything to be seen, but Bearskin would always nod and move on confidently.

It was Shadow John who forged the way, ensuring no obstacles lay in their path so they could advance at speed.

"How the bleedin' hell do you do that?" Veitch asked him as they moved quickly through another square packed with market stalls.

Smiling, Shadow John leaned in and tapped the side of his left eye. "I am more at home in the shadows than I am in the light," he said. "That is where my true nature becomes clear. Best not to look too closely."

Shavi closed his ears to the screams that regularly punctured the dark, but his alien eye would not allow him any respite. It had taken to showing him a constant procession of the spirits of the recently departed as they made their way towards the Grim Lands. In the grey stream, he saw the echoes of the terror of their final moments, and the dismay, and the confusion about their current state, so rapidly had they been snatched from life. The stream was becoming a flood. He wanted to look away, but could not.

"The Enemy are using the darkness as cover to slaughter in their search for us," he said.

Veitch was enough of a friend to catch the hint of distress in Shavi's words, and he gave Shavi's arm a comforting squeeze. "We all knew it was going to get a lot worse, mate," Veitch said quietly. "Keep your head up. We're going to make the bastards pay for what they're doing."

Though he could not ignore the ghosts, Shavi responded to Veitch's words and refocused on the search.

Bearskin came to a sudden halt. "I smell smoke," he said suspiciously.

"Here!" Shadow John had disappeared into the gloom a few paces ahead, but he raced back excitedly. "I think I have found what you are searching for. But we have company!"

Hurrying close behind him, they came to the stone wall of some impressive building, its shape and identity lost to the dark. A small pitched-roof porch protruded from the wall, with Doric columns flanking a gate of iron railings. Three of the Aztec warriors were using their spears to try to break the gate's padlock. Round, staring eyes roving in their mosaic skulls, they turned and brought their spears up sharply to attack.

"What are they?" Shavi asked.

"Don't bother getting into details," Veitch said. "Two categories—friend or foe. And they're not friends." He drew his sword, the blue and black flames fighting for space along the blade. Shavi thought obliquely that there was more of the Blue Fire than he had seen before.

With astonishing speed, Bearskin loaded the blunderbuss that hung from his belt and fired. Flames and a cloud of black smoke exploded from the broad barrel and the head of one of the warriors disintegrated. The body took a couple more steps before realising it was dead.

Coughing, Bearskin wafted the smoke away. "Apologies, friends of the hunt. I must find myself a better gun." He shook his head. "The number of times I have been left with a few flecks of fur and a morsel of meat—"

"You never learn," Shadow John agreed.

Veitch hacked the head and an arm off the second warrior, but the third was causing him some difficulty. It moved rapidly, ducking beneath his attacks and jabbing with the spear. The razor-sharp obsidian blade sliced through Veitch's clothes and drew blood.

As Veitch lunged, the warrior whirled the spear's blunt end against Veitch's calf, upending him. The spear whirled again, ready to plunge into the prostrate Veitch's chest. Shavi grabbed the warrior's arm. As the warrior prepared to drive his wooden sword into Shavi's face, Veitch brought his own sword up into the warrior's gut. On his feet in an instant, Veitch rapidly made sure the warrior was dead.

"What are you doing, you mad bastard?" Veitch raged at Shavi. "Don't ever get involved in a fight again. You'll get yourself killed."

"Sorry. I thought I was saving your life," Shavi replied wryly.

"Well, don't. It's my job to get hacked to pieces. It's your job to be all smart and mystical and bloody Confucius-like." Taking a deep breath, Veitch cleaned his sword. "But thanks anyway."

Shavi grinned. "Perhaps I could get a sword."

"Don't push it."

A loud clank echoed as the padlock dropped to the flags. Shadow John gave a flourish and swung the gate open.

"What's in there?" Veitch peered into the interior. It was even darker than the surrounding city.

"Why, the Labyrinth of the Court of Endless Horizons, of course," Bearskin replied. "It lies beneath the queen's palace. Every year the court would have a challenge with a prize of unimaginable value for any who could navigate the Labyrinth and defeat whatever foul thing the queen had let loose down there."

"You've entered it?" Veitch enquired. "You know your way through?"

"Entered the Labyrinth?" Bearskin exclaimed. "I am no fool."

"No one has ever survived the Labyrinth," Shadow John explained.

"And now you're trying to get us to go in there." Veitch glanced at Shavi. "Is it just me or is there a pattern to our lives?"

"The scent of the Fragile Creature was rising up from the catacombs along our way. It could only be that somehow she has found her way into the Labyrinth through one of its many entrances," Bearskin explained.

Shavi nodded towards the three corpses lying next to the gate. "They were trying to get in there. The Enemy must be after the woman too."

"Looks like Church was right—she is important," Veitch noted. "Not that I doubted him. All right, we haven't got a choice—in we go."

Shadow John shifted uneasily. "But no one has ever survived the Labyrinth."

"The Enemy are right behind us," Veitch said, ignoring him.

"It's what lies ahead that worries me," Bearskin said, fingering his beard. "Still, challenges make us stronger." He clapped Shadow John on the shoulder and propelled him through the gate. "Don't worry, brother—I will look out for you."

"And we look out for ourselves," Veitch said to Shavi before following them into the cold dark.

4

Time seemed to stand still in the constant darkness. Ruth and Tom crept along alleys and down side streets, feeling their way, constantly listening for the sound of any approach. Occasionally they would come across groups of the Aztec warriors searching the empty streets or raiding a building to slaughter the occupants, and then they would be forced to retrace their steps and find another route. The warriors were everywhere and progress was excruciatingly slow.

"They're just running us around like rats," she snapped. "We need to take control."

"Perhaps you should conjure up some of that scary Craft," Tom said sardonically. "Draw a little attention to us."

Ruth glared at him. "I wasn't suggesting that. Besides, I choose the moments when I use my Craft. It's not like some sword you whip out whenever you need it. There are repercussions for every use."

Tom's eyes glinted in the sapphire light from the tip of her spear. "Always a price to pay."

Ruth hoped he didn't notice the shadow cross her face. If she allowed herself a moment's introspection, she realised she was afraid: of what the Craft would do if it was unleashed; of herself, of what she was becoming. Once before, the power had consumed her and she had almost destroyed everyone she loved. She could not let that happen again.

"I smell smoke," Tom said, distracted. "A fire in this situation could be devastating."

"God, I hope the others are okay," Ruth said. "I hope Church was smart enough to stay put."

"He wasn't, and it saved his life."

Ruth and Tom jumped as Laura emerged from the dark at the end of the alley.

"How did you find us?" Ruth asked incredulously.

"Blind luck." Laura glanced at Tom. "All of it bad."

Tom snorted.

"What are you saying about Church?" Ruth pressed.

"I just met him back there. The idiot couldn't sit tight. Massive city, total darkness, everybody split up—the first thing you do is wander around, calling out names, right? Still," she added acidly, "love makes you do stupid things."

"Come on, what are you waiting for?" Ruth was embarrassed by the eagerness in her voice.

"Okay, Jesus, keep your pants on till we get there." Laura strode back down the alley, with Ruth and Tom stumbling behind.

"Is he all right?" Ruth asked.

"Yeah, got out just before that café building burned down. I bumped into him while I was trying to stay one step ahead of those Aztec freaks. Persuaded him to sit still for a while."

"Why did he let you go off wandering?" Tom asked suspiciously.

"Because, grandpa, my plant eyes work better than human eyes. So shut it."

Ruth noted a harsher edge in Laura's mockery; the stress was telling, she thought, though Laura would never admit it.

Laura led them down a side alley to a small courtyard surrounded by three buildings. As they moved cautiously around the edge, they came across Church squatting on his haunches against one wall; he was holding something in his right hand that Ruth couldn't make out.

"Thank God," she said. "I was starting to get worried."

Church stood up to accept Ruth's hug, but as she fell into his arms, Tom called out, "Wait! There's something wrong!"

Church spun Ruth and clamped an arm around her throat; one flex of his muscles and he would crush the life from her. As she struggled to free herself, Church craned his head around to peer into her startled eyes and she could see then that though he looked like Church down to the smallest detail, it was not him; his eyes were filled with cruelty, and his breath against her cheek smelled of raw meat. She was overwhelmed by a sudden feeling of dread so strong it almost made her faint.

"What's going on?" Laura exclaimed.

Tom held her back. "Show yourself!" he urged.

The one who was Not-Church held out his right hand, and Ruth could now see that he clutched a smoking mirror. A glimmer of half-recognition crossed Tom's face.

As he turned the mirror, the hand and arm holding it became that of a jungle cat, black spots against white and orange fur: a jaguar, Ruth thought. And then it changed again, into a human hand, but with grey skin stretched tightly across bone. Afraid to look at the face but unable to prevent herself, Ruth glanced back and was convulsed with fear. It was like looking into the face of a corpse, the skin hanging in tatters from decomposing flesh, unmistakable feline qualities in the shape of the eyes and the tufts of fur clinging on to the skull-like pate. Black lines pulsed beneath the surface of his form, the sign of the controlling power of the Anubis Box; another of the gods the Void, and Janus, had chosen.

"In the Age of the Sun, your kind knew me as Tezcatlipoca," he said. "Three spheres do I bestride." He raised the mirror skywards. "The night. Death, in all its forms." And then he directed a lop-sided grimace-smile towards Tom and Laura. "And temptation."

"I've heard of you," Tom said, unable to hide his fear. "A shape-shifter. You killed the Caretaker."

"I hold this city now in my grasp, as I have held so many others in times long gone. This night will never lift. Death will never leave this place." He tightened his grip around Ruth's throat, forcing her to the brink of blacking out. "And soon one more will join Death's long parade."

5

Church came round tied to a chair in a hot room filled with scores of sputtering lamps. Together, they just about held back the dark that swelled in the corners of the room. It was spartan, with bare boards, plaster walls and only an empty chair across from Church. His head ached and his throat was unbearably dry;

it took him a second or two to recall where he had been when he was last conscious, and another second to recognise where he must be now.

"Where are you?" he called out.

"Right here."

The voice came from behind him. Slowly the Libertarian sauntered into view, his sunglasses reflecting the glittering points of lamplight. He spun around the empty chair and sat astride it.

"I must have seen a lot of bad eighties movies," Church said.

The manufactured flamboyance evaporated and for once the Libertarian stared at Church with cold contempt. "I am not you."

"That's not what you said in Beijing."

"I'm better. Right now I'm what you could never dream of being. In the same way that I could never imagine being you."

The Libertarian continued to stare. Church was puzzled by the barest hint of emotion in a voice that previously had been all role-playing, and he had the strangest impression, although he did not know why, that behind the Libertarian's sunglasses there were tears in his eyes.

"So you've brought me here to debate our different philosophies?"

The Libertarian laughed; the facade returned. "Oh, what's the point in that! Any difference will be over very shortly."

"Not going to happen."

"Yet here I am. And if there was even the slightest chance of you continuing down the primrose path with your unrealistically idealised worldview, I would not be standing before you." He waved a finger slowly at Church to emphasise his words. "Thousands of threads over thousands of years are finally tying together. Oh, if you could only see the full extent of the tapestry you would marvel at the wonder of it all! The rich complexity! I have the luxury of standing on the mountaintop and seeing how a stitch here and another there can create the world we want, while you are mired in the swamp, swatting away insects and wondering when the rain will come."

With as little obvious effort as possible, Church strained at his bonds.

The Libertarian smiled. "I know what you're doing. I remember that quite clearly, as I remembered exactly where you would be this day when my agent brought down the darkness. I find I'm remembering more and more the closer we get to the point of transformation." His lips quirked as if he was tasting something unpleasant. "A small price to pay, I suppose, for being able to interact with you at these vital junctures."

"But there are still a lot of variables, aren't there? Or you wouldn't be bothering with me. These x-factors . . . the little pushes and shoves I'm getting from the Oldest Things in the Land—"

"Forget about those deluded creatures," the Libertarian snapped. "Their days are numbered. As you are aware, we have already eradicated one of them. The rest will follow. You cannot understand the magnitude of what we have achieved. The Oldest Things in the Land! Playing their little games since your world was built out of shit and piss. Always a part of everything, always powerful, and now they are falling before us, one by one by one." He stood up and bowed. "Our brilliance, incarnate. I thank you!"

"What killed the part of you that cared?" Church asked, sickened.

"You think I am the villain of the piece. I am not. There are no villains in life, my young Jack Churchill. Nor any heroes. There are only people who want the things you want, and people who want the opposite. At the moment, you are caught up with your vision that people would be happier if they were completely free. That, in itself, is a trap. The choices, the striving . . . they only bring misery. No, better to be happy with your lot. To be content, and at peace. The Mundane Spell . . . the lack of meaning in everyday existence . . . surely that is a small price to pay for being content."

"War, corruption, abuse, sickness—"

"All small prices when seen from the view of humanity as a whole. They do not affect everyone. Most people have steady lives."

Church thought for a moment, then said, "Don't you miss Sinatra?"

Pausing, the Libertarian appeared to be struggling to recall something just beyond his grasp. A shadow crossed his face.

"'Fly Me to the Moon'? How about your parents' faces, on a summer day, when you were a kid? Don't you miss Ruth?"

"No!" The Libertarian whirled, his features fixed with anger. "I thought I had already strangled the life from her in Greece, that's how little I care!"

"Don't you miss the magic, Jack?" Church said quietly.

In a rage, the Libertarian threw the chair to one side with such force that it shattered into pieces. Hurling himself at Church murderously, he pushed his furious face so close that it filled Church's vision. When he spoke, each word had the stab of an assassin's knife. "I know how much you love her. I know she is the prop that holds your fragile life together. And I know that she is the thing holding you back from reaching your destiny. Which is why I now have her."

Church flinched as if he'd been hit.

"Do I miss Ruth? I'll show you. First I'm going to torture her till the pain blooms in her face and she can see no good in life. And then I'm going to murder her, slowly and agonisingly, and I'm going to dump her body somewhere you will never find it. No chance for mourning. No closure. Your ravens will peck away at her flesh, and then her bones will yellow, and crumble, and she will be gone, as if she never existed."

Tears stung Church's eyes. "I'm going to kill you."

The Libertarian smiled. "That's the spirit."

6

When night fell across the Great Plain before the Court of the Soaring Spirit, the Enemy began its advance. Lost to the gloom, the first sign that Decebalus had of their movement was mounting vibrations in the ground, growing stronger, like the first tremors of an earthquake. The weather had worsened—something to do with the abilities of the remaining Riot-Beast, he guessed—and now torrential rain lashed their ranks and turned the ground around them to a sea of mud.

"They will try to overwhelm us by sheer numbers," he said as he peered into the dark. "I am surprised they did not try it before."

"Perhaps they wisely fear your ultimate deterrent," Lugh responded. Behind him the silent, unmoving ranks of Tuatha Dé Danaan warriors glowed a dull gold.

Decebalus eyed him askance. "You know of that?"

"I am a master tactician, after all. It is what I would have done."

"But would you have been prepared to use it?"

"Thankfully, I will never have to find out. That is now your burden, Brother of Dragons."

As a low, mournful call rolled out across the great plain from somewhere in the vicinity of the city walls, Lugh started and looked around hopefully. "My brother, one of the most powerful of the Tuatha Dé Danaan. Missing for so long. Is he joining the fray?" When he saw Decebalus's puzzled look, he added, "In the time of the tribes, he was known as Cernunnos, but your kind have a great many names for him, as befits his status. The Green Man. Jack o' the Green. He walks in the beating heart of nature, and pulses with the life-blood of Existence."

"Of course I have heard of him," Decebalus said. "He has helped the Brothers and Sisters of Dragons many times. Though, I must say, he has never seemed quite like you Golden Ones."

"My brother is like us, and is also greater than us. His influence straddles many Great Dominions, as befits one of the Oldest Things in the Land."

"He is one of those strange creatures, and also one of you?"

"The Oldest Things in the Land are a higher force, and they draw to them those who can help shepherd the ways of Existence."

"A force for good, then."

"A force for a plan that transcends the concepts of good and evil that Fragile Creatures love to clutch to their breasts for comfort. The universe is not simple, Brother of Dragons, and its pattern is lost to all of us."

The mournful howl rolled out again, but was subsumed by the rising tramp of thousands of feet and the pounding of the downpour.

Rain sluicing from his head, Decebalus said, "Nearly here now." Flickering lights could now be made out in the dark—the torches of the enemy—stretching as far as Decebalus could see in a horseshoe formation from foothill to foothill around the city. "Closing in. Nowhere to run."

"You are a strange being. You sound as if you are almost enjoying this desperate situation," Lugh said.

"We only truly find out what it means to be Fragile Creatures when we are closest to death. Your men are ready for the assault?"

"Of course. This will be as glorious as the Second Battle of Magh Tuireadh, when I slew the great Fomorii god, Balor."

"Then it is time to engage the Enemy." Pulling his sodden cloak around him, Decebalus strode back to his own ranks where a bonfire hissed and crackled, and pitch-soaked torches struggled to stay alight in the storm. The Brothers and Sisters of Dragons sheltered patiently in the tents, looking out of the huge unfurled doors towards the Enemy. As Decebalus moved past them, nodding to the leader of each unit, he saw how alike their expressions were, all of them laced with fear, all trying to hide it, preparing themselves mentally for the battle, knowing that death was likely. Through it all, the Pendragon Spirit blazed in their eyes.

Next to the fire, where everyone could see him, he announced loudly, "The time has come! We go now to meet the Enemy. Our job is to harry down the middle. We strike fast, retreat, regroup, strike again. We have speed and skill on our side. On your left flank will be the Tuatha Dé Danaan, well-drilled, relentless. They will find their line and hold it until they or the Enemy are gone. On your right flank will be the brute force we need to blow the Enemy asunder. The Asgardians have more power than sense—" a laugh ran through the group "—and we will use that, along with a few surprises to keep the Enemy on their toes."

Raising his sword high, he shouted, "We are Brothers and Sisters of Dragons! Though we die, we live on in the Pendragon Spirit. What we fight for can never be destroyed. This day . . . this battle . . . is the reason for our existence. Two thousand years of history leading to this point. Our Brothers and Sisters who are not here are counting on us to drive the Enemy back, to buy them time to save all Existence. We shall not fail. Do you hear me? We shall not fail!"

His voice became a roar that soared up to the heavens, and it was joined by all the Brothers and Sisters of Dragons, one voice of defiance carrying out across the plain. As he turned, they strode out from the tents behind him, those who had taken the role of cavalry to the horses, the others forming ranks for the ground battle. The fear was gone as if it had been washed away by the rain. There was only determination, come what may.

Decebalus summoned one of the Brothers of Dragons, Andy Cairns, a Scottish archer with black wavy hair and a sword scar on his right cheek. "Andrew, prepare your archers."

A moment later a hail of flaming arrows soared across the plain, igniting a liquid that Math had prepared in his tower and which Decebalus had spread in a huge defensive arc around their forces. A wall of fire rose up twenty feet into the air; Math had told him it would burn for at least an hour.

Within fifteen minutes the first lines of the Enemy attempted to break through the fire. Some continued aflame for several paces before they collapsed. Others fell in the midst of the inferno. But wave after wave followed, reminding Decebalus of the red ants he had seen in the forests of Dacia when he was boy; nothing would deter them. Soon the bodies had piled so high they covered the fire-liquid, and the ranks behind rolled over the top of them.

With a roar, Decebalus signalled the attack. To his left, the Tuatha Dé Danaan washed out in a golden wave, silent, focused, frightening in their intensity. The Brothers and Sisters of Dragons were only a step behind. At the heart of them, Decebalus swelled with pride, swinging his axe with abandon as he forced his way to the front.

Within moments they crashed against the rocks of the Enemy, and Decebalus was hurled into such a frenzy of flashing weapons and flailing bodies that it was impossible to see anything beyond a zone of a few square inches. Noise filled his world, the endless shriek of metal on metal, the grunts of exertion, battle cries and the screams of the wounded and dying. Tossed around by a heavy swell, he never rested for a second, swinging his axe into heads, shoulder-blades, arms. Bodies crushed tight on all sides. No thoughts came; there was only time for instinct.

The ranks of the Enemy in front of him comprised the Lament-Brood, dead beings from numerous races with swords, axes and spears rammed into their limbs so that they themselves became weapons that could not be killed, for whom wounds meant nothing; the only way to stop them was to dismember them.

Gradually, his thought process adjusted to the blistering pace of battle, a sublime state where everything slowed and he floated amidst the chaos, able to examine the rich detail, and reflect. Blood sprayed in beautiful arcs. Raindrops on armour glittered like diamonds. Blades caught the torchlight as they whirled, trailing gold. Underfoot, the ground churned, became liquid, a swamp of gore and mud sucking at his legs.

His axe removed the top of a skull, then spun and came down to split the face below. As the Lament-Brood warrior dropped to his knees another was already taking his place.

To his left, Decebalus saw a Sister of Dragons battling furiously, glistening black hair slick from the rain. As she was dragged away by the flow of battle, he tried to remember her name. An unusual name. It was important that everyone was remembered, and seen as individuals sacrificing all, not as a resource to be used up to win.

Demelza, he recalled. Monfries.

He nodded, happy that he had marked her place in his mind. To his right, three Lament-Brood warriors surrounded a Brother of Dragons, his ringletted hair and beard plastered with blood. He had no chance, but he kept fighting to the last.

Decebalus struggled to recall the name, cursing himself furiously until it came. "Stephen," he said aloud. "Harding."

And then Aula was at his side in the white and silver armour of one of the Tuatha Dé Danaan courts, her blond hair darkened by the rain.

"Here?" he bellowed. "You are no warrior!"

With her short sword, she hacked off the arm of one of the Lament-Brood as it attempted to drive a spear into Decebalus's chest. "Answer enough?" she said.

"Not quite, but it will do, for now."

"Even an uneducated barbarian like yourself deserves someone at your back."

They exchanged a brief look that said more than they ever had, or ever would, and then the battle sucked them in once more.

For fifteen minutes of furious exchanges, it appeared as if the Brothers and Sisters of Dragons and the Tuatha Dé Danaan were making no headway against the constant stream of the Enemy; for every one that fell two more took their place. Decebalus saw Redcaps with their clothes of human skin, unrelenting machines of muscle, gristle and bone that exhibited tremendous power and endurance. There were the Baobhan Sith, shrieking spectral figures that shifted shape before attempting to tear out the throats of those nearby; and the Gehennis, shades flapping like sheets in the wind but with more devastating substance than they presented to the world. Towering giants swung clubs that reduced a man to a red mist, while other grotesqueries that he did not recognise ripped apart with claws and teeth.

The explosive bolt of lightning crashed into the Enemy ranks at the point he had planned, when overconfidence had taken the edge off their fighting skills. Body parts rained down from a blackened circle inside which everything had been incinerated. More bolts blasted down at random, bringing fear to the disrupted Enemy ranks.

Decebalus caught the briefest glimpse of Mjolnir smashing through bodies before returning to the hand of its owner, who brought down another lightning bolt before directing the storm towards the Enemy.

Decebalus grinned: the gods had arrived.

Laughing like a madman, his scarred, hairy body completely naked, Tyr waded through the ranks chopping down the Lament-Brood like saplings. Beside him, the Slavic god Perkunas wielded a throwing axe that sent heads flying in unison, while Ares, lost to his bloodlust, had to be continually redirected towards the Enemy so that he did not attack his own side. On a murderous rampage, the Aztecs' Huitzilopochtli tore out the hearts of the living Enemy by plunging his hands into their chests, and the Caribbean war god Ogoun concentrated on the Lament-Brood with his machete, reducing them to quivering chunks of decomposing flesh.

The gods were a whirlwind of fury and righteous vengeance, and every time Decebalus thought he had seen the last descend into the fray another dropped from the skies or drove a wide, bloody path through the ground troops.

Hundreds of the Enemy were falling by the minute, and despite their numbers they were in disarray and being driven back step by step. Lugh was at the forefront of the Tuatha Dé Danaan, serious and dedicated, and though covered in gore he still glowed like the sun. Behind him, the Army of all the Courts fought on, shoulder to shoulder, for the first time since they had left their four fabled homes.

About a third of the Brothers and Sisters of Dragons had fallen, but the rest drove on with renewed energy, faces alight with the Pendragon Spirit.

For the next half-hour, as the Enemy was decimated, Decebalus finally began to believe that despite the odds they could win.

The first sign that events had begun to change was a sudden retreat by the Enemy that left a V of unoccupied ground. Decebalus signalled for the Army of Dragons to proceed with caution; it looked to him as if the Enemy was encouraging them to pursue with abandon, and he never did anything any enemy wanted.

Silence fell across the Enemy ranks, the only sound the beating of the rain on the sea of mud.

"What are they doing?" Aula asked.

"Waiting," Decebalus replied.

After a moment, the Enemy ranks parted and a ten-foot-tall figure stepped through, his identity at first cloaked by the storm. As he neared, Decebalus recognised him from the description Church had given during one of the numerous briefings: brutish features, part pig, part ass, added an incongruous aspect to the elegant clothes of the ancient Egyptian ruling class. Seth, god of evil and the desert, raised a staff mounted with a single golden eye and a flurry of snow swirled around him.

"Fragile Creatures!" His booming voice sounded like a boulder dragged across gravel. "My people were great and wondrous, shining stars in the vast firmament of Existence. Yet you destroyed them, and in your arrogance you thought you could do it with impunity."

"He is talking about the devastation wrought by Church and the others in the Great Pyramid," Aula whispered.

Decebalus barely heard her. Already his tactician's mind was racing ahead, weighing potential options as he tried to evaluate what Seth would do.

"Get back," he said loudly after a few seconds, before bellowing, "Retreat!"

The word had barely left his mouth when Seth raised his other hand to reveal an object that radiated a brilliant white light. There was a second when all the sound appeared to have been drained from the world, and then a shimmering, glassy wave washed out from Seth and the entire battlefield lit up, growing brighter and brighter until it felt as if the sun had crashed to the ground.

And that was the last thing any of them saw.

7

In the Grim Lands there was little to mark the passage of time. Sometimes the quality of light would be a shade darker, sometimes it would have a silvery glint, as though night and day were coming and going beyond the constantly rolling mists. Everywhere was grey, all the time. It left the spirits dampened, and gradually leached the energy from both Mallory and Caitlin. Each incline became a little harder to climb, each graveyard navigated with an increasing number of rest stops, until they started to fear that the mood of the place would eventually bring a critical lethargy that would leave them drifting and aimless like the land's regular inhabitants.

Sitting on the dusty gravel with her back to a tomb marked with the legend Et In Arcadia Ego, Caitlin examined the flickering blue flame of the Wayfinder and tried to ignore the feeling that if she closed her eyes she would sleep forever.

"I wonder if Hal is aware of what's happening," she mused.

Sitting beneath a carved skull on an adjoining tomb, Mallory lazily drew a cross in the dust with the heel of his boot. "That was quite a sacrifice he made. Imagine being a part of the Blue Fire—a part of everything there is and was—and then giving it all up to lock yourself in that little lantern to guide our way. It must have been like being God, and then quitting to become an ant."

"You wouldn't expect anything less. He's always been one of us . . . of our Five." She winced and corrected herself: "Our Four. I wish we'd got a chance to know him better."

"It's even more of a sacrifice than that," Mallory continued. "He can be destroyed while he's in the Wayfinder. He'd escaped from death, and now he's put himself back in the game. That's brave."

The flame continued to point the way across the last few yards of the grave-yard and out into the wilderness beyond, where Callow was on reconnaissance.

"Does this place make you think of your husband and boy?" Mallory asked.

"I've never stopped thinking of them. Not in a morbid way. I remember the good times, and what they meant to me, and I know we're going to be together again some day. Have you ever lost someone you love?"

"Yeah." He paused before realising, "I just don't know who."

The thought clearly troubled him so much that Caitlin didn't press. Chewing on his lip absently, he slipped back into a deep reflection.

In the silence that followed, Caitlin became aware of the presence of her other selves deep in the back of her head. Their whispering always ebbed and flowed like the pulse of her blood, but now she could hear Brigid's voice growing more insistent. Listening intently, she absently spoke the words the second they came to her: "He's coming! Run!"

Mallory started. "Who's coming?"

"I . . . I don't know."

They were surprised to see Callow watching them from the shelter of a nearby mausoleum. "How long have you been there?" Mallory snapped.

"No time for that now," Callow replied obsequiously. "Listen carefully and I think you'll hear to whom the little miss is referring."

Dimly, the scrape of feet on gravel filtered through the blanketing mist. Moving quickly and silently, Mallory and Caitlin kept low, using the tombs and mausoleums for cover. As the mist shifted across a wide expanse of statuary, they saw the Hortha stalking steadily in their direction.

"What does it take to stop him?" Mallory said incredulously.

"He doesn't look like he's been hurt at all. Yet that thing in the mausoleum was . . ." Caitlin's words dried up as she considered the implications of her notion. "How are we going to stop him, Mallory?"

"There's no point thinking about it now. We just need to keep a few steps ahead of him."

"But we'll have to rest some time."

"Maybe we'll think up a brilliant idea on the way."

Returning silently to Callow, they motioned for him to follow as they left the graveyard behind, heading down the rough shale into a bleak landscape of boulders and stones that reminded them of photos they'd seen of the surface of Mars.

After what they estimated to have been an hour, but may only have been a quarter of that time, the going became harder with sheets of shattered slate underfoot that they had to travel over carefully to avoid turning an ankle or cutting themselves on the razor-sharp edges.

This sloped down to an area of towering rock formations that merged until they were moving along the bottom of a deep chasm over large fallen rocks. Through the mist, they could just make out holes cut into the walls above their heads—more tombs, Mallory guessed.

Caitlin thought she glimpsed a head looking down at them out of one of the holes, but the mist closed over it before she was sure. A little further on she definitely did see a figure pulling itself out of one of the dark spaces to watch them pass.

"Yeah, I see them too," Mallory whispered to her before she could warn him.

"The dead are an inquisitive bunch," Callow said. "They half-remember what it was like to be alive and always want to recall more." He glanced at the soaring rock walls. "Probably best not to get caught by them down here. They're not at all like me—witty, vivacious company. They can be a little jealous of what you have, and they have lost."

"How long till we get out of here, then?" Mallory asked sharply.

"Only forwards, just a little way now. If we are lucky," he added.

"I'm starting to question your value as a guide," Mallory said.

A thud resonated behind them, and another: the dead dropping to the rocks from their resting places. Soon the steady tramp of feet followed them. Now whenever Caitlin glanced up she saw the grey, desiccated bodies of the dead levering themselves out of their holes on skeletal arms, some plummeting directly down, others climbing slowly and steadily on near-invisible handholds.

"Let's pick up the pace," Mallory said.

By then the footsteps behind them suggested a small crowd. Others loomed out of the mists on either side as they passed, their hands grasping for the mercurial life. Men, women, children, some naked, others in rags or shrouds or worm-eaten funeral suits. Caitlin was most disturbed by their gaze, heavy, unblinking, not intelligent, but not stupid either—they were the eyes of animals, with instincts for survival, some quicker than others.

She started to wonder about the mythology of the place. Did everyone pass through when they died? The dead she saw around her didn't appear pleasant. Was this instead some kind of purgatory? If so, what did that imply for a system of judgement, for God? The religious teachings of her childhood came back, haunting her with the mystery, troubling her as much as they comforted her. Could Grant and Liam be somewhere in this world? If not, where were they?

As the dead began to crowd along the walls on either side of the chasm, Caitlin grew more anxious. They had the look of wary dogs about them, docile to all appearances but capable of turning savage at any moment.

Mallory kept them moving at a rapid pace, but increasingly she felt hands on her clothes, fingers flexing as if preparing to grab, the dry-wood touch of dead skin brushing her arms. Goosebumps ran up her back. The path between the rows of the dead was growing narrower as they drew in on either side.

And what then? Would they move in on all sides, driving those fingers through her pink skin to investigate the mysteries that lay beneath?

One woman with lank brown hair and a head that lolled onto her chest lunged suddenly and grabbed Caitlin's wrist, but the grip was weak and she shook it off easily. Yet it was a warning sign.

"Mallory, I think we have a problem," she said.

"How much further, Callow?" Mallory barked.

"Oh, not far now. A hundred yards, perhaps," Callow said without looking back. Caitlin wondered why that was: he usually underpinned every line with a studied expression demanding sympathy.

Pushing through a flurry of mist, they came up hard against a dead end. Trapped in a cleft as the rock walls converged, Caitlin looked back fearfully at the dead slowly advancing.

"Oh dear," Callow said. "I appear to have missed a turning."

"You idiot." Mallory faced the shambling figures. As he drew Llyrwyn, they stopped and stared dumbly at the faint blues flames sputtering and fizzing along the blade.

"Back off," Mallory said. "Is there any point talking to them?"

"Oh, yes," Callow replied. "They hear. They understand, though it might take a while for their long-dulled senses to flicker into life. See, here." Callow edged behind Caitlin and shouted, "Look at them, pink and alive! They make a mockery of you! Stop them!"

Mallory rounded on Callow, but by then he had one arm around Caitlin's throat and a razor blade plucked from the turn-up of his dirty trousers gripped between the fingers of his other hand.

Deep in her head, Caitlin felt the Morrigan unfurl her wings and a surge of darkness sweep forwards. Caitlin elbowed Callow in his gut. He let out a pained gasp of air, but instantly slashed her cheek with the razor and then pressed it to her jugular.

Caitlin cried out as blood washed down from the wound, but Callow only dug the razor deeper. "You'll be dead before you can release what's inside you," he whispered in her ear. "I cut one of your kind before, and I am quite prepared to do so again. My shiny friend here can conduct a nice dance across your face and still slit that white throat before you have time to move. You will die ugly, and that thought will eat away at you in this dismal afterlife."

"Let her go." Mallory ignored the dead gathering at his back. He raised the sword towards Callow's throat.

"Oh, the bravado of the heroic man. So false. What can you do? I am already dead. Make me more dead? It is the fault of your sickening brotherhood that I am here, and I have nurtured the desire for the dish best served cold for a long, long time. Give me the lantern."

"Don't, Mallory!" Caitlin cried. She saw him waver. "You need it to carry on. You don't need me."

"Oh, but he does," Callow said slyly. "I've seen it in his eyes as we journeyed together, knights of the road, shoulder to shoulder. He loves you. Perhaps not with the romance of a sexual partner, but with the deeper love of a kindred spirit, a friend you would support to the end. And this, most certainly, is the end."

"Mallory, no!" Caitlin could now see in his eyes the same thing as Callow, and she recognised the same rich depth of feeling in herself. A friend to the end. A deep and complex love. Why did that have to be the weapon that ruined them?

Mallory slowly held out the Wayfinder for Callow to snatch with his free hand. "My little ears hear all sorts of things," he said. "About the genie inside this thing, for one. A vulnerable genie, whose destruction would strike to the heart of the sickening Brothers and Sisters of Dragons."

Caitlin winced at the devastation in Mallory's face. In a cold, murderous tone, Mallory said: "If you hurt him I'll find some way to make you suffer."

"Of course you will." He smiled mockingly. "Now, I know how sly you people are, and I see that pigsticker you're waving around, so . . ." With a flourish, he slashed Caitlin again, missing the vein more by accident than design, but cutting her deeply enough that the blood gushed. Thrusting her towards Mallory, he gripped the handle of the lantern between his teeth and leaped up the wall, clutching on to barely visible handholds before propelling himself through a tunnel that lay half-hidden in the mists just above their heads.

Catching Caitlin in his arms, Mallory desperately tried to staunch the flow of blood. "Not again," he muttered, without really knowing why.

The dead shuffled forwards, their eyes gleaming at the sight of Caitlin's lifeblood. Mallory levelled Llyrwyn at them. "I'll cut you to pieces," he said, trying to keep the emotion from his voice. "Do you understand that? I'll cut you to pieces!"

"I understand."

The voice echoed from further along the floor of the chasm, though Mallory knew who it was before the mist unfurled. A wall of the dead separated the two of them, but the Hortha simply grabbed the one nearest to him, extended his finger of blackthorn and rammed it through the temple into whatever remained of the brain. The dead man slumped to his knees, and the Hortha moved on to the next.

Caitlin found herself slipping to the edge of consciousness as the Morrigan fell back into the dark, but she could see Mallory fighting with his dilemma: the Hortha was unbeatable, but too close for them to make an adequate escape in her severely wounded condition.

"Leave me," she croaked.

"No. Never, ever again."

As he searched around for a solution while trying to hold the dead back and keep Caitlin from bleeding out, his eyes gleamed with a dawning notion. "See him—he's destroying you!" he yelled at the dead. "He hates you. He laughs at what you've lost. He's going to make you suffer even more than you already have. Is that fair? You have to stop him."

The dead paused and turned as one, fixing their unblinking stare on the Hortha as he punctured another head and discarded what remained, not caring whether they saw him.

"He wants to make you suffer more!" Mallory shouted.

The dead moved, tentatively at first but with gathering speed as Mallory's words lit up their sluggish minds. With grasping hands, they pressed towards the Hortha and although the creature tried to drive through the flow, there were too many of them. They began to tear at his form, ripping away the blackthorn as fast as it could regrow, searching for the mystery of his life. Finally, the Hortha went down under a frenzy of tearing.

Mallory tied a handkerchief across Caitlin's wounds and slung her over his shoulder. Grunting with strain and exhaustion, he clambered up the rock wall and stepped into the tunnel, sparing one quick backward glance at the churning pool of grey, dead flesh.

The tunnel was only short, the pearly mist gleaming at the end.

"You love me, and I love you," Caitlin said dreamily. "Platonic. Deep. You're a sensitive soul, Mallory, a good man—"

"Save your strength," he said, embarrassed.

"That's why I love you."

He shifted her weight into his arms to carry her more easily, and she could see the worry in his face. "Am I dying?"

"Not yet. I'm going to sort out that wound when we get out of here. But after that . . ." Shaking his head, he looked away. She knew what he was thinking: how could they find Callow and save Hal in this terrible, bleak land? How could they find the Extinction Shears?

Stumbling out of the tunnel mouth, Mallory came to a sudden halt. Her head spinning, Caitlin craned her neck to see what had brought him up so sharply. Waiting a little way down the slope on the backs of their strange mounts were the Brothers and Sisters of Spiders, their dead expressions grim.

"We've been waiting for you," Etain said coldly.

CHAPTER SEVEN
THE LABYRINTH

1

Caitlin had slipped into unconsciousness. Laying her still form on the rocky ground in the tunnel mouth, Mallory prepared for what he fully expected to be his last fight. He had heard enough about the ferocity of the Brothers and Sisters of Spiders to know he stood little chance of defeating the four of them on horseback.

"Sheathe your sword," Etain said in a low, grating voice. "Ryan Veitch sent us back to this dismal place to give you whatever aid we could."

Mallory tried to read her dead face, but even looking beneath two thousand years of scars and burning it was impossible to read any emotion in her features. "I thought you couldn't talk," he said.

"Here, in the Grim Lands, amongst our own kind, we are at home." Her voice suddenly came alive with a shocking bitterness. "We are allowed some small comforts to endure this place."

Branwen climbed down from her mount and approached in a jerky manner, as if consciously forcing her limbs to move. "Let me help the Sister of Dragons."

Reluctant at first, Mallory eventually allowed her to treat Caitlin's wounds with herbal creams from a bag at her waist, which she applied liberally until the blood flow stopped. "I tended Ryan Veitch's wounds many times across the great gulf of the years," she said. "He cared for us when we were abandoned by all, and we cared for him." She swivelled her head creakily towards Etain. "Some more than others."

"I don't trust you," Mallory said. "I heard how you helped Veitch kill all those Brothers and Sisters of Dragons—"

"We were Brothers and Sisters of Dragons before we sided with the Army of the Ten Billion Spiders," Etain interrupted. "Indeed, we were the very first to carry the Pendragon Spirit into your lineage."

"We followed Ryan Veitch wherever he led, even into the ranks of the Devourer of All Things," said Owein, his muscular, thick-set frame badly scarred. "He would have died for us. We were his only friends."

Mallory didn't think it wise to point out how tragically pathetic it was that a man could only count a bunch of dead things as friends. Instead, he searched for some sign of the direction Callow had taken. "If you're here to help, we need, firstly, to get away from here as quickly as possible because I have this sickening feeling that even a collection of George Romero extras are not going to be able to stop the thing on our trail. And secondly, to find the bastard who did that to Caitlin and took the Wayfinder."

How long would Callow wait before he decided to destroy the lamp and Hal? A while, he guessed. Callow was cowardly and would want to put a lot of distance between himself and Mallory in case the dead were only a temporary setback.

Tannis, who had a warrior's build and a leader's demeanour, said chillingly, "Nothing escapes us."

"Then let's get moving. I want my hands around Callow's throat and I want it now."

With Caitlin's arms tied around Tannis's chest to prevent her slipping, and with Mallory behind Etain, they set off into the mist. After a mile or so, a gentle, stony incline gave way to a steaming, foul-smelling marsh, the brackish water gleaming with oily rainbows. Here Etain slowed her mount to pick a careful course along grassy ridges bordered by thick yellow reeds. Occasionally lights glimmered briefly away in the mists.

"What are they?" Mallory asked. The mood had become even more oppressive.

"Ignore them," Etain responded. "Trapped here are the spirits of those who dedicated themselves to work instead of humanity. They are as jealous and bitter as anything else in the Grim Lands, and they would like nothing more than to entice you into the sucking bog."

Bubbles burst intermittently on the surface of the pools. "Deep?"

"Bottomless. And filled with razor-worms that will feed on your flesh and bones for eternity."

Mallory studied her for a while and tried to imagine what she had been like when she was alive. "I'm betting you'd rather be with Veitch than here with me."

"His affections have turned to another. And why should he not find interest in one of his own rather than a dead thing?" she added pointedly. "Here he was king, worshipped by the inhabitants of the Grim Lands because he understood them. And he cared. Because he has died, and returned."

"That's not as rare as you might think."

"He understands what it is like to be an outsider."

"You're saying that's a good enough motivation to follow him into a life . . ." He paused, couldn't think of a better phrase: "Of mass-murder?"

"I would follow him to the end of the world."

"Which is pretty much where we are."

"He is a good man, whatever you might think of him. But he is as flawed as all mortal beings, and sometimes flaws get the better of us. Of you. It is a constant battle, and judgement should not come easy."

"We judge ourselves. And we do what we can to make amends for our failings, even when there isn't a hope in hell of righting the balance."

"You speak from experience."

Mallory didn't respond.

Pointing to the path ahead, Etain said, "The one you call Callow has passed this way, and recently. We will soon be upon him."

"Good." Mallory glanced back, half-expecting to see the Hortha close behind. "Sometimes you can run as much as you want and never get away," he said to himself.

They rode in silence for another fifteen minutes while Mallory cast an uneasy eye towards the swamp. Every now and then he thought he saw things moving in the black water.

Eventually, they came to a halt. For several minutes Tannis searched the narrow paths amongst the pools before returning to the group. "The trail has faded," he said.

"I thought you said you could track anything," Mallory protested.

"We can, given time. Sometimes the trail can be lost, but by careful scrutiny of the surrounding area it can be located again."

"We haven't got that kind of time." Frustrated, Mallory jumped down and paced the area of solid ground until Caitlin summoned him over.

"We'll find him," she said hoarsely. Some of her strength had already returned.

"Before he destroys Hal? This is all my fault. Why did I trust him?"

"We both trusted him. Don't blame yourself."

"He hurt you—"

"I'll be fine."

"Your face . . ." Mallory traced the line of the wound across her cheek beneath the dressing Branwen had applied.

Caitlin grabbed his hand and held it tight. "A battle scar. There's a part of me that will enjoy having that."

In her eyes, Mallory saw a deep shadow start to grow.

"She's coming, Mallory," Caitlin said quietly. "And she's not going to see a sister treated so badly. There'll be a price to pay, trust me on that."

The shadow filled Caitlin's eyes and moved out into her face. The Morrigan smiled.

2

Deep in the heart of the forbidding swamplands, Callow finally paused and removed the lantern from inside his jacket. He was afraid of retribution—his knowledge of the persistence of Brothers and Sisters of Dragons was extensive—but he was filled with an eager glee for his own retribution.

Sitting cross-legged next to the soupy water, he examined the Wayfinder's blue flame. "Oh, the wonder of it all—a genie in the lamp, and a Brother of Dragons to boot. Can you hear me, little man?" He roughly rattled the lantern in front of his face. "Sadly, I am a mortal like any other, and prone to the melancholies of all men. And yes, the desire for a touch of revenge for being so badly treated. And I have been, oh, how I have been! During that terrible Age of Misrule I was manipulated . . . possibly brutally coerced . . . into helping those misshapen monsters, the Fomorii.

"And did the Brothers and Sisters of Dragons forgive and forget? Did they respond to my plight, and offer a friendly hand in answer to my humble admission of my wrongs and my plaintive desire for redemption? No. They punished me, and brutalised me, and eventually took my sad, sad life. And these are Champions of Existence! How ironic. It is through their cruel machinations that events have conspired to keep me trapped in this hideous place."

He paused slyly. "Or should I say your machinations? It is unfortunate that you will have to pay the price for their sins."

Callow did an excited jig before calming himself. "Now how should I do it? Fling the lantern into one of these sucking pools and watch it disappear forever? Then you would understand the kind of purgatory I have experienced for so long. Or should I smash it and watch the flame flicker and die?" He considered this for a moment, and smiled triumphantly. "I think that would set my world alight."

Drawing one of the many razor blades he had secreted about his person, he attempted to carve his name into the lantern, but he could make no mark on the shiny surface and the razor blunted within seconds. He tossed it angrily into the water where something snapped and spat.

"I was just a humble knight of the road when I met that overinflated Pecksniff Jack Churchill," he muttered to himself. "No harm to man nor beast. Lover of the byways, lover of people, a helping hand to all I met on my way. And look what he did to me."

Callow laid the Wayfinder on the ground, took a running jump and slammed both booted feet upon it. A peal of thunder was accompanied by a fizz of blue sparks. He repeated the assault three times before examining it again. The lantern was dented and the glass on one side was cracked.

"Once more," he muttered. "This may well look like a lantern, but I know its true shape is different from what I see. Yet here in the Grim Lands it is as vulnerable as anything from the places where the living roam. Yes, I think once more will do. I'll say goodbye to you now, oh genie. Enjoy the great hereafter."

Laying the lantern down once again, he paced out a long run-up and then, with a grim smile, hurled himself at the Wayfinder. At the point when Callow hung above the lantern, a column of Blue Fire engulfed him and hurled him back to the edge of the swamp water. Callow let out a high-pitched, shocked scream.

It was only when he picked himself up that he realised the flames were cold, and had done little more than propel him away.

"So it's a fight you want," he said, drawing up his sleeves. "We'll see how long you can keep that up in this place."

3

The blue flash lit up the swamplands even through the mist, followed closely by the echo of Callow's scream across the black water.

Caitlin broke off her examination of the myriad paths through the swamp and removed the axe from its harness on her back. Etain, Tannis, Owein and Branwen were already climbing into their saddles as Mallory growled, "With any luck, something's eaten him."

"That flash—it was Blue Fire," Caitlin said coldly.

Mallory didn't respond.

Another blue flash filtered through the mists, but this time it was accompanied by a shout of gleeful anger.

Callow was so engrossed in his vigorous attempts to destroy the lantern that he didn't hear their approach until the last. With a girlish shriek, he booted the lantern towards the deep water and ran.

Diving at full run, Mallory's fingertips skimmed the Wayfinder before it splashed into the depths, spinning it upwards where it threatened to escape him again. Scrabbling wildly, he eventually snagged it and hugged it to his chest.

"Sorry, Hal," he whispered. "I won't let you out of my grasp again."

With powerful strides, Caitlin caught up with Callow in seconds, brutally kicking his legs out from under him. His frightened pleas quickly turned into sly attempts to explain his actions, but when he saw the dark fury in Caitlin's eyes his voice faded away.

"I bleed, you don't," she said, "so how do I get my revenge against a dead thing?" She pressed the blade of her axe against his face. "I could chop you into tiny chunks, but would there be any conscious thought left in them to suffer?"

"Being in this place is suffering enough, m-m-m-ma'am," Callow stuttered.

"But it doesn't make me feel any better. Where's the justice in that? Where's the lesson learned?"

"Please," Callow called out to Mallory, "have a heart! I made a mistake, that's all. You are Brothers and Sisters of Dragons. You celebrate all that is good about life."

Distractedly, Mallory polished the lantern. "True. But unluckily for you we're not Church's group. They've got compassion in spades. Existence brought us together with specific qualities in mind. They're the good guys. We're the hard bastards." He gave Callow a brutal smile. "All except Hal, and I'm betting he's not feeling very sympathetic towards you right now."

Callow let out a small whimper. Caitlin dragged him to Etain and retrieved a rope from her saddle. His searing cries echoed across the entire swamp as Caitlin bound his wrists tightly behind his back, looped the rope around his ankles, then threw the other end over the branch of one of the spindly trees overhanging the swamp. With a jerk, she whipped Callow's feet out from under him and suspended him an inch above the water, where snapping shapes swam hungrily just beneath the surface.

He cried and pleaded until his throat was raw, and when he finally stopped, Caitlin said, "I think the best thing would be to leave you here where you can't do any more harm. With a few friends for company."

Another jerk of the rope plunged Callow's head into the water up to the bridge of his nose. The water boiled around him as the razor-worms plunged into his eyes and ears, burrowing and eating for what could be eternity.

Half an hour later they could still hear his terrible screams as they made their way out of the swamp and onto a barren plain, once again following the lantern's blue flame.

4

In the hard, silvery gleam of dawn, Decebalus came round deep in the mire of the battlefield. The storm had ended, and a strained quiet lay across the great plain, punctuated by the occasional cry. All around were scattered dismembered corpses of both allies and enemy. It took a second or two for Decebalus's thoughts to flicker into some semblance of cohesion, and then another few seconds to realise he was alive and intact. His first thought was how Seth had been prepared to devastate his own side to achieve a minor advantage.

The remnants of the once-enormous Enemy force trailed across the battlefield towards the city in small pockets, pausing occasionally to slay a survivor.

They skirted much of the area where the gods had fought. Decebalus guessed that if he lived, most of the gods would have survived too. Seth would want to achieve his aims before they returned to the fray.

Drawing his strength back into his shaky limbs, Decebalus was gripped by a flash of memory. Keeping low, he desperately searched amongst the fallen, overturning bodies to peer into blood- and mud-stained faces. Finally he located Aula buried under a heap of dismembered Lament-Brood. She was deathly pale, her eyes closed, her blond hair matted with gore. Decebalus muttered a brief prayer before taking her wrist and locating a thready pulse. Relief flooded through him; the Pendragon Spirit would work its magic; she would survive. Bowing his head to her chest, he closed his eyes and remembered Dacia, so far away in time and space. He wished he could have shown Aula the beauty of the forests on a summer's twilight, the great river at dawn with the sun glinting off the water and the smell of a new day rising. Gently, he kissed the back of her hand. So many things unsaid, so many emotions buried deep in his heart that in his rough ways he had never been able to express. But she knew, he was sure.

Kissing her on the lips, he re-covered her with the bodies to protect her from the Enemy's sight. As he prepared to crawl towards the city, he caught sight of a small group of Redcaps moving his way, emitting their deep, throaty growl as they tore chunks of flesh off dead limbs. If he stood and fought, it would attract other enemies to him, and he would not last a moment, but there was no way he could escape the Redcaps' advance without being seen.

Crawling on his belly, he rounded a larger pile of corpses to find better shelter where he could gather his thoughts. Nearby, two Brothers of Dragons slumped together, bleeding heavily from fatal wounds. Decebalus had nursed high hopes for both of them: Jim Davey, softly spoken and with Shavi's empathic nature, and Michael Koefman, a messy-haired former musician. Decebalus crawled over to them.

"What kind of thing destroys its own side to get at us?" Blood leaked from the corner of Michael's mouth as he spoke. Neither had long left.

"Something that does not care in the slightest about life," he replied. "I have to get to the city before the Enemy's bastards reach the Caraprix. Yet there are Redcaps nearby who will see me when I move . . ."

He let the words hang. Understanding what he was asking, the two

Brothers of Dragons exchanged a fleeting glance of acceptance for their fate, and then Jim said quietly, "You can count on us."

"You are good men, both. I will make sure you are remembered." Decebalus's farewell nod couldn't begin to convey what he truly felt and he crawled away quickly. Not long after he heard them both begin to shout loudly. The roar of the Redcaps followed instantly, and when he heard their savage attack, Decebalus ran for the city.

The remnants of the shattered gates hung raggedly from the twisted hinges. The city beyond was still, the residents cowering in their rooms. At the entrance, Ronnie darted from a hiding place. His wounds were superficial, but his face had a haunted expression as the devastation across the Great Plain ignited memories of his terrible experiences in Flanders during the Great War.

"I was going after that bastard, sir," he said. "He's on his way to the palace and the Caraprix."

"You will not be able to stop him. He is too powerful," Decebalus said.

"And you will? Excuse me, sir, but we're both of a kind."

"Not so much, Ronald. You are a better man than me. My experiences have better prepared me for what is necessary." Decebalus silenced Ronnie's protests. "I have more important work for you. You must find a way to raise the gods."

"To help you?"

"No. The game here is almost played. You must leave this place immediately, do you hear me?"

Ronnie looked unsure.

"Do you hear me?" Decebalus gripped Ronnie's shoulders forcefully until Ronnie nodded, unsettled. "Bring together our own survivors quickly." He told Ronnie where Aula was hidden, and then added, "You must strike out for the Enemy Fortress, to offer what support you can to Church and the others. Time is short. Make haste. Do not wait here a moment longer than necessary."

Decebalus raced through the gates before Ronnie could argue. A brief detour took him to the Hunter's Moon where Crowther and Mahalia waited behind a barricaded door. The teenage girl had been a shadow of herself since Jack's departure, but now her old fire flashed in her eyes.

"Let me help." She drew the small switchblade she carried with her at all times.

"I have greater work for you two," Decebalus said. "You must save an entire city."

"The Enemy's broken inside?" Crowther asked.

Decebalus nodded. "Sound the alarm. God knows, we have practised the escape enough times in recent days. There will be fear, panic. You must show leadership to calm them, and then take them to safety in the foothills. Can I count on you to do this?"

Crowther's heavy-set face glowed; as Decebalus had anticipated, the gift of purpose had brought him alive. "You can count on us."

Within moments of Decebalus leaving the inn, the first tolling bell echoed across the silent city, joined soon by another, and then an entire host. People were already creeping from their hiding places as Decebalus ran up the winding cobbled road towards the Palace of Glorious Light, where he could hear the Enemy advancing. His relief freed him to concentrate on the trial ahead.

In the courtyard before the palace, Seth waited with a few ranks of Lament-Brood and Redcaps. The god's head hung to one side as though he was listening, and then he nodded and forced his way through the palace doors.

Once Seth and his troops had entered, Decebalus slipped in behind and followed one of the many secret passages and hidden stairways that would put him ahead of the Enemy. Math's chamber was silent, but Decebalus sensed the sorcerer was near.

He rapped on the door. "It is I, Decebalus. The time has come."

The door swung open, though there was no one on the other side. Math waited in an adjoining chamber so gloomy that his presence was only revealed by the glint of his mask as it revolved a quarter-turn.

"This is it, then. The end, or the beginning of it." Math's voice was a low rumble. "The Golden Ones always feared that if Fragile Creatures rose up they would destroy what they set out to attain. It is in your nature."

"Be thankful it is. If Existence was left to your spineless kind, the Void would have wiped us all out long ago, and would now be feasting on our bones. Where is it?"

Math took a step into the shadows and returned holding a small iron casket in the palm of his hand.

"That is it?" Decebalus queried.

"Size is no definer of power."

"That has never been an issue for me, in any case." Decebalus took the casket, unnerved by how it hummed beneath his fingertips. "I expected more resistance from you."

"All roads have been leading to these End-Times since the beginning. It is futile to try to avoid it."

"That is another area where I am thankful that we differ. We do not bow down to futility."

"Oh, yes. Hope," Math said with a note of mockery.

"Make peace with yourself," Decebalus said.

He sprinted along the empty corridors towards Doctor Jay's laboratory. As he neared, he could feel the raw power of the Caraprix pulsing through the stone walls.

Seth stood before the broken door of the chamber, bathed in an eerie white light that emanated from within. With the shifting tones playing across his face, the god appeared mesmerised by what he saw in the laboratory, and that, in itself, troubled Decebalus: what power could instil wonder in a god? Behind him, the Redcaps shied away, refusing to look. The Lament-Brood stood in their dumb ranks, unmoved.

"You cannot have them," Decebalus said.

Seth's dark-ringed, unblinking eyes snapped towards him. "You do not know what they are," he said. "If you did, you would not be so quick to defend them."

"I know that you and your master want them, and that is enough for me."

"I have destroyed many Fragile Creatures today, and gods, and beasts. Yet you stand here alone?" Seth fought to stop his gaze being drawn back to the pulsing white light.

"You have never faced anyone like me."

Ringing with more than bravado, Decebalus's words gained Seth's full attention. When he noticed the small iron casket his mood became darker, as though he knew instinctively what lay within. "What is that?" he said.

"This is the end of you, of me, of everything here. It is the weapon I kept in reserve, the one I did not want to use until you drove me to it." The light from the open door changed in quality as if the Caraprix too were aware of Decebalus's intent.

Seth stared at the box.

"I am only a poor, muddy-arsed barbarian from the wilds of Dacia with no schooling and only my common guile to keep me alive, but wiser men tell me that what lies within this box is a Wish-Hex."

A shadow crossed Seth's face.

"This weapon was devised by the bastards in the stinking bowels of the Court of the Final Word. It has the power to bend reality, to ensnare, if you will, or to destroy, and to destroy on a massive scale, or so I am told. This is only a little baby of a Wish-Hex—not like the one those bastards embedded in the boy, Jack, who accompanies Church. But still, I think it will suffice."

"You would not use it. You would not survive."

Decebalus pretended to consider this point, then said, "You gods do not live in the shadow of death, like Fragile Creatures do. It is the thing that defines us. An encounter with death changes us forever, the passing of a loved one, a parent, like the stones the alchemists used to turn lead into gold. We become something sadder, but greater for the experience. Death is a companion to us, and sooner or later we must make our peace with him. I did that a long time ago." He held the box up to eye-level and examined the carvings around it. "I have been told that wish is an old word for soul. Now what do you think that means? Is this a small part of Existence, with all the power that lies in it? I think perhaps it is."

"The Caraprix—"

"If they are destroyed too, then so be it. At least your foul lord will not use them to ensure his unending rule."

There was movement in the room. A shadow emerged slowly from the brilliant light: Jerzy, not conscious, was suspended a few inches above the floor. The light wrapped around him and entered him through eyes, mouth, ears and nostrils.

Seth lunged for the box, and without a second thought Decebalus tore open the lid. His defiant battle cry was drowned out by a deafening roar that made his ears bleed. A brilliant blue light flooded the corridor, and for a second, that was all Decebalus could see, until, strangely, he was walking hand-in-hand with Aula through the forests of Dacia. He was at peace, for the first time. Aula smiled at him, and that was all he knew.

5

Into the Great Plain wound a column of Brothers and Sisters of Dragons, gods and inhabitants of the Court of the Soaring Spirit, stragglers racing from the city to join the tail end. When the soundless blue flare lit up the sky, they came to a halt and glanced back only to see that the city and part of the mountain behind it were gone.

Aula stared at the barren, blackened zone for a long moment, and then wiped away a stray tear. Holding her head proudly, she nodded to Ronnie who waited with Mahalia and Crowther, and the column continued slowly on its way.

6

Rough hands dragged Callow's head from the water. He was briefly distracted by the sensation of the wriggling razor-worms disengaging from his empty eye sockets, and then he cried, "Oh, thank you, oh, thank you! I knew you'd come back for me. Forget about the eyes! They'll grow back in no time, and I'll be as good as new! I forgive you. I accept my punishment for my minor misdemeanour—"

"You encountered the Brother and Sister of Dragons?"

The voice was low and rustling, and inhuman. "Who are you?" Callow asked hesitantly.

"The Hortha."

"Ah. And what is a Hortha?"

"You should know. I have been a step behind you your whole life."

"I think perhaps I would have noticed."

"No. Your kind never notices."

"Perhaps, kind sir, you could help me down from this undignified position, and then we could talk as old friends—"

"My nature is a paradox for all living things," the Hortha said. "Some cross my path at random. Some call me to them, consciously or otherwise. And some I pursue. Once I have been encountered I can never be stopped. It is only a matter of time."

"Why, this sounds like a riddle! What am I? I do like riddle games. Perhaps if I guess correctly, you could reward me in the age-old fashion? In this case, by bringing me down to earth."

"Random or purposeful, that is usually the question that follows me," the Hortha continued. "There is a pattern. There is always a pattern. You can beg and plead, make a bargain with your gods, you can try to bribe and cajole me, or run faster, or hide, or wish, but the pattern can never be changed. And I am bound into the very fabric of it, into the weft and the weave. I have all faces and I have two faces, and in the end I have only one. I am both a being and a symbol."

"Good! Good! I like this. I think I am almost there! Give me another clue."

"Tell me what you learned from the Brother and Sister of Dragons."

"I learned that they are vicious beasts, and that everything they say about their own nature is a lie!"

The Hortha began to lower Callow's head back into the water.

"Wait! Wait! You want information! I understand. A valuable nugget, something that will help you to find them, perhaps? Or . . . Ah, I have it! Something that will give you power over them. Knowledge is power! Yes, indeed."

"Continue."

"They carry a lantern that is not a lantern. Within it is one of their own kind, a genie in the lamp, one who has two faces like yourself—a man and a blue flame! And he is the key to everything they do. Not just their guide, but also a manifestation of that sickening Pendragon Spirit," Callow gabbled. "Is that the kind of thing you want?"

"Yes. It is."

"Then bring me down, my good man!"

Once again, the Hortha began to lower Callow into the water.

"Wait! My reward!"

"You have your reward. You have crossed my path and still you survive. Others, in a similar situation, would not have survived. On this occasion, the great forces of all there is have shifted around you and moved on."

"No!" Callow shouted.

"You still do not understand your good fortune. That, in itself, is unfortunate."

Allowing Callow's head to drop back into the water, the Hortha moved on. The razor-worms returned to their eternal task, and Callow to his screams.

7

Alone in the stifling heat of the room, Church worked at the rope around his wrists fastening him to the chair. Blood slicked the fibres and a deep ache jabbed towards his elbows, but he ignored the pain, focusing instead on Ruth and everything she meant to him.

The Libertarian had grown bored with tormenting him long ago, but that only made Church more anxious, for now his other self might be with Ruth, exacting his promise of torture. Church couldn't think about that, nor his other doubts: did the Libertarian's departure mean his future-self knew Church would not escape, or was this another of his memory blank spots? Where was his sword? Was Veitch already saving Ruth, while he was trapped there impotently? Was that a scream he had heard echoing through the wall, or just his imagination? If he allowed himself, he could get lost in the questions and the infinite permutations.

Focus on the now, he told himself. He used the pain in his wrists to clear his head.

The lamps and candles fizzed as they attempted to keep the dark at bay. Sweat coated his body. But still the rope would not give.

8

"Shouldn't we have a rope or something, or chalk so we can scribble some arrows, or some other shit like they have in all those old stories?" Veitch asked uneasily as they picked their way through the twists and turns of the dusty tunnels beneath the queen's palace. Bearskin and Shadow John had found two torches to light their way, but they revealed no distinguishing features on the stone walls.

"My nose will lead us back out," Bearskin said, before adding with a hesitance that masked a touch of distaste, "Fragile Creatures have a distinct aroma."

"You can smell the woman?" Shavi asked.

"Not yet. But when our paths cross . . ."

Shavi's hand jerked to his alien eye.

"Seeing things?" Veitch asked.

"Just flashes . . . flickers on the edge of my vision. It happens like that sometimes. I cannot tell what they are until they come into focus."

Bearskin held up a hand to bring them to a halt. "I smell . . . something." He listened intently. "The beast still roams this place, but not near, not yet."

As if in response to his words, a low, mournful growl echoed along the tunnels from deep within the Labyrinth, but Veitch understood that the odd acoustics of the place could mean it was much closer than it sounded. He drew his sword in readiness. "How do we know it hasn't already eaten the girl?" he asked.

"We do not," Bearskin replied.

Stooping to avoid scraping his top hat along the tunnel roof, Shadow John peered nervously into the dark. "'Pon my soul, this place is dismal. Can you smell the rotting bodies of the recently departed, Bearskin? How far am I from the parlours I usually inhabit. How very disturbing this all is. At least we have two Brothers of Dragons to save us."

Veitch and Shavi exchanged a don't count on it look.

For the next hour they stumbled around the maze of branching tunnels and dead ends, clambering over piles of rubble or wading through ankle-deep pools of water. Occasionally blasts of warm air threatened to extinguish their torches and Bearskin and Shadow John fought to shield them with their bodies. The origins of the air currents were unknown, but suggested some shift in the Labyrinth's structure, or the opening and closing of doors to the outside.

At every junction, Bearskin's nostrils flared as he searched for telltale scents, and at one he let out a low growl. "More of those skull-headed warriors have entered the Labyrinth," he said, one hand unconsciously going to his blunderbuss.

Their journey was repeatedly punctuated by the low, mournful sound of the beast that lived there, sometimes so distant it was barely audible, sometimes unnervingly close at hand making Shadow John jump and shiver, his long fingers folding into claws.

Finally the endless blur of grey tunnels gave way to a hexagonal area about twenty-five feet across. In the centre of the space was a pile of yellowing human bones arranged in a circular pattern with a hollow at the centre.

Bearskin plucked a thighbone from the heap and gave it a cursory examination before tossing it over his shoulder. "A nest," he said.

Shavi spun swiftly. "Something is here." He came to a halt before one of the six tunnels that led away from the nest. "Gone now."

The mournful growl of the beast issued from another tunnel, so close it raised the hairs on Veitch's neck.

"Hurry, now!" Bearskin insisted. At a rapid pace, he led the way into the opposite tunnel, before a crash of bones and the sound of pursuit echoed behind them. Though the echoes were disorienting, Veitch was sure the beast moved on four feet, but it occasionally issued a rasping laugh that was eerily human. It was fast, drawing closer.

"We're going to have to stand and fight," Veitch gasped.

"Not advisable," Bearskin shouted back. The flames of his torch trailed behind him as he loped, and to Veitch he now looked more animal than man.

Somehow they avoided dead ends as they ducked this way and that down the many tunnel options presented to them, but the beast at their back never slowed. The rasping laugh came faster, accompanied now by the gnashing of teeth.

"Get set now," Bearskin roared furiously, "and run as fast as you can!"

As they raced past the point where another tunnel crossed their path, Veitch glimpsed the pale forms of the Aztec warriors approaching from their left. A moment later the tunnel reverberated with a terrible rending and tearing accompanied by the beast's human laughter as it attacked the warriors.

By the time Bearskin brought them to a halt, the beast no longer followed. Resting his hands on his knees, Veitch filled his searing lungs, but Bearskin was already pacing around, sniffing the air.

"We are nearly there. Yes, I think we are!" he exclaimed. He set off again, and after a few more minutes they proceeded down a short stretch of tunnel that ended in roof-fall. Crouched at the foot of the rubble, hugging her knees and whimpering, was Rachel. Her tear-stained face was streaked with dust and her clothes were dirty. She cried out as Bearskin approached her.

"Let me," Veitch said.

Her blinking eyes recognised on some level that they were the same species, but the fear held her in thrall for several moments.

"You," she said weakly. "I saw you...when I first arrived in this...in this..." She gulped a mouthful of air. "Awful place." Breaking into wracking sobs, she collapsed into Veitch's arms.

He held her tightly until her crying subsided. "Yeah, this place can be a nightmare until you realise how it works. But we'll soon get you back on your feet."

"Home," she said. "Take me home. Please."

"First thing, we need to get you out of these tunnels. Can you walk?"

Nodding, she appeared to see the Labyrinth for the first time. "I don't know how I got here. It's all a blur since I last saw you."

Helping her to her feet, he briefly introduced her to the others, though she shied away from Bearskin and Shadow John and refused even to look at them.

"Understandable," Bearskin said. "Fragile Creatures find it difficult to adjust to the wonders of the Far Lands, if they ever do."

"I do not understand how she got here," Shavi whispered to Veitch once they were back in the tunnels. "Only those with the Pendragon Spirit can cross to the Otherworld without paying a price, and she cannot be a Sister of Dragons."

"That's something we can work out later, if we actually get out of this hole," Veitch said.

Whimpering intermittently, Rachel stumbled along close to Veitch, occasionally reaching out to touch his arm for comfort. He was moved by how quickly she had placed her faith in him.

Following Bearskin's nose, they cautiously retraced their steps, senses attuned for the approach of the Labyrinth's guardian. At the junction of the two tunnels, the half-eaten remains of the Aztec warriors were scattered. Once the nest was far behind them, their spirits eased a little, but the beast's occasional echoing growls still troubled them and sent Rachel into paroxysms of sobs.

It felt as if they had walked miles when Bearskin announced, "We near the exit. This is the most dangerous time of all."

The words had barely left his lips when he pitched forwards to the ground, unconscious.

Shadow John let out a cry of alarm. "Something rushed by me!" He whirled round and round, but his torch revealed nothing.

Veitch prised Rachel's fingers from his wrist and drew his sword. A moment passed as they all waited tensely, and then the staccato laughter rolled out of the dark only feet ahead of them. Shadow John held Rachel tightly against him to prevent her from fleeing back along the tunnels.

"Right, you bastard," Veitch growled, raising his sword above his shoulder, "let's see what you've got."

Veitch only glimpsed a flash of the beast as it erupted from the dark into the tiny, flickering circle of torchlight: a human face, distorted across a broad head, slanting silver eyes, and then the long, lean body of a jungle cat ending in a thrashing, sinuous tail tipped with sharp quills. As it bore down on him, the mouth wrenched open to reveal three rows of snapping teeth.

"The Manticore!" Shadow John cried.

A weight crashed into Veitch's midriff as he prepared to swing his sword, slamming him into the wall and then down onto the flags, winded. It was not the Manticore, for the beast passed over him a second later, turning fluidly mid-leap to rake him with its enormous claws. Instinctively, Veitch rolled out of the way as the creature crashed to the flags, so close he could feel its hot, meaty breath on his cheek.

Disoriented, Veitch heard Shavi shouting, but his words were drowned out by the sound of Rachel's screaming. Scrambling to his feet, he had a split second to search for whatever had knocked him down before the Manticore leaped again. His legs went out from under him before he could even raise his sword. Through his shock, he just heard the last of Shavi shouting, ". . . something else here!" and then the Manticore pinned him down. The distorted human face pressed close, made worse for the lack of any intelligence in the wild eyes. Deep in its throat, the laughter rumbled and then it tore its jaws wide.

Veitch's vision was filled by the rows of teeth. Suddenly the Manticore convulsed and turned on Shadow John, whose fingers were hooked into cruel claws. The Manticore's side had been raked open.

Stepping in front of Shadow John, Veitch said, "Thanks for the help, mate, but stay back. Protect the girl."

"I see it!" Shavi called.

Veitch only had a brief impression of Shavi wrestling on the floor with something he couldn't see before he was surrounded by the Manticore's snapping jaws and rending claws. Rolling to one side, he let the sword dance instinctively, the flames painting a sizzling blue mandala in the dark.

The Manticore's laughter turned to shrieks, and it fell to the floor in a frenzy. Veitch hacked until it was dead.

Shavi continued to roll around the floor, welts and scratches mysteriously appearing across his face and hands. Shaking the daze from his head, Bearskin lifted Shavi with one hand and with the other wrenched out whatever invisible thing was clutched in Shavi's grasp. One snap of his wrist brought the struggle to an end. In his hand materialised a lifeless thing that resembled a small ape.

"The queen of the Court of Endless Horizons needs a lesson in fairness," Bearskin growled. "Two beasts instead of the one she told her contestants they faced. And invisible to boot."

Attempting to staunch his wounds, Shavi said, "So, this eye does have its uses."

Veitch clapped an arm around his friend's shoulders. "Good bit of teamwork there, pal."

"Just like the old days."

Rachel's cries ebbed away, and she looked on Veitch with the wonder only reserved for a true saviour. As he helped her to her feet, she asked with breathless respect, "Who are you?"

"South London's finest, darlin'," he replied.

Within fifteen minutes they were out of the Labyrinth. The city was still gripped by the darkness and the intermittent screams had not diminished, but now there was a new element: a slow drum-beat rolling out across the rooftops. It felt like a call to ceremony, but there was something in the quality of it that left them all inexplicably chilled.

9

After long moments of circling with not a hint of prey, the bird swooped down from the grey sky to land on a slab of granite jutting from the white slopes. The bitter wind ruffled the bird's feathers and whipped up a whirlwind of recently fallen snowflakes that was the only sign of movement on the lonely wastes.

From the niche in the rocks where he had waited with inordinate patience for the better part of half an hour, Miller made a desperate lunge. His fingers almost closed on the bird before it took frenzied flight amidst the high-pitched koo-koo-koo call that Miller had come to know so well during the last few weeks.

It had been there! His fingertips had brushed the grey feathers! And now it was gone.

He collapsed onto the granite slab, sobbing silently, his frozen fingers blue, his eyebrows and hair encrusted with snow. Miller allowed himself one moment to wallow in the despair of his failure, and then he picked himself up, brushed the snow from his trousers and trudged back up the hard-packed track to the cave. It lay on the leeward side of the mountain, protected from the worst knives of the wind, the interior contracting into a tight tunnel before opening out into a larger rock womb. The refuge served the dual purpose of containing the warmth from the small fire he kept alight with kindling from the leafless trees that scattered the lower slopes, and providing protection from the Fomorii that relentlessly prowled the entire mountain range, their oily black forms always visible against the white background.

"Sorry, guys, we'll have to delay dinner," he said breezily, warming his hands near the embers.

There was no response; Miller had only heard his own voice since the terrible plunge from the shattered bridge leading to the Groghaan Gate. Hunter, Jack and Virginia lay around the edge of the cave, their broken bones and burst organs now healed by the ministrations of Miller's hands, but still only a whisper away from death. The rise and fall of their chests was barely visible. Their eyes didn't move. Their skin felt as cold as the rock.

Once the life had returned to his fingers, he moved from one to the other, checking their vitals and, where necessary, placing a hand on their heart to let some of the thin blue glow leak out of him and into them. The healing energy was diminishing as his own strength flagged. A lack of food, the ever-present chill and the constant need to offer up the regenerative force was taking its toll. How long could he keep it up? Death tugged at Hunter, Jack and Virginia and he fought daily to keep them on the right side of life, but he only had enough energy to keep all their hearts beating, not enough to give them vitality; unless he let one of them die. Only then would he have the reserves to save the remaining two. But how could he choose? Who should he choose? If he didn't make a decision soon, his abilities would be depleted and they would all die.

"Turned out cold again!" he joked brightly before investigating the heap of bird bones for any that had not already been picked clean. He was not rewarded.

Lying down next to the fire, he added, "I'll just grab forty winks before I head out again. Don't worry. Everything is going to be fine."

10

For Ruth, only one horizon now existed in the Court of Endless Horizons and that was in the dimension of pain. It had gone on for so long, with such intensity, that it had become the medium in which her body existed, as much a part of life as the air she breathed. She occasionally found herself examining it with a Zen-like detachment, although she knew that was a response to the natural analgesics her brain was flooding through her system. Occasionally, she found herself looking down on her body from high above, seeing her arms yanked over her head and back so that the joints were in permanent agony as she lay stretched across an oaken table, now puddled with her sweat and the blood that had flowed from the thousand tiny cuts made by the obsidian knife. Some went deeply into the muscle tissue, and though she knew the Pendragon Spirit would heal them rapidly, she also realised that Tezcatlipoca would not give her that opportunity. Death would be coming soon.

From her vantage point, she saw Tom, tearful at her suffering, held with a knife at his throat in one corner of the large hall near the top of one of the city's highest buildings, and Laura beside him, her face pale and blank, a spear levelled at her side.

Don't be sad for me, she thought, obliquely. I can survive this. I can survive anything.

Vast windows ran along all four walls, which would once have offered a great vista across the entire city and captured every sunrise and sunset. Now only black lay without. The hall was filled with ranks of the Aztec warriors, their spears banging against the stone flags with each beat of the drum. Ruth knew the beat matched that of her heart, steady, but soon it would be slowing. Soon it would stop.

Where's Church? The notion floated up, detached from any context, and then, Where's Ryan?

In a rare moment of clarity, she realised her instinctive use of the Craft had pulled the essential part of her from her body. A flash of pride came and went: she had never before achieved that state without her ritual and her herbs.

Is this what I'm capable of? From thought to action in the blink of an eye? Is this what we all could do? All that potential in every person. It's a shame I'll never find out.

It didn't matter; in her spirit-form she always had a different perception of what was important, of life and death, and the part all the elements played in what she had heard described as the Great Mystery.

This is what Shavi meant about the patterns, she realised. Rise above it and it all makes a different kind of sense.

Beneath her, Tezcatlipoca raised the obsidian knife again. Ruth was pleased she could no longer smell his decomposing flesh, and she had no desire to witness her body put under more duress so she took her previous thought literally: Rise.

Up to the ceiling, she floated, and then through it into the chamber above, and up until she was inside the dense darkness that enveloped everything. Part of her wanted to keep rising, up past the darkness, past the sky, to search for that welcoming tunnel of light she had heard of so many times, and to see again all those people she missed so dearly.

But she couldn't allow herself to do it, and instead she swooped down so fast that the buildings passed in a blur. When she reached street level, she moved along inches above the cobbles, enjoying the familiar exhilaration. At speed, she ranged through the city, seeing Tezcatlipoca's warriors prowling the deserted streets, slipping into buildings where their victims lay in a jumble and feeling a surge of guilt that she had been indirectly responsible for their deaths; then investigating the other homes and shops, towers, halls and warehouses still packed with the trembling, fearful mass of people who had no idea what was happening around them, but who knew that death was creeping closer. Their faces burned through her dreamlike state and ignited a fierce desire to protect them. She could never give up while a single one remained alive.

The others, she thought. Where are they?

And then the streets and buildings of the Court of Endless Horizons passed in a blur as she searched every corner at speed. Finally she came across Veitch, Shavi, Bearskin, Shadow John and Rachel weaving through an alley to avoid an Aztec patrol as they made their way back to the café where they had arranged to meet Church.

As she floated above them, her hazy mind accepted the futility of what she was doing, for in that state she could neither touch nor be heard or seen. Yet to her surprise, Shavi's head snapped up when she came lower and he stared into her face with a shocked expression.

"Ruth?"

Veitch looked at him askance. "Are you on the mushrooms again?"

"You can see me?" Ruth asked.

Holding off Veitch, who was urging him to move on quietly, Shavi smiled and pointed to his eye. "This thing is proving a better investment than I ever hoped. What are you doing?"

"You have to come quickly," she said. "He's killing me."

"Who is?"

"The god who's taken control of the city. He's been trying to flush us out." She glanced at Rachel. "And, I think, find her. He said he used to be known as . . . Tezcatlipoca?"

Worry underlined the recognition in Shavi's face. "One of the most important gods to the Aztecs. This darkness makes sense now—he ruled the night, and death, and he loved tempting people to do great evil."

"He's got me, and Laura and Tom in one of the tall buildings in the middle of the city. If you can follow me, I can take you straight there."

11

With every beat of the drum reverberating through the walls and floor, Church felt his anger ratcheting up. From the moment it started, he knew it was counting out the remaining moments of Ruth's life, each *thoom* bringing a flash of the woman he loved in pain; he saw each cut, each beating, each agonised expression as if he were standing next to her. The images seared into his mind and pushed him towards the brink of madness.

With his exertion in the heat of the rows of lamps and candles, he had sweated himself dry. He could no longer feel his wrists. The constant drip-drip-drip into the puddle on the floor matched the drum's steady rhythm.

Occasionally his dread for Ruth shifted into blind, red hatred for the Libertarian, who swayed before his mind's eye with his sickeningly mocking grin, and his lies and his contempt, the architect of all his misery. Church knew he could kill the Libertarian without a second thought, the realisation no less troubling than the conundrum of whether it would be murder or suicide.

Thoom. Ruth. Thoom. Ruth. Thoom.

Finally the combustible mixture of dread and hatred exploded in uncontrollable rage. He half-stood, the chair rising with him, and raced backwards, crashing the seat against the wall. The force of the impact jarred every bone in his body, the wood of the upright smashing into his back, but still the rage did not diminish. In a fury, he did it again, and again, falling to the ground, struggling to pick himself up, once knocking himself unconscious.

When he was in the kind of pain he imagined Ruth was experiencing, he heard a loud crack. Barely able to think straight, he slammed into the wall one more time and the chair shattered into several pieces. Stepping through his bonds, he ignored the tattered mess of his wrists and tried the door. It was open. Caledfwlch stood outside.

Stupid, he thought. Do you really think that little of me?

Working the rope against the blade, he was free within a moment and lurching quickly down the corridor towards the drum-beat. His head spun and every fibre of his body ached, but his hatred kept him going.

A maze of stairs and corridors passed in a blur until he found himself stepping out into a small gallery overlooking a great hall filled with several ranks of Aztec warriors. All else faded into a mist when his gaze fell on Ruth, bound to a table on the other side of the hall, either unconscious or dead, her body leaking blood from numerous wounds. The boom of the drum reverberating in the pit of his stomach only added to his queasy despair.

A twitch of Ruth's hand allowed his rage to surface once more, and though the Libertarian was nowhere to be seen—Coward, he thought—his attention fell on what appeared to be a decomposing corpse now looming over Ruth with a black knife.

At the same time, the door into the hall burst open. With a fierce yell, Veitch began to chop and hack at the Aztec Warriors.

Without a thought for his own safety, Church threw himself from the gallery into the midst of the warriors. Several fell beneath Caledfwlch before the warriors realised they were being attacked from behind, and by then Church was cutting a path through them towards Ruth.

In the enclosed space, the warriors' obsidian-tipped spears were useless, and their wooden swords were no match for Caledfwlch. The Blue Fire blazed around the blade with more ferocity than Church had ever seen before, filling his gaze, his mind.

In the chaos of battle, he caught only glimpses of the grotesque grey figure holding the knife above Ruth. His feverish prayers appeared to work, for the knife did not fall. Instead he caught sight of a mirror that appeared to smoke, and then the figure was gone and the Libertarian stood in his place, mocking Church silently.

The sight of the one he hated most in the world drove the last of his rational thoughts away, and then there was only a red haze of blood and bone and flesh as he cut through the final warriors and leaped onto the small dais where the table stood.

Despite the extent of her wounds, Ruth had already come round. She mouthed his name, other words he could no longer hear, and he had no idea why the concern in her face became fear. Slicing through her bonds, he lurched past the table towards the Libertarian.

"You're not going to hurt anybody any more!" he roared.

With a devilish grin, the Libertarian held the smoking mirror towards him, and as the smoke cleared, Church saw what could only have been the reflection of another world. In it, a hellish figure covered from head to toe in blood stared back at him, wild-eyed, in its hands a sword of Black Fire, remarkably like his own. The truth of the reflection did not touch him, or if it did, he did not care, for he advanced on the Libertarian with a renewed rage.

Behind him, he heard one of Ruth's words of power. A flash of lightning and a furious gale assailed the remaining warriors.

Oblivious to the turmoil behind him, Church advanced on the Libertarian. "I'm going to kill you," he snarled.

Someone called his name. He ignored it.

From the side of the room, another Libertarian appeared to knock the mirror from the hands of his twin where it shattered on the floor. A look of abject betrayal filled the face of the first Libertarian, but then his features began to swim.

Church was too consumed by his passions to comprehend what was happening or to wait for an outcome. As the second Libertarian darted towards the window, Church attacked his prey, even as his features began to alter back to those of Tezcatlipoca. An inhuman shriek made his head ring as the blade bit deep, the blue flames a consuming inferno. No cries for mercy would make him relent.

A troubling calm came over him, so he did not hear the thud of the sword that matched the beat of the now-silent drum. Thoom. Thoom. Thoom. The Libertarian was gone, but still Church did not stop. Whatever was before him was now an unidentifiable mass that had to be reduced to the smallest parts possible. So he continued, chopping and hacking and slicing, even when there was only a slurry spread across the dais, and a voice told him that he would never stop, because he could never be sure he could eradicate the foulness he would become. He could never change things, or make them better. He could only destroy.

Rough hands grabbed him, and by then he was too weak to resist. Caledfwlch clattered to the floor and he turned to face Shavi and Tom. Shavi was crying openly, and for some reason Tom would not meet his eyes.

Reeling, his gaze was drawn past them to Ruth, finally worried about her now that his rage had burned itself out. Suddenly he wondered if it was too late, for him, for them, for everything. Veitch held Ruth tightly, comforting her, and they were both looking at him as if he were the monster he had seen reflected in the smoking mirror.

CHAPTER EIGHT
THE WARP ZONE

1

In the ample shade of the roof garden, the ferns, olive trees and date palms swayed in the hot desert wind and the shocking pink and electric-blue tropical blooms released a luxuriant perfume that attracted bees and enormous butterflies. A sense of peace enveloped Church for the first time in weeks. Sipping the hot, spicy tea the grateful citizens brought him, he turned his face to the sun and closed his eyes.

"It's so good to have it back." Rachel sat opposite him, sheltering beneath a large parasol. She, too, had found her first degree of peace in the Far Lands.

"We take too many things for granted until they're gone."

The darkness had risen from the Court of Endless Horizons the moment Tezcatlipoca had been defeated. Church wasn't wholly sure that the god was dead—the vile slurry remaining after he had hacked the body to pieces had vanished shortly after, along with the fragments of the smoking mirror—but it was clear they had bought themselves some breathing space.

The city's diverse inhabitants had gradually emerged blinking into the light, barely able to believe that the immediate crisis had passed, while recognising that the larger one remained; at least the dark had hidden the Burning Man's fiery glare. Soon the streets were packed to the brim once again, despite the numbers slaughtered by Tezcatlipoca's followers.

While the city had quickly returned to the chaos that passed for normal, the tensions amongst the Five had not gone away. Church had found his equilibrium quickly, but Ruth was understandably taking longer to recover from her ordeal, and had insisted on resting alone in a room, refusing all Church's attempts to talk with her. Veitch, Shavi and Laura had been caught in numerous intense discussions, the conversation drying up whenever Church approached, and he had felt their eyes on him wherever he went, as if he would somehow pick up his sword and attack them all with the fury he had shown Tezcatlipoca.

"I am not the Libertarian!" he had shouted at one point, but that only appeared to make them more unsettled, and his inability to show any regret for his brutality or to temper his desire to kill the Libertarian only compounded their suspicions.

Tom had attempted to offer advice and guidance, but Church was not in the mood; time was running out and he was more intent on departing the city and completing his plan as soon as possible.

"This place is unbelievable," Rachel said, her face set, her eyes hard; a great deal of anger was locked inside her. "It's like a dream and a nightmare wrapped up in one. All this beauty, and so much horror at the same time." She focused on a flower, which moved slowly before lunging for a passing bird. "I keep feeling I've been here before, when I was a child."

"Everyone feels that way when they come here for the first time. I don't know why that is—maybe children dream of this place, or they've got some innate connection to it that we lose as we get older."

"Thank you for helping me." Askance, she eyed him, weighing his nature, still not wholly sure. "The elderly man . . . Tom? . . . he told me all about you. I'm not sure how much I believe. But thank you anyway."

"No problem. The next thing we need to do is get you home."

"You can do that? I was afraid I'd be stuck here forever."

"We can try. How did you get here?"

"I don't know where to start." She tugged at the fibres of her dirty jeans for a moment, and then said, "I'm twenty-eight. I've had more jobs than you'd possibly believe—dog groomer, checkout girl, waitress. I'm just one of those people who doesn't feel at home in anything. Always out of sorts. An outsider. Do you know?"

He nodded.

Deep in thought, she remained silent for an uncomfortable amount of time, and then pointed to a scar near her eye. "You see that? I was living in London with this guy. Scott. He used to knock me around, usually when he'd had a bad time at work, or when the car broke down. Or when his team lost. I kept making all these elaborate plans to leave him. Sometimes that's all I'd do—dream up different scenarios, night and day. And I never went anywhere. How pathetic is that?"

238

"It's more complex than that."

"Maybe I deserve this place," she said to herself.

Church leaned towards her sympathetically. "Please—"

She pointed a finger at him aggressively. "Don't patronise me or pity me."

"Okay." He sat back.

"One day I started to notice all these weird things happening. Spiders everywhere." She shuddered. "It was like I couldn't turn around without seeing them. I started to think I was going crazy. All the stress with Scott and the worry had pushed me over the edge. Then this homeless guy came up to me in the street. Filthy, like he was covered in engine oil. And he reeked! He started to rant at me. I can't remember what he said . . ." A hand involuntarily went to her forehead. "It's all foggy. Whether it was that, or the spiders, I just flipped. I went back to the flat, packed a bag and ran out, there and then. All that time planning and I did it on the spur of the moment."

"Where did you go?"

"Salisbury."

"Why Salisbury?"

She laughed bitterly. "More proof that I'd gone nuts. Do you believe in coincidences?"

"Not really."

"For days, everywhere I went, Salisbury kept popping up, along with the spiders. Turn on the TV—something about Stonehenge, an archaeologist being interviewed in Salisbury. Somebody stops me in the street, asks which station for trains to Salisbury. I get a pamphlet through the door for double-glazing—the head office is in Salisbury. This is going to sound stupid, but at the time it felt like—"

"The universe was giving you a message."

"Yeah."

"Some people are receptive to that, some aren't."

"So, you're saying the universe was giving me a message?" she said mockingly.

Church recognised the flicker of uneasiness he saw behind her facade, and recalled the mounting panic that had risen on the day he realised the universe was not at all as he had imagined. "Something else strange happened to you in Salisbury?"

She shook her head, embarrassed now she was verbalising things that had made a half-sense in her head. "Dreams . . . some exactly the same, some with the same sort of feel. There was always a little Afro-Caribbean boy in there. He never spoke, but he always acted like he knew me. Then, one day, I saw him in the middle of town. It was like he was watching me. Yeah, it spooked me. I looked away, and when I looked back he was gone. I was already on edge in case Scott rolled in looking for me, though there was no real way he could have found me.

"After that, the boy kept turning up everywhere, and the dreams kept on going too, and I was starting to feel really creepy. It was in my mind all day, and I was worrying about going to sleep every night. So I decided to confront him—get it out of my system once and for all, and prove there was nothing supernatural about it."

The realisation of what that decision had cost her brought a queasy expression. Church poured her another hot drink.

"Turned out he was a nice kid, told me his name was Carlton. He didn't know anything about the dreams. Pretended he didn't. But he knew lots of things about me that he couldn't possibly have known, and he said he needed to show me something. I gave him a grilling, said I wasn't going to go, but he was just a kid, you know?" She looked out across the desert where the Morvren were circling. "God, it feels like all that happened to a different person, and it was only a day or so ago. I drove him a little way out of town to this place . . . Woodhenge? Not the stones. It was just a few concrete posts in a field as far as I could see."

Church nodded. "It doesn't look like much, but it's one of a series of pointers that the entire area around Stonehenge and Woodhenge was a massive ritual site, one of the largest in the world."

"I never had much interest in that kind of thing."

"There's a theory that Stonehenge was a place where people conducted rituals of death, and then processed along the river to Woodhenge for a celebration of life. An archaeologist called Mike Parker Pearson from Sheffield University led a massive study there called the Stonehenge Riverside Project. He found evidence of a huge temporary living area not far from Woodhenge and lots of animal bones that suggested feasting. It's an important place."

She shrugged, dismissively. "You an archaeologist, then?"

"Once. In a past life." He wondered briefly if the patterns Shavi was always considering extended to everyone, and if, for some unseen reason, everyone was led towards the jobs they were meant to do. He loved archaeology, but after Marianne's death it had felt so unimportant. Yet many of the things he had learned during his studies had helped him in his struggles as a Brother of Dragons. Random or pattern? Meaningless or meaningful?

"I admit, I had a bit of an odd feeling when I got out of the car. The sky looked funny, and there was this sort of swirly mist away over the fields. Carlton pointed to where I should be going and I set off. . . only he didn't come with me. I called him over, but he told me to keep going—that I'd find it soon. So I walked a bit further, and when I looked back he was gone. And so was the car. And the car park. And all those concrete posts. Except, you know, the landscape looked exactly the same, all the hills and fields." The memory was still potent, and she unconsciously hugged her arms around her. "It looked like it would have done hundreds of years ago. I totally lost it, running around and screaming like an idiot. And then all the fields went too, and I was in that mist I'd noticed. And then . . ." Her glass fell and shattered on the floor as she started to hyperventilate. Church gave what comfort he could, but the tears still burned in her eyes. "I don't know what I saw! I don't know how long I was there! I just remember being aware that this thing was after me. . . this thing with a big grin, and horrible eyes, and it was moving low along the ground, and it had this sort of brown skin like a seal . . ." She caught herself, and took a deep breath. "It chased me out of the mist, and suddenly I was standing in the heat out there." She pointed into the desert where the haze shimmered. "It kept coming after me, and I ran as fast as I could. I thought I was going to die. And then I ended up here." She started to pick up the pieces of broken glass, and then hurled them across the roof terrace.

"Do you think you can find your way back to where you first appeared in the desert?" he asked.

"I don't know. Maybe. Do you think there's a way back?"

"Could be." He didn't want to raise her hopes, but his own heart was beating faster.

Leaving her there recovering in the sun, he found Tom and Ruth sitting quietly on another, smaller terrace. Ruth looked paler than he had ever seen her.

"How are you feeling?" he asked her. He hated the uncomfortable space that lay between them, and the way her eyes didn't quite meet his.

"Better, thanks. The Pendragon Spirit works wonders if you let it."

"So what wisdom have you discovered now?" Tom said acidly.

"That boy you saw on the train, Carlton, is working with the Oldest Things in the Land. Maybe he's one of them."

Tom sucked on his roll-up thoughtfully for a moment, then said simply, "Interesting."

"The Oldest Things in the Land conspired to get her here. The Puck chased her into the city. They wanted us to find her, because she can lead us back home. There's some kind of way that isn't one of the regular doors that the Army of the Ten Billion Spiders blocked."

"You're sure you're not reading into this exactly what you want?" Ruth asked.

"With her, we can find our way home!"

Ruth flashed a brief, disappointed look that stung him. "You still want to run away?"

"It's not like that . . . oh, forget it. Why don't you just trust me?"

Tom exhaled a cloud of blue smoke. "It's a good job I'm not embarrassed by your pathetic domestic issues—"

Ruth and Church turned and snapped at him at the same time: "Shut up!" He shrugged, unmoved.

"Let's get the others together," Church said. "We're moving out within the hour."

2

In the dead heat of the morning, they departed the Court of Endless Horizons, past the steady stream of refugees seeking shelter in the city. After the packed, sweltering, noisy streets, the blank, rolling wastes were a welcome relief, stilling the tense chatter of the mind and allowing them all to breathe a little easier.

Casting a threatening shadow across the ochre sands, the black cloud of the Morvren followed them, their cawing a jarring sound in the stillness that lay all around whenever the wind dropped. Lest they be lulled into a false state of overconfidence by the peace of the desolation, the scarlet, orange and gold shape of the Burning Man loomed up ahead of them against the silver-blue skyline, the outline now smudged black with greasy smoke. The closer they got to it, the more charged with dread the atmosphere became.

"What do you think it will look like when the Void fills the space?" Ruth was surprised to realise she was whispering.

"I do not think we should worry about that," Shavi replied. "Once the Void materialises, everything is over."

Soon the gleaming towers of the court and the dark line of jungle disappeared from view, and there was only the rolling dunes scarred with the line of their footprints. They sipped sparingly from their water bottles, all of them aware of the dangers of getting lost.

Leading the way, Rachel pointed to a formation of glassy volcanic rock rising from the sands about three miles distant. "I remember seeing that. I came through somewhere near there. I think."

Laura sighed loudly, eliciting a cautionary glare from Church.

Veitch joined Church shortly after, his gaze fixed firmly on the horizon. "You sure this is the best plan?"

"Have you been talking to Ruth?"

"It's just, none of us can see where this is going."

"You could trust me."

A pause. "I do. Course I do. But everything that's happened since we got here has pushed us all to the limit. I know I'm not thinking straight."

"I hear what you're saying, Ryan. So did you draw the short straw to come and get me back on the rails?"

"It's not like that."

"Because that's a little funny. Not so long ago they were all afraid you'd kill them in their sleep. Now you're the voice of reason, and I'm the bad guy."

"That's not fair."

Church regretted his words instantly. Veitch had been trying his best to make up for his past actions when he had been destabilised by the Void; he deserved better than that, and Church had to do better if he was to be the leader they needed.

"You're right, I'm sorry," he said. "I don't want to tell any of you what

I'm planning. In the Halls of the Drakusa, when we discovered that one of us is helping the enemy, that really hit hard. Once we got back together, I never thought we'd have to deal with a traitor in the group again, even after Tom got his warning from the boy on the train. Now I'm not taking any chances."

"Even though Virginia's dead?"

"I'm not sure it was her." Veitch's silence was pointed. "I'm not saying it was you. I'm not saying it's anybody. I'm just thinking it's wise not to allow any opportunities for our plans to leak out to the enemy." He added, "I don't like to think this way. Mistrust is corrosive. Maybe that's all part of the Enemy's plan—letting it eat away at our relationships and the ties that make us stronger as a group. But I can't see another way to deal with it."

Veitch appeared satisfied with this, and they fell silent again as the heat began to take its toll. Skidding down deep dunes and then climbing up through the shifting sands on the other side made their leg muscles burn and for a long while the rock formation appeared to be drawing no closer. But then they crested a steep incline onto a hardpan plateau scattered with boulders where a stronger wind blew and they saw colours shimmering in the sky like the aurora borealis. Here and there drifted strands of the pearly mist that Rachel had described.

"This is it," Rachel said, turning slowly.

"What now?" Laura asked. Everyone looked to Church.

"We go home," he replied.

3

From a distant dune, the Libertarian watched them make their way across the plateau into the mist. With the *Morvren* swirling overhead, they had been easy to follow, but with each step his anxiety had grown. More than anything he didn't want them to pass through those mists, although he did not know why: another of those annoying blank spots in his memory. He had been so sure that his manipulation of Tezcatlipoca and Church would reap the final rewards he desired, but now his control of events was slipping through his fingers like sand.

When the heat haze shimmered and Church and the others disappeared from view, he broke into a desperate run, stumbling and sliding down the dunes. Cursing, he vowed to let them know that the more desperate they made him, the more he would make them pay.

On the plateau, he didn't slow his pace and plunged into the mists after them.

4

"Stay close together," Church ordered as they moved through an area of bright, swirling colours.

"Wow, trippy," Laura said. "This reminds me of. . . okay, you had to be there."

Aware of the fear in Rachel's eyes, Shavi took her arm reassuringly. "Is this how you remember it?"

"I don't remember much at all, but it feels familiar."

"Do not fight the sensations you are experiencing," Shavi said. "If you allow yourself to go with them, it is not unpleasant."

"That's easy for you to say."

"Tom, what are you thinking?" Ruth asked, seeing Tom's serious expression.

"I'm finding this both familiar and unfamiliar too," he replied, anxiously twisting the ring Freyja had given him. "I have moved through the medium of the Blue Fire many times, across our own world between nodes of power, and between the worlds, but this is different. Yet the same."

"Yep, you lived through the sixties, old man," Laura said.

For once, Tom ignored her. "I've heard talk of this. Somewhere that bleeds around reality, around all the worlds and the connective tissue of the Blue Fire that joins them. Some occultists I encountered in San Francisco believed if you could find a way to this place you could access all places and all times."

"You could run away forever," Ruth said, eyeing Church askance.

"Or you could fight a constant guerrilla war," Church countered. "No one would know when or where you'd pop up."

"What's that?" Veitch pointed to a place where the colours appeared to have thinned so that it felt as if they were looking through a gauze onto the world. The sun was just disappearing below the horizon, casting its dying golden rays on a stone circle surrounded by trees. Beyond were well-tended fields. Figures moved in the circle, hazily coming into view.

"That's Caitlin!" Ruth exclaimed. "But she looks younger. More . . . innocent?"

"And that teenage thug Mahalia," Veitch noted. "And Crowther."

"The past," Shavi said. "Perhaps when she was just beginning as a Sister of Dragons?"

Tom and Rachel hung back, but he flinched and stepped forward when he glimpsed the young boy he had encountered on the Last Train who Mahalia had sworn was dead. Eerily, the boy appeared to be looking directly at him, and smiling knowingly, as if he was aware of all that was to transpire.

Caitlin looked directly at them too, but didn't recognise them, and then the colours swirled back in and the scene was lost.

"I have a feeling we could have gone right there if we'd carried on walking," Church said.

"Caitlin wouldn't need us," Ruth said confidently. "Whatever happened back then, I bet she dealt with it, no problem."

They moved on through an environment that felt both timeless and placeless, the hallucinogenic colours giving the sensation that they were floating. For the briefest moment, Church once again felt as if he was lying on a table, locked inside his own mind, with the odd belief that a group of people were observing him.

"Don't investigate that notion," a voice deep in his head told him. "What you have is better. It will always be better."

Scenes came and went: Celts fighting a furious battle, a World War II pilot standing beside his downed Spitfire, a thick, semi-tropical jungle through which barely glimpsed beasts moved, a castle under siege, a Victorian funeral.

Several times Veitch witnessed himself committing some atrocity in service to the Void and turned away, unable to look. Once he had to be restrained by Church from leaping through the veil to right the wrongs he saw there.

When Laura glimpsed Hunter fighting a furious battle with the Lament-Brood in a past time, she broke down in long, juddering sobs. Nothing the others did could console her.

"I'm concerned we might get lost in here forever," Tom said.

The Rhymer's voice sounded oddly distant and when Church turned, Tom was fading into the swirling colours. It felt like only a step or two away, but when Church dashed back, Tom and the others were nowhere to be found.

There was little point searching in a place that appeared to have no dimension. Putting his trust in fortune, Church continued to walk in the direction he had been following; if they were meant to reunite in the world, he was sure it would happen. If this was a road he had to walk alone, that was fine too. Go with the flow, Tom would have said, followed by some rambling tale of the West Coast in the sixties, but Church felt it was an important lesson he had been taught many times during his long journey.

In the colours, any sense of time passing was lost. It could have been five minutes or an hour when he heard a voice saying, "What is the point of the world?" It was the same voice Church had thought came from deep in his head when he had the impression of lying on a table, but now it appeared to be coming from all around him.

"Where is the meaning in life?" the voice continued.

"Who are you?" Church asked.

"What is real?"

"You don't sound like Tom, but you've mastered his degree of irritation," Church muttered.

"These are the only important questions," the voice said. "Once you consider them, all else flows from them. The answers may seem impossible to find, but it is the same as with any story: the author embeds keys in the text to help the careful reader decipher the true meaning. The rules that apply to the tiniest thing also apply to the greatest. The flower dies, but grows back the next season. Energy cannot be destroyed; it simply changes shape. What does this say for death? And is man a random collection of atoms, like a tree, or a rock, even though his nature is so very different from everything else in the world? In that nature, the key is writ large for all to see if they will only look. The nature of a being is the purpose of a being. If man has the capacity to find meaning, then there is meaning to find."

"Is this for my benefit, or is everybody getting the travelogue?" Church recognised a quality to the voice; once again it appeared to be coming from within his head.

"Is reality a model of a town laid out on a table-top, with each house representing an adjoining world? Is each world a school for souls as John Hicks proposed, and as it was taught to the Knights Templar in the Fortress of Salisbury? How is a world created? By a powerful being? A god? Or in the head of a man, lying on a table, in the last seconds of his life?"

Church flinched. "What are you saying? That all this is my dying dream? That it's all meaningless?"

"And so I return to the three questions: what is the point of the world? What is the meaning in life? What is real?"

Church fought his annoyance at the barrage of questions and considered them for a moment. "A long time ago, I was told that I couldn't be given all the answers—I had to earn them, because only by doing that would I become the person able to utilise that information. Is this part of that? More teaching, but work out the damn answers for myself?"

He walked on a few paces in ringing silence, and then the voice said, "Nothing is fixed in the Fixed Lands. Everything is fluid."

"Yes, I changed reality. I brought Tom and Niamh back." What is real? he thought. He made a new reality. And then: energy cannot be destroyed; it simply changes shape.

Other voices began to echo all around, some familiar, some unrecognised. "We are all stars." That sounded to him like Niamh. "Love turns Fragile Creatures into gods." Niamh again.

"So this is a puzzle?" he said, before adding, "Everything I've been through is a puzzle, right? Like those complex traps that guarded the four great artefacts—the Sword, the Spear, the Cauldron, the Stone. We had to solve them before we got our reward." The rules that apply to the tiniest thing apply to the greatest. "So the keys are embedded in the text of life. Of my life. There's another story behind everything I've been experiencing."

The colours shifted, and for the briefest moment he felt as if he was in a room with opposing mirrors so there were images of him reaching out to infinity; yet each was slightly different—in dress, or in whatever action they were engaged in. It was swallowed up by another flash of him, lying on the table.

"What is real?" he muttered again. "What is real is what's on the inside, not what's around us. That's where the truth lies, where the meaning can be found. Is that what you're saying? We can create our own realities, which are as real as what we perceive to be real around us. We are all stars. We are all gods. So we don't look to the world for answers, because it's fake...and it's real at the same time. It's just...not important. We look inside."

A transcendental sense of revelation overwhelmed him, and while he still couldn't grasp the immensity of what he was discovering, he was sure there was enough there for him to piece it together later.

He was rocked from his contemplation by the sound of running feet. Out of the colours emerged his time-looping double that he had first witnessed in Edinburgh and most recently in the Great Pyramid in Cairo.

As on their previous encounters, the future-Church wasn't shocked to come into contact with his old self. "Is this it?" he said. "Is this the right time? You have to listen to me. This is a warning." Confused, he looked around. "Is this the right place? Am I too late?"

Frustrated, Church said to his future-self, "You're not giving me enough information," even though he knew his double was locked in some constantly repeating cycle in the Warp Zone that made him appear at various points in Church's life.

"When you're in Otherworld and they call, heed it right away. They're going to bring him back. They're—" The future-Church became gripped with fear. In panic, he yelled, "Too late!" and raced away into the colours.

For the first time, the double was close to his current appearance, suggesting that whatever point he originated at was in the near future. "Okay," he said to himself, "when they call, I'll heed it. And then we'll sort out whatever's scaring you, all right?"

Church had a brief sense that someone else was nearby. He considered waiting to see what would turn up until some deep-seated instinct warned him to keep moving. Breaking into a jog, the colours streamed by him.

Am I dying? he thought. Is this just some reality I've created to soothe myself in my last moments?

"That question is not important. Remember the three questions. They are all."

Church was surprised to hear the voice answering him directly for the first time. Before he could respond, the colours around him began to thin and he saw that he was, finally, running into the world.

The voice floated to him one final time, barely audible, and he realised it was his own voice. "Good luck." It faded away with the colours, and then he was jogging through a thin mist and out into a balmy summer night.

Grass lay beneath his feet, and there were trees nearby silhouetted against a sky alive with thousands of stars and a butterscotch moon, full and round, that lit up the field as if it were day. Church came to a halt and filled his lungs with the rich, cool countryside air, revelling in the aromas of hedge and field. As he looked up at the great chamber of the night, he felt an overwhelming sense of peace.

Home.

In a way he couldn't quite understand, every sensation that came to him in that beautiful evening setting reinforced what the voice had told him. His unconscious mind made connections that waited to reveal themselves. Fireflies glinted in the long grass, and as he looked out across the rolling countryside to where the lights of villages glittered, he heard the haunting call of an owl nearby. Here was everything he ever needed, every answer.

The scent of woodsmoke on the wind disrupted his reverie, and he turned to glimpse the flicker of a campfire in the middle of a dense copse. The soft buzz of amiable conversation drifted through the night, and by the time he pushed his way through the trees he knew what he would find.

Sitting around the campfire on which a spit-rabbit was slowly being turned were all the others. Ruth jumped up the minute he stepped into the circle of warm light and hugged him tightly.

"We were starting to worry you were gone for good," she said.

Church caught the brief shadow crossing Veitch's face at Ruth's show of emotion, but he quickly flashed an honest grin.

"What are you talking about? It's only been a few minutes," Church said.

"It's been a week!" Ruth said.

"Time moves differently in that place, just like in the Otherworld, you idiot," Tom muttered as he stirred a bubbling pot of aromatic herbs and hedgerow plants.

"We have been waiting here patiently for your arrival." Shavi clasped Church's hand warmly. "Despite what Ruth said, we never doubted you would catch up with us. Experience tells."

"Yeah, bad news just keeps on giving, Church-dude." Laura grinned at him lazily, hands behind her head as she lay in the shadows just beyond the firelight. "Besides, you're the man with the plan. We couldn't move on because no one knows what's rattling around in that tiny brain of yours. Unless it really is just running away and burying your head in the sand. Which I still think has a lot going for it."

Realising how hungry he was, Church sat between Veitch and Rachel and stirred the pot. "You stayed in one place? With the spiders everywhere?"

"Do you think we're fools?" Tom snapped. "We're on a major ley here. And we've seen no sign of them, or we'd be far away and you'd be damned."

Church laid one palm on the ground. Reaching deep down, he could just feel the faintest hint of buzz. "Not much of a ley. The Blue Fire is pretty dormant. Just like it was before the Fomorii invaded."

"That is the job of the Army of the Ten Billion Spiders," Shavi said. "We awaken the Blue Fire. They exert all their power to reassert the Mundane Spell and stifle the lifeblood of Existence so that it has little effect on the people who live here."

"So that's us, right—pointless?" Laura snorted. "We wake the Blue Fire. They shut it down. We wake it. They shut it down. We do all this suffering and get nowhere." Underneath her irony there was a troubling bleak note.

"That's why we have to stop the Void once and for all," Church said. "That way we change things forever."

"Yeah, stop a god." Laura laughed coldly, then rolled over so no one could see her face.

"You're all funny." Rachel laughed. "You talk about the strangest things!"

They all exchanged glances, but no one felt it necessary to illuminate Rachel on some of the harsh realities they had encountered.

"But you're good company, I'll give you that," she continued. "And you saved my life. I'm never going to forget that." She wiped away a stray tear, the strain of her recent experiences still evident.

Her gratitude was touching, and only added to the warm mood that pervaded the campsite. With the soundtrack of the fire's crackling, the breeze in the trees and the calls of the owls, Church lay back and watched the stars amongst the branches. He would have been happy to stay there forever, with his friends, and the woman he loved, in the beating heart of nature.

They'd all kept going for so long with the promise that such peace would finally await them at the end of their long, hard road, but perhaps this was the last moment they would ever have.

His lambent emotions must have played out on his face, for he caught Ruth watching him with concern. He gave her a reassuring smile. "Let's make the most of this night," he said to the group. "What's out there isn't important. What's here is real, all that matters. Let's celebrate just being alive, being together. Because tomorrow everything starts in force."

5

In the heat of the night, amidst the thick odour of petrol fumes and the regular buzz of traffic heading west along the A30, the Libertarian waited on the fringes of the stark garage lights. For every car or lorry that trundled in for refuelling, he carefully searched the faces of the drivers, filled with barely contained anger that he had no idea what he wanted to find, but convinced he would know it when he saw it, and that it was important. This time, this place. Why? His memory was increasingly and frustratingly patchy, at the point when he needed it the most. He half-recalled a distant memory of sitting around a campfire, and drove its unpleasant taint from his mind; too haunting, too destabilising.

A sleek, silver BMW rolled onto the forecourt, music blaring from the open window. The driver was slim, tanned, with well-cut, sandy hair, wearing an open-necked, light-blue shirt. At first glance, there was nothing out of the ordinary about him, but then the Libertarian caught sight of something subtle that was instantly recognisable: something in his eyes, perhaps, a hardness, too long between blinks, or the way the muscles of his face fell in an unguarded moment. He knew he had his man.

Marching over, he held out his hand. "Simon," he boomed.

"Scott," the driver responded, unsure.

"Of course. Scott. You're looking for your girlfriend. Flighty type. Ran away, left you in the lurch."

The information was so precise Scott was too taken aback to question the stranger.

"I might be able to help," the Libertarian said with a tight smile.

6

At the first light of dawn, Church led the group across the rolling grassland towards Stonehenge. The landscape was still, the rumble of traffic that blighted the ancient site for most of the day not yet rising from the constricting network of main roads. The first light gave a silvery, new-minted sheen to the countryside, with a hint of the warm, golden sun that would soon follow. As they made their way down a slope, summer mist briefly turned the world back in time to the raw, poetic age when the stones were first erected. There was only the grass beneath their feet, sparkling with dew, each step muffled by the soft, drifting mist. For a while, no one spoke, their steady breathing and the gentle melody of birdsong their only accompaniment.

Shavi breathed deeply, peacefully. That moment held all the reasons for the joy he felt at being back in the world.

"Give you a bit of nature and you're in heaven, aren't you, Shavster?" Laura's tone was gently mocking, but her expression remained unusually solemn.

"There is heaven in every aspect of this world, not just in the countryside, if you look with the right eyes. In music heard from an open window on a city street. In the play of light glinting off the windshields of cars speeding down the motorway. In the rainbows of oil in puddles on a building site."

"You're weird."

In the long pause that followed her words, he felt she was desperately seeking something from him, though he had no idea what it was. Finally, she said, "Are we just wasting our time here?"

"Given all I know of Church, I would trust him implicitly and follow him anywhere. What we initially see may not be the true picture."

"That's the point exactly. Maybe we're just a bunch of deluded, woolly-headed losers and what we think we see is just us fooling ourselves. All this power-in-the-land, magic-in-the-heart bollocks. Say it out loud. Listen to it. It sounds like one of those rants you get from the cider-addled dog-on-a-string people you find sitting on the pavement begging for money in Glastonbury."

"You have seen the evidence with your own eyes—"

"I've seen stuff, sure, but who's to say it's right? What if the Void is the right one for our world?" Her voice had a faintly glassy quality that suggested unrevealed stresses deep within.

"It is not right."

"But what if? Just having a little peace, getting a tiny bit of enjoyment out of life before we take the dirt-nap . . . what's so bad about that?"

"Nothing. Except there is the potential for a lot of peace, and a great deal of enjoyment in life. The Void wins by giving people just enough to keep them content. A little less and they would all rise up and change things. A little more and they would see the true potential of what we have, and rise up and change things. The Mundane Spell is very skilful."

"But why do we get to shake things up? Sometimes I feel like we're those revolutionaries who start out trying to make things better and end up consumed by the cause and blowing up babies on a bus."

"We have not hurt anyone—"

"Yes, we have!" She lowered her voice and looked down when Veitch cast a suspicious glance at her. "We've turned people's lives on their heads, all their little happinesses that everyone around here laughs at so much, we've seen people hurt and killed, and we've carried on regardless because we believed it was a necessary price to pay. Because we thought we had the moral high ground. We've not given them anything better to make up for their loss, just the promise of heaven around the corner. You could say there wouldn't have been any Fomorii invasion and world-turned-on-its-head if the Void hadn't been afraid the Pendragon Spirit and its Champions of Existence weren't going to upset the apple cart."

"I would say you are considering things too closely. The big picture—"

"Can't be seen, yeah, yeah, that's our great get-out clause so we don't have to face up to the consequences of our actions. Think of all the misery and suffering that's followed us around. How can we be the heroes? We're not revolutionaries, we're terrorists."

Laura wouldn't meet Shavi's eye, but she couldn't hide how close to tears she was. "It is all right to have doubts," he said gently, slipping an arm around her shoulders. "All of us have doubts at some point."

"Even you?"

"Even me. When you do not know the rules of Existence, and when you cannot see the greater patterns, all you have left is faith in yourself, and faith in your friends."

The words were meant to be comforting, but they only upset Laura more.

Stray tears ran down her cheeks and she wiped them away angrily before accepting a brief, reassuring hug, then marched off to be alone with her thoughts.

The mist turned into a dense fog as they drew towards Stonehenge. Colours glinted in droplets of moisture all around and Veitch asked uneasily, "Are we back in the Warp Zone or what?"

"I don't know, but something's not right." Church slowed the pace as they attempted to orient themselves.

"Someone's here," Ruth said.

"I don't see anyone," Veitch responded.

"I . . . feel it."

"You're using the Craft?" Church asked. "I thought it didn't work so well here when the Blue Fire is dormant."

"I don't know . . . it feels stronger, somehow. I was using it instinctively, like I learned to do in the Otherworld."

Lurching out of the dense fog, a figure brought them to a sudden halt. His long hair tied in a knot at the side of his head, he wore a fur cape over a woollen tunic that had been dyed brightly with berries. They bristled for an attack, but he grinned broadly and waved before hailing them in a musical language that only Church understood. With a flourish, he disappeared back into the fog.

"What the fuck?" Laura said.

"Iron Age Celt," Church said, recalling with a pang his time in Carn Euny almost two thousand years ago.

"In Wiltshire, now?" Ruth said.

"Something is strange here," Tom muttered. "And we are still not alone."

Footsteps circled them, ebbing and flowing through the muffling shroud of the fog so that it was impossible to pinpoint their location. But they could all tell that whoever was making them was following with caution, perhaps even a hint of threat. They drew into a tighter knot, unsettled by how fast the footsteps moved. At times they wondered if they were mistaken and it was really an animal prowling around just beyond view.

The fog folded and briefly revealed a dark shape that did not assuage their doubts; it was long and lean, moving low, so it could have been rising from all fours or falling from two feet. It loped back into the fog as soon as their gaze fell upon it.

Church drew Caledfwlch and was shocked by the whoosh! as the blue flames leaped around the blade.

"That cannot be right," Tom said. "In the times when the Void has been most dominant, the Blue Fire in this area has always been more dormant than at other sites. Human encroachment, the roads and the abuse bled the land of its sacred quality."

"Maybe," Church said thoughtfully, "the Void isn't as dominant as we thought."

The figure erupted from the mists in a whirl of limbs brandishing a weapon that moved too fast for them to see. A blow creased Church's forehead; another upended Veitch; and the final one came to rest at the skin of Ruth's throat.

Her gaze ran along the gnarled wooden staff to the just as gnarled figure holding it, arms and face mahogany-brown from the sun and wind, grey-black, greasy hair hanging lank around his head, a stained cheesecloth shirt and mud-spattered trousers and the fiercest eyes Ruth had ever seen.

Familiar eyes.

"Wait!" Shavi called exuberantly. "It is us!"

The Bone Inspector eyed them suspiciously, then slowly lowered his staff. "These are dangerous times," he growled. "Upheaval. Constant change. Damned spiders coming and going. And now...this." He nodded around him. "We're going to have all hell on us in no time." His steely gaze scanned every face until his eyes rested on Tom and a small smile sprang to his lips. "I'd heard you were dead."

"It was overrated. I came back." They hugged each other briefly like old friends.

"Two grumpy old bastards together," Laura muttered. "This is hell in stereo."

"We'd also heard you lot were gone from this world," the Bone Inspector said to the others. "I wanted to be sure you weren't some trick of the spiders. A Trojan Horse."

"Who is he?" Rachel whispered to Shavi.

"You've got nothing to fear from me," the Bone Inspector said. "Not unless you get on the wrong side of me. I watch over the old places, the burial mounds, the wells, the stone circles, the cairns. Make sure no one interferes with the treasures they've held since the old times. From Shetland to Scilly, Neath to Norfolk, I'm there. Always have been. Will be till I die."

"You said 'we.'" Church rubbed the bump on his head. "You're not alone."

"If you're here, then I suppose you need to see this." He turned and loped into the fog, and the others hurried to keep up.

After only a few yards, the fog began to thin, turning back into the low, drifting mist, now golden in the light of the dawn sun, and within a few moments that too was gone. Behind it lay a landscape that took their breath away, so ancient and wild that it appeared as if they had walked two thousand years into the past. But when he squinted, Shavi could see pylons in the distance and the air still had the taint of petrol fumes.

Stonehenge was no longer a ruin, eroded by centuries of wind and rain and man's poor stewardship. The megaliths stood tall and proud, the lintels complete, and all around the outlying stones were erect, their surfaces gleaming and smooth as though they had been hewn by the stoneworkers only recently.

A sprawling crowd faced the rising sun in silent adoration. The reinvigorating dawn rays shone brightly along the precisely aligned avenue. The people wore the Iron Age clothes of the man they had encountered in the fog, and there were young and old, men, women and children, strong and frail, all side by side in the solemn congregation.

The sun hit a point where it was framed whole and round between two stones, and a man—some kind of priest, Shavi guessed—raised his arms and called out to the sky. As one the people raised their heads. Loud drumming began instantly, a perfect, complex rhythm, but within seconds Shavi realised there was more to it than a simple celebration. The peculiar alignment of the stones created strange acoustics that amplified and distorted the pounding so that it appeared as if the stones themselves were singing to the heavens, the sound rolling and muffling, then growing louder as it shifted around the circle like a living thing. It was hallucinogenic, transcendental; though he was well away from the ritual, he was transported, and he wondered what awe those at the henge would be feeling.

When the drumming reached a crescendo, it stopped suddenly. The ringing silence was just as potent, but it only lay over the circle for a second before there was a soaring whoosh as Blue Fire burned in lines along the paths of the ancient leys. In the distance they interconnected to create the Fiery Network. Above the stone circle, the sapphire flames rushed up to create a structure that appeared to reach towards the stars, a cathedral of fire that made their chests swell and brought tears of awe to their eyes.

For a moment, they basked in the wonder of the display and then the Blue Fire washed back into hiding, but the effect it had on their emotions did not disappear. A cheer rose up from the crowd, children whooping and playing, adults hugging each other, or kissing, as they turned from the stones and made their way towards the shimmering line of the river.

As the congregation dispersed, Shavi was surprised to see several people in modern dress following the throng, their faces as alight as their ancient ancestors'.

"They'll make their way back to Woodhenge for a feast that will go on till tomorrow." the Bone Inspector grunted. "This is the Summer Solstice. A celebration of life and death, and how the two are tied together." He glanced at Tom. "Nothing ends. There is always something higher, always something beyond the horizon."

"What's happening here?" Church asked. "Those Iron Age people . . . the megaliths—"

"All time is folding together," the Bone Inspector replied. "Don't ask me how, but I hear this is how it is in the Otherworld."

Rachel wiped the tears from her cheeks. If anything, she had been more affected by the sight than the others. "I never guessed," she whispered. "So much potential . . . all around us. And we never saw it."

"It won't last long," the Bone Inspector said. "The Army of the Ten Billion Spiders won't let it. Things like this could destroy the Mundane Spell in a minute. Once you've seen this, why go back to your offices?"

"We can't let that be destroyed!" Rachel said desperately.

"Then you need to get busy," the Bone Inspector said, "because you lot are the only people who can stop that happening."

"The Brothers and Sisters of Dragons, you mean?" Rachel enquired.

"Humans." He turned back to Stonehenge. "Come on. There are people you need to meet."

7

As they passed through the fringes of the crowd streaming towards the river, the mood of exuberance was infectious. Once their dress was forgotten, Church could have believed they were all from the modern world enjoying the festivities of some summer carnival. Many hailed him and the others as they went by and entreated them to join them at the feast.

The Bone Inspector was untouched. Keeping his head down, he marched past the last of the crowd towards Stonehenge. Electricity filled the air as they walked between the megaliths of the outer circle and into the heart of the ring. Amongst the stones, ten men talked quietly. Most were in their fifties, though a couple were very elderly indeed. They wore grey robes tied with a cord at the waist, and on their heads were circlets of oak and ivy.

Church recognised their dress from his time in Carn Euny. "The Culture?" he said, referring to the secretive society that had guarded the knowledge of nature and the Blue Fire since ancient times. "I thought most of them were wiped out during the Roman invasion."

"You and me both," the Bone Inspector growled. "I always thought I was the last of them. But then a few days ago, they reappeared."

One of them came over eagerly the moment he saw them. He was in his sixties, tall, with piercing grey eyes, a totemistic staff indicating he was the leader of the group.

"Brothers and Sisters of Dragons!" he said, shaking each of their hands in turn. "We never expected to see you here! My name is Matthias, leader of the Culture." He nodded to the Bone Inspector. "Brother, you were wrong."

"Sometimes I am, and this time I'm glad."

"Walk with us," Matthias said. "Join the feast."

"We've got work to do—" Church began, but Tom interrupted him.

"Not so fast. You might learn something."

A note in Tom's voice suggested the Rhymer had some hidden knowledge. "You've seen something in the future," Church said.

Tom nodded slowly. "I've seen a lot of things. This is the last step of the journey. Don't go rushing to finish it up too quickly. Savour it. Besides, it's the Solstice. The Blue Fire swirling around beneath Stonehenge is at its peak. You don't want to be going down there until it's abated, a little at least. Tonight will be fine."

"You want to go beneath Stonehenge?" Ruth said.

Church couldn't answer. He looked briefly from face to face, searching for any hint of potential betrayal, and finally his gaze came to rest on Tom, who recognised what was going through Church's head and looked away, disgusted.

"Come on," Tom said. "I'm hungry, and I need a rest and a smoke."

They joined the tail of the group processing along the river towards the Durrington Walls henge and the nearby Woodhenge. It was going to be a beautiful day. The sky was a clear blue and an age-old peace lay over the fields, copses and hedgerows; five thousand years wrapped up in one moment. Church wondered briefly if the magical transformation that had come over the site had something to do with the power infused into the land through generations of reverence, a store of sacred energy that, right at the end of time, had started to transmit.

His thoughts were brought to a halt by their arrival on a ceremonial path leading from the river into a bewildering chaos of noise and activity. For thousands of years the site, unlike Stonehenge, had been buried beneath the rolling Wiltshire countryside. Now temporary roundhouses and ramshackle huts stood side by side, specially constructed for the Solstice celebrations of life and death as they had been in the distant past. Within a week they would all be dismantled, the tribes that had gathered there returning to their homes across Britain, and even across the sea to mainland Europe.

It reminded Church of the Glastonbury Music Festival, families and friends gathered in small communities amongst the larger sprawl of their people, campfires everywhere, the smell of cooking food, impromptu music performances with drum and voice, and a general sense of celebrating life.

The contemporary people Church had witnessed earlier wandered around the camp in a dream, welcomed by their ancestors and called to the fireside where they were offered meat carved from the roasting animals.

Shavi beamed. "If only it was always like this."

While Shavi took Rachel, Ruth, Laura and Veitch to explore the camp, Matthias and the other members of the Culture guided Church and Tom to a peaceful enclosure slightly removed from the chaos. Allowing himself one backward glance as Veitch took Ruth's arm, Church fought a pang of jealousy.

In a roundhouse, beside a fire, a warm herb infusion was served in wooden bowls while the Culture sat on the straw. Church was increasingly concerned about Tom, and couldn't shake the feeling that the Rhymer was receiving visions he didn't want, or couldn't bear, to share. Occasionally, he would drift into a reverie, jerking himself alert a moment later with tears in his eyes.

"It is good to be back in the world," Matthias said when all had received their drinks. "Our society has existed since the dawn of mankind. You knew of us, True Thomas, before you were stolen from your home, but by then we were only spoken of in whispers."

"I could have done with you then. We all could have over the last few centuries," Tom said. "We were left alone, without teachers. That made us children trying to find our way in a dangerous world."

"If we could have found a way to survive here, we would have," Matthias replied. "But it wasn't gods or beasts who tried to destroy us, it was our own kind. Fragile Creatures. The seekers of power. The warmongers. Our work was to cater to the spiritual needs of the people, to guard the knowledge they need to grow and prosper, and to stand as sentinels, and guides, to the invisible worlds that cluster close to our own. We were a tremendous force for good, yet we were seen as a threat by those who wanted control."

"The Void saw you as a threat," Church said. "Those who bought into the Void's philosophy were just the tools that carried out the dirty work."

"Driven from our groves, hunted to the point of extinction, we fled to the Otherworld where we survived on an island in the Dismal Marsh. Unable to tend to our people, we were dissolute and broken in spirit." He bowed his head. "It took time for us to renew our purpose. But then we became aware that the Brothers and Sisters of Dragons were active once more, and that knowledge brought the Blue Fire back to our hearts. If you were fighting to oppose the Void, how could we remain in hiding?"

"See?" Tom said pointedly to Church. "You keep thinking of yourselves, with your own shallow perspective, only looking around the tiny sphere of your immediate influence. You don't realise that simply by moving through the world you are changing all of Existence. The connections ripple out, altering the pattern." He sighed. "How am I supposed to drum some sense into your head? Step back and see the big pattern, and all your petty little concerns fall into perspective."

"It's hard to believe everything happens for a reason when you're wading through life's little miseries," Church snapped.

"That's the point." Tom took out his tin and methodically began to roll himself a smoke.

"One other thing was responsible for our return to the world at this time," Matthias continued. "The First called to us."

Church was shocked. "The First called? To you?" The oldest and greatest

Fabulous Beast was the recipient of the full power of the Blue Fire, and Church had been convinced he was the only one who shared a link with it; even then, when his mind intertwined with the Beast's, he saw with its eyes and felt what it felt, but he never gained any sense of its consciousness. They were always together, and separate.

"We were as astonished as you, Brother of Dragons. We protected the First in the Far Lands when it was most under threat, and during all that time it made no contact with us. Indeed, we thought it was incapable of communication with humans. But it summoned us back here, to this place, to help empower the land, and through that to empower the First. Our ritual today, at the dawning of the Solstice, focused the full force of the Blue Fire in this land on the greatest of the Fabulous Beasts."

"That's why I'm here," Church said. "To take the First back to the Far Lands to help us in the battle."

"Hmm," Tom mused. "Do you think there are any coincidences?"

"When all the Brothers and Sisters of Dragons gathered in London, I hid it close to the city so it could make its way here to Stonehenge when the Void was looking elsewhere," Church said.

"There is a secret you must know," Matthias said. "The First has two forms. It is a Fabulous Beast, and it is the purest form of the Blue Fire that speaks through a human avatar. A force for Life, and a force that can be used for destruction, both interconnected. The First told us that this is important. It is a mystery that is also a key to what comes next."

"You need to think about that," Tom said.

"Is that one of your subtle hints?"

"Time is running out for subtlety. I haven't been able to tell you anything because it's important you learn all this yourself. We're never going to get to heaven if you haven't learned how to find the path."

Church was puzzled by Tom's odd choice of words. It prompted another flash of himself lying on a table being observed, and he rubbed his temples forcefully to drive it away. "It's not all about me," he said with irritation.

"Actually, it is. And it always has been." The weight of Tom's gaze upon him was almost unbearable, and so much lay behind it, a sucking vacuum that he had to resist or be lost in it forever.

"I don't want to know." He stood up suddenly and marched out of the roundhouse and into the crowd where he lost himself physically in the celebration. But he couldn't escape his thoughts, which increased in gravity during the course of the day until he became filled with dread about what lay ahead. Everything was about survival in the face of the Void, but somehow, in a way that made no sense to him, it was really about even more than that.

Towards the end of the day, he found Matthias standing beside him as he watched the sun moving down the sky. "The mysteries will never be revealed to you. They can only be discovered by your own contemplation," the leader of the Culture said.

"My mystery?"

"All mysteries. We are all stories unfolding. The author, be that your unconscious or some higher power depending on your point of view, will leave clues for you to decipher the meaning beneath the chain of events. But no good author would make everything plain. Revelation is passive and easily forgotten. Discovery is active and imprints on your mind and soul forever."

Breathing in the woodsmoke and the smell of cooking meat, and listening to the sound of jubilant voices, Church realised how much of an outsider he felt. "I've had enough," he said. "Of the mysteries. Of the struggle. The heartache. I want it all to end. A happy ending, like they have in the stories."

"Happiness is found in the strangest places," Matthias said. "For some people, it can only be felt by seeing it ignited in others."

"I don't want to be a hero either."

"But you are. It is in your nature—you could not be anything else. You have risen above your flaws. You have kept travelling along the road when the obstacles would have driven others to the wayside. As you will keep travelling now, even though you feel this way. Am I right?"

Church nodded dismally.

Not far away, Ruth made her way through the crowd, the Spear of Lugh resting jauntily on her shoulder. She looked at peace, and that made Church happy to see. She caught sight of him and came over, giving him a kiss on his cheek as she slipped her arm through his.

"I can't believe how well the Craft is working for me here," she said. "I've been practising. It makes me feel so alive to use it. If only it was always like that."

"It's inversely proportionate," Matthias said. "If the Mundane Spell is working strongly, using the Craft, getting closer to nature, bringing the Blue Fire alive is harder, if not impossible. The two are different faces, like the Void and Existence, but they're linked. One pulls one way, the other loses ground, and vice versa. For the majority of human existence on this planet, everything pulled in Existence's direction, the Blue Fire thrived and humanity was better for it. After the Industrial Revolution, everything changed. The Mundane Spell got a grip on the land, and the Blue Fire went into a long decline. Eventually magic disappeared from the world.

"It was always within the power of humanity to keep the Blue Fire alive, but the Mundane Spell is very seductive. It speaks to the worst instincts of human nature, and good men and women are required to overcome it. People should have taken a stand long ago. They did not. And so the Mundane Spell whispered in the night, and gradually draped on them responsibilities and needs that did not make their lives better, but which seemed at first glance attractive. By the time humanity recognised that, it was too late.

"But that is how the other side has always won. Not by direct confrontation, but by an arm of a 'friend' around the shoulder. The foolish, the unthinking, the tired and worn down—they always listen. Only now, as it sees its control ebbing away for good, is the Void turning to destruction."

A black cloud passed briefly across the setting sun, swirling up and then back to circle around the camp. The revellers stopped what they were doing and faced the sky as the Morvren settled on the trees all around.

"An omen?" Matthias said.

Church felt a shiver of darkness touch his heart. "He's here," he said.

His comment was underlined by a scream rising up on the edge of the crowd.

"The Libertarian will go all out to stop me reaching the First," Church said. "He knows it could be a turning point."

"You do what you have to do," Ruth said. "I'll round up the others and try to head off the Libertarian."

Before she could move, Veitch ran up. "That scream—I think it was Rachel. I can't find her anywhere."

"She's under our protection," Ruth said. "If the Libertarian has hurt her, he's going to pay." She reluctantly dragged her gaze away from Church and left with Veitch before any questions were asked about what she was thinking.

Church decided he didn't need to ask; increasingly, they were seeing the Libertarian as him—not as some other character shaped by an as-yet-unrealised crucible, but as him: his thoughts, his motivations, his hatred. And perhaps they were right.

Matthias grabbed his arm as he made to leave. "You must ensure no harm comes to the First, or else all is lost."

Church gave his assurance, and then ran off towards the long fingers of twilight reaching across the landscape. Behind him, the sounds of celebration continued unabated, but night was falling fast.

CHAPTER NINE
ICE AND FOG

1

Beyond the marshes, the Grim Lands reverted to rocky shale for a few miles before the ground descended along a steep slope to a desert of grey dust that had the same texture as ashes. Occasionally, blackened, twisted trees stood in lonely vigilance on the desolate wastes, giving the impression that the entire area had been swept by a massive conflagration that destroyed even the tiniest particle of life.

"Don't you see," Caitlin said to Mallory when he raised this thought, "that everything we pass through is just a different symbol of death and decay. I don't think any of it is real—it's just what we project onto it." Her voice had the clipped tones of the Morrigan, her eyes dark and unblinking as she searched for any threat in the folds of the dense fog.

Though it was still unmistakably Caitlin, Mallory missed the warmth of his friend when the Morrigan was riding her; he had even grown to miss her separate personalities, as irritating as each of them was in turn. Even calm, the Morrigan cast a frightening shadow; there was always the sense that violence could erupt at any moment.

Ahead of them, Etain and the other Brothers and Sisters of Spiders roamed through the mist, searching for potential danger. The Wayfinder continued to point its path ahead, but they had no idea if they were any closer to their destination, or if the shifting quality of the Grim Lands would keep them wandering forever; their own brand of purgatory for the sins they had committed in life.

And somewhere at their back was the Hortha, never wavering, eternally vigilant, driving forward until he could take their lives; that, too, was part of their personal purgatory, as frightening in symbol as it was in reality. There would be no rest for either of them, and only death at the end. Bitterly, Mallory wondered if that was a metaphor for life.

Cruel fingers of wind plucked up the ashes and swirled around them, stinging their eyes and pitting their faces. Choking, they wrapped handker-chiefs across their mouths and noses, put their heads down and continued in silence for another mile, fighting against even more limited visibility. Howling, the gale increased in intensity the further they advanced, as if attempting to hold them back.

Thundering hooves brought them up sharply as Etain skidded from the mist to a sudden halt next to them. "Do not take another step!" she yelled.

The moment she spoke, the wind died and left an eerie silence that reminded Mallory of a just-vacated room. Leaping from her mount, Etain took Mallory and Caitlin's hands and led them forwards a few feet to the edge of a sheer drop. Plucking a pebble from the ashes, Mallory dropped it into the dense fog. There was no sound of it hitting the bottom.

"The Abyss," Etain said.

Caitlin took the Wayfinder from Mallory and held it aloft. The flame continued to point ahead across the gulf. After exploring in both directions along the edge for several yards, but finding no immediate sign of an end to the drop, he said, "This makes no sense."

Tannis, Owein and Branwen dismounted and continued to explore while Caitlin and Mallory conferred with Etain. "What do we do now?" she said.

"We never thought it was going to be easy," Caitlin said. "Whoever, or whatever, took the trouble to hide the Market of Wishful Spirit out here was never going to set up signs for us to find it."

"So we climb down? That could take forever," Mallory said.

"Everyone in the Grim Lands knows there is no bottom to the Abyss," Etain observed.

"So it's on the other side," Mallory said.

"There is no other side. This is the boundary between the Grim Lands and the unknown. Nothing passes beyond this point."

"Ask Hal," Caitlin said.

"The Blue Fire has little strength here. It might weaken him if he has to mani-fest himself." Mallory weighed his options, then peered into the glass panels of the lantern. "Hal? You there?" He glanced at Caitlin. "I feel stupid talking to a lamp."

Caitlin couldn't suppress a smile. "You telling me your life hasn't pre-pared you for that?"

"That's right—mock me." He unhooked the hinge and opened the door that gave access to the wick. The familiar burned-iron odour of the Blue Fire drifted out.

With a fizz, the flame flickered larger and licked out of the lantern, but there was none of the surging whoosh and crackle of flames that Mallory had experienced before; and Hal was no longer the searing figure of raging fire. He resembled a ghost, so intangible that his form flickered and guttered to reveal the grey dust behind. The only sign of the Blue Fire was a thin halo limning him.

"You survived Callow's attack," Mallory said.

"Just. It took nearly all my reserves. I'm barely hanging on now." He gave a wan smile. "Not much use to you any more, if I ever was."

"What happens when the reserves go?" Caitlin asked.

He raised his hand and waved almost-fingers gently towards the Abyss. "Gone, gone, gone." He saw her face fall, and added hastily, "Don't worry, I'm ready for it. The time I've spent in the Blue Fire—which to me feels like all-time—has been . . ." He laughed quietly. "There's no point me trying to explain it. Let's just say, I've seen all there is to see, experienced all that's on offer and know the answers to every question I ever considered. Even the big ones."

"A few tips wouldn't go amiss," Mallory said.

"It'd be like cheating in an exam—you'd get banned. All right if you work out the answers for yourself, but no insider dealing." Hal's face grew serious, and a little sad. "Don't worry, Mallory. Really. Don't worry."

"Can you help us now?" Caitlin asked. "We can't see what we're supposed to do next."

"Yeah, the Wayfinder flame's a bit of a blunt tool," he replied. "I can't get it to point down."

"That's it? We climb down?"

"Not all the way. You'll see what I mean." A crackle like static disrupted Hal's indistinct form. "Not much time left for me." The words broke up.

"Then get back in the lantern," Mallory said. "We're going to return you to the world."

With a nod of thanks and a smile, Hal faded away. Mallory fastened the Wayfinder to his belt before inspecting the drop, and after a few moments' preparation he eased himself over the edge, feeling for hand- and footholds. Under the deft, fearless control of the Morrigan, Caitlin came next, followed by Etain and the others.

Progress was slow, and soon Mallory's joints were aching from the strain of clinging on to the rock face, while reaching out all around to find nooks that would support his weight. From time to time, they had to go back up to take a different route when the footholds disappeared.

"One good thing about this fog, you can't see the bottom," he gasped. "Saves me blacking out from the vertigo."

After each few feet, Mallory paused and checked the Wayfinder. When they had descended for about half a mile, he realised he had passed the point of no return for his exhausted limbs, but just as he began to worry, the direction of the flame moved from upright to the left. Relieved, Mallory edged horizontally across the cliff face.

"Mallory!" The timbre of Caitlin's voice had changed to the rasp of her crone-like Brigid persona. "Danger approaches!"

From deep in the fog, a high-pitched screech emanated. "Etain!" he called out. "What threats have got—"

The words caught in his throat as something swooped out from the fog, passing so close that it ruffled his hair before disappearing in a flash. A bird? he guessed, but he had an after-image of something bone-white and near-skeletal, as big as an eagle.

Bracing himself, he clung on with one hand and drew Llyrwyn just in time as the thing burst from the fog again. Missing both eyes, what little skin it had was pale and desiccated, wrapped tightly across bones that were visible all over; it looked as if the carcass had been left out in the sun for weeks. With the wild flapping of enormous wings, it attacked him with beak and talons, lunging and snapping, again and again. Mallory lashed out with his sword, but each swing threatened to pitch him off the cliff-face.

Caitlin arrived behind him just as two more of the bird-creatures emerged from the fog. Balancing so precariously on her toes that Mallory was sure she would fall, Caitlin lashed out with her axe and chopped one of the attackers neatly in two. As it plunged down into the fog, they heard the screech of more arriving.

Bringing his sword up sharply, Mallory despatched one bird, but the other had dug its talons into his shoulders and was driving its beak into his head as it attempted to tear out his eyes.

Struggling to defend himself from the bird's frenzy, his fingers detached from the cliff-face and he began to lurch out over the gulf. As his stomach flipped, Caitlin's hand snapped tightly around his wrist and held him fast.

Blood streamed down Mallory's face from the bird's furious assault. Then, as he fought and failed to get a purchase on it, the creature was torn away. Above his head, Etain clung to the cliff-face like a spider. Gripping the thrashing bird in her left hand, she snapped her teeth onto its scrawny neck and tore its head off. Both parts flew down past Mallory, but by then he was wiping the blood from his eyes and moving as fast as he could along the cliff before any more of the creatures attacked.

Their shrieks made his skin crawl, and he could hear them swooping just beyond the limit of his vision, circling as they looked for the right moment to strike.

Before they made their next move, he located a narrow fissure in the rock from which a cold wind blew. He dragged himself in quickly, with Caitlin and the others pressing close behind. The fissure opened out into a dark tunnel just big enough for them to walk upright.

Caitlin resisted Mallory's attempts to keep her away and tended to his wounds. "Stop being such a man," she said. "At least you didn't say, 'It's just a scratch.'" Her voice had all the warmth of the real Caitlin, free of the Morrigan's hardness. In the middle of that cold, miserable place, it touched him deeply, and he gave her arm a quick squeeze. She smiled back.

"After what Callow did to you, I have the feeling they're just trying to whittle us down, a bit at a time."

Once the wounds had started to dry, they set off along the tunnel. After several yards, they became aware of a subtle change. The Grim Lands had a claustrophobic feel, as if the very environment was pressing in on all sides, but that had lifted. Mallory found he was breathing easier, and the air had richer odours—vegetation, he guessed—and was damper than the dry atmosphere they had been breathing for so long.

"This is weird," Caitlin whispered. "Etain, have you any idea where we're going?"

When there was no response, Caitlin looked back to see that the Brothers and Sisters of Spiders had reverted to the same mechanical movements they had exhibited in the Far Lands. Their staring eyes swivelled to lock on to Caitlin, but they registered no sign of any intelligence.

"Uh, Mallory—" she began.

"Hush," he hissed. "The tunnel's coming to an end."

They emerged near the foot of a hill. It was dark, and there was a forest all around, but ahead of them Chinese lanterns glowed in the trees surrounded by fluttering moths. An autumnal chill hung in the air, and the aroma of ripe fruit, damp leaves and fern.

"I don't think we're in the Grim Lands any more," Mallory said quietly.

Cautiously, weapons drawn, they made their way down the remainder of the hillside. The Brothers and Sisters of Spiders walked steadily behind.

The lanterns cast a peaceful ambience over the forest setting. Not far away, high in the branches, an owl hooted and was answered immediately by another.

"How can we be in the Land of the Dead, and somewhere else at the same time?" Caitlin asked.

"Some kind of pocket?" Mallory suggested. "If the Market was tucked away here to stop anyone stumbling across the Extinction Shears, the people would need some kind of atmosphere in which they could thrive."

"Because only the dead can exist in the Grim Lands."

"Exactly."

"Who has the power to do that, Mallory?"

He had no answer for her. They found themselves on a track that wound into the forest where more of the lanterns clustered. In the soft, golden glow, they could just make out the shapes of the first market stalls, and as they neared they could see that it spread out far into the trees ahead.

"Why is it so quiet?" Caitlin whispered.

"Deserted?" Mallory suggested, but as they reached the first stall he could see he was wrong. Skulls, crystals, candles, mirrors and other magickal items were loaded onto the table under a dark-green awning. Behind it stood the owner, a man in a broad-brimmed black hat and dark coat. He wasn't moving. Pearly, glistening trails of spider webs covered him, reaching from the brim of his hat down to the table.

Mallory edged closer to him and touched his hand. "Still alive," he said. "Sleeping."

"Give him a kiss. See if he wakes up."

"Sure. And if we come across a spinning wheel, you get to play with it first."

The scene was the same at the next stall, where books and maps were loaded on the creaking table. The dusty, web-covered owner was a squat old woman with a warty nose and a scarf holding back her grey hair. Hesitantly, they advanced through the market, but everywhere the owners were locked in a deep sleep that appeared to have struck them where they stood.

"At least it keeps resistance to a minimum," Mallory said. "We just have to search through all this weird shit, try not to get our hands blown off by stuff that looks perfectly normal but is totally lethal, find the Extinction Shears—"

"And do it before the Hortha gets here."

"Okay, ticking clock—I get it. You look over there, I'll do here." He glanced at the Brothers and Sisters of Spiders watching them, unmoving. "No point asking them. You keep guard!" he added with a shout. He was surprised when Etain and the others obeyed him and shuffled back along the path.

Mallory moved quickly along the stalls. He had no idea if the Extinction Shears would be out in the open or hidden away, although his knowledge of the Market suggested the owners had scant regard for the dangerous nature of the items they sold. Caveat emptor was the sole motto.

The wonders on display were so dazzling that he had to fight not to be seduced by them. Some, he guessed, were entrancing him magickally on some level beyond conscious thought, and he kept his attention skittering across the objects to prevent them from hooking him in.

Everything he could imagine was available. Sometimes, when he returned to a stall for a second look, the objects on it had changed, adding another disconcerting twist to his search. There were weapons of all kinds—swords, magic axes, hammers, daggers; poisons and potions to achieve any outcome; maps of every place he'd heard of, and many he was convinced only existed in stories; stuffed animals; statues whose eyes followed him as he passed; musical instruments—flutes made from human bone, lyres, skin-covered drums; medical instruments; implements of torture; mysterious creatures in cages that slept just like their owners; Tarot cards, playing cards, talking greeting cards, curse cards; hats, cloaks, belts—some magic, some perfectly normal; and, in the main, a host of artefacts that Mallory couldn't begin to comprehend.

Behind one stall, a beautiful, voluptuous woman stood with one hand on a cobweb-festooned cat. At the front of her stall was a crystal ball. Mallory gave it only a cursory glance, but it snared him instantly. Mesmerised, he peered into its depths where he saw not the distorted reflection of his face, but the skull beneath his skin. The more he stared, the more it drew him in, whispering, "This is who you are."

He was thrown roughly to the ground. Caitlin hauled him to his feet and shook him until his sense returned.

"Sorry, but I've been trying to rouse you for ten minutes," she said. "You were gone. That's not all—it was as if you were trying to pull the flesh from your face."

The skin around Mallory's jaw was sore to the touch. Even so, he found himself irresistibly drawn back to the crystal ball, until Caitlin shook him again and dragged him, half-stumbling, across the path to the stalls she had been inspecting.

"I've found them," she said. "At least, I think I have. This is the only thing that comes close."

Tucked away incongruously behind a pile of rags was a pair of shears with ornate gold handles, and though they appeared to radiate no light, Mallory saw a white glow wash over Caitlin and himself. As he examined them, Mallory had the impression that he wasn't looking at a pair of shears at all, but something infinitely larger and more mysterious; several potential images—an intricate clockwork machine, a crystal—skittered across his mind, but it always came back to a pair of shears.

"What do you think?" Caitlin asked.

Mallory had the strange impression that he had seen the shears before, as though in a dream. He decided it was instinct, but he was much surer than he ought to have been. "That's them."

As he reached for them, a silver candlestick on the table in front of his fingers moved. He cried out and leaped back. "What the fu—!"

The candlestick flowed like mercury, rolling itself into a silver egg and then, sprouting legs, it scurried across the table to the edge and dropped to the ground.

"A Caraprix!" Caitlin exclaimed. "I thought they were all in that room at the court with Jerzy."

"Not all of them, apparently." All across the market, the tables became alive with objects moving, changing shape, glowing with a silvery light. As the Caraprix scuttled to the ground and streamed towards the far side of the

Market, Mallory saw in them an eerie reflection of the Army of the Ten Billion Spiders.

Delicately plucking the Extinction Shears from the table, Mallory was unsettled by how warm and yielding they felt under his fingers. Hastily, he slipped them into the bag at his belt, then turned his attention back to the Caraprix.

The stream of shape-shifting creatures led to a point where the forest came to an end, and only rock walls lay beyond. A glassy quality to the air right along the boundary gave the impression that they were standing in a bubble.

The Caraprix spread out along the boundary and came to a halt, exuding a bright white light that slowly spread upwards into a ten-foot-high rectangle. As the quality of the light changed, Mallory and Caitlin realised they were looking through a window onto the terrain of another world, where steaming jungle came up hard against a vast golden desert.

"The Far Lands," Caitlin said in the hard-edged voice of the Morrigan.

"A doorway back," Mallory noted. "So we don't have to go through that ritual Math forced us to learn. I'm not even convinced he was sure it would work."

"So the Caraprix brought the Market here?" Caitlin said.

"Looks like it. The perfect hiding place."

Caitlin slipped her hand into Mallory's and gave it a squeeze. He was troubled by how quickly she appeared to be flipping back and forth between her true self and the part corrupted by the Morrigan, as if she was assimilating the goddess into her being. "Then that's mission accomplished," she said. "Let's go—"

Caitlin was interrupted by the sounds of fighting behind them. Racing back the way they had come, they found the Brothers and Sisters of Spiders in fierce combat with the Hortha, which was just inserting one extended, thorny finger through Tannis's forehead. With a dry, cracking noise, it burst through the rear of his skull and Tannis crumpled to the ground, the dim light in those dead eyes finally extinguished.

Instantly, it turned its rustling, papery face towards Mallory and Caitlin. "Nowhere to run now," it called drily.

Owein and Branwen attacked it with their swords, hacking through the dense blackthorn body only for it to sprout and grow back almost instantly.

Etain glanced back, questioningly, and Mallory shouted, "Can you hold it off till we get away?" For the first time, Mallory saw deep in her eyes the merest hint of the Sister of Dragons she had once been. It brought a pang of conscience, but he reminded himself that her time had passed.

Yet she continued to stare at him with a hint of desperation, and he realised she was trying to communicate with him. He knew instinctively what she wanted to say. "I'll tell him," he called.

Branwen fell as the Hortha avoided her strike and punched the twisted spike into her forehead. As Mallory and Caitlin ran, they glimpsed Owein dropping too, and then Etain was fighting alone, sacrificing herself for the people she had once been driven to destroy.

The atmospheric conditions of the forest setting were altering fast; it was warmer, and Mallory and Caitlin felt as if they were running through treacle. Spatial dimensions distorted, and time itself came in stuttering fits and starts so it felt as if they were speeding towards their destination, then frozen as the world around them moved. Trails of light flowed from the Chinese lanterns swinging wildly in the branches. The Market began to compress and stretch towards the door created by the Caraprix.

The view across the Far Lands was now much clearer, and they could feel the tropical heat of the jungle and the dry wind blowing across the desert.

Pausing, Mallory grabbed Caitlin's hand. "You ready?" he asked.

"We've come this far together. Why stop now?" She gave him a warm smile of deep affection.

"Back to life," he said. "Back to reality. Of sorts."

They took the great leap together.

2

Though the small campfire burned continually in the cave, it couldn't dispel the bitterness of the unending winter outside, nor the chill in Miller's heart. He had tended to Hunter, Jack and Virginia night and day, but had now reached the point of ultimate despair: their decline had accelerated and he was forced to accept the impossibility of keeping them all alive.

Surviving on occasional birds and rabbits he trapped in the snow while constantly evading the roaming Fomorii had taken its toll, both physically and emotionally; drawing on his healing force so often was also sapping his own powers of recuperation. The futility of it ate into his bones much more deeply than the aching cold. While there was life he had to keep on trying, but now he had to make the choice he had dreaded: sacrifice one in the hope that it would leave him strong enough to save the other two.

Tears froze on his cheeks. He'd been crying on and off for most of the afternoon while he wrestled with the arguments and his own corrosive guilt, but finally he had made the decision he'd known he would have to make all along.

Crawling over to where Hunter lay, eyes closed as if he were sleeping, Miller laid one hand on his friend's barely beating heart. Choking on the words, he whispered, "I don't know if you can hear me . . . I hope you can. I'm so sorry, Hunter." He took a deep breath. "I've thought long and hard . . . I've prayed. I can't see another way out. Every life is equal to me, Hunter, but not every life is equal for what Church wants us to do.

"You're a Brother of Dragons . . . you're important, but Jack is one of the Two Keys. Him and me, we're needed somehow if we're ever going to stop the Void. And Virginia . . . if I can ever get her back to Church . . . she knows a way into the Fortress. She's vital to us striking right at the heart of the Enemy. And that leaves you. We need you, of course we do. But not as much as we need the other two."

Laying his head on Hunter's chest, he whispered, "Why do I have to make this choice? It's not fair." After a moment, he sat up and dried his eyes. "No, I'm up to this. That's what's expected of me. Hunter, I'm going to have to stop keeping you alive, and transfer all the power I've got left to the other two in the hope that I can cure them completely. If you can hear me, please forgive me."

There. It was done.

Taking a moment to steady himself, he went to Virginia and drew up the searing blue light inside him. Once that was done, he moved on to Jack, and then flopped, exhausted, against the foot of the cave wall, and cried some more.

His eyes had barely dried when he noticed blood trickling from his nose. It was accompanied by the sickening sensation of a heaviness in his head as if something was moving around inside his skull. Faces of departed friends and family flashed across his mind, but it was Hunter's that came back repeatedly, looming larger each time.

"Leave me alone," he whispered, scared now.

The death-images came harder, threatening to destroy his sanity.

"Bring him out." The voice rolled in from the wilderness beyond the cave mouth, colder than the winds of Winter-side.

"No," Miller whispered defiantly.

"My brother. My death-brother. Bring him out."

Miller was too weak to fight. With a last, great effort, Miller dragged Hunter into the swirling snow.

Further down the slope stood the giant that Hunter had freed from its prison far beneath the Halls of the Drakusa. He still wore his hood, but although Miller had never seen him before, his brain crackled with images of the devastated, melted-wax face that lay beneath, as the cold, alien intellect teased and probed. Dread consumed him so deeply, he thought he would die from the weight of it, but the giant would not let him; his thoughts were too weak to resist its control.

"I am El-Di-Gah-Wis-Lor, the final judgement of the Drakusa, the dark at the end, the breath of the grave," the giant said. "I am death, and I bring death. Brought to being for one purpose, to end the plague of the Caraprix, I was not allowed to fulfil my destiny. But now, in that one, I see another purpose."

"You can't have him," Miller croaked futilely.

"He whispers on the edge of death. I hear him now, when I could not hear him before. His whispers ring out across the mountains of this place, and deep into the darkest places beneath the mountains. He is death, and I am death, and we share a destiny. He can teach me. He can give me purpose."

Miller realised that a connection had been forged between the giant and Hunter once the healing had been withdrawn.

"Give him to me."

"No."

"Give him to me, and I will give him life, so he can join me in the pursuit of death."

"You . . . you can save him?"

"That I cannot do. But I can give him life."

Hesitating for just a moment, Miller stumbled through the thick snow to the giant without a thought for his own safety. The giant took Hunter from his arms with surprising tenderness and turned back down the slope. Miller followed.

In the lee of some rocks, there was a large cave entrance that Miller had not come across before in his random searches for food. Striding into the dark, the giant continued into a tunnel large enough to accommodate his height. It drove deep into the heart of the mountain through a series of forgotten chambers once occupied by the Drakusa, their floors now covered with shattered masonry and discarded weapons.

For what felt like miles, the tunnel sloped down sharply until Miller became convinced they were going to the core of the world. Finally, they entered a chamber in the deepest part of the complex. It stretched far into the dark on all sides, the echoes so dim it could well have gone on forever.

Fear gripped Miller when he saw that the chamber was filled with an army of Fomorii warriors, waiting silently in ranks, their black skin gleaming over shields and weapons grown from their own bodies. They could have been glorious obsidian statues except for the humming waves of power that washed off them.

Miller trembled as he followed the giant amongst the horde, but they never even acknowledged his presence. Can the giant control so many ferocious beings? he wondered. How powerful is he?

The giant came to a halt before a large stone well more than twenty feet across. Blue light radiated from the depths, shimmering like the sun off water. Miller could feel the rejuvenating force of the Blue Fire long before he neared the lip.

"What is this?" he asked in awe.

"The Well Between Worlds." Standing with his head bowed and his body tense, the giant remained in the shadows just beyond the pool of light. "This was the last desperate act of the Drakusa. Their last great act. While they created me to destroy the Caraprix, they also constructed this conduit to the very heart of Existence itself."

"Why?"

"They thought if they could not destroy the Caraprix, they could return them to the Source."

"The Caraprix come from Existence?"

"The Caraprix are Existence."

"But I...I thought they were a danger. They destroyed the Drakusa, didn't they? How can they belong to Existence if they go against Life?"

After a moment of humming silence, the giant said, "The well shows that the Drakusa were capable of miraculous things, yet they were given over to war and destruction. This...To reach into the very heart of all there is...How great is that achievement? So many have tried to touch Existence, even to begin to approach it, and in their last desperate hours the Drakusa did what no other had." An odd note of regret laced his voice.

"Bring Hunter here, then," Miller said excitedly. "I can use this to heal him."

"I cannot approach. The Blue Fire is anathema to me. I am death."

Miller took Hunter from the giant's arms and staggered towards the well, his head reeling from the tremendous sense of well-being that rose up from it. As he rested Hunter on the small stone wall, he had a moment to reflect on the irony of the situation—death giving life to the dying—and then he placed one hand on Hunter's chest and thrust the other into the aurora of sapphire light. His instant invigoration was overcome by the sensation of the currents of power moving through him. The cold touch of the giant in his head disappeared, and in its place he heard warm whispers; though he couldn't make out the words, he felt reassured and at peace. He looked down into the brilliant light and thought he saw things swimming there, deep down; whatever they were, they uplifted him too.

Hunter spasmed and coughed, and slowly the pale-blue tinge of his skin flushed a healthy pink. His eyes flickering open, he looked into Miller's face.

"Hunter—you're going to be okay."

Hunter's lips moved so weakly that Miller couldn't hear what he was saying. He pressed his ear close.

"I said, 'Bring me wine and a woman. I've got some catching up to do.'"

3

The warm midsummer night was filled with the exuberance of the feast, but Ruth pushed her way through the revellers with mounting frustration. "We're never going to find Rachel in this chaos," she said. The campfires blazing amongst the makeshift huts only illuminated the milling bodies, and beyond their light the shadows were deep.

"I do not understand why she is of any interest to the Enemy now," Shavi replied. "In the Far Lands, yes—she was the key to our returning here, but now?"

"I don't even get why they wanted to stop us coming home," Veitch said. "You'd think they'd be happy with us running away."

Tom muttered something acerbic under his breath.

Shavi came to a halt when he saw Laura was falling behind. "Keep up. In this crowd it will take all night to find you if you get lost."

Laura smiled, didn't reply.

With an exclamation of irritation, Ruth stopped outside a roundhouse. "Keep watch outside," she said at the doorway. "I'm going to fly."

Puzzled, Shavi began, "But you do not have any of the balms . . . and the ritual takes—"

"I don't need any of that here." Her eyes blazed.

"You need any help?" Veitch said hesitantly.

Ruth smiled. "I'll be fine. Just watch over my body. I don't want the Enemy attacking it while I'm out of it."

In the cool of the roundhouse, she sat cross-legged against one wall and closed her eyes, letting her breathing become measured as the sounds of the revelry receded. Reaching deep inside herself, she became still, concentrated, focused. She was surprised, and a little scared, by how easy it was becoming to use the Craft. When she was being tortured in the Court of Endless Horizons, she had put her ability to fly down to the pain and the fear disengaging her mind. But now she knew the truth: she was getting stronger; she was getting better.

But the power was seductive. Once before it had almost consumed her; could she control it now, even though she was older, wiser, honed by experience?

She reached down even further, through her body and into the earth where she could feel the gentle, reassuring pulse of the Blue Fire. Her fears faded, and were supplanted by the rightness of what she was doing. In the cool cavern of her mind, the primal sanctuary of the human against the terrifying dangers of the unknown beyond, she envisaged the symbol that had come to represent both the Ritual of Flight and a word of power; it was a blazing blue mandala that was image and word and will and act rolled into one.

A second later, her essence rushed up out of her head, through the round-house roof and into the night sky. In the first hallucinogenic dislocation, she felt a wave of affection for Shavi, Laura, Veitch and Tom, waiting anxiously by the door, and then another wave of love for the wild, feasting throng; she didn't know any of them, but she was linked to them all, individually and as a group, on the deepest levels.

Rising up higher, she saw the campfires and the village in the context of the broader landscape, the dark canvas of fields, the strips of roads, the lights of Salisbury and the subtle lines of Blue Fire connecting it all. Her chest swelled as she took it all in, and understood, deeply, for the first time in a long while, why they were fighting so hard.

With an effort, she wrenched herself from the revelation and swooped down low over the camp, seeing everything, hearing all. Systematically, she searched until she reached the fringes of habitation, where the lonely country-side eventually lapped up against the well-lit A-roads. The full moon painted the grassland a magical silver, against which lay the charcoal strokes of trees and hedges.

Flying low over the ancient, grass-covered monuments of the ritual land-scape, Ruth scanned for any sign of movement. In a dense copse, her attention was distracted by a large owl, seemingly watching her from the low branches.

In its huge eyes, she saw echoes of her own familiar, slaughtered by the Libertarian in Greece, a companion, if not a friend, whom she still missed acutely. She was not surprised when it spoke to her: "Sister of Dragons. You know what I am?"

Ruth floated an inch above the ground in the centre of the clearing. "Not exactly."

More owls flapped down to settle on branch after branch, and there was constant movement in the grass as a flood of cats, rats, hares, frogs, snakes and mice drew near to observe her with eerily intelligent eyes.

"Our kind are as old as time." The owl had developed unsettling human characteristics during the time her attention had been on the other creatures. "We have always shepherded the sisterhood of the Craft, guiding and teaching, and punishing where necessary. Every sister needs a guide on the dangerous path you walk. This is the role we have been given, and some of our kind have even developed a fondness for those we shape. Some. We have demanded little in return, save obeisance to the weft and the weave. When all is connected, to harm one harms all."

Ruth shivered at the weight behind the eyes that lay upon her. In her spirit form, sometimes, when she looked askance, she could almost glimpse their true shapes, but it was too frightening for her to give it her full attention.

"You, of all our charges, understood that. You, of all, have proven yourself the greatest, and the most deserving of our guidance. After the death of our cousin, your companion, you were left bereft. The bond, unfulfilled. That slaughter, the first in long years, struck at the very heart of our kind, and so the Council of Yekyua was summoned."

Ruth was now surrounded by people with the characteristics of animals, squatting like beasts, yellow and green and red eyes ranging, fur, and talons, and fangs.

"This world is in peril. This magickal land that we have helped protect for so long, this crucible for Existence's greatest force in the long war. And so we must act. Sister of Dragons, you no longer stand alone. You do not have one companion on the hard road, you have many. The Blue Fire burns in the Craft. The Blue Fire burns in our hearts. Know this world will be protected, come what may."

Silence fell across the assemblage. Ruth was surprised and empowered by the clear respect she could sense they held for her. "Thank you. I'm grateful. The Brothers and Sisters of Dragons need your help now more than ever." She paused, looked deeply into the faces before her, seeing endless possibilities. "Then I have a request for you."

Not long after, as Ruth returned to her body, the moon-washed countryside was alive with wildlife sweeping out into every hidden nook and cranny. Overhead, the owls flew, majestic, fierce, with eyes that could see an insect a mile distant.

Beneath the turf, the Blue Fire pulsed, and grew stronger.

4

Rachel regained consciousness on a public footpath winding across Salisbury Plain to where a silver BMW was parked on the side of a quiet lane. Dragged across the turf by her wrist, every joint in her body burned. Her left eye had closed up. Blood ran from her nose and into her mouth from her pulped lips. One tooth was chipped. There was a sharp pain in her ribs, and her right knee had ballooned.

"Please, Scott," she began, but it hurt so much to talk that her voice was little more than a rasp.

"What the fuck did you think you were doing?" he growled. He was angry; bloodstains spattered his neatly ironed blue shirt.

Not so long ago, she would have cried and begged for his forgiveness, offered him her body, promised he could do whatever he wanted. "I can do whatever I want."

He stopped and kicked her sharply in the side. Pain shot up her spine bringing hot tears, but she hid her face from him.

"I'm not going back with you," she blazed.

He punched her on the side of the face. "Why do you keep opening your stupid mouth? Can't you see? Every time you say something moronic, it hurts. You don't want pain, you keep quiet."

"I'm not staying quiet any more," she gasped. "I've got a right to be who I want to be."

Letting go of her wrist, he grabbed a handful of her hair, dragged her a few more feet and then threw her down on the turf. Standing over her, he said with conviction, "You need me. You can't survive without me."

"I can."

"That's the way it's always been. Women need men. We have to do all the things you're too weak and pathetic to tackle. You try to drag us down, but we're the real power." He bunched both his fists. "I don't want to do this. I love you, Rachel. Despite all your stupid ways, I love you. But you've got to learn that you can't carry on like this or we'll never be happy."

As he prepared to swing his fist, he realised Rachel was looking past him with an expression of awe.

The first thing he saw were the roiling clouds, and jagged bolts of lightning dancing wildly across the grassland, though the rest of the sky was as clear and star-sprinkled as it had been all night. Thunder boomed, and then out of the tightly localised storm walked a woman, her hair flowing around her like snakes, her face blazing with an inner light. She was a ghost, a demon;

she terrified him. On either side of her, a carpet of animals undulated towards him, their eyes glittering.

Her face, he thought. I can't look into her face.

As she rushed across the landscape towards him, an unaccountable feeling of dread filled him. Rachel was forgotten; and when he saw that the woman was floating an inch or so above the grass, he wanted to turn and run, but his legs would not respond.

"You're going to get it now," Rachel croaked, with a note of glee.

Old instincts surfaced and he cursed and ran towards her, ready to punch and kick. A blast of wind smacked him in the chest with the force of a car, flipping him up and over. He heard a rib break, as he had heard Rachel's crack earlier.

His fear obscured any pain, and he scrambled to his feet too late. The woman was upon him, her eyes filled with fire.

He swung out, but she ducked and brought the staff of the spear she was carrying up hard against his chin.

"My name is Ruth Gallagher." Her voice appeared to be echoing from the bottom of a well. "The rules have changed now. No man gets to do what you've done here."

"Don't hurt me," he pleaded.

Ruth examined the mess he had made of Rachel, barely recognisable as she attempted to heave herself up to her feet, and when Ruth looked back at him there was no hint of compassion in her gaze.

"Your kind can't be taught," she said. "You can't be socialised, or have the violence drained out of you. It's who you are. People like you. . .you're the ones who give the Void the power it needs to keep ruling this place."

Scott whimpered, and shook his head pathetically. Just as Ruth thought he was about to fall to his knees and beg, he lashed out at her with a short kitchen knife he'd pulled from his belt.

The knife lanced towards her belly and came up hard. She watched his bovine expression as he tried to force it into her, then the flicker of fear when he realised he couldn't withdraw his hand either.

"The Libertarian brought you here, didn't he?" she asked.

When Scott didn't answer, one of his fingers uncurled from the knife against his will, bent back and snapped. He howled in pain.

"Yes!" he cried. "Yes!"

"He wanted you to hurt Rachel. He wanted you to mess her up badly."

"Yes!" Scott shouted.

Ruth snapped another finger for good measure. Scott howled again as the knife fell to the ground.

Ruth thought of Callow slicing Laura in the back of a van so long ago, of Demetra and the women in Greece, brutalised but trying to carve a life for themselves, of the pain she'd suffered in the Court of Endless Horizons, and she said, simply, "I've had enough."

Rachel hesitated, but Ruth nodded to her to make her way to the BMW. Limping, she set off and never looked back, even when she heard the screech of the owls, the spitting of the cats and the fierce rending of claws and fangs, even when she heard Scott's scream, high-pitched and reedy, going on too long.

Briefly, the violent sounds paused and there came a terrifying voice she didn't recognise: "You gave no one any chances, but I'm giving you one. I'll leave you with an inch of life, a slim space where you can choose to make a difference, or not. Crawl away in your own blood. Learn a lesson. Keep it for the rest of your life, because if you ever backtrack . . . ever . . . these creatures will be watching you, wherever you are, and they'll act with all the fury of the natural world, and none of your pleading will do any good."

The birds and the beasts resumed their attack, and the cries rose up once more.

5

Perched on the top of a five-bar gate, the Libertarian watched the churning fur and feathers and the little black storm moving back across the grassland towards the distant campfires. "Sometimes justice comes red in tooth and claw," he mused wryly.

Manipulation sometimes involved big gestures, and sometimes only a little shove, particularly when one knew the subtle motivations, deepest fears and heartfelt hopes of a person, the kind only voiced to a lover in the dark. He was growing increasingly desperate as events moved towards the final reckoning without the clear outcome he required, but here he felt success.

Ruth knew he had guided the vile boyfriend to the woman purely so that the well-dressed thug could beat her until she bled. But the Libertarian knew Ruth would not blame him for that, oh no. Unconsciously, she would draw connections between Church and the Libertarian. She would know Church had passed on the knowledge of Scott and Rachel's relationship, had brought the two together so that sickening violence could ensue.

For if she believed that the seeds of the Libertarian were already in Church, it was only a small step backwards from the terrible, monstrous Libertarian arranging for a woman to be near-beaten to death to the current love of her life. What lurks in Church's mind? she wonders. He laughed. What hidden hatreds? What ability for abuse? What contempt and violence? Perhaps he doesn't even recognise it himself. But is it there, ticking away, ready to explode?

A small thing, the thin end of the wedge, perhaps, prising her apart from her love, pushing her towards Veitch—a simple man, but always a protector of women. And thereby pushing Church towards the Libertarian.

Yes, he thought, a fine outcome for a night's work.

6

Church stood just beyond the outer ring of Stonehenge. High above the megaliths, the moon cast intricate shadow-patterns across the surrounding grassland. It was still, and quiet, and it felt to him as if there was magic everywhere.

How long it felt since Tom had first revealed to him the secret of the Blue Fire at these stones, and he had become a willing supplicant to the numinous spirituality that pervaded these sites across the world. A few rocks, roughly shaped and proudly raised towards the stars millennia ago, yet they provided a window to the heart of Existence.

Breathless after his run from the processional river path, he approached the stones as any supplicant would have thousands of years ago, looking from the dark silhouettes to the stars and the moon, breath held in awe, and feeling the charge of well-being rising from the earth.

This is our land, he thought defiantly. This is who we are. This is why we fight.

The seemingly random connections and coincidences that had brought him back to Earth to recover the First had served another effect: renewing his purpose. In the Far Lands, the Libertarian had done everything in his power to break his spirit and drive him off the path. But here he could see clearly; think; breathe.

He moved into the circle. Electricity buzzed around his fingertips as he stroked them along the megaliths in passing, and once out of the direct moonlight he could see the faint blue light limning every stone.

Narrowing his eyes, he let the Pendragon Spirit drive his perception. After a moment he saw the serpent amongst the stones, as his ancestors had done so long ago: a sinuous trail of Blue Fire forming a spiral pattern that had so entranced the Celts they had carved it into stones and worn it on their jewellery. A symbol for the path a human takes through life, which was also a real manifestation, which was also a symbol for life itself. Did it have other meanings too?

He walked to the centre of the spiral—death and rebirth into a new life—and drove both hands palms down onto the turf. Blue sparks flew, and within seconds the ground trembled and a large area rose up to reveal a tunnel leading into the depths: the womb from which all life emerged. Quickly, he scrambled inside.

The tunnel led to a large cavern, the glistening rocks overhead washed by a sapphire light emanating from a lake of Blue Fire, one of the reservoirs that fed the searing leys criss-crossing the land. Scattered all along the rocky shore was treasure beyond imagining: gold coins, chalices, plates, jewellery, ornaments, silver artefacts, weapons, helmets, chain mail—ritual offerings to the great power from across generations.

Beneath the waves, a dark shape swam sinuously. The liquid fire cascaded off the Fabulous Beast's head as it surfaced in front of him, as majestic and awe-inspiring as the first time he had encountered it. Scales, tines and horns glimmered in the blue light, and the leathern wings gradually unfolded from beneath the fire. Behind it, he could see smaller, newer Beasts swimming.

The creature towered over him, the heat from its breath enough to bring him out in a sweat, but he wasn't afraid. Looking it deep in the eye, he let their consciousnesses merge, coping with the queasiness of processing two images in his mind: him looking at the Fabulous Beast; the Beast looking back at him.

"I know there's more to you," he said to the creature, to himself. "What are you?"

"Existence." A deep, masculine voice rang out strong and clear across the cavern, but when Church turned, he saw the same woman he had encountered with the Fabulous Beast in the cavern under Boskawen-Un in Cornwall more than two thousand years earlier. Pale skin, black hair, eyes burning with the Blue Fire. "I gave you knowledge and purpose the last time we met," the woman continued, although her lips did not move.

As the Fabulous Beast moved beside the woman, its scales and bone and tissue changed until it appeared as if it was made of the Blue Fire.

"Two of you," Church said. "Two faces. There's that duality thing again—another of those patterns that keeps repeating through the universe."

"The dark and the light are spread throughout all there is, in every fibre, every atom," the woman said. "But to enable direct change, the two powers must focus upon one place, one time. The Devourer of All Things has chosen the Burning Man—"

"And Existence manifests in this form," Church interrupted. "You've been influencing things directly all along."

"There is a reason why all things have happened, from the very smallest to the greatest. In your own personal story, there is a reason. You have been shaped, schooled, prepared for everything that lies ahead. You were chosen Brother of Dragons—the first and the last, the once and future. Of all the Brothers and Sisters of Dragons, only you can join your consciousness with the essence of Existence in this corporeal place. Only you."

The words stung Church as he began to understand their deeper meaning. "The murder of my girlfriend, Marianne—?"

"Necessary."

"Being torn apart from Ruth and hurled back in time, having to fight my way back to her, seeing her torn between Veitch and me?"

"All necessary. All part of the shaping of the hero . . . the king . . . who will save the land."

"The Libertarian?"

There was a long pause before the rich, deep voice continued, "There is always a risk. Death is a powerful catalyst. The experience of it shapes the soul, but its potency can sometimes lead to corruption and despair. The other factors in the transmutation should mitigate against that—love, friendship, support—but in the final account, the landscape of a human heart, and a human mind, is unmappable."

"So I could still ruin all your careful planning?"

"The fate of everything rests with you, Jack Churchill."

"Shavi was right. The pattern . . ." Church said to himself, his head spinning as he tried to accept the weight of what he was being told. "How much has been manipulated?"

"Everything, in every life. Sometimes Fragile Creatures make choices against the direction of the plan, choices with unforeseen but enormous consequences, and other changes must be made to reaffirm the pattern.

"But, essentially, everything. Everybody plays a part. The person they choose to hurt, the one they choose to help. The work they do, the things they create, the words they pass on, which then get passed on to others. Everything.

"The pattern materialises in seemingly random events and coincidences, in ancient tales and contemporary stories and music and works of art. In the patterns in nature, the patterns on the landscape, the patterns men make in life. Numbers are key. The hand of Existence is clear if one only looks with care."

"But we always dismiss it," Church said. "The human brain has evolved from the earliest time to see patterns in everything, but we dismiss it as a quirk, a throwback, in the same way we dismiss random events and connections as coincidences."

"There are no coincidences."

His thoughts raced. "The legends, the old stories, are the key to the pattern. The king shaped by events to be a great hero, who waits in some symbolic under-hill to be called back in the world's darkest hour, with his knights, to beat the forces of darkness. The king who represents both a man and the Blue Fire. The same story repeated over and over in different legends, even in modern religions in a slightly different form. There's the pattern in its biggest form. There's . . . me."

"You are the legend. You are at the heart of the pattern."

Church looked into the woman's face, and then into the shimmering features of the Fabulous Beast, and was convinced he saw a glimmer of something important that was unspoken. "If this was all the creation of a dying brain, then I would be the heart of the pattern—because I created everything. I'd be the true god of this world."

"What is life, what is death? What is real, what is not?"

Church could see he wasn't going to get anywhere with that line of questioning. "And this pattern that's been building . . . it's designed to overthrow the Void?"

"Yes."

"And it began . . . when?"

"At the beginning. And it will end at the end."

Deep in the lake of Blue Fire, the dark shapes swam closer, some large, some small.

"Tell me," he began, "how the pattern developed. Then maybe I can work out how it's going to end."

"In the beginning, tiny shards of Existence were placed in every Fragile Creature. Hidden in plain sight from the Devourer of All Things. These sparks, in some, would eventually fan into the blue blaze of the Pendragon Spirit."

"And in everyone, over time," Church added. "That's part of the Gnostic secret . . . and the key to humanity reaching the next level. That's why the Tuatha Dé Danaan were so afraid we would equal, then surpass them."

"Fragile Creatures gradually ascended, shaped by their experiences, and the spark inside them flickered into a flame, still beyond the perception of the Devourer of All Things. Forged by the many challenges in the crucible of life, the Pendragon Spirit became stronger, and Fragile Creatures became stronger and more able to face the demands that would be made of them."

"Existence set everything going from the start," Church realised. "The good and the bad. A cascade of events, each one impacting on the next."

The woman smiled.

"Everyone has been manipulating everyone else—the Tuatha Dé Danaan and the Fomorii manipulating humanity. But you and the Void were manipulating them, and us, and each other. Nothing is clear. It's all movements in the fog, and you only find out the consequences much later." He considered this. "The Tuatha Dé Danaan used the Fomorii so that the Brothers and Sisters of Dragons would bring about the Golden Ones' return. And the Fomorii god Balor was supposed to stop humanity rising up the ladder.

But...but...because we got involved, Shavi ended up getting killed and Veitch went to the Grim Lands to bring him back, and that break in the rules of the universe attracted the attention of the Void. And brought it back here. And that's exactly what you wanted!" His thoughts raced away with him, and he had to steady himself. "Existence arranged for the Brothers and Sisters of Dragons to play a part in all of this, and you directed the Tuatha Dé Danaan behind the scenes because you wanted the Fall to happen."

"The Fall removed your Brothers and Sisters of Dragons from the heart of the pattern so that a new Five could arise, who would also play a vital part. Mallory, Caitlin, Hal, Hunter and the Forgotten One, brought together with particular skills so they could operate, for a time, beyond the perception of the Devourer of All Things. So they could bring their peculiar skills to this time, this fight, at the End.

"This was all present, right from the start. The Golden Ones had legends of this happening. So did humanity. The final pattern was fully formed at the beginning, and embedded in everything, from the smallest part to the greatest. There to be discovered—"

"If you only had eyes to see," he repeated. "So, right back in the Iron Age...me setting up the Brothers and Sisters of Dragons, the rise of the Culture, who are here now, protecting this site, and you, the formation of the Watchmen...you directed all that, with a subtle push here and another there." His proximity to the reservoir of Blue Fire soothed him, but there was still a dull spike in his gut. "All the pain we suffered, all that terrible heartache, you caused that. Indirectly or not."

"To a definite end."

"That doesn't make it any easier!" Steadying himself, he tried not to think of all the awful things he had gone through to become the force that Existence wanted. It felt so unfair. He could have lived a quiet life, untouched by strife, lived and died and left no mark by his passing, but he could have been content.

"Is being content enough?" the woman said, reading his mind. "In the final reckoning, do you judge the value of your life by what you had, or by what you could have had?"

His head knew the answer; his heart dragged him in another direction.

"That is the eternal dichotomy of the Fragile Creature," the woman said perceptively. "The curse and the gift."

"What happens at the end, when we can all see the final pattern?"

"That is up to you."

"How did I guess?" he said bitterly. For a moment, the ringing cavern was filled only with the faint hiss of the flickering Blue Fire, and then Church said, "I came here to take you to the Far Lands with me."

"And I have been waiting for you to come for me, Brother of Dragons. We are joined, inextricably, for all-time-to-come, and all-time-gone."

"Then let's go." His thoughts were still swimming, but everything that had been planned for so long was so close to a resolution that he could put his doubts and fears to one side. It all came down to him; whether he was capable of navigating what lay ahead, whether he had learned enough; and whether he was prepared to make the final sacrifices that would be demanded of him.

Church strode from the cavern. Behind him, he could hear the torn-sail-cloth sound of wings, growing louder, not just one pair, but more, and more joining every second until the sound was deafening, and the cavern shook.

Emerging into the summery night in the moon-shadow of the ancient stones, Church was surprised to find the Morvren waiting for him in an eerie crescent of blue-black feathers, unmoving, every beady eye fixed upon him. They had always appeared as a portent, following him in a detached manner. This was different. As he looked around the semicircle, he felt a similar connection to the one he had experienced in the cavern. They were a part of him now, this symbol of death joining him at the same time as he had raised the spirit of life. Two sides, two faces.

"I am the Raven King," he said, quietly. "I can do anything."

He smiled. The heavy beat of a different kind of wings grew louder far behind him, tearing out of the hidden caverns of the soul and into the harshness of the real world. Underneath his feet, the Blue Fire surged into the land. It was now so powerful in the leys that he could see it glowing through the grass.

Battle had been declared.

7

"Bleedin' hell! Would you look at that!" Veitch pointed beyond the circle of campfire light to the wild, dark countryside beyond. A swarm of spiders seethed towards the celebrations and Stonehenge. But they had come to a halt in a vast arc around the ancient sacred complex, swirling around an invisible wall that sent them spilling in all directions as they searched for ingress.

"The Blue Fire's holding them at bay." Tom's faint smile was lit by the hot coal of his roll-up. "And that's not all—look."

The reignited leys burned across the landscape, and where they crossed the stream of spiders there were flashes of blue light as the spiders burst into flames.

"Never seen that before," Veitch said in awe.

"Neither has the Army of the Ten Billion Spiders." Ruth had arrived behind them. Veitch and Tom could both see she was changed in some way they couldn't quite define; she appeared to be carrying a great weight. "This place is crackling with power, like it was before the Mundane Spell took effect. The spiders have lost their grip."

"Yeah!" Veitch said. "This is our turf now!"

"Don't get too wound up," Tom said. "Every time you have reignited the power in the land, the Spiders have changed everything to reinforce the Mundane Spell and drive the Blue Fire back into a dormant phase."

"This is still different," Ruth said. "It's never been this strong. Something has changed."

"This is what we're fighting for," Veitch said. "This. Here. Now."

They were interrupted by a breathless Shavi. "Laura has gone."

"She's probably just on the lash with that homebrew alcohol this lot are swilling." Veitch jerked a thumb towards the revellers singing loudly amongst the huts.

"I do not think so." Shavi appeared devastated.

"What's wrong?" Ruth slipped a comforting arm around his shoulders.

"She was last seen walking back towards the Warp Zone. I am afraid . . . I am afraid she has gone to warn the Enemy of our plans. I am afraid she was the traitor amongst us." He wiped away a stray tear.

"Nah!" Veitch said. "She's a bitch, all right. But a traitor—no chance. Her heart was always in the right place. She'd never sell us out." He could see Shavi, Ruth and Tom were not convinced.

"What's Church going to think?" Ruth said. "If she has done it, I mean. Betrayed by someone we all put our faith in, someone Church was once really close to."

"Does it destroy hope in the Pendragon Spirit?" Tom asked. "Does it breed despair? Hope is what keeps the spirit alive."

Before they could consider it further, the night was torn by the thunder of wings. An awed silence fell across the camp as all eyes turned to the sky. Glimmering in the moonlight, the Fabulous Beasts moved steadily towards the Warp Zone, their scales glinting like jewels, occasional bursts of golden liquid-fire illuminating the land beneath them.

"He did it," Tom said, smiling to himself.

"Bloody hell." Veitch's strained voice reflected the wonder that was heavy in all their faces.

"Yes," Ruth said. "Yes."

"This is it." Veitch grinned broadly. "This is where we take the fight back to the bastards!"

CHAPTER TEN
TOWARDS THE FORTRESS

1

In the dead heat, a stifling desolation choked the blasted lands. The dry, ochre dust of the hardpan licked up to jagged rocks and dead, twisted trees reaching blackened hands towards the bleached sky. In the craters, pools of foul-smelling, rainbow-streaked oil attracted clouds of fat, lazy flies, droning constantly.

This was the land that the Void had built.

Just visible through the haze hanging in the distance was a structure so large that at first it appeared to be a part of the landscape, a soaring bluff stretching across the whole length of the horizon, its brown granite charred here and there by great fires. Above it, black birds swirled like gulls scavenging a refuse tip. But as the eye adjusted to the perspective, jarring details emerged in opposition to natural law: disturbing angles, unsettling proportions, materials with the gleam of plastic or metal, or the sickly resilience of meat; and the birds could not be birds: much larger than any known living creature, their scavenging took on a menacing air.

It was the Fortress of the Enemy, known by some as the House of Pain, a complex as large as a city, constantly under construction, with no end in sight as it crept relentlessly across the landscape exuding a potent atmosphere of black depression. For all its artifice, there was still a sense that in some way it was alive.

The Burning Man towered above, black smoke pothering from the flaming outline.

Scrambling down the scree of a steep hillside, the first sight of the Fortress brought Church, Ruth, Shavi, Veitch and Tom to a sudden halt. They told themselves it was the imposing sight that affected them so deeply, and tried to ignore the unsettling alien whispers that insinuated into the back of their heads.

"Big." Veitch shielded his eyes against the sun. What he didn't say told them more about his feelings.

"Swarming with Lament-Brood, Redcaps and God knows what else," Ruth said. "I mean, how many of them must be inside a building that size? Are we expected to fight past every one?"

"Yes, go right up and knock on the door," Tom said tartly.

"Virginia could have shown us the secret path into the Fortress," Church noted, "but she's not here so we've got to find another way. We know the path exists. If we could find it—"

Tom snorted derisively. "Stumble across it, perhaps."

Veitch flinched, and Church steadied him with a subtle nod. "Whatever, if Laura is in there, they'll be ready for us."

He felt the skitter of quick glances upon him. He knew why: he could barely believe Laura had betrayed them, and the more he allowed the concept to settle upon him, the more despairing he felt. They needed to be Five united as One for the Pendragon Spirit to be most effective. Every new development destabilised them a little further, causing fissures to spread throughout relationships he had considered solid. He felt the hand of the Libertarian upon it—sickeningly, his own hand. He had underestimated his alter ego's capability for subtlety: the brash, theatrical exterior of the Libertarian had been a distraction, and now looked clever and carefully designed.

They skidded down the remainder of the scree and raised clouds of sticky yellow dust as they trudged across the hardpan towards the Fortress. After ten minutes, Shavi brought them to a halt.

"Movement," he whispered, subtly indicating a crumbling rock formation that resembled a finger pointing at the sky.

"That eye's a bloody good deal, mate," Veitch said.

Veitch and Church kicked up a large cloud of dust, which allowed Veitch the cover to approach the rock on the blindside of where Shavi had seen the movement. When he disappeared behind the outcropping, they waited for the sound of a fight, but within a few seconds Veitch was hailing them from a ledge on the side of the rock.

They found him with his arm around a ruddy-faced Brother of Dragons with a thatch of wiry blond hair, who was grinning broadly. John Baker was a seventeenth-century farmhand. Church had discovered him lifting a cart to mend a broken wheel, a remarkable feat of strength that was matched only by the depth of his good humour.

"Never thought I'd see the day," he said in a broad Cornish accent.

"The rest of the Army of Dragons is here," Veitch said.

"Ar, what's left of 'em." The grim note in Baker's voice was quickly replaced by the grin. "I've been out on patrol for a day and night. Orders were to find you and bring you in, but we were afraid you'd already gone inside there, and that'd be the last we'd see of you."

"We wouldn't leave you out of the fun," Veitch said. "Let's go and get everybody tooled up. This is where it all kicks off."

2

An expanse of rocks, dust and haze gave way suddenly to a colourful camp as they passed through the boundary of the glamour. With a pang of regret, they saw it was smaller than they had hoped, but the cheers that rose up the instant they were seen wiped away any dismal thoughts for a while.

A knot of about ninety Brothers and Sisters of Dragons were suddenly swallowed by a significantly larger crowd of jostling gods, the commotion quickly devolving into a number of fights and arguments. Church was pleased to see Lugh, a wan smile lighting a face that had grown too grim.

He shook Church's hand heartily. "Welcome back, Brother of Dragons. I knew you would not be deterred from your mission."

"How are your people?"

"Less than a tenth of the army survive. The Court of the Soaring Spirit was destroyed. Many fled. How many survive across the Far Lands, I do not know."

Lugh accompanied Church and the others into the leader's tent. Church expected to see Decebalus planning strategy around the large wooden table in the centre of the tent, but instead it was Ronnie, his First World War uniform giving him some gravitas, but his face showing the weight of expectations upon him.

Aula was with him. "Decebalus is dead," she said bluntly. "He sacrificed himself to prevent the Enemy gaining the Caraprix. He will always be remembered as a great hero." She held her head proudly, but her grief was clear.

"I'm sorry," Church said. "He was a good man. I was proud to call him my friend."

Aula nodded curtly, and restrained a sad smile.

"Pleased to have you back, sir," Ronnie said, relieved. "I presume you'll be taking control of the forces now."

"You're going to have to keep that responsibility, Ronnie. We're entering the Fortress as planned. We need someone on the ground to marshal the troops. You're the best man for that with your experience."

"I was afraid you were going to say that, sir. I've heard it once already today."

The explanation for his comment was revealed as Mallory and Caitlin marched in, throwing themselves into unrestrained hugging and back-slapping.

"Mission accomplished," Mallory said. "Though not without a few minor hiccups." He handed Church a package tightly wrapped in purple velvet. Church could feel the buzzing energy of the Extinction Shears even through the material.

"I'd like to say it was nothing," Caitlin said with a smile, "but it really was something."

Mallory turned to Veitch tentatively. "Etain is gone. And the other three. She sacrificed herself to save us."

"That sounds like her."

"I think she loved you, in her own way."

Veitch nodded slowly. "She was a good person who had a raw deal. We . . . found a lot in common. I'll miss her." He hesitated. "Thanks for telling me."

"No problem. I was wrong about her. Maybe I'm wrong about you too. Everybody deserves a second chance, right?"

Cautiously, with a brief nod, they came to terms with each other.

For a few hours, everyone exchanged details of the battles they had fought, the ones they had won and the others they had lost, mourned friends who had fallen and drew up plans for the fight to come. Most of all they enjoyed being reunited with old friends, and new ones, men and gods together, at peace in each other's company. It was a bittersweet time, for though they had overcome all odds to be together once again, they knew it could well be the last time.

That knowledge generated a heightened mood where deep emotions thrived. Once dark had fallen, Church led the others through the camp. In each little enclave, the gods sat around campfires, telling stories in grave voices, or drinking and feasting, fighting, having sex, whichever were the peculiarities of their own particular group. The Norse were the most raucous, followed closely by the Greeks in an adjoining camp, and at times they appeared to be in competition with each other as to who could revel with the most abandon. The Chinese were measured and introspective, weighing the lessons of the past before considering tactics for the following day. In some of the groups the rituals were alien and unsettling.

The Brothers and Sisters of Dragons were welcomed by all the gods they encountered. Church declined offer after offer to join this group or that, and once they had toured the entire camp, he led the others back to the Tuatha Dé Danaan, where they felt most at home.

Around the fire, stripped of their arrogance and facing the harsh reality of their position in the universe, the Golden Ones appeared smaller in stature, but somehow more noble than Church had ever seen them. The mood was restrained, but positive, and after a while they began to sing. The songs stirred the emotions in ways far beyond the simple arrangements of music and words, evoking their yearnings for the four lost cities of their homeland—Gorias, Finias, Falias and Murias—the only places where they would ever feel at peace.

When they had finished, Church saw tears in Ruth's eyes. "I don't know your homeland, but we all long for the same thing," she said to Lugh. "We just give it different names. A place or a relationship where we can be who we really are. Somewhere we can put aside the constant struggling and the fears and the anxiety and find peace."

"We will all find our home one day," Lugh said. He turned his attention to Church. "Never in our long existence have the Tuatha Dé Danaan known hopelessness, but now we all feel it pressing tight against our backs. The Devourer of All Things has haunted us since the earliest stories told by my people. In our hearts, we know it is the End. Should we fight this battle, or would it be best for us to walk away and seek out our homeland, attempt to find at least a little of that peace before all falls away?"

Every one of the assembled Tuatha Dé Danaan turned their attention to Church; he could see this was a question that had been troubling all of them.

"Over the last few days I've been forced to consider a lot of big questions...why we are here and what all this around us means," he began slowly. "And I've learned to study life in the smallest detail to find the big answers. I don't know if I believe in an End. The science of my people suggests there is no such thing. The universe starts with a bang, expands, collapses and then restarts—a constant cycle of life and death. And that's what we see in nature. The big answers are written small." He looked to Shavi, who was nodding. "All the information encoded in every aspect of everything, like every part of a hologram contains all the information possessed by the whole. There is no end. We can see it around us, in the turn of the seasons. We can see it in the Tarot cards, where the Fool goes on a journey of enlightenment, and when he thinks he's learned everything, he's back to the start as the Fool again, learning once more."

Lugh nodded. "Then the End may be a new start. But for the Devourer of All Things and his followers. Not for us."

"Fair enough. But I think the Void can be beaten," Church said. "The Void loves the mundane, the normal. For all its spiders and its weird army, it hates magic. And that, essentially, is what the Blue Fire is. Look around you. Here we are, in the heart of this landscape devastated by the Void, and magic is still here."

Everyone shifted their intense concentration from Church's words and looked around, and they saw that he was right. The campfire crackled and sent golden sparks swirling upwards in the fragrant woodsmoke, tiny stars shimmering with beauty. High overhead, the real stars shone like ice in a glacial sweep across the black velvet sky. As one, their breathing slowed, and they listened, and they felt. There was silence in their tiny circle of light, and the peace that only came where magic lay.

"We have to use the magickal lessons we learned on our long journey," Church continued, but now he was talking directly to the Brothers and Sisters of Dragons. "The secret knowledge that kids know and adults forget, because it's encoded in their stories, their books. Don't stray from the path. Trust your heart. Three times is the charm, say the name three times, call three times. And the rest. That information comes from the Far Lands. This place is the receptacle of that knowledge, for our world to tap into. So we learn it, for this time, this battle. The magic is in here." Church rested his fist against his heart. "That's what we've learned, isn't it? On the road, after we all got together that first time." He looked Ruth directly in the eyes. "On that long trek I made from the Iron Age back to our time." She didn't look away. Church saw the campfire reflected in her eyes, and himself, and the past, as the frostiness he had sensed since Stonehenge slowly slid away.

"Friendship," she said. Then, hesitantly, "Love. It sounds sickly, sentimental, simplistic." She looked to Shavi and Veitch, and then to Tom. "But that's what we learned, isn't it? Five forged into One. That's where the magic is. And we don't stray from the path." She felt for Church's hand out of sight of the others and squeezed it tightly. "We don't stray from the path," she said quietly to herself.

A low, mournful call rang out across the camp that sent goosebumps up Church's arm. Gradually, the tone changed until it became uplifting, growing louder, a roar of defiance. The Tuatha Dé Danaan jumped to their feet as one.

"Our brother!" Lugh exclaimed.

Peering into the dark beyond the campfire, Church's eyes gradually became accustomed to the gloom. He could just discern a large figure circling the camp, occasionally throwing its head back to roar into the night; at times it appeared to be an animal, with horns silhouetted against the lighter night sky; on other glimpses, it appeared to be nothing more than vegetation.

"Cernunnos," Ruth said quietly. "The Green Man, he's here. That should give us hope—he's a god, one of the Oldest Things in the Land, and he's so closely linked to the Blue Fire."

Church looked up at the spray of stars. "This could be the last time we see this." He put an arm around her shoulders. "Let's make the most of it."

Ruth folded into his arms and rested her head on his shoulder. "Sometimes everything feels such a mess, Church. Everything between us should be perfect, but I'm scared that there's some real darkness inside you—"

"The Libertarian waiting to come out?"

"Yes. I was all ready to keep you at arm's length, but what you said at the fire . . . about the magic. It made me realise what we had, and what we've got to fight to keep. We've come a long way, from beneath Albert Bridge to this God-forsaken place, and everything feels as if it's been trying to tear us apart. But here we are!"

"It just shows how fragile everything is. We can't take anything for granted. You and me. What we feel for each other. There's always a threat waiting, beyond the path, in the forest." He kissed the top of her head, closed his eyes and indulged himself in the warmth from her body. "I think you're right—there is a darkness inside me. And you. We know what happens when you get caught up in the power of the Craft, right?"

She stiffened, realising the truth of this for the first time.

"And that's how it should be. Because without that darkness we wouldn't be able to fight. We'd be useless. That's where we find our anger, our drive. I've been thinking more and more about the rules hidden in life about us, and particularly in that whole duality thing. It's everywhere, in every aspect of life. Two faces. Light and dark. Summer and winter. Even Cernunnos has two faces—his light side and his dark side, the Erl-King. We need both. The trick is not to let that darkness dominate. I . . . we . . . have to fight every day to keep it under control because there's always a chance it could break through. I could become the Libertarian. You could destroy everything! But we can fight, and we can win. We just mustn't . . . stray from the path . . . of you and me, and what we believe in."

She was silent for a moment; he couldn't see her face in the dark to judge her mood. Then she said, "But doesn't that mean Existence is wrong to destroy the Void? We need both of them."

"I don't know. I do know that the Void is going to destroy us and Existence if it gets its way. This battle has been building since the beginning of time. Who knows what the outcome's going to be?"

She kissed him deeply. "I'm sorry," she said, "for almost making a mess of things."

"That's what we do, right?"

Behind a tent, away from the buzz of people returning to the campfire, she pulled him down and kissed him again. Within moments, they were deep in passion, an act of love that was also an act of magic. The world flashed by, the sounds of the camp and the jubilant roar of Cernunnos, all lost to the rhythm of their bodies and the beat of their blood. When they were finished, they held each other in silence and remembered what they had overcome to be there. Neither of them thought about what the following day would bring.

In the hazy half-world on the edge of sleep, Church had an impression of someone circling them slowly, close to the ground. He saw bright eyes and a wide grin filled with mischief.

The voice rolled out, rich and wry: "The Merry Wanderer of the Night looks after fools and lovers. Dream on, sweet children, and dream the world a'right."

3

Dawn came up hard on the blasted lands. The red sun turned the desolate landscape to blood and within an hour the heat was unforgiving. The remnants of the Army of Dragons gathered to see Church and the others off. Church felt undeserving of the awe he saw in their respectful faces, but he understood their need for inspiration and moved through them, shaking hands and exchanging comments with the ones he knew personally.

Finally he came to Ronnie who gave him a formal salute. "Sir!"

"You're going to be fine, Ronnie."

"I miss Decebalus, sir."

"We all do." He glanced at Aula in the crowd, who had swapped her white Roman gown for black armour; her face was scrubbed and her hair cut short. "But you're a Brother of Dragons, Ronnie. And you'll be a better leader than most of the others here. You've seen what heartless leadership can do."

"I hope I can do you proud, sir."

"Just watch out for the Fabulous Beasts. You'll know when to make your move."

Church was surprised to see that many of the gods had turned out too. Tyr clapped him hard on the back and roared with laughter. Freyja seductively kissed his hand, to Ruth's annoyance, and Lei-Gong bowed formally.

"The thunder and the lightning are at your disposal, Brother of Dragons," he said.

Church was increasingly disturbed to see the other gods watching him with hints of the same awe that had gripped the Army of Dragons; before, they had viewed him with contempt or humour. Was he that changed?

Finally, on the edge of the camp, the Tuatha Dé Danaan waited in gleaming ranks. Lugh stepped out and took Church's hand, and then shook the hands of each of the Brothers and Sisters of Dragons and Tom's too. "This may well be the last time we meet," he said. "I am proud to have known you. Fragile Creatures no more—you are the equals of the Golden Ones. You are prepared to sacrifice all you have for our race. We can do no less for you. And if, this day, the Golden Ones are eradicated, keep us in your hearts and remember us fondly, Jack Giant-Killer, for we were spoiled and arrogant, but we brought joy and magic to the lands and that should be our monument."

"It will be." Church hesitated and then gave Lugh a hug. The god appeared surprised at first, but accepted the bond.

As they moved out into the blasted lands, Church and the others could feel the eyes of the Tuatha Dé Danaan on their backs, and the attention of the other gods and the Army of Dragons. Despite their best intentions, it felt like an ending.

4

Her face streaked with tears, her clothes filthy with the sticky ochre dust, Laura staggered across the blasted lands. She had no idea where she was going, just that she had to get away, away from the consequences of her terrible betrayals and the lies and the guilt. If she had stayed with the others she knew she would only have betrayed them again, and again, until they were all dead like Hunter, and the dreams of the Blue Fire and the hopes of all those who believed in Existence were ashes. She would do that. She would destroy anything, friends, strangers, entire worlds. She wouldn't stop until there was nothing left.

She was pleased the blasted lands were so free of moisture. She'd cried herself out, and her abilities needed her to be hydrated to work properly. If she kept walking, she wondered if she might finally dry up and die like any plant left too long in that place.

"I'm not human," she muttered to herself. "The girl I was is gone. What's here is nothing. It doesn't matter any more if I die. Who would care, right?"

Her rambling was disturbed by a long, low call rolling out across the hardpan. Through her daze, she thought it sounded familiar. Glancing back, at first she saw only the dust and the haze, but eventually a dark shape emerged from the glare, bulky, moving fast towards her. She watched it for a moment as her skittering thoughts coalesced and then recognition surfaced from the murk.

"Shit. Shit. Shit!"

Drawing energy from depths she didn't know she had, she broke into a mad scramble. Cernunnos, the god of the green, the power in nature itself, was her patron and her guide. He owned her. And now he was coming to destroy her for her grand betrayal.

Choking on the dust, Laura dived behind a tower of rock, hoping it would hide her from view long enough to decide on an alternative course. She'd taken only four steps when the ground shifted under her feet and a hand snapped around her ankle.

"Bastard! Get off!" She kicked out, only to be thrown roughly onto her back by a brutish, hairless figure rising quickly from where it had been lying hidden in the dust. It was the colour of the rocks, with skin like a lizard's and double-lidded eyes that would protect it from the dust-storms that blew across the blasted lands.

Before Laura could fight back, it had clamped one large, rubbery hand over her mouth and pulled her up under its arm as if she were a doll. Then, with a lurching gait, it loped rapidly across the hardpan. Laura's struggles were quickly contained with a few hard punches, and by the time her senses had stopped reeling, they were below ground level on a dry river bed.

Rounding a bend, Laura saw a force of around two hundred—Lament-Brood, Redcaps and many more like the brutish creature that held her tight. The ranks parted to let her captor run deep into their midst and then closed behind them. Laura was thrown roughly onto the pebbly bed. Dazed, she staggered to her feet, cursing loudly, not caring if they turned on her and killed her there and then.

"Well, a Sister of Dragons." The voice was rich and mocking; and familiar.

"Holy shit," Laura snarled bitterly.

As the warriors parted again, Niamh strode out to stand before Laura, a sadistic smile twisting her lips. Despite the heat, she wore black armour and the black, horned headdress that emphasised the beauty of her features. "Here I truly am the queen of the Waste Lands."

"Bitch of the Waste Lands," Laura snapped.

"So bitter. And you have helped us so much. Now, I think, you can help us some more." She nodded to the brutish creatures and said, "Hurt her, a little. When she is more compliant, we shall return home and see what else she knows."

5

Though they were still a mile away, the Fortress of the Enemy loomed up high above their heads, casting a long, dark shadow across the blasted lands. Above the walls, the flying creatures swooped and soared, calling out harsh, mechanical cries. The air smelled like stagnant ponds on a hot day.

Church and the others had spent half the day seeking an alternative path that had allowed them to approach with a modicum of cover. A crevice cut through the hardpan towards the walls, and though it was not particularly deep it allowed them to get close without discovery so they could search for some point of entry.

Church brought them to a halt at the point where the crevice narrowed and rose over boulders. Crawling on his belly with Veitch beside him, he reached a vantage point where he could scan the remainder of the approach. A towering door of beaten black iron was set in the wall, but there was no other sign of access.

"See there?" Veitch indicated rows of small windows on the upper storeys. "They'll be able to pick us off with arrows before we're halfway to the door. There's no way we'd be able to slip through anyway. There's probably an army of guards on the other side."

"There's no point trying a frontal assault," Church replied. "We'll get nowhere. It's got to be subterfuge or nothing."

"You're using big words again. What are you saying—we sneak in, in disguise or something?"

"Or something."

"You're a crazy suicidal fucker."

"Better idea?"

Shielding his eyes against the glare, Veitch looked along the length of the wall. "I saw you sneak off with Ruthie last night," he said incongruously.

"This isn't the time, Ryan."

"Yeah, it is. We're not all coming out of this in one piece. We probably won't have another good time."

Church sighed. "We don't want this getting between us when we're inside."

Veitch bristled. "You think I'd let it? I know my duty."

"I didn't mean to imply—"

"Yeah, you did. Nobody'd think you'd do that, but me—I'm just the thug, the right-hand man, the psycho who always lets his emotions get in the way of business."

"What do you want, Ryan?"

"I want to be the good guy. I want to be the hero like you. I want everything you've got. Respect, just . . . people thinking well of you. I want Ruth."

"I know you do."

"And I know I'm not going to get her. I can see that, and wishing doesn't make it all right. Fairy-tale endings, they're for people like you. Not me."

"Don't do yourself down. You're as good as any of us."

"You've always stood by me, I know that. Makes me feel even more of a stupid bastard for the fucking awful things I did. And there it is—you're better 'cause you think things like that. And I'm worse, 'cause I think things like I did, and do things like I did. You're the hero deep inside. And I'm the fucking psycho. You always do the right thing, 'cause that's who you are. And I do the wrong thing. Give me two choices, and I'll always pick the wrong one."

"You're here now. You came back to us. You didn't have to."

"Yeah, but did I do it for the right reason, or because I wanted Ruth to think I was a big man? A good man. That's all I've ever wanted to be since I was a kid, and I want it even more now I've been such a nasty, vicious wanker—I want everybody to know that deep down I'm all right. That I can do the right thing. That I'm the hero."

The emotions were so raw that Church didn't know how to answer him.

"I've had a bit of a wake-up call these last few days. I don't know where it'll take me yet, but I'm going to do my best not to be a selfish bastard. I won't try to steal Ruth away from you, however much I want to. Not that I even think I could, but I'm not going to try. I want you to know you don't have to worry about that. About me. I'll have your back in there. I'm trying to learn from you, because you're the best fucking example I've got in this world."

"I'm a mess, Ryan."

"Yeah, but you get over it. And I don't. And that's the difference between a hero and a wannabe. I don't want to be a wannabe. I want people to know

I'm all right. And I want you to be the first. I'm going to be better than I was."

"I trust you, Ryan. You don't have to worry about that."

"Stop being so fucking noble, you cunt. Jesus. I'm never going to live up to your standards." A grin broke through his troubled expression, and Church realised how much he liked him. "It's you and me together, buddy. The last gang in town is going out fighting. We'll do our best. And if we don't win, we'll still have done our best."

"That sounds like a better motto than mine."

"What's yours?"

"No happy endings."

"That's crap. At least I'm better than you at something."

Breathlessly, Mallory slid in next to them. "You need to see this."

They crawled back on their bellies and pulled themselves up on the wall of the crevice where they could see a column of the Enemy approaching across the hardpan. At the head, Niamh rode on a black reptilian horse. Just behind her, Laura trudged, head down.

"She is with them," Church said. "I tried to believe there was some other explanation."

"Still might be," Veitch replied. "Things aren't always how they seem. I should know."

Church was distracted from his mounting despair at Laura's betrayal by the sight of Mallory's knuckles growing white where he gripped the rock.

"That bitch." Mallory blinked away a tear of rage. A shudder ran through him.

"Laura?" Church asked.

"Niamh." Mallory steadied himself. "I don't know why I feel so bad. But I see her, and I just want to get out there and kill her." He looked away. "I don't understand what's wrong with me at the moment. I keep feeling really strong emotions, but I don't know where they're coming from."

In contrast, Church felt a damp sense of dismay when he saw what had become of Niamh, all-pervasive like the cold of a midwinter day. He recalled her on their long trek across the years together, on a warm night on the road from Rome, or in a New England autumn, when she had been consumed with love for him. He had never felt the same depth of emotion back, but her attention and care for him had been endearing, and had kept him going during his darkest hours.

Her transformation was baffling, and he fought to comprehend it. The answer came when he saw Tom crouched down at the foot of the crevice, lost to his dismal thoughts, not the Tom he recalled either but one who yearned for death.

"I made her that way," he said quietly. Devastation descended on him. "I turned the Axis of Existence and altered events, saved Tom and Niamh, and probably a load of other stuff I don't even know about. But every change has unforeseen consequences." He chewed his lip in dismay. "Every bad thing she's done in this form, it's my fault."

The confession hit Mallory hard. Staring at Church, he struggled with the mysterious tides of his powerful emotions, then, unable to comprehend or contain them, he gave in and with an anguished roar drew his sword and half-scrambled over the lip of the crevice.

Church and Veitch dragged him back, too late. A cry went up and the ground vibrated with feet running in their direction.

"That's torn it!" Veitch wrenched out his sword, the blue and black flames surging, entwining.

"Sorry. Hell, what's wrong with me!" Mallory raged.

Church gripped his arm, steadied him. "Forget it. Fight!"

Blue Flames whooshed as they drew their swords together. All three of them were stunned by the way the fire from the three blades funnelled together, twisting in complex shapes, interacting, throwing out bolts of crackling energy.

It echoed within each of them, feeding the Pendragon Spirit so they felt unbelievably stronger, more confident.

"The Three Great Swords of Existence!" they heard an awed Tom exclaim behind them. "In use together for the first time in generations. Three become one!"

They had no time to consider what it meant. The first brutish creatures appeared at the lip of the crevice.

"We've got to get out of here!" Veitch yelled. "They'll just pick us off one by one trapped down here!"

Church scrambled back along the crevice with Ruth, Shavi, Caitlin and

Tom close behind, and Mallory and Veitch protecting the rear. Scrabbling for footholds, Church propelled himself up the opposite wall of the crevice and out onto the hardpan. The roar that greeted him from the enemy was deafening. At the same time he saw activity along the rows of windows in the Fortress wall. In the midst of the action, his attention alighted on two things: the delight that came to Niamh's face, not that of someone who spies a former lover, but something cruel and sadistic; and the devastation that marred Laura's battered features.

Battle cries that sounded like the roars of hungry animals filled the air. The enemy streamed across the narrowest gap in the crevice, and within seconds Church was fighting for his life. The brutish creatures moved with the speed and strength of gorillas, using their long arms to propel themselves forwards before slashing in a frenzied manner with short, serrated swords. Bracing himself, Church hacked with Caledfwlch, but each collision was so bone-jarring that he was almost thrown from his feet.

Within seconds, Veitch and Mallory were at his side and he felt his strength and stamina increase proportionately. The air was red with blood-mist and lit with the electric sizzle of the Blue Fire, dancing around them as though it was alive.

"Nice one, Mallory," Veitch shouted between attacks. "Why didn't you send up flares while you were at it?"

"I didn't want you to get lonely doing all the screwing up." Mallory's Templar swordsmanship was more controlled than the other two, and he carved through two for every one Church and Veitch took down with their self-taught skill.

For several minutes, the world was just the hard-fought few feet around them, where the dismembered bodies piled up and their own lives were challenged every second. But then they each became aware of activity beyond their sphere.

A gap in the attacking bodies revealed Ruth transformed into a furious elemental force, her hair whirling about her head, Blue Fire crackling off her and the Spear of Lugh, which she wielded with brutal efficiency. Attackers she didn't even touch flew back from the force of invisible hands. Others were turned inside out, or had their eyes boiled in their heads.

"Bleedin' hell," Veitch said. "You're not going to want to get in a fight with her."

312

Beyond Ruth, Caitlin was a force of nature too. Her eyes blazed as she carved a path through the brutish creatures with her axe, which whirled so fast it was barely visible. Heads split in two, limbs were cleaved, and while she was striking with one arm, she was tearing out throats with the other. When one attacker broke through her defences, Caitlin effortlessly clamped her teeth on his jugular and ripped it away; blood drenched her hair and face, but she never missed a step. The savagery of her attack was counterpointed by the eerie calmness of her face.

"We're the A-Team," Veitch said, gutting another attacker.

As the waves of brutish creatures thinned out, Church dared to hope they had survived the onslaught. But then Niamh's shrill laughter echoed nearby, and the attackers came to a halt.

Through some trickery, Niamh had got the better of Ruth, who now slumped in a daze at Niamh's feet, a knife at her throat.

"My rival of the heart for so long, through all those years of my awakening to the pain of human existence, and here she is, finally at my mercy." Niamh laughed. "Oh, how different things would have been if I had cut the life from her all those times ago." Niamh looked directly at Church, no hurt in her eyes, just cruel glee. "And now she is here, I have no true need of her death, for I have already got you, my sweet, in a form that is better than the one you now occupy, stronger, more attuned to me. I have won. And she has lost, because I will have you forever, and she will not. Though she no longer matters to me one jot, I will kill her anyway, because I can. Because it will drive you into my arms, soon now, just a little way along this road."

Church froze. Was this it? The moment of shattering devastation that would transform him into the Libertarian? He looked at Ruth, the knife at her throat, and his heart broke. Nothing mattered more than keeping her alive; not the destruction of all Existence, all his friends, his sanity, his soul. Nothing.

At the great Fortress wall, the enormous gates rattled open slowly. The black gulf grew wider, like a monstrous mouth, and then light flooded in to reveal a sea of misshapen creatures poised to spill out across the hardpan.

Mallory let his sword drop to his side. "This is starting to look like game over."

Church turned his attention from the reinforcements back to Niamh's hard smile, and then to the knife poised a fraction of an inch from destroying his world. And then Ruth's eyes snapped open, her lips moved and after the disconnection of a second, a word of power boomed out. A bolt of Blue Fire seared across Niamh's face and into the silver sky where it exploded like fireworks. Screaming, Niamh staggered back, clutching her face. One side of her shimmering golden features was seared black, the sun being eaten by the moon.

Caitlin grabbed Ruth's arm and hauled her towards Church, Veitch and Mallory. In the lull, Shavi and Tom clambered out of their shelter in the crevice and faced the oncoming horde.

"Hundreds of them," Veitch said. The bleak edge to his voice stung them all.

"No point running," Mallory said. "Got to die sometime."

"I always planned on picking my moment," Veitch said. "Fuck."

"The bad news never stops coming." Tom was facing away from the Fortress, looking out across the hardpan. The others turned to see what had caught his attention.

Glistening like oil, a black wave washed across the hardpan. On skittering insect legs, the Fomorii came, their forms changing as they moved, plates clanking into place, spikes bursting from the gleaming carapaces, wings unfurling. Thousands of the shape-shifting beasts converged on the Fortress gates.

"They found their way through the Groghaan Gate," Church said.

"This is just overkill." Mallory turned slowly to take in the full weight of the forces ranged against them. On the lip of the crevice, the tiny knot of Brothers and Sisters of Dragons was at the eye of a hurricane of savage enemies. Amidst a deafening, full-throated clamour, the Void's army continued to surge out of the Fortress, like the flow from a disturbed anthill. The Fomorii were almost upon them too, the low rumble of their call and response now resonating in the pits of their stomachs.

Church felt for Ruth's hand, and they exchanged one brief, painful look of regret.

"We always knew it would come down to this, right?" Veitch said. "People like us, we were never going to win."

"Speak for yourself," Mallory muttered. He eyed Caitlin, wishing his friend was there, but seeing only the grim face of the Morrigan.

"Laura ought to be here," Shavi said. "We should all be together at the end." Searching the swelling ranks, Shavi finally glimpsed her casting one desperate look his way before moving towards the Fortress gates of her own accord. His heart sank.

As Church prepared for the wave to break over them, he realised something odd was happening. The Fomorii had moved into a crescent formation, the twin horns bypassing the Brothers and Sisters of Dragons. His first thought was that they were completing the circle, but they continued with mounting speed until they crashed with the force of a tsunami on the disoriented ranks of the Enemy.

Church had forgotten the sheer ferocity of the Nightwalkers. The Fomorii ripped through the brutish creatures, the Lament-Brood, the Redcaps, as if they were sheep. Razor-sharp limbs and snapping jaws churned up a fountain of body parts, bones and blood, as if the Enemy had been put through a giant mincer. A red haze came down, making it impossible to see more than a few yards ahead.

The unthinking enemy army put up a fierce resistance, seemingly oblivious to their own impending destruction. By sheer weight of numbers they bought down several of the Fomorii. But soon paths were being carved through their ranks and the flow from the gates was reversed: the retreat had been announced.

Church and the others shielded themselves from the wild, bloody storm in the reaches of the crevice, but as it moved towards the Fortress wall, they clambered out to witness the carnage. A red slurry lay across the ochre hardpan. Along the walls, some of the Fomorii harried the last of the Enemy left out in the open after the gates were closed, while others threw themselves at the walls, attempting to break through or scale them.

"What the hell?" Mallory said. "Never saw that one coming."

"I...I think that may explain it," Ruth gasped.

Making his way across the hardpan with a piratical swagger was Hunter. Behind him trailed Miller, Jack and Virginia, all in the bizarre shadow of a hooded giant.

Stunned, Church and the others could only gape as Hunter offered a broad grin and a wave. "Missed me?" he said.

"We thought you were dead," Shavi replied. "All of you."

"Takes more than a few-hundred-foot fall to kill me. I'm a hard, hard man." He nodded towards Miller. "Besides, when you've got Doctor Miller here with his healing hands, anything is possible."

Church shook his hand forcefully. "It's good to have you back, Hunter."

"Who's the big guy?" Veitch asked.

"My new brother. Yeah, probably wouldn't be a good idea to antagonise him. He gets under your skin and into your head, and not in a good way."

Ruth looked towards the Fomorii. "How did you—?"

"Him too."

While Mallory hugged Miller, then Virginia, and clapped Jack on the back with honest relief, Shavi said with cautious sensitivity, "We feared you had been murdered by Laura. She has not been herself."

"You always did have a way with words," Hunter said noncommittally. His grin remained broad.

"Did she attack you?" Ruth pressed.

"Not something we need to think about right now."

"It's something you need to think about very shortly," Tom said sharply. "She's working with the Enemy. She's inside the Fortress. With all she knows about us and our plans, she could cause untold damage."

"I'll deal with her," Hunter said. He removed the Balor Claw from his backpack and slipped it on.

"What's that?" Church asked suspiciously.

"Nice, isn't it?" Hunter turned it so it caught the harsh light. "I think it adds to my flamboyant appeal. Got to look good going into battle."

"Hunter, I know how much you cared for Laura," Ruth pressed. "I know you must be devastated by what she did to you. It's okay to let it out."

"Nothing to let out, beautiful."

"Just . . . just don't hurt her. Whatever she's done, she's still one of us," Ruth said, unsettled by his calm demeanour.

"Don't worry, I'll be gentle."

"Virginia can lead us inside the Fortress?" Church asked.

"There's a dry river bed about a mile that way." Hunter indicated east. "It runs close to the walls. Somewhere along it there's the remains of an underground tributary. Follow that and it'll bring you through run-off channels to the lowest levels of the Fortress. Apparently it's pretty deserted down there, so we should be able to move quickly to a good proximity of where we need to be."

"I don't think we should travel together," Church said.

"I agree."

"Are you mad?" Ruth said. "Haven't you seen a hundred horror films where the team splits up only to get picked off one by one?"

"We need to maximise our chances of somebody getting through," Church said. "If we're all travelling together we're easy to find—and to kill."

"If you want my advice, you should lead your original lot," Hunter said. "Mallory and Caitlin work well together. Looks like they've still got Hal in the lantern. That makes a team. I'll take Miller, Jack—the Two Keys—and Virginia. We've got a good rhythm going."

"Mallory can take the Extinction Shears so we haven't got all our resources together," Church said.

"I'll look for Laura first," Hunter said. "Neutralise the fact that she could upset the apple cart. Then I'll head for the reunion." He ignored Ruth's searching gaze.

"How will we know where and when to meet up?" Shavi asked.

"My new pal." Hunter indicated the giant who was standing motionless on the fringes, his head cocked to one side. "He's some kind of mentalist—reads minds, talks to you in your head. Weird as hell, but it works. He's the link for group communication, and he can also perceive any potential threats upcoming on our routes. And guide me to Laura."

"Sounds like a plan." The relief in Church's voice was palpable. "I thought we were done for. Now we're back on course. I'll tell the others."

Veitch and Hunter were left alone. "You and me, we're alike," Veitch said, gently clanking his silver hand against the Balor Claw. "Same basic abilities, same psycho-skills for killing. You're smarter by a long way, and I'm not going to be copying your fashion sense, but we're on the same wavelength, right?"

Hunter nodded, wondering where Veitch was going with this line of thought.

"I might be a thick-headed git from South London, but that doesn't mean I don't learn from my mistakes," Veitch continued. "So whatever you're planning for Laura, give her a break. Things might not be how they seem. I know how you can end up doing stuff that you'd never normally do. Her and me, we've never seen eye to eye, but deep down her heart's in the right place. For her sake...and for yours...don't do something you'll regret for the rest of your life."

"Thanks for the advice."

They nodded curtly and separated. Veitch hoped he'd done enough; Hunter was impossible to read, but Veitch was afraid they really were too much alike.

While Mallory and Caitlin examined the unnervingly weak flame in the Wayfinder, and Hunter regaled the others with a brief but dramatic version of his journey from Winter-side, Church and Ruth returned to Veitch.

"Everything is going in the right direction now," Ruth said. "We've eased the tensions amongst us. We've turned you away from the Libertarian—"

"No, we haven't," Church said bluntly. A shadow crossed his face. "If everything was going fine, he'd be here, making our lives a misery every step of the way. But he's not, he's sitting back somewhere, and that means he still thinks things are on course."

"But what can go wrong now?" Ruth said. "We're together." She squeezed his hand tightly. "You said that it was something to do with you and me that tips you over to become the Libertarian—we're not going to let that happen."

The defiance in her voice failed to move him. A black mood welled up in Church, all his fears laid bare, and Ruth realised how much he had been suppressing it. She couldn't bear to see that raw emotion etched in his face.

"We don't know what's ahead," he said. "We can mitigate against it as much as possible, but...we don't know. One thing's for sure—I will never let myself become the Libertarian. I've already seen some of the misery my stupid, thoughtless actions have caused. I'm not going to have any more on my conscience. I'll do whatever it takes to make sure the Libertarian's future doesn't come to pass."

Grim-faced, Church marched away. Ruth watched him go, her heart breaking.

"We're going to keep an eye on him, all right?" Veitch said.

Ruth cast a quizzical glance his way.

"Nah, it's not some ploy to win your heart. I'm a simple bloke—I don't do things like that." He watched Church kneel and hug Virginia tightly, as much to find comfort for himself as for her. "Our lives are like some bad soap most of the time, but here we're right down to the wire and everything has to change.

We've passed the point where we can indulge ourselves with little games. It's about survival now. And we all need to look after each other, because we're friends. More than friends, maybe. Family, in a stupid, screwed-up kind of way. From here on in, we're looking out for each other, watching backs, carrying the weight."

"What's come over you, Ryan?"

"You know us working-class boys—we're hard as nails but we're sentimental as fuck." He paused. "I love you."

"Ryan—"

"Don't say anything, you stupid tosser. I love you and I want you to be happy, all the time, ever after, and if that means you're with Church, well, that's the way things are meant to be." He glanced after Church. "And I love him too, like a brother. He's blood. The bloke I admire most in the world. That's why I was so desperate to kill him. Make sense?"

"Only in your strange, warped world, Ryan." She tried to make light, but she felt all her emotion on the point of bursting out. Too much stress, she told herself. Calm down.

"We're all he's got—you, me, Shavi, Tom. He needs us to look out for him, to keep him safe, to stop him doing something stupid. And that's what we're going to do, right? We're going to look after him, and keep him safe. Whatever it takes. Because he needs us."

"You're rambling, Ryan."

"Yeah, sorry."

"I love you too." She surprised him with a kiss on the cheek and then went after Church.

He knew what it really meant and he wasn't disappointed. It was, quite honestly, the best moment in his entire life, better even than the mermaids swimming beside the boat on the way to Caldey Island. He didn't need anything more now.

6

Along the great Fortress wall, the Fomorii swarmed. Some climbed and ripped out chunks around the windows, ignoring the clouds of flaming arrows that emerged from within. Others crashed against the great gates. It was only a matter of time before they broke through the defences.

"Death is all around, brother," said El-Di-Gah-Wis-Lor, the final judgement of the Drakusa. Blinded by his hood, the giant saw everything. "I feel it circling, shifting the patterns of this world, leaving marks and symbols that tell of its passing. A shadow where none should be. A cloud in the shape of a skull. Random grains of sand that spell a dead lover's name. The others do not notice these things, but they feel it, sometimes. A shiver. A moment of emptiness. A question on their lips."

"Yep, this time we're bringing death on a grand scale, and you're helping me do it," Hunter said. "I've always hated my strength, but sometimes you've just got to recognise what you're good at and go with it." He watched the Fomorii in action. "I hope they're enough to get things moving."

"They will suffice for now. There are more things on the way."

"Yeah?" Hunter shrugged. "Funny how things turn out. All these little coincidences. Me stumbling across you, you saving my life. Your presence saving the lives of the others. Now this."

"There are no coincidences, brother."

"Maybe you're right."

The giant turned and looked into the sky behind him.

"What do you see?"

"The opposite of us, brother."

Beyond the deafening rending and tearing of the Fomorii, Hunter could just make out another sound, drawing nearer. "Wings?"

From the far horizon came the Fabulous Beasts. He counted seven; there could be more behind. The one at the head was larger and even more magnificent than the rest, the steady rhythm of its leathern wings like a heartbeat. Its jewelled scales gleamed, and the myriad colours, and the sheer wonder that it evoked deep inside him made the desolation of the blasted lands insignificant, a grey shadow that would fade in the first rays of the sun.

Hunter watched the Beasts pass over and for the first time in his life felt at peace. The downdraught from the wings ruffled his hair and the shadows passing over were cool and refreshing. Sinuously, the Fabulous Beasts arched and then drove down towards the Fortress, performing an intricate, breathtaking ballet in the air above it.

The greatest one was the first to release a blast of liquid fire that sent a geyser of rubble blasting into the air and set alight a large area of the Fortress. Soon the others were diving and releasing their terrible flame. The Fortress shook and large sections of the wall fell away to reveal the swarming insect life within. The glorious blaze leaped up to the sky, pouring thick black smoke that for the first time obscured the shape of the Burning Man. The heat was so intense that Hunter could feel it on his face a mile distant.

"Game on," he said.

CHAPTER ELEVEN
THE GREAT HOUR OF DESTINY

1

As the glamour faded, the world rushed in to greet them. Overseeing the hellish scene with a sick fascination, Ronnie recalled the Somme with a clarity that made him shudder, the carpet of bodies so thick you could walk across it without touching earth, the pall of choking smoke, the plague of rats and the rain-lashed trenches.

"Ronnie? You okay?" Doctor Jay shook his arm.

"Yes. Of course. Fine as a fiddle."

The sky was black with greasy, sulphurous smoke, the harsh red and gold glare of the blazing fortress like a dying sun in the depths of space. In the gloom all around, the Army of Dragons and the ranks of the gods waited patiently for Ronnie's order.

Bitterly, he recalled Haig's plan that could not fail: a seven-day bombardment to destroy the German defences and then the order to advance to pick off the disoriented survivors. So terribly flawed. Fifty-eight thousand British troops dead or mutilated in one day alone. The machine guns cutting bodies in two. Was Haig haunted by his failure? Ronnie wondered. How could he possibly live with himself after that?

"War demands the best of us." Aula was at his shoulder, calm and steady in a way that he had never seen her before; there was more of Decebalus in her than she liked to reveal. "We fight for the right reasons, and it demands sacrifices," she continued. "And sacrifices of our own souls, for we are forced to give up a part of ourselves that we would never have relinquished before. It destroys the person we were and we can never recover, but we do it so that others can live the lives we cannot."

"I'm prepared for my own sacrifice, ma'am."

"And everyone here has signed that compact too. Trust yourself. Never forget why we do what we do. Never forget the humanity of the people who fight. With those two things in mind, your decisions will be true."

Ronnie took a deep breath. "Doctor Jay...Aula...thank you for your counsel."

"We're all in it together, man. Don't forget that," the Doctor said.

Ronnie strode out along the lines and gave the order. There was only a briefest tinge of self-doubt, and then he turned his attention to the battle. Thor, Tyr and Ares raced ahead with insane glee. The Japanese war god Bishamon was more measured. But those who marched into the fray with the greatest dignity were the Tuatha Dé Danaan, Lugh at their head, glowing like a sun. There was a great sadness about them, but also a fierce determination; for the first time Ronnie thought they truly did resemble gods.

As they neared, a thousand thousand flaming arrows erupted from the Fortress windows, the stars coming down to earth.

The final battle began.

2

Even far underground, the tremors reverberated from the constant fusillade. Dust and fragments showered down until the Brothers and Sisters of Dragons feared that the rock overhead was on the point of collapse. They had made their way along the dead riverbed and through Virginia's network of crawl-spaces into the lower reaches of the Fortress with speed. Their parting of the ways had been swift, with nods and hugs, none of them knowing if they would ever see each other again.

Now Hunter climbed steps that had the sickly texture of meat with the whisper of his brother giant in his head. Following in his footsteps came Virginia, seeming to carry a great age with her now that she was back in the place of torment, then Jack, serious and intent, and a frightened Miller at the rear.

The steps opened onto a narrow corridor running along the Fortress wall overlooking the battle. The heat there was intense. Charred bodies lined the way, and thick smoke rolled in through gaping holes. A few Lament-Brood fought mechanically with Fomorii warriors clinging to the outside wall.

The Balor Claw sang as Hunter moved swiftly down the corridor, taking apart any Enemy he met. A branching corridor led them deep into the heart of the Fortress. At one point the route was blocked from wall to wall by a solid column of Lament-Brood marching towards the front line. The Balor Claw reduced them to nothing in minutes. Hunter pushed on relentlessly. Jack, who knew him best, could not read his mood: anger, desperation, grief, something of all three? Mostly, he appeared impassive, as though the enemy warriors he was despatching were little more than a distraction, and for the first time Jack felt chilled by what he saw there.

They emerged into a courtyard where a carpet of bones covered the flags. In the centre stood a wooden post from which several chains hung.

When Virginia saw it she began to sob, sucking in huge mouthfuls of air. Jack and Miller tried to comfort her, but she broke free from them and raced towards a low building on the right-hand side of the court.

Hunter cursed loudly. "That's the wrong way!"

"You can't leave her alone in this place!" Miller protested.

Without hesitation, Hunter raced in pursuit of the young girl. Fleet of foot, she moved rapidly through the low building to a dark, stinking room on the far side. Hunter caught up with her standing in the doorway, still sobbing. She flinched when he placed a hand on her shoulder.

As his eyes grew accustomed to the gloom, Hunter saw that the room was filled with people wearing clothes from many periods of Earth's history. They were dirty, bloody, beaten down; some had lost eyes, limbs, some had been so hideously scarred they didn't lift their faces from the floor. The room was thick with their own filth, and around the edge many decomposing bodies lay.

"Who are these people?" Breathless on his arrival, Miller quickly came close to tears.

"People the Void stole from Earth to work here in the Fortress." Jack's grim face resembled a skull in the half-light. Hunter knew he was remembering his own kidnapping from his mother's side and his long, agonising incarceration in the Court of the Final Word.

"Are your people here?" Hunter asked gently.

Virginia was rigid; it was somehow worse than her crying.

"Virginia?" The voice was barely more than a croak rustling out from the depths of the dark.

"Mama?" Virginia started, and then hurried into the room. She came to a halt next to a woman who could have been in her forties but looked thirty years older. Kneeling amidst the filth, she had lost half her hair, and her forearms were so badly scarred they were pink and raw. Virginia buried her face in the woman's neck, whimpering.

"Virginia, why did you come back here?" her mother said. "You were free of the pestilential torments inflicted in this place."

"Mama, Mr Hunter is here to save us."

The woman looked up at Hunter with eyes that scarcely dared believe. "You are here to deliver us from this place?"

Whispers leaped from person to person, spreading rapidly around the room. Desperate hands clutched at Hunter's legs. Others tried to stand, or dragged themselves towards him.

"No pressure, then," Hunter muttered to himself. "Yes, I'm here to help," he announced. "That noise you hear is this place being taken apart brick by brick. There'll be no more suffering. Stay here a while longer—it's dangerous out there. But don't worry—we're going to free you."

Anguished cries of relief were joined by loud prayers of thanks. "Don't worry, Mama," Virginia said, stroking her mother's head. "Mr Hunter and his friends are good and true. Our saviours. God has answered all our pleas." Her mother began to cry silently.

Hunter crouched down and said to Virginia reassuringly, "You stay here and look after your mum, okay? I'll be back for you when this business is finished."

Smiling for the first time since Hunter had met her, Virginia nodded eagerly.

Out in the courtyard, Miller said, "See, Mr Hunter, everyone can see you're a good man."

"Shut up, Miller, or I'll be forced to slap you around."

Miller winked at Jack. "Just like my friend, Ryan."

The giant's whispers returned to Hunter's head, guiding him quickly through a maze of buildings, corridors and stairs until he reached a tower of gleaming obsidian. Barely able to keep up, Jack gasped, "Is this where Laura is?"

"On her way to the top. You stay down here."

Racing into the tower, Hunter took the steps two at a time, the Balor Claw scraping loudly on the stone as he rounded the spiral. Footsteps echoed from above. The stairs opened out into a room covering the entire floor of the tower, with large windows ranged around the circumference. Through one Hunter could see part of the Burning Man, unsettlingly close; figures writhed in agony within the outline. Through the others the Fortress blazed, the Fabulous Beasts sinuously riding the air currents. The beat of their wings was deafening.

Her face tear-stained, Laura stood in a daze near one of the windows. She started when she saw him and then lurched, on the brink of a faint.

"I'm not a ghost. Or the walking dead."

Stunned, her fear subsided and she gulped for words that wouldn't come. Hunter rapped his temple. "Indestructible. Solid bone."

Her shock passed quickly and she moved rapidly to the window and clung on to the frame. "I should have guessed. I can't even kill someone properly."

When Hunter took a step towards her, she placed one foot on the ledge ready to propel herself outside. "Get away from me," she said flatly.

"Come away from the window."

"What? So you can cut me to pieces with your killer glove?"

"I'm not going to hurt you."

"Right." Her laugh was laced with bitterness. "I tried to murder you. God, all this time I thought I had. You, and Jack, and Miller, and . . . and . . . little Virginia."

"They're all fine."

A sob broke through; her expression was shattered. "You loved me. You're the only person I've ever met who loves me for who I am, not what I can give you, and I betrayed you. Of course you're going to kill me. And you're going to make me suffer first. And why the hell not! I deserve it." She pushed herself fully into the window, glancing at the dizzying drop.

"What are you doing, Laura?"

"What does it look like I'm doing? You think I can carry on—" The words caught in her throat.

"I still love you."

Laura flinched as if she'd been slapped.

"I've never said that to anyone before."

She gulped back a sob. "What's wrong with you, you crazy bastard? I tried to kill you!"

"I know you. I know how your mind works. I know how your heart works. I know every tiny, twisty turn of your maze-like personality. And I know that once you peel back all the protective layers you've wrapped yourself in, deep down inside you're a good person. I believe in you. Whatever you tried to do to me, that's not you."

Laura began to cry. "It's the end of the world out there, and we're having a boyfriend-girlfriend talk! For God's sake, get a grip! You're supposed to be the hero!"

Laura hovered on the brink for a moment, and then collapsed onto the window ledge. Hunter pulled her up, holding the Balor Claw behind his back.

Looking deep into his eyes, she said, "You always were a good liar, Hunter. Do it, then. I won't stop you."

Hunter pushed her against the wall and ripped her T-shirt down the back. Embedded in her shoulder-blade was a shiny black spider. As he watched, it dug its legs deeper into her flesh. With relief, Laura began to cry silently.

"You'll never get it out," she said.

"How long has it been there?"

"After you saved me from the Court of the Final Word and I went back to Earth . . . no one asked how I found the others so easily in New York. Everyone takes so many coincidences for granted, nobody questions any more. They caught me and fixed that bastard into my flesh. I was their fail-safe. Every time things looked like they were going in the wrong direction, I was forced to give a little shove, make a comment, do whatever it took to destabilise. Brilliant, wasn't it? Because that's what I do anyway!"

"Hold still." Hunter deftly manoeuvred the Balor Claw so that he could plunge it into the spider without touching Laura's flesh. With a sizzle, the spider was wrenched from Existence.

Gasping for breath, Laura clutched at the wall for support. "It was whispering in my head all the time. It wouldn't let me speak . . . do anything to show it was there. I let everybody down."

"You couldn't help it."

"Why couldn't I fight against it? I gave Veitch such a hard time when the Caraprix controlled him, and now . . . I'm so sorry for how I treated him."

"Hush." Slipping the Balor Claw into his backpack, Hunter held her tightly.

She remained silent for a moment and then said quietly, "You bastard. How could you believe in me? Now I've got no excuse."

"You never had any—you were just too dumb to see it." He kissed her on the forehead. "Hmm. I guess this isn't the right time for sex. We have a bit of a job to do first. You up for it?"

Laura pulled herself away from him, gradually finding her equilibrium. "So, who do you want killing?"

3

From the parting of ways in the lower levels of the Fortress, Church, Ruth, Veitch, Shavi and Tom were guided by the hooded giant's whispering directions to take the most direct route to the location of the Burning Man at the heart of the sprawling complex. They stayed in the network of sewer-like tunnels, vaults and natural caverns that formed the base of the Fortress, where they were sure they would meet no resistance.

"All right," Veitch said, "they're going to send their reinforcements to the walls to hold back our forces, but that doesn't mean they're stupid. They're not going to leave an open channel right into the most sensitive part of their operation."

"They don't know we're coming," Ruth argued. "Why waste troops when they could be putting them to good use? Church, what do you think?"

"I agree with Ryan." Caledfwlch's flames provided Church with just enough illumination to pick his way through the oppressive gloom. He was distracted, increasingly brooding the deeper they progressed into the Fortress. "At the very least the Libertarian is going to be shadowing us. He might not remember everything that led up to his transformation, but there's a chance he recalls how we got into the Fortress."

Tom, too, was increasingly introspective, and he compulsively twisted the ring given to him by Freyja.

When the corridor led into another cavern in the bedrock beneath the Fortress's foundations, they came to a slow halt, unnerved by what lay ahead.

The previous caverns had been bare rock, but this one resembled a cemetery, with jumbled mausoleums and crypts, and graves in the grey dust floor. Lanterns hung from some of the houses of the dead, the pinpoints of illumination stretching out far into the dark ahead. An autumnal chill hung in the air and there was an odour of damp vegetation, although none was visible.

"Now this is...strange." Church scanned the cemetery for any sign of movement; it was still and silent.

"It's like the Grim Lands," Ruth whispered. "This is just how Mallory and Caitlin described it."

"What's with all this death stuff?" Veitch asked. "Grim isn't the word. We become Brothers and Sisters of Dragons when we experience death. We keep getting topped, then coming back—some more than others. And people keep telling us it's in the air and all about us."

"Death is the key to everything," Shavi said. "It always has been; it is just that we have been unable to see it, because of the way we have been brought up to consider it. We think of death as grim, terrible, the ultimate harsh reality, but anyone who has experienced death knows there is magic circling around it. It is almost as if death clears a space, in reality, in the mind, and allows magic to enter. Because death is not mundane, anything but. It is the opposite of mundane. It is, quite definitely, the key to everything. Change. Transformation. We only fear death because we think of it as the end. But if it is only a doorway...the entrance to another room, another house, another street, another town, what then? What then?"

After searching the entrance to the cavern, Church said, "No way around it. We'll have to go through it."

"What is this? We're all Going on a Bear Hunt?" Ruth said.

Cautiously, Church led them into the cemetery, the dust soft underfoot, the air growing damper the further they advanced.

"Try telling that to someone who's just lost a loved one," Veitch said to Shavi. "Magic? No chance."

"Of course we feel grief at those times," Shavi replied, "and that emotion is so potent it often crushes our senses so much that we fail to appreciate what else is happening. Before I left home, I had to drive my aunt on an emergency trip to the specialist spinal unit at a hospital in Sheffield. My uncle was dying. He had fallen downstairs a few years earlier and paralysed himself from the chest down. From that moment on, it was a constant fight against infection, one that he was losing. The antibiotics were not working. My aunt received a call at midnight to say he did not have long left."

Shavi's calm voice soothed them, and though Veitch knew it was one of Shavi's kindly acts to keep them at ease during a time of tension, he still appreciated it.

"The M1 was deserted," Shavi continued. "The hospital was immense, but completely empty too, when we arrived at two-thirty a.m. And I could tell the moment I stepped out of the car that there was something special in the air. A stillness, a sense of the infinite peering in to see us in our glass tank. I swear there was magic there. And in the ward too, devoid of the usual bustle of waiting relatives, there was a completely different feel. It was buzzing with a power that made my heart beat faster. The occasion was so desperate, so sad, so grim, but yet so different from the life we knew. I loved my uncle. My heart went out to my aunt, who had not been separated from him for forty years. But in that moment we touched an aspect of life we never experienced in our normal days. It had a charge, like electricity, and we felt so strongly—not just emotions, but the quality of the light, and the sound, and the stillness, and there was meaning all around us, so powerful we could touch it."

Shavi grew animated. "There was magic, Ryan. Magic is meaning. A lack of meaning is mundane. Once you have the meaning, anything is possible. You can change the world, yourself, those around you. You can make things better. If there is no meaning, you are locked in a world without feeling where everything is as it is. Nothing can be changed. Those who advocate no meaning are sealing themselves inside their own cell, locking the door and throwing away the key."

He fell silent, but his eyes gleamed. Veitch dwelled on his words; they had touched something deep inside him, although he still could not work out exactly what. "So you're saying we shouldn't fear death?"

The deep, rumbling laughter may have been in response to Veitch's question, but it made goosebumps rise on all of their arms.

"I just knew it," Tom muttered.

"Who is that?" Ruth whispered.

The laughter came from just beyond the large mausoleum ahead of them. Two figures waited in the warm, yellow light of a lantern. On a tomb sat a

Caribbean man in a black tailcoat, shiny top hat and sunglasses, and carrying a silver-skull-topped cane, his face painted white to resemble a skull. He clutched a cigar between two knuckles, and blue smoke drifted from his pearly-white grin. The one behind him had more of the grave about him than elegance: grey, desiccated skin, baleful red eyes, a necklace of human finger-bones and grey hair tufting from a scalp showing patches of the yellow bone beneath. Bearing the taint of the Anubis Box, they were both under the Void's control.

Church and Veitch advanced, swords drawn.

The one in the top hat laughed louder. "No worries, boys! We are no threat to you. That lies ahead. We just watchin' over our domain, makin' a little place for you, a-while from now."

"Who are you?" Church asked.

"We got names and names, boys, but on the island they called me Baron Samedi and my silent partner is Baron Cimetière. He is me and I am he. I am head of the Guédé family of the Loa. We stand at the crossroads to watch the souls of dead humans pass."

Church shivered. "Is this the crossroads, then?"

Baron Samedi grinned wider.

"We're not dead yet," Veitch said defiantly.

"Maybe you are and maybe you not. I am a wise judge, boy, even with these marks upon me. I say you pass now. And so says he."

Baron Cimetière leaned across the tomb to inspect each of them in turn. When his gaze fell upon them, they each felt a cold breeze.

Tapping his nose, Baron Samedi added, "I am also Loa of sex and resurrection. Ring any bells?"

"Time is slipping away, Brothers and Sisters," Baron Cimetière said in a whispery voice. "The Devourer of All Things is nearly come. Any moment now . . . any moment—"

"Don't let them distract you!" Tom shouted. "Move on!"

Amongst the mausoleums and the crypts, something—someone?—drew near.

"Don't look at it!" Tom cautioned, too late.

Church was caught by the sight of a familiar face, and was suddenly flooded with recollections, the smell of her hair, the softness of her skin, lying in bed on a Sunday morning, slick with sweat after sex. "Marianne?" he said.

"I deserved to live, Church," his long-dead girlfriend said. "And I would have, if you hadn't been chosen to be some stupid hero. Why couldn't someone else do it? Why did I have to die to set you on this path? It's not fair."

Her words resonated with his own doubts. So many people had suffered because of the manipulation of the Great Powers in their sprawling millennia-long campaign.

"We're all just pawns, Church. The gods manipulated Veitch to kill me. The Void manipulated the gods and Veitch. Existence manipulated everyone. None of them can be trusted, so why play their game? Why follow their rules? You have the power to walk away. Do it, and save someone else from having to go through what we both suffered."

She was right. It wasn't fair; he could see fault on both sides, and strength on both sides, and it was always humanity caught in the middle. If he walked away, what would the Powers do then? Only dimly did he feel the Blue Fire when his hand went to his sword; he could throw it away, a symbolic gesture—

"Church!" Tom was shaking him roughly.

Where Marianne had stood, there was now a hideous yellowing skeleton with staring eyes, its claw-like hands clutching long tendrils of mist that reached to the heads of Ruth, Shavi and Veitch. The one that had been fastened to him was now breaking up and drifting away.

"Lee . . ." Shavi mouthed.

Ruth muttered the name of her dead uncle, tears streaming down her face.

A queasy guilt was carved into Veitch's features at the memory of all the people he had killed.

"I am Mictlantecuhtli, God of Death, and all who walk the cemeteries are my servants. In your arrogance, you raised a sword against my little brother Tezcatlipoca, and now a balance must be struck," the skeleton intoned. "Choose one of your comrades to join me here for all time, in service to the Devourer of All Things."

As Church made to draw his sword, Baron Samedi laughed heartily. With a flick of his wrist, Mictlantecuhtli drew the tendrils taut and Shavi, Ruth and Veitch crumpled to their knees, their faces drawn as if the life was being sucked out of them.

"Your grief for your lost loved ones traps you," Mictlantecuhtli said. "You cannot see that they are inside you and around you forever. You cannot break this thing. It sucks the life from you."

Church continued drawing his sword until Tom stopped him. "They'll be dead before you can do anything," the Rhymer whispered.

"You want me to choose one of them to die? I can't do that. And they'd never let us go anyway."

"Stay calm. Think. This is the land of death. What has power here?"

"Choose now!" Mictlantecuhtli ordered.

"Why don't you just tell me what you're thinking?" Church snapped.

"Because I can't—don't you understand!" He showed Church his ring. "The deal I did with Freyja was that I would not help you at any turn. As my power of prophecy returned after you dragged me back to this life, I could have helped you so many times. Lives have been lost . . . lives will be lost . . . and I could have prevented it. I see them so clearly. And I have had to live with that knowledge." Tears sparked in his eyes. "But that witch didn't want me to aid my friends . . . the only people I have ever cared about . . . because that way you'd be truly tested."

"Why?"

"If you were weak, the Void would have won easily. She wanted to know you were strong so she could decide if she should side with you."

"Now!" Mictlantecuhtli drew the tendrils tighter.

"Wait," Church said. "Give me time." His mind raced as he turned over Tom's words. "Why didn't you tell us this before?"

"You would have spent all your time wondering what I knew." He looked away. "I would have been even more alone."

"Power in the land of death," Church repeated. He looked around, examining the symbols of death on every mausoleum and crypt in the cemetery; and then he had it.

Closing his eyes, he whispered, "I am the Raven King. I can do anything."

It sounded like a storm approaching across a great plain. The thunder rolled closer, magnified by the echoes along the network of tunnels and caverns through which they had walked. Within moments, a black cloud rushed into the cemetery, the swirling tempest of black wings bringing darkness and chaos. The Morvren attacked with one mind, tied to Church's consciousness as strongly as the Fabulous Beast.

In the confusion, Church and Tom managed to drag Shavi, Ruth and Veitch free, and they scrambled across the cemetery beneath the cloud of swirling birds.

Fighting to repress the memories that had been torn free, Veitch turned in a rage, sword drawn. "I'm going to cut that bastard to bits!"

"Forget it—we'd never beat three of them," Church said. "We'd be lucky to overpower that Aztec one on his own. The Morvren won't hurt them, but it should keep them distracted until we get away."

Ruth, too, was altered by her experience. The dredged-up memories of her grief, and whatever lies her dead uncle had told her, had left a deep-seated anger rooted in her eyes. Spits and crackles of Blue Fire flashed around her, and Church could see she was struggling to maintain control. He went to comfort her, but she turned away.

He noticed Tom hanging back, and said quietly, "You took on a huge burden to help us. I won't forget that."

Tom nodded sullenly, but his relief was apparent.

"They said the Void was nearly here. Have we run out of time?" Ruth wiped away stinging tears.

"I don't know," Church replied. "But I do know that now we've been discovered every rogue god the Void has under its control will be trying to stop us reaching the Burning Man. And probably every single warrior in this entire Fortress."

"Bring 'em on," Veitch growled. "They got me mad, messing with my head like that. They're the ones who should be scared."

4

"We are not safe! She comes!" Doubled-up, Caitlin clutched at the wall, the crackling, ancient voice of Brigid echoing from her young mouth.

Every switch in persona always caught Mallory off-guard. Throughout the journey from the parting of ways, he had been dealing with the cold, brutal efficiency of the Morrigan, who gave little response to his attempts at warmth and friendship. "Who is coming?" he asked.

Dazed, Caitlin shook her head. "I . . . I don't know. Brigid is scared. She's hiding . . . so are the others." She shook her head again and her eyes darkened. The Morrigan looked back at Mallory. "Move quickly," she said. "We need to find a defensible position."

Mallory sighed with frustration. "Any chance you could stay with one personality for more than three seconds?"

He drew his sword. The sound of many running feet coming their way was already clear. Instinctively, a protective hand went to the bag containing the Extinction Shears.

They were in a section of the Fortress that appeared to be constructed entirely of the spoiled meat, gloomy and foul-smelling, the floor spongy underfoot. Nowhere to hide.

Snatching her axe from her back, Caitlin ran along the corridor. When the Morrigan was riding her, Mallory had difficulty keeping up; she was stronger, faster, her reactions more finely tuned, and she was more savage. The best person to have at your side in a fight, but Mallory valued the companionship of his friend more. The Caitlin he knew always reminded him of the real reason they were fighting; she kept him going when things became too bleak.

The corridor came to a dead end at a large doorway leading onto a stone and metal balcony. Beneath them, the Fortress stretched out for mile upon mile, an insane jumble of forums, towers, grand halls, industrial-scale factories, obelisks, barracks and many other structures Mallory couldn't identify. The sky was scarlet and black from the fires blazing everywhere, the air chokingly acrid. Creatures that resembled pterodactyls but with skull-like heads swooped overhead, screeching, as they attempted to fend off the Fabulous Beasts. Occasionally, the pall of smoke would shift to reveal the Burning Man looking down. Ten storeys below was an extensive forum paved with white stone, across which the Enemy streamed as they reinforced their defences or scattered to avoid the fiery blasts from above.

"How many of them are here? Millions?" Mallory gaped.

Another balcony could just be reached with a leap across a gulf, and there were other balconies in a line alongside the building they were in. Before he could point this out to Caitlin, she had turned and was swinging her axe at two of the sallow-skinned brutish creatures who had approached silently. Two heads flew off the balcony to the flags far below, but before the bodies had crashed to the soft, sticky floor the corridor was already packed with the rest of the pursuers. In the middle of the throng stood Niamh, the charred half of her face emphasising her fury.

Mallory's blood ran cold. Why did he hate her so much? In the depths of his mind, recollections shifted, ratcheting up his anger, but no solution to the mystery surfaced. Overcome with the desire for revenge, he gripped Llyrwyn and prepared to attack.

"The Brothers and Sisters of Dragons have broken into our home," Niamh shrieked. "Sound the alarm! Leave the walls. Here is the real threat!"

"That's not good," Mallory said. "We're going to have to cut our way through every bastard in here to get where we're going."

The air was filled with a deafening siren that sounded like the cry of a tortured animal. Across the Fortress others began in sequence.

Mallory and Caitlin darted forwards at the same time as the hanging wave of their enemies broke. Within seconds, the corridor was filled with furious battle. Without room for delicate swordplay, Mallory hacked and slashed his way through anything that appeared before him, his blade sizzling through flesh, severing limbs and unleashing geysers of sticky black blood.

Despite the frenzy, he was aware of Caitlin beside him, hypnotic in the fluid rhythms of her savage ballet. Sidestepping, ducking and pirouetting at the same time as she whirled the axe in glittering arcs, she removed heads and limbs, crashed through shoulder-blades and tore open guts. Within a few seconds, she had carved a path ahead of Mallory. As two of the creatures fell, she rammed her fingers into the throat of another and ripped it out. Blood soaked her from head to foot. The axe came up instantly into the jaw of another, rending through its skull and out of the top of its head.

Mallory kept his focus on Niamh, standing cold and aloof at the rear of her guard. His blazing hatred was a distraction, and he made two errors of judgment in rapid succession. One of his enemy's short, razor-sharp swords broke through his defences and ripped open his chest. Another caught him a glancing blow on the side of the head and he pitched backwards. Instantly, they were upon him.

Through the crush of bodies, he had a brief glimpse of Caitlin striking out towards Niamh. The cold, unfeeling eyes of the Morrigan flashed briefly upon him, dismissed his plight and moved on, and Mallory realised his last chance had passed.

A sword cut through the top of his ear. Another tore open his temple. But their weight upon him made it difficult for the enemy to strike a killing blow.

Stupid bastards, he thought obliquely.

Just as he had given up hope, the weight pressing on him eased as bodies were torn off, had their throats cut and were discarded.

Caitlin looked down at him with eyes that contained only a hint of the Morrigan. "I couldn't leave you," she said with a smile.

As she offered a hand to pull him up, a sword burst out through her left shoulder. A look of startled incomprehension crossed her face. She glanced down at the protruding steel and watched the blood gush.

"Not again!" Mallory raged. He hacked through two more attackers, then grabbed Caitlin as her legs gave way. Her axe slipped from her fingers.

"I'll be all right," she gasped. "It missed the artery. Just . . . look out for yourself."

Leaning her against the wall where she slid slowly to the floor, Mallory turned his attention to the few remaining attackers. This time his hatred and anger became fuel. He cut through warrior after warrior until only Niamh was left. She showed no fear.

"Pathetic Fragile Creatures. Your time has passed," she spat. "You taught me to feel emotion and defiled me for life. You deserve to be eradicated from Existence for the poison you have inflicted on all wondrous things. Love." Fury filled her. "Love! See what it has done!" She indicated Caitlin, who was attempting to staunch the flow of blood from her shoulder. "It has destroyed you too, though you do not realise how or why. It has destroyed me. In the end it will destroy Jack Churchill, the vile and deceitful last chance of humanity."

With a flourish, she tore a dagger from her belt and attacked. At the last moment, Mallory turned and it tore open his upper arm. Instinctively, he brought Llyrwyn up and with a sizzle of Blue Fire he separated Niamh's head from her shoulders. After a second, the body exploded in a wild flurry of moths, their brilliant gold corrupted by black as they swirled up to the ceiling, and through it. When they had gone, there was nothing left of Niamh.

Mallory had thought his mysterious urge for revenge would be sated, but he only felt deflated, and strangely sad. He hurried back to Caitlin, who gave him a forced smile. She was deathly pale.

Blood streamed from his own wounds, but he was certain that, given time, the Pendragon Spirit would heal him. Of Caitlin, he was not so sure. "I'm afraid to remove the sword. It might cut the artery," he said.

"Don't worry. Let's get out of here, find somewhere we can rest a while." As he lifted her in his arms, she added, "You can go on ahead with the Extinction Shears, come back for me later when it's all done."

"No," he said, denying the practicality of her suggestion. "You and me, we're a team. We've travelled across Earth, the Far Lands and the Land of the Dead. We're not going our separate ways now." He added, "I need you with me."

"No, you don't."

"Yes," he said firmly. "I do."

Bracing his foot on the edge of the balcony, he propelled them across the gulf onto the next balcony. Landing hard, they spilled onto the ground. Caitlin cried out as the sword twisted.

"Don't worry," she added hastily. "You did great."

Carrying her into the adjoining corridor, he laid her at the foot of the wall. Her clothes were sodden with blood.

"A good infusion of the Blue Fire could turn you around quick as anything," Mallory said. He unhooked the Wayfinder from his belt and examined the flame, which flickered even more weakly than the last time he had scrutinised it.

"Doesn't look too good, does it?" Caitlin said. "For me, or Hal."

"Don't be so negative." Hiding his despondence, Mallory wondered where else he could find another source of Blue Fire in that God-forsaken place.

Taking his hand, Caitlin appeared to read his thoughts. "You mustn't worry about me. There are more important things to deal with right now. I can wait." She saw his face, and smiled. "And even if I can't, I'm proud I've played my part. I'm ready, Mallory."

"No!"

"I've buried my husband and my son. I've seen so many people die. There's been so much suffering, but so much good too. Friendship like I never imagined. And love . . . Everything that's happened has made me see life and the world in a completely different way. It's not mundane at all. There's so much wonder everywhere, it's just so well hidden. But once you find it . . . everything really is magickal." She smiled. "And then there's you."

"Will you be quiet?" Mallory tended to her wound, but the blood pumping out around the sword was not diminishing.

"Life was dark after Grant and Liam died, but you made it worthwhile for me again. You've been a good friend, Mallory. My best friend." She took his hand and squeezed it tightly.

He didn't like the way she appeared to be drawing an end to the story of her life. "Stop it. The Pendragon Spirit is all about hope, and while your heart's still beating that's what there is. No more talk like that."

Her smile was sympathetic. She nodded as if she agreed, but that only made him feel worse.

A noise from further along the gloomy corridor disturbed them. As Mallory drew his sword, the shadows retreated from the blue flare, but he still couldn't see who was there.

"No one's going to get past me," he said. "You'll be all right."

The darkness unfolded to reveal a blue light way down the corridor, drawing closer. Puzzled, Mallory held his breath and watched. It was Blue Fire, he was sure of it, but it moved like a person. As it neared, he saw it was indeed a man in a column of the sapphire flames.

"Is that Hal?" he asked quietly. Flicking open the lamp's glass door, he saw only the faintest flame guttering inside.

"It is!" Caitlin said. "That's why the Wayfinder flame was dying. He was taking on form."

"Hal!" Mallory called. Sheathing his sword, he ran to greet their friend. "Come on! Caitlin needs your help!"

The burning blue figure was a beacon of hope in the grim Fortress, but as Mallory skidded to a halt in front of him, the blue flames licked out. The figure beneath didn't resemble the Hal Mallory had seen in the flames, but even as he struggled to recognise the face, the features were growing fluid, changing. A moment later the Hortha stood in front of him.

Before Mallory could react, the Hortha extended an arm and plunged the rapidly growing spike of blackthorn through Mallory's chest. Caitlin's voice was so weak, her scream barely carried. In his shock, Mallory felt nothing. He staggered back a pace as the spike withdrew, and examined the hole in his chest from which blood now pumped.

Dazed, he scrabbled for his sword, but the Hortha rapidly punched another spike into his gut. This time the agony lanced through him and he yelled, fighting to stay conscious. His hand twitched and thrashed, but couldn't reach Llyrwyn.

"And so one of the Great Swords of Existence is consigned to search for a new master," the Hortha said.

Impaled on the spike, Mallory was lifted off the ground and carried back to Caitlin where he was dumped unceremoniously on the floor, and for a moment he did black out.

When he regained consciousness, the Hortha was crouching beside him and Caitlin was crying weakly. The pool of blood around her had spread too far and her eyelids struggled to stay open. Mallory could tell from the position of his wound, and the speed at which his blood was rapidly joining Caitlin's pool, that he could not recover.

"You had to trick us," Mallory said. "I'd have hacked you to pieces and kept hacking and then dumped you over the balcony if I'd known it was you."

"I know." The Hortha's crumpled paper face showed no emotion. "Your resistance has been strong. I needed a small seed of information to get through your defences. And I found it. Your attachment to the genie in the bottle."

"How did you know about that?"

Uninterested, the Hortha waved his comment away. "This end was fixed the moment I tasted your blood in the Court of the Soaring Spirit. It was only a matter of when," the Hortha said. "You could never outrun me."

"You can kill me, but you'll never win." Mallory coughed up a mouthful of blood. "And I've got a whole bagful of clichés where that came from. Stick around—I'll bore you to death."

"I have fulfilled my commitment to the Devourer of All Things, and now I will wait until I am called again." The Hortha took the bag containing the Extinction Shears. Mallory was too weak to prevent him. "Without these, your cause is lost," the Hortha continued.

"Never," Mallory said. "The others will find another way."

The Hortha glanced at Caitlin, who was fading in and out of consciousness. "She is gone too. And now there is only this one to eradicate." He plucked up the Wayfinder and prepared to snuff out the dying flame.

Blue Fire erupted from the lantern and engulfed the Hortha. A high-pitched wail leaped from him as he staggered backwards, flapping madly to extinguish the flames. But they burned so furiously that Mallory couldn't bear to look at them, and soon the high-pitched wail was consumed too. After a moment, the flames sucked back into the lantern and there was nothing left of the Hortha but a few charred twigs and a pile of grey ashes.

Mallory spat more blood. "That'll teach you, you bastard. We win. We always win," he croaked.

Beside him, a shadow was moving across Caitlin's body. It took a glimpse of red eyes in the umbra for him to realise it was the Morrigan vacating her host. The gaze fell on Mallory and for the first time he saw a hint of warmth within them.

"Don't leave her," Mallory pleaded. He knew. If the Morrigan left the body it was a clear sign that it was too late for Caitlin; the goddess would move on to another mare to ride. "Please. Stay here. She'll live. Really."

The shadow hovered for a moment, and then slipped away. Once it had gone, Caitlin stirred and gained a degree of alertness, but she appeared oblivious to Mallory and was staring into the dark as if she could see something. "The Knight. He's here. And...and . . ." She gave a warm smile, which lingered for a while, and then her life slipped from her.

Mallory stifled a sob, and reached out for her still hand. His own life was draining from him fast, but he didn't feel sad. It would be good to expunge the one terrible thing he had done in his life, to rest finally, free from the struggle and the worry. His only regret was that he wouldn't be there to help Church and the others win. But he still had the Extinction Shears, and soon one of his Brothers or Sisters would find them and use them as they were intended. He had no doubt about that.

He closed his eyes, listening to the slowing beat of his heart. Steady. Easy. Finally. But after a moment he realised he was no longer alone.

Standing beside him, smiling fondly, was the young boy the others had discussed. The one who had died, but hadn't, who was now one of the Oldest Things in the Land. He searched for the name in his fragmenting mind. Carlton.

"That's right, Mallory," the boy said.

"You can read my thoughts?" Mallory said weakly.

"Thoughts aren't as ephemeral as you might think." He laughed.

"That's a big word for a kid."

"I'm not a child. Never was, really."

"What are you, then?"

Carlton only smiled.

"So, what? You're an angel? Here to take me by the hand and lead me to the Promised Land? You ought to know I don't believe in God."

"I know. You don't believe in anything."

"That's served me well. Why are you here?"

"Because you've reached the end of your story."

"I know that. I'm ready."

"And you've accounted for the thing that troubles you the most."

"How would you know? You're a kid. But thanks anyway."

Carlton broke into a grin. "I like you, Mallory. You were always a lot of fun."

"We've never met before."

"Oh, we have. Many times." He waved gently to catch Mallory's fading attention. "I want to show you something that no living person ever gets to see."

Carlton motioned towards Caitlin. She was still dead. The dark pool around her had become a sea, and he realised that much of the blood was his.

"Look closely."

Darkness pressed in around his vision. He peered at the still form of his friend and saw a hint of movement—not in Caitlin, but on her—and a strange light in the vicinity of her belly that had no clear source. The light coalesced, grew harder, became solid: a silver egg emerged from Caitlin as though it was insubstantial and passing through her. It lay on her for a second, then ran like mercury into a new shape before moving quickly away into the dark of the corridor.

Mallory knew he had seen such a thing before. He searched his memory—thought of Miller and Salisbury and a strange yearning in the office of Steelguard Securities—and then it came to him. "A Caraprix," he said. "What . . . what was it doing in Caitlin?"

"There's one in you too, Mallory. Indeed, in all humans." Carlton knelt beside Mallory and brushed the hair tenderly from his brow. "Before you go, I wanted to let you into a secret. A big one. Part of the huge pattern that nobody ever gets to see while they're alive. You've earned it."

"There's a Caraprix in all of us? Like the gods?"

"The Caraprix is in you. The gods only get to be friends with them for a while. What did you think they were, Mallory? Where do you think they came from?"

"No idea. Don't care."

"The Pendragon Spirit is an amazing thing. A shard of Existence lodged in every human being, a reminder of their potential and their potential all wrapped up in one. But it's even more than that. It's a seed, waiting to be nurtured. Every experience a human has in their life is sunlight and water to that seed. It grows, and develops, and becomes something wonderful."

"The Pendragon Spirit becomes the Caraprix?"

"Humans tend them, and grow them, and then, at the point of their death, set them free. And if they've done a good job in their life, the Caraprix thrives and moves off to its destiny. That's the point of life, Mallory. That's the reason for the tough road, the hardships and the suffering and the misery. As you fight to overcome them, you're growing these wonderful, brilliant things."

"But what do they do? What are they for?"

"You'll see, Mallory. You'll all see. And then you'll understand why human beings and their fragile, hard lives, and their loves and friendships, their troubles and strife, their passing irritations and great achievements, their lows and highs, their fears and wonders and awe, are all so absolutely vital, and so amazing, and so much more important than you ever dreamed while you were going through them."

"There's one in me?"

"There's one in you, Mallory. It'll be emerging soon, and it'll be a remarkable thing because you've nurtured it so well. It'll be one of the strongest, and it will have a part to play."

"Well, that's weird. . .and. . .unexpected. And I still don't believe in stuff, but . . ."

Carlton laughed.

The world had grown dark.

"You close your eyes now, Mallory, and be content. You've done a great job, everything that was expected of you and more. You're a hero, Mallory. You won't be forgotten, ever."

Mallory died.

Carlton watched him for a moment, studied the growing light and then gave a satisfied smile. He had been right.

Afterwards, he picked up the Wayfinder and blew on the dying spark that burned at the end of the wick. It winnowed into a small flame, and then grew larger and stronger until finally it burst from the lantern as it had when Hal attacked the Hortha with the last of his strength.

This time the flame folded in on itself and disappeared with a zzzzip, leaving a bemused Hal staring at his hands in incredulity. He was human, exactly as he had been up to the moment when he gave up his body to enter the Blue Fire.

"What?" he said, dazed. "I'm here."

"I'm sorry to pull you from the Blue Fire, Hal. I know exactly what you've lost. But you had it for a while, and that's more than anyone else."

"Of course," Hal said. "But. . .I thought I was dying. I'd given up every part of me."

"Exactly. Like every Brother and Sister of Dragons, you've been on your own personal road to enlightenment and transformation. Everything you've experienced has been preparing you for this moment. And your last, great sacrifice was. . .the final exam, I suppose. You passed."

"Yeah?" Hal thought for a moment, and then said, "I miss it, but in a way I'm still part of it. I was a part of it for all time."

"Exactly."

"What now?"

Carlton handed Hal the Wayfinder. "Existence needs a Caretaker, Hal. Someone to walk the boundaries, watch over the fabric, close some doors, open others. Someone to turn on the lamps of hope in the dark of the night, and extinguish them when dawn's light touches the sky. Will you accept?"

Hal took a moment to assimilate the magnitude of what Carlton was offering him, and then he beamed. "Of course I will!"

Carlton grinned. "I knew you would. Now pick up the Extinction Shears, and let's be away. Everything is coming to a head, and you'll want to be there at the end."

CHAPTER TWELVE
ONCE AND FUTURE

1

When Church looked back at the cemetery cavern, it wasn't a cemetery at all, just bare rock covered by a thin, grey dust. Lost in the shadows of the upper reaches, the *Morvren* flew, calling to each other in voices that reminded Church of grief-stricken mourners at a funeral. The three gods were nowhere to be seen.

A distant roaring was revealed to be an underground river that lay at the end of a short tunnel. Their path continued along the bank.

"Don't go near the water—it's poisoned," Tom cautioned as he examined the oily, foul-smelling flow.

Church took him to one side and asked, "I understand you can't tell me any details of what your visions are showing you, but is there anything you can give me that might help?"

"Everything hangs in the balance. It could go either way."

"If I choose to become the Libertarian."

"Yes."

"The Void wins."

"For all time. Existence won't recover." Weary, Tom's shoulders sagged. "I'm sorry. It was always my role to be your guide. I was supposed to help you become the person you were always meant to be, but I'm not much use."

"You made the right choice in Norway when you did that deal with Freyja. We wouldn't have the Two Keys, Ryan would probably still be a threat to us and Ruth could well be dead."

"It might be better if she was dead."

Church flinched. "How can you say that?"

"Love has two faces. It gives us the power to do remarkable things, and it can turn our minds from the right choices and damn us forever."

Church gripped his shoulders. "Let me teach the teacher. I've learned a lot of things since I found myself back in the Iron Age. It's not about good and evil—it's not that simple. Everything has two faces, like Janus, like Cernunnos, like me with the Fabulous Beasts and the scary, carrion-eating Ravens of Death. Different views of the way forward, one always influencing the other. The trick is walking a fine line between the two. It all comes down to how skilful we are at staying on the path."

"It sounds odd."

"What?"

"Wisdom coming out of your mouth."

"I've got one more question." Church steeled himself. "Is anyone else going to die?"

Tom hesitated, then replied, "Yes. Don't ask me any more." He walked quickly away before Church could pursue that line of questioning.

"It's getting hot," Ruth said. A mist rolled across the river and the walls dripped with moisture. "Does that mean we're getting closer to the Burning Man?"

"There is movement ahead." Shavi came to a halt, two fingers resting against the bottom of his alien eye as he searched deep into the dark.

A low, mournful, wolf-like howl rolled along the rocky walls.

"I know that sound." Church recalled a smoky London night in the middle of the Blitz.

Bounding from the shadows on all fours came a lithe figure that could have been either man or beast. Grey hair trailed behind it, pupils glowing golden in the gloom. Snarling lips curled back from rows of gleaming fangs.

"Loki!" Church called to the others. "Trickster and shape-shifter! Don't trust what you see!"

As Veitch braced himself, sword drawn, the god barrelled towards him, shifted onto the rock wall without missing a step and then continued forwards along the tunnel roof. Wrong-footed, Veitch clumsily swung his blade upwards, but Loki had already passed overhead. He dropped behind Veitch, lashed out with a long, muscular arm that sent Veitch flying towards the river's edge and turned instantly on Shavi.

Shavi dived beneath raking claws that would have taken his head off. Rolling along the ground, he helped Veitch to his feet.

As Church attacked, Loki flashed a lupine smile and disappeared.

Baffled, the next thing Church saw was a golden eye mere inches away from his own, and then pain erupted in his chest as claws raked upwards. Staggering back, he saw blood spread across his ragged shirt. Loki lashed out again, and though Church pulled back at the last, he caught a glancing blow that made him see stars. His vision cleared when he was on his back, Loki hunched over him, ready to tear out his throat.

The blast of Blue Fire blinded him.

Blinking, he saw Loki's smoking, twisted body lying on the river's edge. The god was still alive, but he had lost control of his form; it oozed like melting toffee into turrets and sticky strands. The golden eyes still rolled in a head filled with holes.

Ruth moved towards him, though it took a second for Church to recognise her, so altered was she by the raw power of the Craft, her eyes all black, her hair snaking.

"You won't hurt him!" she raged.

The transformation had been so rapid that Church was stunned. How close to the edge was she if she could become so elemental so quickly? She reminded him of the Ruth who had almost been consumed by her power during the Battle of London, the same erosion of rational thought, the same passion for the sheer coruscating force she wielded.

Clutching at his stomach wound, Church sat up and croaked, "Ryan, she's losing it. Talk her down."

"Ruth, darlin', you've beaten him, all right?" Veitch ran to her side.

She turned her fierce gaze on him, and for a second both Church and Veitch thought she was going to kill him on the spot.

After a moment some connection was made and her power receded, her eyes returning to normal.

"Oh, bravo." The Libertarian stood further along the river's edge, clapping mockingly. "What a fine fighting force you are! A conflicted leader, a psychopath, a woman on the edge of a breakdown and . . ." He glanced curiously at Shavi and Tom. "Not quite sure what you two are. Irrelevant, I suppose."

With mounting unease, Church saw the crackling force around Ruth begin to grow more intense again; her face darkened, her eyes glared.

"Oh, look. The trickster has torn open your true love," the Libertarian said to Ruth mockingly. "Why, it's a miracle he still lives. Ah, but then wait and see what little surprise I have waiting for him next—"

In her anger, Ruth lost control once more. Eddies of Blue Fire crackled above her head as she levelled the Spear of Lugh and released a blast of energy that the Libertarian avoided easily.

"Is that the best you can do? He'll be dead before you know. Frankly, you all will."

"Ruth!" Church called. "He won't kill me! If I die so does he!"

Filled with fury, Ruth didn't hear. Floating an inch above the floor, she raced towards the Libertarian, who stood, arms folded, unmoved.

Church couldn't understand what the Libertarian had planned until he saw emerald clouds unfolding rapidly further along the river channel. Rushing forwards, churning, the clouds were accompanied by the sound of doors being slammed open.

Lurching to his feet, Church called Ruth's name as Janus appeared from a door in the air beside the Libertarian, his dual faces shifting between black and white.

As Ruth bore down on the Libertarian, Janus used his key with a flourish and another door opened in the air directly in front of her. She disappeared into the gulf, and after a brief, mocking wave, the Libertarian followed, shouting, "I really do need a new queen—that last one got a little damaged. And now I have one!" Within a second, Janus was gone too, and the only sound was the door in the air slamming with a terrible finality.

2

Time passed, though Ruth was no longer aware of it. Her eyes rolled back so that only the whites were visible. Behind her, Mictlantecuhtli extended a skeletal hand to draw the misty tendril that would play with her memories of grief and loss, corrupting her thoughts with their toxic load.

The Libertarian watched with a faint, mocking smile, as bogus as everything else about him. Inside, he was in turmoil. The peaceful equilibrium he had achieved since he had accepted his transformation was gone. Apart from the odd stray memory, he had thought that every part of his old life had been wiped away, but ever since he had been compelled to kiss what he thought was a just-dead Ruth in Greece, he had felt incomprehensible stirrings. Apparently, love crossed more barriers than he'd thought. He didn't want to believe that was true, for it would set up a disturbing sequence of self-analysis that could destroy his reassuring sense of what he had become: better. It meant he was still grounded in all that had gone before. It meant he was still corrupted by the foul stuff that eventually destroyed humans.

Yet now he could see a certain symmetry. Niamh and Ruth, the opposing faces of his former romantic life. One had come and gone, and now he could have the other, finally. By transforming her to become like him, they could be together, and the past could once again be eradicated.

And, as he had long believed, it would be the final act in his becoming. If Church could not have Ruth as a human, and could only gain her as the Libertarian, it was a choice he would always take. The future was sealed. All hope was gone.

3

"Church, mate, you've got to get a grip," Veitch urged.

They'd raced along the bank of the stinking river until the roof had become too low to proceed further, and then had been forced to take winding, rough-cut steps back into the Fortress. The entire city-wide building appeared to be on fire. Choking smoke swept through the gloomy corridors, and the heat was rising by the minute. They had to shout to be heard above the noise of warfare, the blasts of fire from the Fabulous Beasts, the collapse of massive buildings that shook the ground, the constant, jarring rise and fall of the siren.

Church was consumed by his fears for Ruth, all thoughts of the destruction of the Burning Man now gone. With Caledfwlch drawn, he ran ahead of the others, moving inexorably towards the heart of the complex.

Veitch eventually caught up with him and dragged him to a halt. Church rounded on him, on the brink of striking out until Shavi interposed himself between the two. "Church, we will rescue Ruth—"

"Don't you get it?" Church raged. "This was the Libertarian's plan all along . . . my plan. Ruth will be consumed by her dark side and join with the

Libertarian. I won't have lost her to you . . ." He shook his sword at Veitch. "I'll have lost her to the worst aspects of myself. The only way I'll ever get her back is by becoming the Libertarian."

Tom and Veitch's briefly exchanged glance was not missed. "That's right," Church continued. "The only way you're going to stop me is by killing me."

Weaving through the corridors ahead of them, he emerged from a large door into a vast circular area in the centre of the Fortress. It sloped down to an abyssal pit from which emerged the Burning Man, a wicker structure towering so high that the top was lost in the pall of smoke. Within the flaming structure, the bodies of gods writhed, their essence fuelling the focus of power that would soon attract the Void. The portion of the wicker structure Church could see was already filled with flames; the moment of arrival could not be far off.

Overhead, the Fabulous Beasts released random blasts of flame before they disappeared back into the smoke. Everything was painted with the hellish red glare of the fire.

Surging into the arena from every door on the perimeter was the Army of the Void, thousands upon thousands of Lament-Brood, marching with their mechanical undead step, Redcaps, roving like packs of wild beasts, and a tidal wave of the sallow-skinned brutish creatures.

"Okay, then." Veitch had arrived at Church's shoulder. "We just need to get through that lot and we're on course to give the Burning Man a bit of what-for."

Shavi searched the surrounding buildings. "No sign of Mallory and Caitlin with the Extinction Shears or Hunter with the Two Keys."

Above the milling army, the air boiled, and amidst a thunderous sound of slamming doors that drowned out all other noise, Janus appeared. Floating in the air, he brandished the gold key, and from another door emerged a figure whose image eventually coalesced into that of a rotund oriental man at least ten feet tall, with a white moustache that drooped down to his feet. He was naked apart from a loincloth, but strands of human skulls hung down his body, clattering every time he shifted his bulk.

"Who's that git?" Veitch asked.

"His appearance suggests he is Yen-Lo-Wang, the Chinese god of death and ruler of the Fifth Level of Hell," Shavi replied. "A very powerful god, with an aptitude for tormenting souls."

As Yen-Lo-Wang raised his arms, the chaotic army became instantly silent and fell into step, as though he were a puppeteer pulling their strings. As one, the army turned to face Church and the others.

"Ragnarok," Tom whispered. "This is it—all the prophecies lead here."

Shavi was distracted by the white stone flags of the arena. "Something is not quite right here." Deep in concentration, he caressed the flesh around his alien eye before he said, "Beneath the flagstones there is a force, like the Blue Fire, but opposite. Black as the flames on Veitch's sword."

"The Libertarian calls it 'the Bad Blood,'" Veitch said uncomfortably. "It comes from the Void, like the Blue Fire comes from Existence. Normally there's not much of it around, but it's been getting stronger the closer the Void gets. You step anywhere near that, you're dead."

"How are we going to get across there?" Church said.

"There is some kind of pattern," Shavi said hesitantly. "But I cannot see it."

The Army of the Void moved forwards.

"Holy fucking shit," Veitch said. "What are we going to do now?"

"We fight," Church said.

"I thought I had a bleedin' death wish."

"I think I can beat you all on that front." Hunter was sitting on the edge of a balcony above them. Behind him, Laura stood sheepishly, with Miller and Jack hanging back where Hunter had ordered them to wait. "Come on, a little applause at the very least. I've fought my way through. . .ooh. . .thousands of these ne'er-do-wells. And I got the girl. That amounts to Epic Win in my book."

"Shut up and get down here," Veitch said. He nodded to Laura. "You better now?"

"Better enough to give you a good kicking." She clambered down with Hunter close behind, and immediately gave Shavi a hug, and then, surprisingly, Veitch.

"What's that for?" he asked, taken aback.

"I thought you needed to know what a woman felt like. You know, final treat before you die."

Distracted and on the edge of sanity, Church said harshly, "We can trust you now?"

Stung by his tone, she forced a grin. "Scout's honour, Church-dude."

Slipping on the Balor Claw, Hunter turned towards the advancing army and pretended to count heads. "I'll take the first hundred thousand. Split the rest up as you like."

"You people are going to die! What is wrong with you!" Tom snapped, but there was a hint of pride in his voice.

"You're going to die too, old man," Laura replied.

"I'm going to be running back through those corridors as fast as my arthritic knees will carry me while they're turning you into mulch," Tom said.

"Oh, come on," Hunter said. "It's not about winning or losing. It's about dying in such a spectacular manner that it becomes high art."

"Actually, it is about winning for me," Veitch said.

"Shut up!" Church gritted his teeth and raised Caledfwlch over his shoulder. "And fight!"

The tidal wave broke against them.

Church fought like a fury with Veitch barely a foot from his side, one troubled eye always on his friend, noting with each passing moment how quickly Church was moving down the road towards becoming the Libertarian; it was etched in his face, in the brutality with which he despatched the Enemy, in his cold, unflinching focus.

But soon both were left behind by Hunter, who moved through the ranks with the Balor Claw, bodies falling apart with every sweep of his hand; no one got near him.

"Blimey, where can I get me one of them?" Veitch shouted.

"Sorry, one of a kind," Hunter responded. "Just like me." He moved with the easy grace of a fieldworker scything through long grass, but with every death his lips moved as he consigned the face to memory.

"They're too efficient," Veitch said. "It's that bleedin' god controlling them. They should be going crazy with us ploughing through them like this."

"Leave that to me." While the battle raged around her, Laura achieved a moment of absolute calm. Her attention focused on Yen-Lo-Wang floating above. The skulls hanging from him appeared to move with a life of their own as he controlled every thought of the advancing army and directed them towards one purpose: death.

Plucking a seed from her pocket, Laura tossed it into the air. As it spun towards Yen-Lo-Wang, it sprouted shoots, its momentum increasing.

Yen-Lo-Wang did not see it until the last. Inches from his face, a woody tendril burst forth and prised its way between his lips. An expression of surprise flourished on his face and then Laura let the Blue Fire rise up within her and shift through the spectrum towards green. Growing at an incredible rate, the tendril searched the intimate byways of Yen-Lo-Wang's body, filling every space as it passed. When it reached its limit, Laura gave one burst of concentration and the tendril doubled in size. A loud PAK accompanied the explosion of Yen-Lo-Wang's corporeal form.

A wave of disorientation ran through the ocean of bodies. Church, Veitch and Hunter renewed their attack, so many dismembered corpses piled around them that they had built their own defences.

"Nice one, darlin'," Veitch said, "but we're only scratching the surface here." The glance he exchanged with Hunter expressed more clearly his fears that they would be overwhelmed in a very short time.

Hunter brushed his forehead as his mind felt the gentle touch of his "brother." "Cavalry's coming. Maybe it's not the Alamo after all."

From the rooftops, the Fomorii swarmed. Dropping into the arena, their gleaming black bodies snapped, shifted, mutated, sprouting wings, fangs, armour, razor-sharp cutting spikes, crab-like claws, barbed blades, hooked drills, crushing jaws. Efficient machines, they plunged into the middle of the packed bodies and were instantly lost in a whirl of activity that sent limbs and blood spraying high into the air.

The utter confusion they caused was only the beginning. Close behind the Fomorii came the gods. Gleaming gold in the hellish gloom, the Tuatha Dé Danaan burst from doorways around the arena with Lugh at their head and set about the Enemy fiercely. Behind them were the others, wielding hammers, axes, spears, filled with the hopes of different cultures but all connected by the same threads of Blue Fire.

Viracocha, burning like the sun come down to Earth. Ogoun, surrounded by the heat and smoke of a furnace as he wielded his machete. Benten, the sheer power of her beauty forcing the Enemy to lay down their arms. After a while, they became like flashes of light reflected off burnished metal, flitting through the darkness. Soon the Army of Dragons raced from the maze of corridors to join them, their power limited to the courage in their hearts, but no less for that.

The blue light that surrounded the Brothers and Sister of Dragons dimmed as Church lowered Caledfwlch. Oblivious to the others around him, concentration turned his face to stone. An instant later he was looking at the churning army from the perspective of the Fabulous Beast, while at the same time facing the ranks of the brutish creatures struggling to get over the mound of bodies.

Down he dived, swooping low over their heads, and then released a blast of purifying fire that gave him a shudder of pleasure. A smoking, blackened path scoured through the Enemy towards the Burning Man. As Church returned to his body, the Morvren flocked down to form a swirling black cloud around him, cawing and shrieking with voices that sounded almost human, and gleeful.

Veitch was forced to back away a step. He eyed Tom and Shavi uneasily, and weighed his sword in his hands. Neither gave him the guidance he needed.

Church's angry voice broke through the deafening wings—"I can do anything!"—and the birds rushed as one towards Janus. The god disappeared in the storm cloud and when the birds dissipated, he was gone.

Veitch caught Church's arm as he prepared to advance down the smouldering path. "You gotta watch out for the Black Fire, mate. One wrong step and it's game over."

"When I was up there a minute ago I saw a pattern," Church replied. "We've had prophecies of this day tied up in the old stories for millennia, but there's also been clues hidden in it."

"How so?"

"Spirals carved into rocks from Neolithic times. Spiral patterns in Celtic artwork. Their story of the spiral path as a journey through life. Those things were put there so we'd remember them, and think about their meaning. The Spiral Path marks how the Blue Fire runs in the land, but it's also the way through the maze of Black Fire. Those clues were left for us to read now."

"Church, you have to prepare yourself for the possibility that Ruth may already be dead," Shavi said. "The Libertarian may be tricking you with hope."

Church glanced at Tom, who gave nothing away. "If she's dead—"

"If she's dead and you let yourself become the Libertarian, you killed her." Laura caught his hand. "Don't go down that road, Church-dude. You can fight it. That's why you're the big old chosen one, and not the rest of us losers."

Church turned and moved away along the Spiral Path before any of them had the chance to see if he had accepted Laura's words.

They followed him, as they always had, as they always would, cutting down any of the Enemy that attempted to impede their route. Around the arena they raced, always moving closer to the acrid smell of burning that was worse than any of the other fires raging across the Fortress.

The feet of the Burning Man disappeared deep into an abyss separated by the bridge that ran between them. Beneath it a tunnel plunged, following the line of the bridge. Church knew he would have to descend into it even before he reached the yawning entrance. The vision he had received in the Forbidden City was as clear as if he had lived it: broken, on his knees before the Libertarian, in the dark beneath the arena with the abyss on either side and the legs of the Burning Man turning the cavern into hell. Despair gripped Church as he realised he couldn't see any way that that future would not come to be.

Steeling himself, he raced into the dark with the shrieks of the Morvren echoing in his ears.

4

Anxious, Hunter, Laura, Shavi and Veitch paused briefly at the entrance. Nearby, Tom held his head with both hands.

"This is it," Hunter said. "We can't hold back any longer. If it looks like he's going to become the Libertarian, one of us has to stop him. And by that, you know what I mean."

"I'll do it," Veitch said. "It's my responsibility."

"You can't," Laura said desperately. "He's the king. That's what you keep calling him. The king."

"Throughout history, when the land has to be saved or renewed, the king has to be sacrificed," Tom said.

"Shut up, you old git!" Laura glared at him.

"I'm just saying. If you can find another alternative . . . If not . . . ." Tom looked to Veitch.

A roar echoed above the clamour of battle. Shivering, Laura watched a figure silhouetted against the flames on one of the rooftops, part-beast, part-vegetation.

"Oh God, he's come for me," she whispered.

Cernunnos, the Green Man, bounded into the throng. He was not alone. A flash, low and lean on the edge of vision, signalled the arrival of the Puck. A glimmer of blue light. A small figure, filled with a power that dwarfed the world.

Time appeared to stand still. There was silence and a cold, cold wind as the Oldest Things in the Land drew rapidly closer, never in plain sight. And then Cernunnos was towering over Laura, and all she could see was his eyes filling her vision.

"I'm sorry," she said.

"Do not be afraid, daughter," his voice boomed, "I harbour no ill feelings. You played your part well, and bore your own personal pain like a true Sister of Dragons."

A tear of relief sprang to Laura's eye.

Cernunnos turned to the others. "This road is nearly done, your parts played out. An end fast approaches, but its outcome is yet in doubt. Existence holds its breath, and here, in the heart of the final battle, all is still."

The shimmer of the Puck's grin, there, then gone. "Fools and lovers, all. The clock has turned, the final moment beat. Stay your hands now. Only three—that magic number—can stand."

Cernunnos towered over Veitch. "You have learned of death, Brother of Dragons. That was your role. Go now, and put into practice all that you know."

Veitch nodded, and raced into the dark after Church.

"Lovers," the Puck added in a quiet, enigmatic tone, "and fools."

5

It was dank and dark for the first section of the tunnel, but eventually it opened out onto a broad stone bridge framed by the glare of the Burning Man, whose arms reached down into the abyss on either side. When Church glanced over the edge, it was impossible to see more than a few feet into the darkness, as though some quality of the place was draining the light away. The strip of rock overhead appeared to be pressing down upon him, adding to the claustrophobic atmosphere. Torches flickered all around in the gulf.

Caledfwlch's flames danced as Church advanced across the bridge, but even the blade's light was dimmed.

This is where it all happens, Church thought. Be ready now.

Red eyes glimmered in the gloom ahead and he realised the Libertarian was there.

"Where's Ruth?" he said.

"Why do you care?" the Libertarian mocked. "She's moved away from you. She's with me now. Which is you. Oh, what a strange and sweet paradox. If she's attracted to you, she'd be secretly attracted to me. I don't know why you never thought of that."

"Ruth's stronger than me . . . and you. Whatever she might feel for us, she'd walk away rather than pick the wrong side. She'd sooner see us both dead and suffer a broken heart."

"I love it!" the Libertarian exclaimed. "The romanticism! A broken heart! It's like listening to yourself as a child. All that innocence. All that ignorance."

Ruth was nowhere to be seen, but Church knew she had to be close at hand.

"You see, both you and the lovely Ruth have been on a learning journey," the Libertarian continued. "She has seen the real you, not the good, decent, pure-hearted hero that legend would have us believe in. Within you lurks the seed of me. And without that knowledge she would not have been so easily turned."

"What do you mean?"

The Libertarian gestured flamboyantly. Behind Church, at the entrance to the bridge, Ruth stood, in the tight-fitting black outfit that Niamh had once worn. Consumed by the power of the Craft, bolts of energy crackled around her as she floated inches above the floor, her eyes on fire.

"She's mine now," the Libertarian said. "The only way you can get her back is by becoming me. You see, even though I've moved on, I still understand the human heart, and its many, many weaknesses. Despite all the battles and the great adventures, that, in essence, is what it's all been about: love. It means more to humans than saving the world. It means everything."

"There's a reason for that," Church said. "It really does mean everything. That's what you don't get."

The Libertarian laughed. "Still playing the innocent, with your syrupy philosophies. Life has harder edges than that."

Church looked from Ruth to the Libertarian, weighing whether he could reach either one before he was struck down.

"This moment, right at the end of time, is fluid," the Libertarian said. "It will already be deviating from the vision you had in the Forbidden City because your knowledge of your destiny now alters your choices, but without changing the outcome. You were never up to doing what needed to be done to prevent me coming into being. Because of love." His words dripped contempt. "You've reached the end of the pattern and found that it's a maze that always leads back on itself. The only way to prevent me defeating you is to kill Ruth, and then kill me. Ruth is my Key. The key to your heart, your hopes. When I toss your bleeding body into the flames of the Burning Man, it is her power that will help you be reborn as me. Kill her, and end this now."

Church glanced back at Ruth and knew the Libertarian had won. Ignoring the futility, he turned and raced towards his future-self with sword held high. The blast from Ruth came just as he had anticipated, hurling him up into the air. Blood splattered all around from a score of wounds.

Next to him, Caledfwlch lay shattered, the Blue Fire extinguished. The outlines of the sword blurred and changed continually, not a sword at all.

Church tried to pull himself to his feet, spat a mouthful of blood and collapsed on the stone. His body felt drained of energy.

In the distance, a pack of dogs howled, their voices joining to become one gut-wrenching, mournful cry for what was about to be lost. The Libertarian cupped his ear. "The Hounds of Avalon," he said. "Every time the world ends, they get to sing it out in style, and the Void has ended it many times, pressing the reset button and starting again. But this is the last. The ultimate. The end. So let them howl their hearts out one final time."

The Libertarian caught Church by the lapels and pulled him up. "Three minutes to go, Brother of Dragons. Three minutes until the final, absolute victory of the Devourer of All Things. The end of all hope for Existence. That is what you have thrown away with your stupid love.

"You never realised how important you were to everything or you wouldn't have made so many stupid mistakes. You were always the key to Existence succeeding, both as a man, in the things you did, and as a symbol of everything that Existence is.

"But when I throw you into that abyss, you will be wiped from Existence. No one will remember you. You will not have existed, you will never have existed, and reality will reshape itself around the vacuum you leave behind, with me. Without you, without the very symbol of Existence, nothing can ever change again. Existence is destroyed. The Void wins forever."

"No," Church croaked, "I'm not that important."

"You always rattled on about the power of symbols and failed to see how crucial you were. The king. The power in the land. The hope of all reality in its darkest hour. With you gone, with you never having existed, there is no hope. And without hope there is only despair."

The Libertarian hauled Church to the edge of the bridge. "I should say something poetic, like 'Prepare to come to nothing, like all your dreams,' but I think I'll settle for die, you bastard. Die, and be gone, so I can forget about you, finally."

6

From the dark, Veitch watched Ruth launch her attack on Church. In the dying flare of the light, he dashed forwards and threw himself at Ruth, clamping a hand over her mouth as he dragged her back into the dark. The shock of the attack prevented her from using her Craft, and by the time she had recovered, he had his sword at her throat.

Across the bridge, he could hear the Libertarian mocking Church as he talked about wiping him from Existence, but he kept his focus on Ruth. Her eyes crackled with power, but he continued to whisper her name and slowly the subtle manipulation of Mictlantecuhtli ebbed away to reveal the Ruth with whom he had fallen in love. Right then he understood his role in the pattern. If he and Ruth had not shared affection, she would never have responded to his quiet words, would have fought him and probably killed him. There was a reason for his heartache, and that made it a little more palatable.

"It's all right, darlin'. You're back."

"Church—"

"He's still alive." Veitch could see she was aware of everything that had transpired.

"You have to stop Church becoming the Libertarian, Ryan." Tears flooded her eyes. "If you kill him, Church can't be wiped from Existence. He'll always be a symbol. He'll always have the power to affect things, even from death. And the Libertarian will never come into being."

Veitch glanced over at the Libertarian counting out the seconds as he held Church close to the abyss. "There's a better way," he said.

"You can't take any risks!"

He gave the cocky smile that she had always loved. "There's always a better way."

Yet she saw in his eyes something deep and mature and very unlike Veitch and it troubled her deeply. "What are you planning?"

He whispered it in her ear.

"You can't, Ryan!" Gripping his arm, she fought to stop herself becoming distressed.

"I don't matter here," he said. "Church matters. You matter. I was always along just to make sure you two made it through to the finish line. And that's what I'm going to do now. My last act."

"Ryan, if you go into the abyss, you'll be wiped from Existence. No one will ever remember you."

He grinned. "Not the end of the world."

"But that was all you ever wanted—for people to remember you as a hero."

"Yeah, that was all I wanted." He glanced back to check on the Libertarian and Church. A minute to go. The fires of the Burning Man were growing more intense; the Void was coming. "I've learned a lot from Church, and you, and the others. I'm a better man now. I know what's important. It's not what's out there, or what people think. It's what's inside. I've got a whole world in here. In the past, I could never look inside myself—it was too frightening. But now if I know I'm going out a hero, well, that's good enough. That's important."

"Don't do it, Ryan—"

"There isn't any other choice, darlin'. This is the whole reason I'm here. I know that now." He wiped a tear from her cheek. "A kiss?" he said. "Won't mean anything. I know you love Church, and that's right. I've got my head around it now. But it would be. . . nice."

She pulled his head down and kissed him deeply.

When he broke away, his smile melted her heart. "I can die easy now. There's nothing else I want."

He tore away from her grip as a roar began to fill the cavernous space. The heat from the Burning Man increased sharply, the flames turning a deep scarlet. Dropping his sword, Veitch ran. He thought of his father and his mother, of the mermaids swimming by his boat and the tiny people with gossamer wings who always instilled such peace. And he thought of the woman he loved more than anything else in the world, more than life itself.

Hitting the Libertarian full force, they both went over the edge of the bridge while Church slumped against the side, clinging on. At the last, Veitch thought he saw relief in the Libertarian's red, lidless eyes. His adversary had time for one word—"Ryan . . ."—and then they plunged down into the dark.

7

"Ryan!" Church yelled as he watched Veitch and the Libertarian fall.

Ruth scrambled to his side. "Remember him, Church! Don't let his memory die! Don't—"

The words died in her throat. They stared at each other in incomprehension for a moment, and then Church dragged himself to the centre of the bridge. "What just happened?"

Ruth shook her head. "I don't know." She looked around. "We . . . we must be . . . The Burning Man. We have to destroy it."

Church nodded, although he instinctively knew that was not the correct answer. "Where are the others?"

On cue, Miller and Jack ran in accompanied by Shavi and Tom. "Hunter and Laura are guarding the entrance," Shavi said, "but there is no sign of Mallory and Caitlin. We do not have the Extinction Shears."

"Yes, you do." Walking along the bridge from the opposite side, the Wayfinder held high so that the blue light lit his path, came a cloaked figure.

"Hal?" Church said, baffled by his human form.

"The Caretaker," Hal said with a smile. "The new one. There's no time to explain. Here." He handed over the Extinction Shears.

"What do we do?" Church asked.

"You use the Two Keys to destroy the holding matrix for the Void. And then you use the Extinction Shears to untether him from reality. The Void will be lost forever."

The roaring became deafening: the Burning Man glowed so brightly they could barely look at it. A deep dread closed in around them, and a feeling that a terrifying presence was only a room away.

"No time!" Hal stressed.

"The Wish-Hex in me won't be enough to destroy that!" Jack peered over the edge of the bridge into the fire.

"I can help," Miller said calmly. "Of course. I can see why I'm here now. As the Wish-Hex starts to destroy you, I can heal you so you can keep releasing the power. You can do that?"

"I. . .I think so," Jack said. "Keep the chain reaction going."

Miller looked around the others. "We always knew it was going to come to this. Don't worry about us."

"But if you go into the abyss you'll be wiped from Existence," Ruth said. "No one will ever know you existed." Just like no one knew of. . .A name began to come, then faded rapidly.

"Good," Jack said. "Then Mahalia won't feel any pain. She can get on with her life."

His maturity brought a swell of pride to Ruth and Church.

"I wish Hunter was here," Jack said. "He was . . ." The word choked in his throat. "Never mind."

Jack stepped onto the edge of the bridge, and Miller wrapped his arms around him tightly.

The roaring was so loud they could barely hear themselves speak. "Go!" Church yelled.

Jack and Miller threw themselves off the bridge. Instantly, a white light washed out, and a moment later a blue glow, the two intertwining, merging. A burst of the white light rolled upwards, and the bridge shook and then cracked, huge chunks plummeting down into the abyss.

As Church, Ruth, Tom and Shavi ran back the way they had come, Church snatched up a sword. It wasn't the shattered Caledfwlch, and he had no idea who it belonged to, but it felt right in his hand. He sheathed it. The Caretaker was nowhere to be seen.

As the bridge fell into the abyss and the white and blue light continued to roll out in waves, the structure of the Burning Man began to break up and fall apart. The scarlet flames leaped out with a life of their own, no longer able to maintain any shape.

"We did it. The matrix is breaking up." Church opened the Extinction Shears and felt their pulsing energy rush up his arms and into his heart. He knew he wasn't really holding shears. On the edge of his perception, images shifted constantly, hinting at something much bigger, something that reached across worlds. "Now we just need to get rid of the Void forever."

As the frame of the Burning Man plunged into the abyss and the flames roiled out of control, a voice rang out far behind him. "Church! Stop them! Use the Shears! Stop them!"

He didn't turn. His concentration was fixed on the flames; he was convinced he could see a face in them that would haunt him for the rest of his days. Part of him knew the voice was Hunter's, that the warning was important. But he didn't turn.

Crying out in shock, Ruth thrust Church to one side as a seemingly endless army of spiders streamed towards the furiously churning flames, their metallic bodies glinting in the ruddy furnace light.

"Stop them!" Hunter called, closer now.

Church glanced back to see Hunter and Laura racing behind the flow of spiders. Beyond them, Cernunnos, Carlton and the Caretaker all looked on with deep concern. He realised, too late, that it was the moment his future self had warned him about so many times: when you're in Otherworld and they call, heed it right away.

The spiders flowed around the weakened essence of the Void lost in the flames, carving through reality to create a door in the air leading to the superstructure behind everything where the spiders moved freely across all time and space.

As Church raced to the edge of the shattered bridge, the swirling flames were sucked through the gaping door. Falling through, the spiders worked rapidly to seal the opening behind them.

They had taken the Void to another place, perhaps another time. They would be bringing it back.

From the doorway behind reality, coloured lights leaked out and Church felt the very nature of the cavern alter. Mists rolled all around and suddenly he was in the Warp Zone again, and there were numerous versions of himself at different points in his history, wandering, baffled, determined, scared, fighting. Desperate to send a message to himself to change what had occurred, he raced from one to the other, calling, "Is this it? Is this the right time? You have to listen to me. This is a warning."

But, of course, he knew it was futile.

That didn't stop him. Confused by the shifting reality of the Warp Zone, he added, "Is this the right place? Am I too late?" To the multiple Churches, he insisted, "When you're in Otherworld and they call, heed it right away. They're going to bring him back. They're—" Suddenly he glimpsed the spiders closing the door in the air and remembered where he was. "Too late!" he yelled, racing out of the colours to the edge of the abyss.

With only a sliver remaining, Church brought the shears together. There was a moment when everything seemed to hang, and Church felt as if he was floating in a brilliant white light. But with a sound like the crystal-clear chime of a bell, he was snapped back into the harsh reality of the cavern and flung head over heels in a rushing wind. His head hit stone and he blacked out.

8

"Will he be all right?"

Silence.

"Please come back to me. Please!......"

"Don't worry—it's nearly over. There'll be peace."

"Peace . . ."

9

Surfacing from disturbing dreams, Church found himself lying out in the wastelands, surrounded by his friends. On the horizon, there was a smudge of scarlet, gold and black where the Fortress of the Enemy burned and above it the Fabulous Beasts swooped majestically, caught in the rosy light of the setting sun.

"We did it?" he asked, still dazed.

"I don't know what you did exactly, but the Enemy's army lost all heart for the fight." Squatting beside him, Tom looked more at peace than Church had ever seen him. He pulled off the ring Freyja had given him and tossed it down a dune into the ochre dust.

Looking up into the darkening sky, Church said, "The stars are coming out."

Ruth brushed a hair from his forehead. "I never thought I'd see that again."

Levering himself onto his elbows, Church asked, "Are we all here?"

"Yes," Ruth replied. "You, me, Tom, Shavi, Laura and Hunter. Five Brothers and Sisters of Dragons, one hanger-on." She smiled at Tom, but it was gradually replaced by a puzzled, sad expression.

Church understood. "Strange—it feels as if somebody's missing." Shrugging off a sharp pang of grief, he clambered to his feet.

Nearby the Army of Dragons and the gods celebrated loudly. The Brothers and Sisters of Dragons moved amongst the knots of strange beings, surprised by the camaraderie and the hugs and back-slaps from ones who may well have tormented them only a few days earlier. Not far away, Virginia and the other refugees stared at the sky in mute disbelief.

Lugh saw that Church had recovered and made his way up the dune with Rhiannon close behind. "Brother of Dragons, you have the thanks of all of the Golden Ones, indeed of all living things in all the lands." He shook Church's hand warmly.

"The Void isn't gone for good," Church said.

"Yes and no," Lugh said enigmatically. "This is the dawn of a new age. A golden age. You will soon understand."

"It is a new age, too, for the Brothers and Sisters of Dragons," Rhiannon added. "You were forged to prevent the victory of the Void this day. You will have a new role now, and in that spirit we, the Golden Ones, have a request, equals to equals."

"Go on," Church said.

"The great sadness that lies at the heart of our people is the loss of our homes—Gorias, Finias, Falias and Murias," Lugh continued. His eyes blazed with a hopeful excitement. "Help us find them. Help the Tuatha Dé Danann return to their ancestral homes and bring joy to our hearts again. It would be a quest that would live up to the great legend of the Brothers and Sisters of Dragons! The filid would sing songs of such an achievement until the stars came down!"

Church glanced around the others and saw the silent answer. "We owe you for your help and sacrifice," he said. "Once we've rested, we'll start to plan."

Lugh and Rhiannon could barely contain their joy. They thanked the Brothers and Sisters of Dragons profusely and then hurried back to the ranks of their people to spread the news. Soon their celebration dwarfed even that of the Army of Dragons and the other gods.

In the growing gloom, a blue light gleamed across the wastelands. "Wait here," Church said to the others. "I'll be back in a while."

As he set out towards the light, he was distracted by the strange but familiar sight of a puppeteer standing alone on the blasted terrain. Eight feet tall, wearing black robes and a white mask with a nose that arched like a bird's beak, he looked just as Church had seen him in Venice in the sixteenth century. His hands moved rapidly above five dancing puppets, though there were no strings. The puppets' lifelike faces were exactly as Church had guessed.

Church approached him and for long moments watched the silent show. Then he reached up and removed the puppeteer's mask, without any resistance. His own face looked back at him, though that too resembled a mask.

"It's true, then?" Church asked.

The puppeteer only gave an enigmatic smile.

Realising he would get nothing more, Church headed once again towards the light, and when he glanced back briefly the puppeteer was gone, no marks in the dust to suggest he had ever been there.

Soon all thoughts of what he had seen faded, to be replaced by the unexpected sensation of a great weight lifting from his shoulders. Could it be all over? After so long, he scarcely dared believe it.

Night came down quickly in the desert. Hal waited for him, the Wayfinder a blue beacon of hope in the desolate landscape. His cloak was wrapped about him against the plummeting temperatures.

"You're the new Caretaker? How did that happen?" Church asked.

"Long story. It's a big job, an important job. Someone needs to do it, and I guess I passed the entrance exam."

"Don't do yourself down. You deserve it."

"Walk with me." Hal held the lantern high to guide their way across the wastelands.

"It's not over, is it?"

"No. I'm sorry, Church. It's never over."

"Never?"

"Never."

Church's heart sank.

"On the bright side, you get to spend eternity with the best friends you could ever wish for. You get to be a tremendous force for good in the universe, shaping the lives of untold millions. And you get to be king, now and always."

"So we didn't win today. Despite all the deaths and the pain, we didn't win," Church said wearily.

"Oh, you won." The Wayfinder's sapphire glow gave Hal's smile a strange, transcendental quality. "You won bigger and better than you ever dreamed."

Hal's words resonated with what Lugh had said about the Void and the new age, and Church had a strange sensation of something of incomprehensible magnitude drawing around him. He shivered, although he had no idea why.

On the crest of a rise, Hal indicated the shifting colours of the Warp Zone ahead. "That's still here?" Church said. "I thought it was some bizarre side effect of the Void."

"It's going to stay here. And it'll be your new home." Hal laughed when he saw Church's baffled expression. "In a way. It's time I told you everything."

They sat together on the ridge in the chill desert night under the lamp of the full moon. Across the heavens, the glorious sweep of stars brought a shiver of magic and a feeling that anything could happen.

Hal set the Wayfinder in the dust and watched the blue flame dance. "Destroying the Burning Man weakened the Void immensely. If there'd been time to use the Extinction Shears, the Void would have been cut from this reality forever."

"I don't know if that would have been such a good thing. Everything needs two sides, two faces. One to define the other and to give it value. We need the Void and Existence. It's just a matter of balance."

Hal nodded slowly. "They said you were wise."

"So is this how it was meant to have turned out? All part of the pattern?"

"Who knows? I don't. What I do know is the spiders took the Void to safety in the past. That dark force can reappear at any time in Earth's history to try to change things so that what happened today . . . never happened."

Watching the drifting colours of the Warp Zone, Church thought he understood.

"It's the job of the Brothers and Sisters of Dragons to oppose the Void wherever it appears," Hal said. "In the Renaissance, the seventies, the Norman Conquest, the Jurassic era, for all I know. Whenever the Void starts to exert its influence, calling on new allies, creating new threats, trying to shift the pattern, you and your Brothers and Sisters will be there to stop it."

"Through the Warp Zone, we can reach any time and any place."

"Exactly. It was always going to be this way. You read all the legends, the old stories. The king, waiting across the water . . . the ocean—of time and space—at the darkest hour when the call would go out and he would return with his knights to vanquish evil and save the land. The Brothers and Sisters of Dragons become the ur-myth."

"Yes, I know that story." Church drew the sword he had picked up near the shattered bridge. After Caledfwlch, it had a strange feel, but it felt right, as though it had been held by good people, despite the way the blue and black flames appeared to fight along the length of the blade. "So we don't get to rest."

"You get to live forever with the people you love the most because time never passes here in the Far Lands, or there in the Warp Zone. Always young, always strong, the greatest hero Existence has, fighting the true fight for all time. Does that not feel good?"

Church considered it for a moment and realised it did. It felt, in a strange way, like heaven. The best reward of all.

"Lugh and the Tuatha Dé Danaan have asked for our help," he said.

"You'll have time for that. After all, you've got an Army of Dragons to help you out. And more gods than you can shake a stick at. If you really need them." He laughed quietly.

"So we keep repelling the Void at every turn. But we can't destroy it, because without the Void we would never have been challenged enough to grow and become what we are today. We needed that dark side to learn how to be good. That was part of the plan too, right? Existence needed the Void to achieve its ends. There's irony in there somewhere."

Hal began to say something about the Caraprix, but then caught himself and would only shake his head enigmatically when Church pressed him.

"But something happened when I used the Extinction Shears. I felt it," Church said.

"Something amazing. You severed the Void's connection to the warp and the weft. It escaped into the pattern of the past, but from this day on it has no connection."

"The Void can't exist in the future?"

"You freed all the worlds, Church. The Void's influence will always be felt through the infinite connections, but it can have no control. There is no Mundane Spell. What lies ahead is the Kingdom of the Serpent. Existence will rule the balance for the first time since time began. It really will be a golden age."

The possibilities were too vast for Church to comprehend.

"The future hasn't been written yet," Hal said. "There's still a very important job to do. But that's for tomorrow. Right now, enjoy the knowledge that every sacrifice has been worthwhile. You won, Church."

They sat in silence, watching the moon make shadows across the desert, and the stars glinting like jewels in the vast chamber of the night, and Church felt at peace. For the first time.

He felt at peace.

EPILOGUE
HAPPY EVER AFTER

1

After Church had explained what the future held, he took Ruth away into the desert and left Shavi, Tom, Hunter and Laura sitting around a large campfire, drinking a potent brew that some of the Norse gods had brought with them.

"So, an eternity of fighting. Could be worse," Laura said.

"It's going to play murder with my plans for a Caribbean holiday." Hunter prodded the fire and sent a cascade of sparks shooting towards the stars.

Laura saw Shavi smiling to himself as he looked around the circle. "What are you thinking, Mr Enigmatic Seer?" Laura prompted. "Or is it more of your weird sex fantasies?"

"I am thinking that this has ruined Church's motto for his T-shirts. No happy endings, he said. And here we are. This . . ." he gestured expansively ". . . is more than I could ever have hoped for. The best of friends, a family, even. We faced death, we faced heartache, and we moved beyond them, together, by relying on each other. And we built bonds that have enriched us all. I am very, very happy."

Nobody spoke for a while as they reflected on Shavi's words and realised the depths of those bonds. But then Laura glimpsed Tom's face in the firelight. In it were fears and doubts she recognised.

"Don't think you're getting away, you old bastard," she said.

Tom flashed a suspicious glare her way.

"You're one of us. If I haven't got you, who am I going to torment?"

"I am not a Brother of Dragons," Tom said.

"No, you are our guide, our wisdom, our conscience," Shavi responded. "Jiminy Cricket! We need you."

"That'll teach you, old man," Laura said. "You're going to have to spend an eternity listening to Shavi ramble on about the philosophic connections between the fluff in his belly button and the way a bumblebee dances. We can all wallow in our misery together."

Laura saw the relief on Tom's face as his fear of loneliness drained away, and she felt a sense of satisfaction that she had secretly helped him. They were more alike than either of them would have cared to admit.

"Then I will accept my miserable responsibility and attempt to drill some sense into all of you," he grumbled. "Have pity. My life is over." He took out his tin and carefully constructed a roll-up from his dwindling supplies, a smile playing on his lips.

Laura stood up, stretched like a cat and took Hunter's hand.

"Sex?" he said.

"Like you stand a chance with me. It's only been charity, didn't you realise that?"

She hauled him away from the light, enjoying the feel of his hand in hers. "You're not inviting your friend over for a drink?" Laura indicated the silhouette of the hooded giant away in the desert.

"He's not a great socialiser."

"He going to be joining us in the Great Beyond?"

"It'll be like having children without going through the whole childbirth thing."

"That's how I always wanted children."

In the shadow of a dune, they held each other, and kissed.

"I've got a question," Hunter said after a while. "What's your name?"

"You know my name."

"Not that DuSantiago bollocks. That's for the idiots you wrap around your little finger. This is me."

"Privileged information. I've never trusted anyone enough to tell them that. Once someone knows your real name they have power over you. Don't you listen to any of Church's crazy ramblings?"

He waited.

"Smith." She sighed. "Laura Smith."

"You see, the reverse is actually true," he said. "Now you have power over me."

They kissed again, and it felt as if it would go on forever.

2

Hand in hand, Church and Ruth walked out of the Warp Zone into a misty morning just before dawn. Familiar, comforting smells of exhaust fumes, damp vegetation and the heavy, deep aromas of the river reached them. They breathed deeply, soothed by the silky sensation of the mist on their faces. The city breathed slow and easy too. It dreamed good dreams.

"Where are we?" Ruth looked from the hazy street lamp to the parked cars covered in dew.

"Don't you recognise it? Come on."

As they walked along the road, the trees eventually revealed the lights of Albert Bridge, and Ruth smiled. "London. Where we met," she said with a smile. "God, that seems so long ago. We were different people then."

"If we knew what lay ahead, do you think we'd have carried on down that road?"

"You're joking, aren't you?" They walked to the railings and looked down at the slow-moving river. "Miss that chance to peel back the boring, real world and see the magic that lies behind it? I remember . . ."

A Fabulous Beast swooping out of the night over the lights of the motorway. Stone circles, still and peaceful under the stars. Hidden doors in crumbling castles. Secrets encoded in the landscape thousands of years ago. Old knowledge shining new light on life. The Craft. Flying. Magic swords. A boat that sails between worlds. A Welsh night and a being as old as time, eyes burning in a face made of leaves, ushering her into a new life with a brand on her hand. Friendship. Love. And the Blue Fire burning just beneath the surface of the land, and in the stones, and in hearts.

"The world is better than it seems. And so are people," she said. "We've been allowed a glimpse into the biggest mystery of all. The knowledge that there's so much more . . . I wouldn't trade that for anything."

"The Void's influence is still here. It's going to take people a while to open their eyes and pull themselves out from under the effects of the Mundane Spell. But once they have, there'll be no going back. This is the start of something big and new, and—"

A fox trotted out of the mist and paused when it saw them. In its eyes was a light Church hadn't noticed before; it was filled with secrets. The fox looked them over as if greeting fellow travellers and then moved on. In that moment was a strange magic that neither could explain.

"Why have you brought me here?" Ruth asked.

"I wanted to remind myself what was important, before . . ." He looked around at the trees and the lights and the still, dark houses. "Whatever lies ahead."

He was interrupted by a splash in the river below them. Glowing with a dull golden light, a low, long boat drifted slowly in the flow, and aboard it were the Seelie Court, returning once again to the land they loved. Each mysterious member looked around in awe at the scenery, but the queen caught sight of Church and gave a slight, enigmatic bow.

Once they had passed, Ruth slipped her arm around Church's waist and rested her head on his shoulder. "Since we met here, things got so complex. We've been through cynicism, darkness, we've become more troubled. But in the end, innocence wins out," she said. "That was always the message."

In the circle of misty light beneath a lamp, Tom waited. "It's time," he said.

"It was always going to be you, wasn't it?" Church said.

"Of course. I'm your guide."

"Can Ruth come?"

After a moment's hesitation, Tom nodded. "She's the one who kept you on the path."

Looking around one final time, Church glanced up and thought he glimpsed a brief light somewhere through the layers of fog, so high, so fleeting, it would have been easy to miss it. A burst of fire.

3

"I've been here before," Church said.

"Of course you have. We all have at some time," Tom replied. "We leave here and we return here."

A cavern, a space deep in the earth, the smell of damp and the chill of the dark. A blue light guided the three of them forwards until they encountered Hal holding the Wayfinder aloft.

"I am the Caretaker," Hal said. "I keep a light burning in the darkest night. I serve all who come to me, whether their hearts are filled with hope or tainted by despair."

Church recognised the words, and now understood that it was a ritual greeting.

Beyond Hal lay a cave where a cauldron bubbled over a small fire. Poised over it was a man with wild grey hair clutching a long staff and an old woman in a black dress who could have been his twin, her face smeared with dirt or grease so that her eyes stared with a terrible intensity.

"Look into the cauldron," the woman said.

Uneasily, Church ventured beside her and peered into the depths. He saw himself lying on a bed, eyes closed, with people watching him. There was an air of uncertainty to the image.

"Is that the truth, then?" he asked. "Am I really dying?"

"The real question is, does it matter?" the wild-haired man said.

"Nothing is true, except what you make it," the old woman cackled.

Church wanted to see more, to try to understand, but Tom gently pulled him away. "Where are we going?" Church asked.

"You have learned the ability to alter much," the wild-haired man shouted after them.

As Hal led them along a tunnel, there was a flash beside them, a fleeting grin, mischievous eyes. "Fools and lovers are the greatest heroes," the Puck said. "This Merry Wanderer of the Night will wander alone no longer." He gave a flourishing bow and disappeared.

A feeling of dread fell across them as they approached another cave. Cernunnos waited outside it, his eyes glowing within the vegetation of his face. He indicated that Church should enter. "You have something that belongs to the Daughters of the Night," he said.

Inside the cave, three hooded women stood, their faces hidden. They were the source of the dread that made Church's flesh crawl.

"One spins threads. One measures them," Cernunnos said. "And the other . . . ?"

From the small bag at his belt, Church pulled the Extinction Shears. They sang as he brought them into the light. When the third woman reached out a bony hand and reclaimed the Shears, Church took care not to brush her fingers with his own.

At the side of the cave a silvery thread stretched from the shadows above down to the floor. The third woman opened the shears around the thread, and waited. Slowly she turned to look at Church; he bowed his head, afraid that if he looked into the depths of her cowl he would die.

"What is that thread?" he asked, unsettled.

"You don't need to know that." Hal's tone was sympathetic. "You've returned what belongs to the Daughters of the Night. Let's move on."

Outside the cave, Carlton waited. Beaming, he shook Church's hand, and then Ruth's and Tom's. "We're nearly done now," he said. "But I wanted to let you know that what you have achieved is no more than what was expected of you, and, in the final reckoning, remarkable. You've earned the faith that was placed in you, Church."

"What do you want me to do?" Church asked.

"Destroy the world. Destroy all the worlds."

"What?" Church said incredulously.

"Turn the Axis of Existence, as you did once before."

"I don't understand."

Carlton smiled. "Destroy what's out there, Church. Do what the Void could not do."

Church gaped.

"Remake the world, as you would see it made."

"Remake . . . ?" For a long moment, Church tried to comprehend if there was some hidden meaning in Carlton's comments, but the honest innocence in the boy's face told him the truth. "That's insane! I can't do that!"

"You are the only one who can."

"How long are you giving me—seven days? I'm not God!" The insanity of what was being proposed left Church reeling.

"Why Church?" Ruth took his hand, supporting him.

"Everything that has happened to you has been preparing you for this moment," Carlton said.

"I'm not prepared. How can you say anyone is prepared to change the world?" Church looked from Ruth to Tom.

Tom rested a reassuring hand on Church's shoulder. "During my travels I read the story of the Pilgrim's Progress," he said, "and that is essentially what you have done. You've journeyed around Britain, across time, around the world and across the dimensions, meeting humanity, and life in all its forms, learning valuable lessons from your experiences. You know what it is to be human, to feel, to love. That is what has prepared you for this moment."

"Destroy the world and remake it? I can't do that. It's too . . . big! I'm not up to it."

"Then leave it just how it is, but maybe with a few slight changes," Tom prompted.

Slowly, what Tom was saying dawned on Ruth. Her eyes gleamed. "Yes," she breathed. "Think of it. A world that's about magic not money. That's about friendship and love, not power. And you're the best person to do that."

"How can you say that?" Church tried not to feel betrayed. "Nobody should have that kind of power. The ultimate power. I could be as bad as the Void. What if I didn't like . . . I don't know . . . people who walked with a limp, so I made sure they didn't exist in this brave new world?"

"Because I know you." A quiet confidence suffused Ruth's face. "I know in any given situation you will always do the right thing. You've proven that over and over again."

"I trust you too," Tom said.

"Is that why they brought you along? My mentor. To convince me?"

"They could have brought any of the others. They all would have said the same thing."

"I'm not the person you think I am."

"You've never had confidence in yourself," Tom said. "You've doubted at every turn, but your actions have shown the truth. On the long road, you were presented with numerous opportunities to go the wrong way. You could have given it all up to pursue your love for Ruth, the sole, defining factor in your life. But you kept going. You kept true. You're a hero."

"I'm not!" Church snapped. "I'm . . . nobody. I'm just an ordinary bloke."

"And maybe that's what's needed here," Ruth said quietly. "Somebody who knows the right thing when he sees it. Somebody who understands simple, uncynical, easily mocked concepts—like love. Or innocence. Or duty. Sacrifice."

Her admiration for him was so powerful he could barely look at her.

"We need a better world," Tom said. "Everybody on the planet wants that. They don't want a world ruled by those desperate to make money or seek power. They want something true, and honest. And it's your responsibility to give them that."

"Don't say that!"

"It's your duty," Tom insisted quietly.

The words hung heavy on Church's shoulders. Desperate and isolated, he lowered his head and closed his eyes, wrestling with his answer. After a moment, he sighed, "How does it work?"

"Come with me." Carlton took Church's hand and led him to a large cavern filled with a brilliant light. It took Church a while to realise the cavern was filled with Caraprix, all of the mutating creatures in a state of flux. Amongst them stood Jerzy, blank-eyed but alive.

"God, you manipulated that poor bastard," Church said. "You made sure one of those shape-shifting things was stuck in his head to call all the others home."

"The Mocker will live," Carlton said. "He's been a good servant."

"How are those things going to help?"

"The Caraprix are like the spiders, if you will," Carlton said. "They are the agents of Existence. They can unpick the weft and the weave, and then weave a new reality. They are machines of creation."

Church watched the silver creatures continually change shape. "So they're like angels?"

Carlton laughed.

"I decide what the world's going to be like and they go out and make it a reality."

"Something like that."

"Where do they come from?"

"That's not for you to know right now."

"But they destroyed the Drakusa," Church said. "They were a real threat. The Drakusa did everything they could to wipe them out, but the Caraprix committed genocide."

"The Drakusa had the potential to become agents of change, but they chose to direct all their abilities to their own ends. They ignored the greater good. They desired power, for themselves. They crushed other races that fell before them. If they had been true to who they were, perhaps the golden age could have been ushered in a long, long time ago."

"So you destroyed them?"

"Me? No. The Oldest Things in the Land are agents, just like you, Church. We worked and strove and failed, sometimes. But did Existence wipe out the Drakusa? Yes. They chose to work for the Void, though they didn't understand it in their terms. Innocence does not mean weakness."

"How many races fell, like the Drakusa?"

"Every race has a choice: act for the greater good, bring magic back into the world, or support the aims of the Void," Carlton said. "Free will, Church. There is a pattern, but everyone has a choice. The only rule is they must accept responsibility for their actions. If you seek out personal power and lay others low, do not be surprised when a higher power decides to do the same to you."

"Sounds very Old Testament to me." Church watched the Caraprix change and for the first time felt awe: he could see something wonderful in the very essence of them.

"Everyone has a choice. Fragile Creatures didn't fail. You didn't fail."

Church steeled himself. "There's no point talking. Let's do this."

"You're ready?"

"No. But I'll do my best."

"That's all anyone's ever asked of you, Church. And you've never let anyone down."

Carlton led Church back to Ruth and Tom who waited by the cave he thought he had visited in a dream when he had been in the Sleep Like Death. Whatever lay inside made his perception skew wildly. He saw a network of lights, a mandala, a rotating crystal, and then the image his mind found easiest: an enormous machine of cogs and gears with a protruding lever.

"Just like before? Pull the lever?"

"It'll be easier this time," Carlton said.

"Symbols," Church whispered to himself before announcing, "This could be the last gasp of my dying brain. The final shape of the hallucination. Pull the lever and it's all over. Is that what it is? The lever is death?"

"It's whatever you believe it to be," Carlton said.

Ruth kissed him on the cheek. "Just remember, whatever happens, we've won. Against all the odds, we've rid the world of corruption. It's been a long, hard struggle, but we've won."

"What kind of world will you make, Church?" Carlton asked.

"A good one," Church replied. "I hope."

"Jack?" Tom caught his attention. "You're a good man. Don't forget that."

Church placed both hands on the lever and steadied himself. He looked to Tom and then Ruth and drew strength from the absolute trust he saw in their eyes.

"Every happy ending is a new beginning. Come on, Church—pull the lever," Ruth encouraged.

He hesitated for a long time.

Her final words were a whisper, a prayer, a promise from the depths of her heart. "You can do it, Church. I trust you. I love you. I'll love you always . . . and forever."

He pulled the lever.

ABOUT THE AUTHOR

A two-time winner of the British Fantasy Award, Mark Chadbourn was raised in the United Kingdom's East Midlands and studied Economic History at Leeds University before becoming a jouranlist. Now a screenwriter for a BBC television drama, he has also run an independent record company, managed rock bands, and worked on production lines. He is the author of the celebrated The Age of Misrule, The Dark Age, and Swords of Albion sequences. He now lives in a forest in a two-hundred-year-old house filled with books.